Praise for
THE LONELY PLACES

"A compendium of titillating terror . . . Morris's hallucinatory mixture of memory and nightmare, aggression and submission, pain and excitement will intrigue . . . as will the ending." —*Publishers Weekly*

"Convincingly surreal and involving . . . a satisfyingly mysterious gothic that leaves enough strings dangling spookily in the wind." —*Kirkus Reviews*

"Morris is a first novelist, but he writes like an old pro, building suspense slowly, almost imperceptibly. The story's resolution is exciting . . . and emotionally satisfying. Fans of character-driven psychological thrillers by such British authors as Mo Hayder, Minette Walters, or Frances Fyfield will be pleased by this first effort."
—*Booklist*

"Morris's experience in writing horror is evident in the very tightly plotted story. Whether Ruth is awake or dreaming, each detail fits precisely into the story. . . . Recommended." —*Library Journal*

"A blend of sexual intrigue, hallucinatory sequences, and unusual sleuthing add up to . . . a sense of foreboding menace. . . . Readers looking for an offbeat detour into a twisted physical and mental landscape will be happily sated." —*Pages*

"The sense of paranoia is cranked up inexorably, along with growing sympathy for Ruth, a character with real depths subtly revealed . . . a small masterpiece of compassionate writing." —*Time Out*, UK

"Masterful . . . the tension remains at a screaming pitch until the very end. . . . Always believable and intriguing . . . the story's resolution is both startling and satisfying. . . . Morris has written a masterful psychological suspense that explores the depths of the human mind and its capacity for horror."
—freshangles.com

"*The Lonely Places* comprehensively demonstrates that J. M. Morris has all the assurance and authority of a seasoned veteran; this is a truly chilling debut. . . . Morris adroitly reinvents tricks of the suspense novelist's trade and delivers a brilliantly orchestrated narrative. Morris is particularly successful in the first-person narrative chosen for the increasingly concerned Ruth: her growing psychological tension is perfectly matched by the ever-darkening trajectory of the mystery."
—Amazon.co.uk

"Eerie, assured and utterly compelling, this is a novel you will not forget."
—Michael Marshall Smith, author of *Spares*

"The suspense, the how-will-it-end keeps us lashed to the pages . . . you will not find a false step in this book."
—I Love A Mystery.com

The Lonely Places

J. M. Morris

A DELL BOOK

Published by
Dell Publishing
a division of
Random House, Inc.
New York, New York

Library of Congress Catalog Card Number: 2001053798

ISBN: 0-440-23736-X

Manufactured in the United States of America

Published simultaneously in Canada

February 2003

10 9 8 7 6 5 4 3 2 1
OPM

The Lonely Places

One

"SO WHY ARE WE here?"

My tone was light, almost playful. I wasn't afraid of him back then. We were still in our honeymoon period. I didn't analyze each sentence, each word, each *syllable* before I uttered it for fear he would fly into a rage. For three months we'd been happy. We'd laughed a lot. We'd developed what I'd believed was a real bond of friendship, of understanding. Later, despite his behavior on this day that I always think of as Day One, I blamed myself not only for rousing the darkness inside him to life but for actually creating it. I convinced myself that he became angry and violent not through any fault of his own, but because of me, of something in my makeup, of some lethal ingredient I was bringing to the rich, warm stew of our relationship. I was a poisonous mushroom. A chunk of spoiled meat. Without me, with someone else, he would have been happy and loving and well-balanced.

All blinkered, self-deprecating crap, of course. Classic

victim mentality. It's obvious to me now that this day—
Day One—was the day on which the alarm bells began
to ring loud and clear, but that I was simply too flattered
to pay them any heed. Flattered by his bringing me here
once I'd found out why; by his willingness to confide in
me, to share his darkest secret. What happened afterward was not entirely his fault, I suppose. Men are not
born evil, they are molded by their experiences, blud-
geoned or teased into shape by what happens around
them and to them.

I looked at him when he didn't answer me immediately. I was shocked by what I saw. He looked . . . I don't
know . . . haunted. His features pinched, his skin pallid,
his shoulders hunched, his hands clamped on to the
steering wheel. The engine was still running, and I half
expected him to slam the car into gear and hightail it out
of there, gravel spurting from beneath our squealing
wheels. I touched his arm. The muscles beneath his
fleece jacket were rigid.

"What's wrong, Matt?" I asked. "What *is* this place?"

His head made a small, darting turn to the left and
for the briefest of instants there was a look in his eyes
which dried the words in my mouth and smothered the
consoling smile rising to my lips. All at once an understanding smile seemed grossly inappropriate, as improper
as a beatific grin if he'd just told me that his mother had
died, or that he had terminal cancer. The look he gave
me was one of . . . the only way I can think to describe it
is cold contempt, though it was less stark than that, as if
he were in a partial trance, and yet all the more disturbing because of it. There was something almost primeval
about the way he looked at me.

Silly? Maybe. But how do you describe that moment when the lights go out in someone's eyes and the darkness takes over? They become something you can't reason with, something whose conscience you can't appeal to—like a shark or a machine. They look human, but they're not. Not in the sense that the majority of us understand anyway. They have no moral code. They become less than human—inadequate, incomplete. And what is missing can make them dangerous, even deadly.

But I'm getting ahead of myself. I'm applying hindsight to what was actually nothing more than a fleeting impression. All I was aware of at the time—and this only peripherally—was that as Matt glanced at me, something slipped free of him, some essence that changed him from the man I had grown to love and trust to . . . to what? An emotional void. It was enough to make me suck in a surprised breath and hold it there, to not release it again until he spoke.

"What does it look like?"

I looked away from him then, *tore* my gaze away from him, and surveyed the place we'd arrived at. The drive from London to Preston had taken over three hours. Matt had been subdued for most of the ride, but when I'd asked him if he was all right, he'd simply said, "I'm just tired," or "I'm concentrating, that's all." Later, a little awkwardly as if he wasn't sure how to broach the subject, he'd said, "I want you to know everything about me."

"Is that why we're making this trip?" I asked.

"Yes. There's a place I need to show you."

"Couldn't you have described it to me?"

He scowled, emotions chasing one another across his

face. A touch of exasperation, a hint of anguish. He seemed on the verge of launching into some kind of explanation for his secrecy, but in the end he just shook his head.

"Okay," I said, settling back, feeling an urge to be flippant. "Magical Mystery Tour it is, then."

I hated (hate) tension—I'd had enough of it at home—and so I was always the first to lighten a dark mood with a joke, to offer the peace pipe in an argument. Sitting in the car outside that place, I wanted to punch Matt playfully on the arm, to say something silly to make him laugh. But I couldn't. Not because I was afraid of him—not then—but because I was afraid *for* him. Afraid that, for whatever reason, he was only just holding himself together. And because of this I had to be strong and steady, sensible and composed. So, trying to keep my voice light but neutral, I said, "It's an old railway station."

He didn't answer, but continued to stare broodingly at the building in front of us. Then he leaned forward and twisted the ignition key and the car's engine sighed to silence. Matt sighed, too, shoulders slumping a little as if he had also turned off his internal tension. "Yes," he said. "Yes, that's all it is."

We sat in the car, quiet now except for the clinking of metal as the engine cooled down. The place didn't look like much, was simply an old branch line out in the sticks, evidently derelict for some considerable time. The car park was strewn with weeds and rubble, the stonework of the long, low station façade so black it looked charred. The roof had been stripped of slates like the meat from the back of some vast creature, leaving mottled brown ribs exposed. The building huddled at the bottom of a slight valley, down a side road that time had reduced to little more than a dirt track. It was early October, chilly. Wind moved stealthily through the spindly clumps of grass that were staking a claim to the land, and through the shell of the building itself, whispering secrets.

Before I could ask Matt again what we were doing here, he abruptly opened his door and got out. Although he'd said it was important for him to bring me here, he seemed oblivious now to my presence, as he started striding stiffly toward the station entrance. I considered leaving him to it, but then I got out of the car and followed him. It was obvious that something momentous had happened here. Momentous and bad. I played out a little scene in my mind as I went after Matt, envisaged him telling me of a boyhood game that had got out of hand, of one of his friends—perhaps even his best friend—losing his footing on the platform, falling in front of a train. A tragic accident that Matt had always blamed himself for. A game of Dare with terrible consequences. I was practically rehearsing my words of solace when I finally caught up with him. He was standing just inside the station entrance, in the ticket office, staring at the rusty turnstile that led to the platforms.

"Hey, wait for me," I said softly, wrapping both my arms around his right one, pressing myself against him. I could feel the back of his hand resting lightly against my pubic bone, but he didn't react—not to my physical presence anyway. He nodded somberly toward a turnstile and in an oddly hollow voice said, "It's through there."

What is? I wanted to know, but decided not to push him, to let him tell me in his own time. "Okay," I said. "Let's go and see."

We moved through the ticket office, a square space where journeys long past had begun and ended. There was a ticket booth to the right, the glass—surprisingly still intact—now cloudy as cataracts. The area stank of stale urine despite a breeze, strong enough to ruffle hair, that swooped down on us through the gap where the roof had been. The floor was strewn with cans and bottles and broken glass glittering like a fortune in diamonds dropped by a fleeing thief.

"When did this place close down?" I asked.

Matt shrugged. "It's always been closed. Ever since I was a kid."

"So it's stood like this for what? Twenty, thirty years?"

"I suppose so."

"Did no one ever think to knock it down, to develop the land?"

"I don't know," he snapped, turning on me. "I'm not a fucking expert!"

His anger made me jump—but at that time not through fear, merely surprise. I let go of his arm, which had become rigid with tension again.

"All right," I said, torn between placation and irritation. "I was only asking. Look, Matt, you've got to see this from my point of view. You drag me halfway across the country without any real explanation and then behave as though you don't really want me here. I mean, it's hardly what I'd call a fun day out."

"It's not supposed to be fun," he muttered, and then

that weird emptiness came into his eyes again and his voice choked. "It's not supposed to be fun, you stupid . . ." He took three stumbling steps away from me. Then he did an odd and scary thing. He turned back around to face me, slowly raised his hands, and began to jab the tips of his fingers into his forehead, both hands moving in deliberate unison, reminding me of a machine whose function was to punch holes in sheet metal.

He did this at least eight times, and might have gone on indefinitely if I hadn't lunged forward and grabbed one of his hands, shouting at him to stop. He did stop, though his eyes were still expressionless, his mouth set in a compressed line. He had eight angry circles of red skin on his forehead, a vivid contrast against his otherwise pale flesh, like war paint.

"Matt, what's wrong? *Talk* to me!" I pleaded.

His eyes jerked up in their sockets and he finally seemed to see me. His mouth opened, but at first no sound came out. Then he murmured, "This is so . . . hard for me."

"Then don't do it," I said soothingly. "You don't have to, Matt. Let's go away from here."

"No," he said. "I *do* have to."

"Okay. But not here, eh? I mean, I've seen the place, haven't I? You can tell me what happened somewhere else. Over a drink, a nice meal."

"No." His eyes and his voice were suddenly full of alarm. "It can only be here. It can't . . . it can't *be* anywhere else."

He seemed to be talking about the memory as if it were a caged animal, as if it could only be allowed to roam within certain confines. I stroked his arm as if *he* were the animal, skittish and unpredictable, needing to be calmed.

"Okay," I said. "Okay. Let's get it over with, then."

We walked together up to the turnstile, feet grinding into broken glass. The turnstile shifted a squealing inch when Matt shoved against it, but then jammed solid. We climbed over. The platform beyond was a wind tunnel, causing my skirt to snap against my stockinged legs hard enough to sting. The rails were barely visible through the long grass that grew wild for as far as the eye could see. At the far end of the platform was a crossing point, presided over by a traffic light which was bent at an angle (forcing me to gulp back a comment about the wind being *really* strong around these parts), its eyes long since blinded.

"This way," Matt said, pointing to the left. He led me to a door which must once have been royal blue, the words WAITING ROOM lovingly rendered in gold script across the upper panel. The paint that hadn't peeled or blistered had faded to the color of sludge and the letters IT had been scraped away and replaced with NK in black marker pen that itself had faded to gray.

As Matt reached for the handle I noticed that it wasn't coated with the gritty dust that covered everything else. Spooked by Matt's behavior, and by the sudden thought that maybe we weren't alone here, I darted out a hand, placing it over his.

"Be careful," I said.

Matt regarded me coolly for a moment, but said nothing. His hand was motionless under mine, as if waiting for me to release him, though I wasn't gripping him tightly. Matt has big hands. Strong. The fingers long, the knuckles prominent. I didn't know then how much I would come to loathe them, to fear them. After a moment I let go of him and said, "Sorry. This is starting to freak me out a bit."

He didn't comment. Just turned the handle and pushed the door open.

The stench of urine was as pungent as mustard gas. The lack of a roof had allowed the elements to attack the ceiling above us. It was yellow-brown, pulpy as porridge, sagging and bulging and cracked. It looked as if one good sneeze would bring the whole lot down on us. Fingers pinching my nose, I said "Don't" as Matt stepped back to close the door.

He looked at me, and though his face was deadpan I felt a need to justify myself. "I can't stay here if you don't allow some air in, Matt. It stinks."

He left the door open and crossed to the middle of the room, where two rows of metal chairs were screwed to the floor. He sat down without even inspecting the seat. I hovered by the door, anxious to get this over with, to get away from this vile place as quickly as possible.

As Matt leaned forward, resting his elbows on his knees, the room suddenly darkened. I glanced out of the open door, and saw battalions of grime-gray clouds drifting across the pearly haze of the sky, colliding and entangling. A few fat drops of rain began to fall. I thought of the ceiling above us enduring yet more punishment, and asked, "Are you going to tell me what this is all about now?"

Matt had been staring into space, but his eyes now swiveled to regard me. What little light there was in the room clung to the oily whiteness of his eyeballs, making them gleam. Although Matt is good-looking, he is also tall with a long, sharply boned face, and too much shadow can make him appear cadaverous. Now his cheeks looked sunken, the skin on his nose and forehead stretched tight across the bone. He opened his mouth and darkness flooded in.

"I was ten when it happened," he said.

I waited for a moment, but he lapsed into silence again. Finally I asked, "When what happened, Matt?"

His response was immediate, as if I had flicked a switch. "I used to come here with my mate, Steve. But this one day he was off school. Tonsillitis. This place tempted us. There was never anyone here. It was creepy, but exciting too. We thought of it as our secret hideout. We were young enough, naïve enough, to think that no one else knew about it. That anyone who *had* known had either died or forgotten it was here.

"We used to come into this room and read each other ghost stories, scare ourselves silly. After a bit we used to think we could hear things outside. Dragging footsteps. Creaks and moans. Imagination.

"Often we'd stay here until dusk, until the place had filled with shadows. That was when we'd start to see things too. Dark things moving. Through the window. Out on the platform. Not clearly, but from the corners of our eyes. I could never really describe them. They were just shapes. Not there, not really. Just shadows.

"More often than not we'd end up running out of here, our hearts pounding. Terrified. But not really terrified. Exhilarated. *Alive.*

"We'd always come back. We'd always look forward

to coming back. I'd lie in bed at night and the thought of it would give me a delicious thrill. This place existed on the edge for us. It was full of ghosts, but they were *our* ghosts. We controlled them. We defined their limits. They scared us, but they couldn't hurt us. It was the best kind of fear. *Our* fear."

Matt's tone was flat, his body as motionless as the chair on which he sat. I shivered and told myself it was the chill that the rain, now pattering outside, brought with it. Matt's story seemed to have consumed him so completely that he had become oblivious to his surroundings. I thought that even if the ceiling above his head suddenly started to groan, even if an avalanche of sodden plaster started crashing down around him, he'd continue to sit there, staring into space, his story seeping from him.

"One Monday morning I got to school," he said, "and Steve wasn't there. I hadn't seen him all weekend. He lived a couple of miles away from me, so it was hard to get together. I wanted to come here. I was aching to come. You know how, as a child, you sometimes want something so bad it hurts? But Steve was off ill. I wanted to cry. I spent the morning in a daze, thinking that my whole world had been shattered. It sounds silly now, but when you're ten having to wait an extra day for something you've been longing for can seem like an eternity. And what if it was more than a day? What if Steve was away for the whole week? The thought of having to wait that long made me so angry, made me hate Steve even though he was my best friend. And then in math that afternoon an idea came to me. It was like a revelation. Just because Steve couldn't go to the station didn't mean I had to stay away too. What was to stop me coming here on my own?

"Once I'd realized that, I couldn't get it out of my head. I felt sick with excitement. When the bell went at the end of the day I was off and running, my stomach turning cartwheels. It took me twenty minutes to get to the station and when I reached the bottom of the dirt track and saw it, I thought straightaway that it was waiting for me.

"I was hot and sweaty, panting because I'd run all the way, and the strap of my satchel was digging into my shoulder. It was summer term. May. The days were warm and long. There were flowers among the weeds. Butterflies and bees flying about. The station still seemed to squat, though, like a dark secret in amongst the long grass, hidden away to everyone but me.

"I stood there for a while, scared to go in, because once I went in I'd be giving myself over to it, trusting it not to hurt me. Without Steve it felt as if the balance of power had shifted. Steve was my safety net and I was his. For the first time I wondered whether coming here on my own had been a mistake.

"Then I heard a noise behind me, a rustling in the grass, and I turned round. I didn't see anything. I nearly called out Steve's name, but I was worried about drawing attention to myself. It sounds odd, but hearing that noise behind me gave me the courage to move forward, towards the station. I went the way I'd always come, through the main entrance, across the waiting room, through the turnstile onto the platform, until I finally ended up here.

"I shut the door behind me, wondering all the time why I'd come. I was already regretting it. It suddenly seemed like an enormous distance to go back if things started to . . . go wrong. I didn't feel good being here without Steve. I didn't feel excited. I put my satchel on the floor and sat down on one of the seats, wondering what to do for the best. I'd brought a book of horror stories to school with me and I'd been looking forward to reading a story I'd read in bed the night before, about a man who is dared to spend a night in a waxworks museum. Only now that I was here on my own, I didn't feel like reading horror stories. Didn't even feel like getting the book out of my bag and looking at the cover. I thought if I did that, then it would wake up the ghosts, and without Steve here I knew I'd have no chance of controlling them.

"So I decided to leave, and was just picking up my satchel when I heard another noise outside. It was the sound of someone moving about. I saw a shadow blot out the line of sun from under the door. The next moment the doorknob started to turn.

"I was petrified. Everything shriveled up inside me. I couldn't move. I just stood there transfixed as the door started to open.

"The door opened all the way, and I saw a figure standing there: bulky and shapeless, made of the dark. Then it stepped forward into the room and the light it had been blocking shifted and fell on it and I saw that it was a man.

"He was about forty-five. Fat and red-looking. Nice suit. Shiny shoes. Glasses. He was carrying a brown leather briefcase, which he placed carefully by the door as though it contained something fragile. He was looking at me the whole time, and he seemed sort of nervous, as if he thought I might attack him or something. Then he smiled and said, 'Waiting for a train, are you?'

"When he spoke my terror seemed to sag out of me. My head began to swim and I thought for a moment I was going to faint. I felt sick, but I managed to shake my head. Too strung out to realize he was joking, I said, 'There aren't any trains. No one uses this station anymore.'

"He smiled. Not a nice smile. It seemed somehow forced. Like he was just stretching his lips to give his teeth some air. I knew straightaway there was something creepy about him. He was giving off a vibe that made me want to get out of there. But he was standing between me and the door. 'So why are you here?' he asked.

" 'Me and my friend come here after school sometimes,' I told him.

" 'Ah,' he said. 'So where's your friend now?'

" 'He didn't come to school today. I think he must be ill,' I said.

" 'So you decided to come here on your own,' he said.

"I nodded and he looked at me as if he were a teacher who'd caught me out of bounds and was trying to decide how I should be punished.

"I moved to pick up my satchel. 'I need to go home for my tea,' I said.

"Straightaway he took a step back toward the door. 'Not yet,' he said.

"That was when I started to feel really scared. A big

thick ball of fear started moving around in my stomach like the oil in one of those lava lamps.

" 'I have to,' I said, my voice cracking.

" 'Do you know why I'm here?' the man asked, his voice suddenly soft and intense. His eyes stared at me. They didn't blink. And I said, 'No,' and he said, 'I'm here because I followed you.'

" 'Oh,' I said. I couldn't think of anything else. I didn't want to talk to this man. I knew things were badly, badly wrong, but I couldn't see a way out.

" 'Do you know why I followed you?' the man said.

" 'No,' I said.

" 'I followed you because I wanted to talk to you.'

" 'Oh,' I said again. I wanted to say, *Well, I don't want to talk to you, you big, fat pig.* But I'd been told to respect my elders. And I'd been told never to talk to strangers. I didn't know what to do, I was afraid that he would get mad.

" 'I wanted to talk to you about what you and your friend do here,' he said.

" 'I have to go home for my tea,' I said, my voice so quiet I could barely hear it.

" 'Soon,' he said. 'You can go home soon. First I want you to tell me what you and your friend do here.'

"I shook my head. 'We don't do anything.'

" 'You must do *something,*' the man said.

" 'We read,' I said. 'And we talk. And we just . . . muck about.'

" 'And how do you muck about?' he asked.

"I shrugged. 'I don't know.'

" 'Do you masturbate?' "

I gasped. I couldn't help it. I'd become mesmerized

by Matt's story, by how he'd gradually, unconsciously, come to adopt the two personas—the fat, middle-aged man and the frightened younger version of himself— during the course of his narrative. I'd been expecting something like this, but the bluntness of the fat man's question, as Matt told it, still came as a shock.

Matt, as before, didn't even register my reaction. He was no longer with me. He'd traveled back twenty years in time. He was ten years old, and about to relive the ordeal that would wrench the rest of his life—and the lives of those he touched—hideously out of shape.

"I didn't answer him," Matt said, my gasp overlapping the "I" of his sentence. "He leaned a bit closer to me and his eyes were jumping, dancing. They were dark, but they seemed so bright, so shiny. He was sexually excited, but I didn't know that then. To me he just looked crazy.

" 'Do you know what that word means?' he asked, panting out the words, as if he were trying to talk after he'd run for a bus. 'Do you know what it means to masturbate?'

"I did, of course, but it wasn't a conversation I wanted to get into, so I didn't say anything.

" 'Masturbate means wank,' he said. 'Do you and your friend wank when you come here? Do you wank each other off?'

"I think I started to cry then, but I was trying not to. I could feel the tears crawling up my throat, pushing at the backs of my eyes. I picked up my satchel and bolted for the door, but he reached out and grabbed me by the shoulder and shoved me back.

" 'Where do you think you're going?' he said, and he sounded not angry but . . . indignant. As if by trying to leave I was the one doing something wrong.

" 'Home,' I managed to say, and I tried to twist away from him, but his grip was too strong.

" 'Not yet,' he said, still sounding offended. 'I haven't finished yet.'

"I tried to tell him again that I had to go home for my tea, but my tears were forcing their way out of me now. I was crying and shaking so hard I couldn't get any words out.

"He pushed me right back against the wall, his big fat hand on my chest. With his other hand he started fumbling with his trousers, and as he did so he carried on talking, each word gasping out of him. 'When I was a boy,' he said, 'I used to come here too with my friend, Simon. We used to wank each other off. It was the best time of my life.' "

All at once Matt fell silent. He didn't alter his position, didn't bow his head; the expression on his face didn't change. But the oily shine in his eyes started to run down his cheeks. He was crying.

I was about to go to him when he started speaking again, his voice even softer, more measured, than before.

"I tried to struggle, tried to fight him off, but he was too strong for me. He grabbed me round the back of the neck and forced me down onto my stomach. I felt the weight of him on the back of me and I thought I was going to suffocate. I could smell him; he smelled of heat and aftershave—something sharp and noxious.

"I didn't know he'd got my trousers down until he

shoved his hand between my legs from behind and grabbed me. He started to pummel and yank at my cock. I suppose he was trying to wank me off, but he wasn't having much luck. After a bit he gave up and I felt what I first thought was a fist forcing its way into me from behind. The pain was horrible, unbelievable. I started to scream and he shoved his fat, smelly fingers into my mouth to stop me.

"Halfway through the rape I blacked out—or at least I went into a sort of world of my own. I could hear him somewhere above me, grunting and snorting like a pig. At some stage he must have taken his hand out of my mouth, because I threw up on the floor and then just lay in it until he had finished.

"I don't know how many times he raped me, but it seemed to go on for a long time. Afterwards he tied me up and left me there, naked from the waist down, lying in a pool of sick. He kept telling me to promise not to tell anyone, like he was some schoolkid who'd done something a bit naughty. Then he left and I lay there for the next seven hours until the police found me.

"It was Steve who told them where I might be. I was cold with shock and bleeding from my anus and the circulation had virtually stopped in my hands, which were tied behind my back. Another few hours and I might have had to have one or both of them amputated. I might even have died of hypothermia."

Matt sighed, shifting slightly in his seat as if to denote that the main body of his story was over, that the rest was simply epilogue. "They never caught the man that raped me. To this day I have no idea who he was. I recovered slowly, but I was off school for a long time and ended up having to drop down a year, which meant that Steve and my other friends moved on to the secondary school and left me behind. By the time I got there they'd all made new friends—which is something I lost the knack of doing before I got to drama college."

He glanced up at me, acknowledging me for the first time since he'd sat down. "So now you know. My big secret. Hi, I'm Matt. I was fucked up the arse by a pervert when I was ten. Bit of a conversation-stopper, isn't it?"

I went to him, put my arms around him, stroked his short hair, pressed his face against my chest. "Oh, Matt," I whispered. "Oh, Matt."

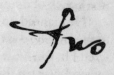

THE HARDEST THING ABOUT people who have problems—and I'm talking about real problems: health-threatening, *life*-threatening problems—is getting them to admit what they are. Not what the problems are; I don't mean that. I mean getting people to admit what they themselves are. You know what I'm talking about, I'm sure. You've seen the films and the soap operas and the TV dramas. You've seen some much-loved character standing up in front of a roomful of people and (usually after a dramatic pause) announcing, "I'm Joe Bloggs, and I'm an alcoholic." And if it's done well, you feel like applauding or weeping. Because that's it. That's half the battle.

Well, here goes me. Get ready to cheer.

My name is Ruth Gemmill, and I'm a victim.

All that I've told you so far—that afternoon in the station with Matt—took place three years ago. Almost to the day, in fact. October '97. I can't remember the exact date, but I know it was early in the month, just like it is now. The first hint of a winter chill in the air. Leaves turning to fire on the trees. The darkness muscling in on the light, claiming an increasingly larger share of each passing day.

That afternoon changed my life, or at least began to, but I didn't know how devastating and terrible its effect would be until later. At the time, as I've mentioned before, I felt flattered after I'd got over the initial shock. Flattered that he had confided in me, that he had trusted me enough to divulge his awful secret.

Day One. Over a thousand days ago now. Plenty of time for wounds to heal, you might think, and yet there were still days, like today, when those wounds had to be bathed and tended, days when I had to constantly remind myself that it was finally over, long gone. And my relationship with Matt *was* over; it was merely its ghosts which walked within me now. They were restless spirits, but I was doing my best to deal with them, and most of the time I think I coped pretty well, thank you very much. It was just occasionally, when my mind didn't have enough to occupy it, that the spirits grew bold. Idle moments; the vulnerable time before sleep; long car journeys like this one.

I was on my way from London to Greenwell, a small market town in North Yorkshire, to look for Alex, my brother. Some people might welcome four hours' thinking time, but not me. For the first hour or so I'd tried to quiet the ghosts with the happy clamor of Radio One, and when that didn't help, with the more cerebral entertainment of a talking book—E. Annie Proulx's *The Shipping News,* if you care to know. Yet even though it was a good book, it wasn't long before I could barely hear it above the clanking of chains and the wailing of tormented souls.

In some ways I hate Matt for this more than anything else. Hate the way he's crushed and killed the simple pleasure of being relaxed enough to allow my mind to drift. In my old life there was this café I used to go to near Covent Garden. I'd sit there with my cappuccino, staring out of the window, watching the world go by. If I tried to do that now, it wouldn't be very long before the phantoms, sensing the silence, would creep out of their hidey-holes and begin anew their restless roaming. They prefer the quiet, lonely places. They don't like bustle and clutter. Thanks to Matt, I have to take medication before I go to bed every night to help me fall asleep. The pills are bitter and though I'm ashamed of my hatred, I can't help but revile his name each time I swallow one.

If it hadn't been for Alex, I wouldn't have survived it all. Alex is two years younger than me. We've always been there for one another. Even when we were kids we didn't fight like siblings are supposed to. Instead, like lovers, we opened ourselves up, made ourselves vulnerable. We told each other our hopes, our desires, our dreams. And, long before Matt took me to the abandoned railway station, Alex and I were telling each other everything.

I knew Alex's greatest secret well before anyone else did. Sometimes I think I knew even before Alex had admitted it to himself. Certainly I found it far easier to accept than he did. I remember the words he used when he first told me. He said, "I think I might have something wrong with me."

He was seventeen and I was nineteen, and in my second year at university. I'd come home from London to spend Christmas with my family. But home didn't feel much like home anymore. I found it parochial and stifling. My parents' lives seemed stagnant to me. I spent my time trying not to allow my feelings of superiority to manifest themselves as contempt, trying not to allow their dismal, petty concerns to drag me down to their lowly level. That makes me sound like a snotty cow, I know, but I was simply at that age when we all think we're God's gift. Funny how time shifts us round in a slow circle. Back then all I wanted was the bright lights, the noise, and the smell and heat of life. Now, twelve years later, I find I'm beginning to tire of that. London is beginning to seem transient. It's not the place where I want to spend the rest of my life. A few months ago, when Alex told me he was getting out, that he'd got a job in a small market town I'd never heard of, I felt a touch of wistful envy.

"But what will you do there?" I asked him.

"I'll teach. It's a nice school."

"No, but what will you *do*?"

He smiled. "I'll walk in the meadows. I'll breathe clean, fresh air."

"You'll hate it. You'll be lonely."

"Don't you mean that you will?"

I don't think he really said that. I think that that was simply the thought I was ashamed to admit I was thinking.

It was twelve Christmas Eves ago when Alex said, "I think I might have something wrong with me." We were in The Malt Shovel, a pub about a mile from our parents' house, where I had illegally bought my first alcoholic drink at the age of sixteen. The place was packed, the air hazy with smoke, the liquid in our glasses shivering as the music from the annual Christmas Disco thumped through from the function room next door.

We'd got in at seven, grabbed ourselves a table, and started drinking. I was having pints of lager and Alex was on Pernod and Coke. This worked out well because when Alex went for a round, the rugger buggers propping up the bar assumed the lager was for him, so he didn't get any hassle.

We had been drinking steadily for three hours and were pretty pissed when Alex made his announcement. I looked at him uncomprehendingly. "What do you mean?"

He looked down at his drink morosely as if it had asked the question and not me.

I punched his arm, a squirm of anxiety in my belly. "Alex, what do you mean? Are you ill?"

He lifted his head, but refused to catch my eye. "No, no," he said quietly, "nothing like that."

"What, then?" When he didn't answer immediately, I punched his arm again, harder. "Come on, Alex, you're scaring me."

"I . . ." His voice faltered. He pursed his lips, then looked at me. "You won't laugh, will you? Or think badly of me?"

"I'll try not to," I said. "What is it?"

"Well, I think . . . well, it's just that . . ." He leaned forward, lowering his voice. "I don't fancy girls. I mean, I like them and everything, but I never fancy them. I've tried to, but I can't."

"I see," I said. Suddenly I felt sober and mature. I'm not sure how else I felt. Not shocked or upset. Not even surprised. Matter-of-factly I asked, "So what are you telling me? That you're gay?"

He blushed in abject misery. "I don't know. I suppose so."

"Do you fancy other men?"

He winced, then nodded dumbly, toying with his glass.

Realizing that the onus was on me to keep the discussion going, even though he was the one who had instigated it, I reached out and stroked his hand. "Well, that's okay," I said. "It's nothing to be ashamed of. Don't they reckon ten percent of the population is gay? No big deal."

Again he didn't say anything, just continued to stare forlornly down into his glass, his face crimson with embarrassment.

"Have you got a boyfriend?" I asked.

He looked as though he'd been stung. His shoulders jerked, his head snapped up. *"No!"* he said, glaring at me as if the very idea were preposterous.

"Okay, I was only asking."

Making a vague circular motion with his hand, he mumbled, "I've never . . . done anything. I've never acted on how I feel."

"Why not?"

He grimaced. "Too scared, I suppose. Besides, how can you tell if . . . well, if another bloke's the same as you?"

"Depends where you go. In London there are pubs and clubs you can go to."

He laughed humorlessly. "There's nowhere like that here."

I leaned back and looked at my brother. I remembered him falling out of Gran's apple tree when he was six and breaking his ankle, remembered how his screams of pain had been so full-blooded and intense that they had caused the hairs to rise on the nape of my neck. I remembered him and his friends making homemade parachutes for their Action Men and throwing them out the bedroom window onto the patio. I remembered how once at school he had squared up to a boy called Pete Kershaw, who was two years older and a foot taller than him, because Kershaw had reduced me to tears with a relentless campaign of sneaking up behind me and lifting my skirt.

What am I trying to say here? Only that Alex had never been a loner or an outsider, had never been "different" from his friends. Growing up, he had given no hints as to his sexuality; he had even had girlfriends, though admittedly none of them had lasted very long. And yet somehow I had always *known*. Or at least, when he told me about himself that Christmas Eve, I felt as though a series of vague and mysterious components were clicking neatly into place. "So what will you do about it?" I asked.

He gave me a pained, defeated look. "What *can* I do?"

A solution entered my mind immediately, but I paused for a moment, allowing myself at least a few seconds of reflection. Then I decided to give it voice, to allow the notion to sink or soar of its own volition.

"You could come back to London with me," I said.

Alex stared at me for a moment, searching my face for signs of duplicity. Finally he shook his head. "No, I can't."

"Why not?"

He flashed an intentionally self-deprecating smile. "You don't want me around."

I gawped at him in indignation. "Al, I *love* having you around. I always have. I thought you knew that."

"Yeah, but . . . things are different now."

"Different how?"

"You've got your own life in London. Your own friends. You don't want me cramping your style."

I didn't know whether to hug him or hit him. How could my beloved brother think this of me? Reaching across the table and grabbing his hand, I said, "Alex, listen to me. Believe me. There's nothing I would like more than for you to come to London with me. I would be proud to introduce you to my friends. And you could really open up there. Be yourself. Not like in this shit-hole where everyone's so . . . so fucking insular."

Alex clutched my hand. "Keep your voice down," he urged.

I looked around. A couple of heads were turning in my direction and I realized that I wasn't quite as sober as I'd thought. "Sorry," I hissed, and leaned toward him. "But what do you reckon? Please say yes."

"I can't just up and leave. I've got to finish my A-levels. If I don't finish my A-levels I'll never get into university."

I sighed. I couldn't argue with that. I couldn't justify persuading him to abandon his studies, not even for some much-needed personal freedom. "Okay," I said, "but you'll be finished in six months. What about applying for London then? You could come and stay with me until you get yourself sorted out. We could have a fantastic summer."

A slow grin spread across Alex's face. He's got a real heart-melter of a grin, my brother. It makes him look about eight years old.

"Yeah," he said. "Yeah, that'd be good."

"Six more months to endure at home before then, though. Will you be okay?"

He shrugged. " 'Course I will. Mum and Dad aren't so bad."

"You reckon?"

"I mostly keep out of their way and they keep out of mine. It's okay."

I scowled. "I don't think *I* could stand it, not anymore. They're . . . I don't know . . . like vampires. They suck the spirit out of you. I'd be wanting to tear the place apart within a week."

"I suppose I've never known any different," Alex said noncommittally.

I took a long swallow from my pint. "Will you tell Mum and Dad that you're gay?"

Alex looked horrified at the prospect. "What do you think?"

"I don't think it would be a good idea," I said, deadpan, then I grinned wickedly. "Mind you, it wouldn't half jump-start them out of their lethargy."

Alex looked alarmed. "You're not going to tell them, are you?"

" 'Course not," I said. "Do you honestly think I

would?" I paused, then asked, "Do you think you'll ever tell them?"

"I don't know. I suppose so, one day. Maybe I'll write them a letter. From London."

"Coward," I said, then giggled. "I know. Maybe you could put an announcement in the local paper. It'd certainly give Dad and his friends something to talk about at the golf club."

Alex laughed. It was good to hear, though it made me realize with a pang that I hadn't heard him laugh for a while. "Can you imagine it! He'd die of shame," he said, warming to the idea. Then suddenly the humor drained from his face. "Shit, he's going to hate me, isn't he?"

" 'Course he isn't. You're his son. He loves you."

"Yeah, but he thinks I'm *normal*. When he finds out his son's a poof, he'll go fucking Beirut. He'll think I've done it just to spite him."

He's not that bad, I almost said, then didn't. Because the thing was, he *was* that bad. I mean, he was my dad, and he'd always done the best he could for us, and despite the fact that he and I hadn't really seen eye to eye since puberty (mine, not his), I loved him for that. But there was no getting away from the fact that he was a bigoted bastard—albeit in a repressed, passive, middle-England sort of way. I couldn't watch current affairs programs with him anymore because the merest glimpse of dreadlocks or facial piercings or politicians who wore red ties instead of blue ones would elicit grunts of disapproval from him, or dismissive shakes of the head. A report on the AIDS epidemic, intercut with footage of guys dancing together in a gay nightclub, had once prompted him to blurt out contemptuously, "They've brought it on themselves, these people." Last time I'd been home we'd had a blazing row about single mothers and I'd ended up calling him a walking *Daily Mail* article before storming out of the room.

In Dad's defense I'd say that he'd had a pretty sheltered upbringing, and that much of his bigotry was due more to a lack of understanding than anything else. However, I think you get the idea that perhaps he wasn't—and isn't—the most tolerant person in the world.

None of which helped Alex, of course. There was no getting away from the fact that his announcement would be a bitter blow to our decent, upstanding, right-thinking, fiercely heterosexual father.

"Do you think he'll punch me?" Alex asked.

I shook my head. "No. He'll probably just shout a bit."

"What about Mum?"

"She'll cry at first," I said, "but she'll be all right once she gets used to the idea."

Alex looked worried. "I'm really not looking forward to telling them."

"Well, you don't have to yet," I said. "There's plenty of time."

In fact, Alex didn't tell our parents for another five years, but that's another story. Six months after our Christmas Eve conversation, he did indeed move to London, and there—as I had predicted—he flourished. Well, maybe not at first. He had a lot of adapting to do, and for the first three or four months he was on an emotional roller coaster. He would climb to heights of dizzying self-discovery only to plummet to new depths of doubt and despair. But just as he had always been there for me, so I was there for him. I talked and listened, and as best as I could, I comforted and reassured.

And gradually he got through it. He said I'd helped a lot, but I think he'd have got through it anyway. Over the summer he stayed with me and my friend, Keri, in our shared flat, and then in September he started his zoology course at London University and moved into student accommodations. He started having relationships—proper relationships—the first of which was with a sweet Welsh guy called Dave, who had bleached hair and a tattoo of a rose on his bum. Alex loved his studies, and stayed on afterwards to do some postgrad research or other, which culminated in him writing a book about fiddleback spiders (called, appropriately enough, *Fiddleback*), which, Alex assures me, is regarded as the definitive work on the subject.

When all that was finished, he was offered a job on the lecturing staff, which he took, and subsequently wrote a couple more books—one about scorpions and one about the breeding habits of some kind of carnivorous fish whose name I can't remember. Whenever anyone asked him what he did for a living, Alex would say, "I'm a naturalist," and as they started to grin, he'd add, "And no, that doesn't mean I walk around with no clothes on." Sometimes, if he was talking to some guy he fancied, he would meaningfully raise those perfect eyebrows of his and murmur, "Although that can be arranged."

God, I loved my brother.

Except that now he'd gone and I didn't know where. He'd got the job in Greenwell a couple of months ago. I couldn't believe it at first. It seemed a backward move to be going from London University to some obscure comprehensive in a northern backwater. But Alex was adamant. He said he'd always wanted to teach kids and had been wanting to get out of London for a while, move back up north (our family home was in Newark, near Nottingham), and live in the country. Meeting guys would be harder up there, I told him, but Alex shrugged off my protestations. He was older now and wiser. He knew where to go, what to do. He knew how to recognize the signs. At least, that's what he told me.

"But won't you miss me?" I asked.

" 'Course I will. But you'll be able to come and visit. And I'll visit you. We'll have the best of both worlds."

For the first six weeks we talked a lot on the phone. Every day, in fact. And then one evening last week I called him and he wasn't there. I left a message, but he didn't ring back. I called again the next day, left another message, but again he didn't respond. I felt hurt and disappointed and worried, though I told myself I had no reason to be. He'd probably gone away with the school for a few days. Or maybe he'd met someone and was staying with him, too caught up in the euphoria of a new relationship to give me a call. I admit I felt a bit resentful, but I wanted Alex to be happy. I left it another two days and then I rang him again. Answering machine. Message. No reply.

I rang Directory Inquiries to try to get the number of his school, but there was nothing listed under Greenwell Comprehensive, so I could only assume that the school went by some other name. It infuriated me that I had no way of contacting Alex at work. I was sure I'd written his work details down at some point, though God knows where. Probably on some scrappy piece of paper which I'd accidentally thrown away.

I sat and brooded for a bit longer, and then last night, waiting restlessly at home, willing the phone to ring, I finally thought: bugger it. I was a freelance production designer, and currently between jobs, so it didn't matter about taking time off work—not that that would have stopped me anyway. I packed a bag with enough stuff to last me for a few days, set the alarm for five, and went to bed.

And now here I was, nine-thirty in the morning, five miles from my destination, stone-walled fields to either side of me. It was a bright, clear morning, sunshine enlivening the land, even though much of the foliage was withering and browning, mournful of summer's end. The air smelled verdant, the breeze that slipped in through the open window sinewy, vigorous with life. If I hadn't been anxious about Alex I would have felt good. Cleansed. But my stomach was tight with trepidation even though I told myself time and again that there was no reason for it. What, after all, did I expect to find when I got to Greenwell?

I was doing fifty, the road a winding gray thread in front of me, when out of the corner of my eye I glimpsed a scarecrow in the field to my left. It was a couple of hundred yards away, and my eye was drawn to it because it was the only splotch of darkness amidst the glow of green. As I half turned my head I became peripherally aware of something darting out in front of the car. Suddenly I was slamming on my brakes, my leg rigid as my head snapped back. Instantly there was a thump of impact, the sound—real or imagined—of bones splintering, and the car juddered slightly. A cold wash of nausea coursed through me as I screeched to a halt maybe twenty yards farther up the road. What had I hit? A dog? A sheep? A child? Whatever it was had sounded pretty big.

I sat in the car for a moment, trying to catch my breath. My head was spinning, and it took me a few seconds to work out how to turn the engine off. I managed to get out of the car, feeling weak and wobbly, not quite with it yet. I turned to face back up the road, dreading to see what I had hit.

There was something there, but it wasn't as large as I'd feared. A bundle of brownish fur with a thick streak of red trailing from it like the tail of a comet. The redness was vivid in the sunshine. I took a deep breath, then started walking toward it. It wasn't until I was a couple of paces away that I realized what it was.

A hare. The biggest one I'd ever seen. Wiry and rangy, built for speed, like a cross between a rabbit and a greyhound. Only this one had run its last, had had the unbelievable misfortune to encounter possibly the only moving vehicle in several square miles. Its sleek, bony head and its front and back legs were intact, not a mark on them. But its abdomen, which must have borne the brunt of the impact, had been ripped open, and an eruption of glistening bodily contents now lay smeared across the pitted tarmac.

My hand flew to my mouth. I knew there was nothing I could have done to prevent it, but I still felt terrible for inflicting such a violent death on such a beautiful creature.

And then the creature's back legs abruptly kicked, its glazed eyes opened wide, and it began to make an awful, high-pitched squealing sound.

I jumped back in horror. For one ludicrous moment I thought the hare's outrage at its sudden and meaningless death had granted it the power of resurrection. Then I realized that the animal must simply have been stunned and that it had now regained consciousness. Its back legs continued to thrash and jerk as if they knew nothing other than to run even as it squealed out its agony. I had to do something. I couldn't stand by and watch the poor thing suffer. The animal was clearly beyond help, but at least I could put it out of its misery.

I looked around, feeling sick with nerves, my thoughts slow and gelatinous. I needed a weapon. No, mustn't think of it like that. This was to be an act of mercy, not violence. For a few seconds I stood, my eyes searching the area helplessly while the creature shrieked in pain. My somnolent thoughts began to race, and a desperate mantra ran through my mind: *There's nothing here, there's nothing here.*

Then, as though someone had whispered the solution in my ear, I stepped onto the grassy verge and crossed to the stone wall that boundaried the field containing the scarecrow. I leaned forward and, using both hands, lifted up a capping stone. It was thick and heavy as a stack of dinner plates. I was desperate to stop the animal's pain, but I forced myself to move carefully so as not to stumble and drop the stone on my toes. I moved back across the grass verge and onto the road where the hare lay, kicking and screaming. I positioned the rock directly above its head, then shuffled my feet back so that my shoes wouldn't get spattered when the stone crushed its skull. I told myself to do it now, to let go of the stone, but my arms seemed locked, and I couldn't bring myself to let go. The longer I held on, the louder the doubts echoed in my mind. What if the stone wasn't enough to kill it? What if it simply fractured the animal's skull, prolonging its agony?

I don't know how long I stood there dithering. I can't honestly say how long I might have stood if the hare had not given a final convulsive shudder, belched out a gush of blood which fanned out around its head, and died.

My strength seemed to ebb with the loss of the creature's life. The stone in my hands was all at once unbearably heavy. I could barely find the strength to turn away before letting it drop to the ground. It hit the tarmac with a crack and split open, revealing a crumbly core, the color of golden sand. My hands felt scoured by the stone's surface. I felt internally scoured, too, scraped out, nausea harsh in my belly.

I turned away from the eviscerated animal, and the brilliant green of the field ambushed me, making my eyes sting. It was the sun, hanging high above the field, which made the grass burn like green fire. I squinted, my head aching. At first I thought the gray blot I could see in the green was some fleck of dark matter in my eye. Then my vision shifted, refocused, and I realized it was the scarecrow I'd briefly noticed earlier.

Only it couldn't have been a scarecrow, because its arms, previously outstretched, were now falling slowly to its sides. I blinked again and shielded my eyes with my right hand, but the figure was difficult to focus on. If it was a man standing out there in the middle of the field he looked unnaturally gray—his clothes, his skin, even his hair seemed to be the color of clay. I shook my head as if it would help clear my vision, and saw the figure half raise its hand as though greeting or marking me, then begin to walk in my direction.

All at once I was inexplicably terrified. There was something about the way the figure was striding toward me that was indefinably horrible. Sick with panic, I turned and ran for my car, my ragged breath seeming to scrape the back of my throat. My body heavy and lethargic, I seemed to be moving in slow motion. Pulling open the car door, getting into my seat, turning on the ignition—each of these functions seemed to last an age. Petrified to look in my mirror for fear of what I might see behind me, I tore away with a screech of tires, and didn't slow down until, three miles later, I finally reached Greenwell.

Three

MY FIRST IMPRESSION OF the town was that it seemed designed to discourage visitors. Greenwell's center, such as it was, could only be reached via a circuitous, badly signposted route of narrow, potholed streets. The desultory buildings lining these streets hardly made it seem worth discovering the hub. For the most part they were stolid and unattractive, made of grime-blackened stone that even in the sunshine conveyed an air of foreboding and neglect. There was no greenery in evidence; in fact, wherever I looked I saw merely dark colors—or rather, a negation of color. Greenwell seemed as though it were generating its own hazy canopy, beneath which it dozed, murky and forgotten.

I couldn't understand why Alex had wanted to leave London to come here. The town seemed not only dead but stagnant, rotting. Perhaps it had hidden charms, though the few people I could see walking about looked as depressed as the place made me feel. Hunched over and colorless, they reminded me of wood lice, perambulating mindlessly. "The Greenwell shuffle," I said to myself just as a sign reading Wedge Square appeared in front of me, pointing to the left.

Wedge Square. That's what Alex had told me to look out for if I ever popped up for a visit. I'd insisted on directions as soon as he moved in. "It's a bit complicated," he had said on the phone. "If you can get to the Square I can give you directions from there."

Wedge Square. An ugly name in an ugly place. I turned left and found myself at the barely beating heart of the community.

The Square was remarkable only in that nothing had been made of it. There was no statue, no war memorial, no ornamental fountain, no grass, no flowers, no trees. There was simply, as the sign stated, a square, whose cracked, uneven flagstones had created hollows where muddy pools of yesterday's rainwater had collected. Perhaps in days gone by the area had been a center of commerce, a marketplace, but now that mantle had been assumed by the sorry, run-down collection of buildings that bordered it.

There was a pub, a post office, a butcher's, a baker's, a greengrocer's, a bank, a chemist's, and a hardware store. The pub was called the Solomon Wedge, and boasted a painting of its namesake on a hanging wooden sign above the door. If the likeness was accurate, then the original Solomon Wedge had been a fat, bewhiskered, fierce-looking Victorian. I wondered who he was. The town's founder? No, the place must date further back than the last century.

As I got closer to the pub, I noticed a square of white

paper Scotch-taped to the inside of one of its dark windows. Written on the paper in thick black marker pen were the words: ACCOMMODATION AVAILABLE. *I can stay there,* I thought, *if . . . if what?* If I didn't find Alex? But then, why shouldn't I? Even entertaining the thought that there might be something sinister about Alex's silence made me angry with myself.

I parked in front of the pub, opened the glove compartment, and grabbed the folded sheet of notepaper resting on top of the car manual. I spent the next two minutes reading the directions to Alex's flat; my brother had been right when he'd said it was complicated. For a small town Greenwell was crammed with streets. Parks, gardens, and playgrounds had seemingly been sacrificed to accommodate more buildings. Why, I couldn't begin to guess. It wasn't as though the place had a thriving local industry, nor was there any evidence that it ever had. It didn't even have the feel of a commuter town; the houses were too small and neglected for moneyed townies seeking a bucolic retreat. In fact, from my admittedly brief impression of it, Greenwell didn't seem to be *anything,* a town without purpose. A place to live and a place to die, and that was all.

From the Square, streets radiated outward like the spokes of a wheel. If Alex's instructions were correct, then the fourth turn after the pub should be Coldpike Lane. I started the car and pulled back out onto the road. Though mine was the only moving vehicle in the vicinity, none of the half dozen or so people I could see wandering around paid me the slightest heed. I counted the roads as I passed them, murmuring the numbers under my breath as if afraid that if I stayed silent I'd be somehow deceived. Sure enough, when I came upon the entrance to Coldpike Lane I felt a fierce surge of joy, as though the mere sight of the words on the metal street sign meant I was already closer to Alex.

Alex's directions were spot on, and five minutes later I parked in front of the building where he lived. It was a tall, narrow house, one of a terrace of dark Victorian properties that had been converted into flats. In keeping with the rest of the town's houses, there was no front garden, just a tiny yard with a low brick wall in front of it, which at least meant that the front door did not open directly onto the pavement. I got out of the car and walked into the cold shadow of the house. Beside the front door were six buttons, each labeled with a small white rectangle of waterlogged card. No names, just flat numbers.

I pressed the top left-hand button, the button for flat 6, and waited. I wasn't surprised at the lack of response. It was Monday morning; if Alex wasn't ill in his flat, then he'd be at the school now. I tried the other buttons in descending order. When I got to 3, a voice so crackly with static that it was impossible to tell whether it was male or female said, "Who is it?"

"Oh, hi," I said, trying to sound bright and friendly. "I'm trying to get in touch with Alex Gemmill. He lives in flat six. I'm his sister, Ruth."

There was no reply, and I wondered if whoever I'd been talking to had stopped listening when they realized I wasn't here to see them. "Er . . . are you still there?" I asked.

"This is flat three," said the voice bluntly, its sex still indeterminate.

"Yes, I realize that," I said. "I've tried my brother's flat, but he's not in. I was wondering if you could buzz me in so I can leave him a note."

Again I thought the person in flat 3 had gone without bothering to reply, but then there was a sound like an angry wasp and I pushed at the door, which opened with a click. I went inside and shut the door behind me.

The hallway I walked into was clean but featureless. It had cream walls and a thin but hardy light brown carpet which must have been laid fairly recently because it retained a fresh, new carpety smell. I was quite surprised, actually. I'd expected to walk into somewhere dingy, with scuffed, dirty walls and a manky old carpet. There was nothing in the hallway except a low IKEA-style table with a few envelopes on it. I sifted through them. Bills and circulars mostly. Nothing for Alex.

Ahead of me, taking up two-thirds of the width of the hallway, was the staircase. There was an unmarked door tucked into the corridor to the left, which I vaguely recalled Alex telling me was a laundry room. I went upstairs, the old steps creaking under my weight. There was no other sound in the house, not even from flat 3. I had a mental image of the occupant of that flat standing motionless, ear to the door, listening as I ascended. It gave me the creeps, particularly as I couldn't imagine what sex they might be. I thought again of the gray figure in the field and of my absolute terror as it had come striding toward me. I found it hard now to recapture the intensity of that emotion. It had happened less than half an hour ago, but already I was beginning to wonder if it had really been as nightmarish as I remembered it.

At the top of the first flight of stairs was a square landing with a door on either side. The door to my right had a black plastic number 1 screwed to it, the one on my left a number 2. The back wall was dominated by a huge window with an old-fashioned latch which overlooked a small yard bordered by a crumbling brick wall. Beyond the wall the ground sloped away steeply, which made the descending rows of smaller terraced houses built on it look precariously perched. I wouldn't have fancied living at the top of one of those streets, though if you were a kid getting to the bottom on a bike would have been fun. Beyond the rows of terraces, which looked like dominoes waiting to topple, were undulating fields and thick green clumps of woodland.

From here, with the sun shining on it, the place looked peaceful, incongruously idyllic. Even though he chose to live in London, Alex had always been in his element in the countryside. "Food for the soul," he called it, whenever he managed to drag me out of the city. Alex was great to be with in the country. When it came to flora and fauna he was a mine of information. He could recognize birds both by their song and their plumage, identify different types of trees and plants, and was always pointing out dens and nests and small animals, once even a snake curled up in the grass—stuff that the majority of us clodhopping townies tend to miss.

I went up another flight, which took me onto the landing containing the doors to flats 3 and 4. I stared at the door numbered 3, again wondering whether I was being listened to or even spied upon. Not wishing to appear intimidated, I turned my back and climbed up the next flight of stairs, making a conscious effort not to tiptoe.

This was the top of the house, but it was the same layout—square landing, a door on either side, a window on the back wall. I went up to Alex's door, number 6, and did all the usual things. I knocked, I called his name, I had a peek through the keyhole. I hadn't expected him to be in, but I felt disappointed all the same. I suppose I'd hoped to see some evidence of him—some funny little sign he'd put on the door to make it less austere than all the others. Or a pair of his muddy walking boots sitting on newspaper on the landing outside. Or . . . oh, I don't know. Just something different, something to distinguish him, to let me know he'd been here. Silly, I know, but I missed my brother. I'd come all this way, I was standing right outside his flat, but I still felt as if we were hundreds of miles apart.

I might have come here on impulse, but at least I'd had the foresight to realize that I might have to write him a note. I took a notepad and pen from my shoulder bag and, after a moment's thought, wrote:

Hi Alex!
Surprise! I've come all the way up from London to see you, but you're not here. I thought I'd stay for a few days if that's okay. I'll book myself into the Solomon Wedge pub, so give me a ring when you get home from work. Hope you're free tonight. I'll look forward to seeing you later.

Love you,
Ruth

I shoved the note under his door and started back downstairs. Despite not having found Alex, I still felt positive, purposeful. I'd head back into town, book myself into the Solomon Wedge, and see if I could find out which school Alex might be teaching at. Not that I'd disturb him at work, not today at least, but it would be useful to have the information.

I had descended the first flight of stairs, and turned the corner onto the second, when I saw the spider. It was halfway down, motionless, almost as if it had been waiting for me. It was about eight millimeters long, with long, slender legs, and light fawn in color—practically the color of the carpet it was standing on, in fact, so it looked fairly innocuous. Maybe my eye was drawn to it because it was the only thing in front of me that wasn't all flat planes and sharp angles. I'm not keen on spiders— I mean I wouldn't pick one up—but they don't bother me too much. Ordinarily, I wouldn't have paid the thing much attention. I'd have probably just stepped over it with a shudder. This was different, though. On this occasion I halted with a gasp and felt a prickling sensation run up my legs and through my body. Thanks to Alex, I knew without a shadow of a doubt that the spider on the stairs in front of me was a fiddleback.

The reason it shocked me so much is because you don't get fiddlebacks in Britain. You get them in Australia, North America, hotter parts of Europe. They're not that impressive-looking, and they're actually quite shy, reclusive creatures. They can give you a nasty bite, though. Their venom doesn't usually kill—though it has been known to—but it can cause illness and horrible, pustulating skin ulcers that sometimes take months to heal.

I stared at the fiddleback, and for a couple of seconds I felt as though it were staring back at me, marking me. Then it became a blur of brown, and was gone.

I'm not saying it vanished into thin air. Nor am I saying it was a phantom spider or a hallucination or anything like that. All I know is, one moment I was looking at it, the next it had eluded me. And that—suddenly not knowing where it was—was worse than seeing the thing in the first place.

All at once a horrible thought struck me. Had Alex not been getting in touch because one of his spiders had bitten him? Maybe he was sick, or even paralyzed, and couldn't get to the phone or the door. I started to feel a familiar panic rising in me for a moment, and then I fought it down. No, be sensible. Alex knew how to handle his creatures. He was always ultracareful. Besides, he had antidotes for every type of insect and spider venom. He always kept a vial and a needle right beside him whenever there was the slightest chance that he might get bitten or stung.

Then again, he was careful—no, more than careful, obsessive—about making sure his creatures couldn't escape from their glass tanks. And yet the fiddleback had escaped, hadn't it? So something, somewhere, had gone wrong.

I ran back upstairs and pounded on Alex's door. "Alex," I shouted. "Alex, it's me, Ruth! If you're in there, please find some way to answer."

Again, there was no response, so I ran back downstairs, keeping a wary eye out for the fiddleback, and knocked on the door of flat 3.

I waited for thirty seconds, but the door remained

closed, so I banged again, harder. I think I've already said I don't like conflict—I'd had a bellyful of it from my dad, and my relationship with Matt had hammered whatever excess stuffing I might have retained out of me—but at that moment I felt ready to take on anyone. If whomever I'd spoken to on the buzzer had continued to refuse to answer, I would probably have shouted something along the lines of "I know you're in there and I won't go away until you open this door." But then the door *did* open—albeit only slightly—and a face peered out.

It was a small face, pale and gaunt, with pinched, narrow features and sunken, red-rimmed eyes that made me think of chronic insomnia. A few minutes earlier I hadn't been able to discern this person's sex from their voice, and now that I was confronting them face-to-face I still couldn't. The crack he or she was peering through was so narrow that all I could see of their hair were a few greasy strands of fringe. I felt my irritation seeping away, to be replaced by a sense of shame at my own robustness, a feeling that I'd used it to bully my way into this person's life.

"I'm sorry to disturb you," I said with what I hoped was an ingratiating smile, "but I need your help."

For a few seconds the person stared at me expressionlessly. If they were scared or suspicious or even just pissed off at me for interrupting what looked on the surface to be a pretty miserable existence, then they didn't show it.

I thought I was going to have to repeat what I'd said, but then the person asked, "What help?"

Female, I thought as soon as she spoke, and suddenly

my perception shifted and I wondered how I could ever have been unsure. Of course it was a girl. The soft line of the jaw, the delicacy of the features—it was obvious.

Despite the nervous fluttering in my stomach, I forced myself to keep smiling.

"My name's Ruth," I said. "My brother, Alex, lives upstairs."

"You already said that," said the girl.

Taken aback by her bluntness, I started to stammer. "Did I? Oh yes, well, I was just putting things in . . . well, it's just that . . . well, I'm worried about him."

I expected her to say "Why?" or "Are you?" but she didn't, she just looked at me. I stumbled on, simultaneously intimidated by her silence, and annoyed by it, and anxious for Alex.

"I'm worried that he might be ill, in his flat." I almost told her about the fiddleback, then decided not to; I didn't want to get Alex into trouble. "So ill that he can't get to the phone or the door. And I was wondering . . . I don't suppose you have a spare key?"

"No," she said shiftily, looking at me as though I were accusing her of something.

"The landlord's number, then? Do you have a number for your landlord? He can let me in."

The girl now looked suspicious, as if I were trying to trap her. "He won't like you ringing him."

"Well, if I don't ring him, I'll ring the police," I said, feeling suddenly angry. "I'm not just leaving this."

The animation that had briefly flickered across the girl's face now disappeared again and she gave me another of her deadpan stares. Then she said "Hang on," and her face receded into the darkness as the door closed.

A minute later it opened again, and she thrust a strip of paper that looked as if it had been torn from the corner of an old yellowing newspaper at me. "Don't tell him it was me," she said, then retreated once more, shutting the door.

Clutching the paper, I ran downstairs, my head darting this way and that as I looked for the fiddleback. The front door of the house was on a heavy spring, which meant I couldn't get out to my car to get my mobile without it clicking shut behind me. Not trusting the girl in flat 3 to let me in again, I propped the door open with my left boot and hopped out to my car.

When I got back, I put my boot back on and laced it up, then dialed the number I'd been given. It was only when a brusque voice said "Cressley" that I realized I didn't know the landlord's name.

"Oh hello," I said. "I'm trying to get in touch with the landlord of 5 Moxon Street."

"Yeah, that's me."

"Hi, my name's Ruth Gemmill. My brother's a tenant of yours. Alex Gemmill. He lives in flat six."

"What of it?"

Cressley's manner was snappy, impatient, as if I'd interrupted something very important that he wanted to get back to. I paused, refusing to be rushed. "Well, it's just that I'm worried about him. I think he might be ill."

"What's that got to do with me?" asked Cressley.

"Well, nothing, except that . . . I'm worried he might be so ill that he can't get to the phone or the door. I was wondering whether you could possibly come over and let me in?"

"Look, love, I've got a business to run here. If I was expected to show up every time some tenant of mine had a personal crisis, I'd be chasing my bloody arse around all day," Cressley said contemptuously.

I felt my throat constrict. I hated this kind of confrontation, but at the same time, for Alex's sake, I wasn't going to give up on this one.

"It's not a personal crisis, Mr. Cressley," I said. "I really think my brother might be ill. I'm extremely worried about him."

"And what makes you think he's ill?" Cressley asked condescendingly.

"He's not answering his phone. He's not been in touch for days. It's not like him."

"Did it ever occur to you that he might have gone on holiday?"

"Of course it did, but he would have let me know."

"Maybe he wanted a break."

"You're not listening to me, Mr. Cressley. If my brother had gone away he would have told me. We're very close."

"No, love, it's you who's not listening. Maybe he wanted a break from you."

"What?"

I was flabbergasted by his rudeness. Cressley gave a snort of what sounded like satisfaction. I imagined him to be the kind of man who enjoyed getting a rise out of people.

"Now, don't take this the wrong way, love," he said, "but you come across as the clingy type to me. I think if you were *my* sister I'd want a break from you now and again."

I couldn't believe what I was hearing. For a moment my throat was so tight that I couldn't speak. I could feel my anger boiling over in my head. Then the pressure of it made the lump in my throat burst out like a cork from a bottle, and I managed to make "How dare you!" sound like the snarl it was intended to be.

Cressley laughed. "Whoops," he said. "Have I gone a bit far? I only speak as I find, love."

"You . . . you . . ." For a moment I had so much venom rushing through my head I wasn't sure what was going to come out. Then the floodgates opened and it all emerged in a torrent. "You don't know anything about me! How dare you make assumptions about our relationship. I am *not* the silly, fussy woman you obviously think I am. I have a genuine cause for concern here. Now, are you going to come over with a key or do I have to call the police?"

There was silence for a moment, then Cressley sighed and said, "Keep your knickers on, love."

"Don't be so bloody rude!"

He was silent again, and I wondered whether I'd managed to stun *him* with the force of my anger. Encouraged by this, I demanded, "Well, what is it to be? Shall I call the police?"

I heard him groan with either exasperation or defeat, or maybe a bit of both. "I'll send someone round," he said, "if only to shut you up."

"Thank you," I said, not entirely sure whether he'd intended it as a threat, "I'll expect someone shortly." But he had already put the phone down.

I sat on the front step of the house, trying to look cool and businesslike in case Cressley suddenly showed up—after all, I had no idea how far he had to come. I was quite pleased with how I'd handled myself on the phone, though my hands were now shaking with a delayed nervous reaction. I was aware that my cheeks were burning, too, and tried to think calm thoughts; the last thing I wanted was to appear flustered when he arrived. I'd been sitting there about ten minutes when a highly polished maroon Espace with a personalized number plate—MC 15—drove up. It was the sort of vehicle you saw a lot of in the exclusive little village just outside Newark where my parents had retired to three years ago. Slim, smart, sophisticated-looking mums with corn-colored hair, pearls, and gigantic wedding rings used them to take their children to their private schools before heading off to the gym or the riding stables, or to have lunch with the girls.

It was pretty obvious that whoever was driving this particular vehicle wasn't in their league, though. The Espace didn't cruise to a sedate stop behind my car, but roared right up to the rear bumper as if to ram it. I wondered whether the driver thought I was sitting in my car before the Espace came to a lurching stop, the hand brake ratcheting so harshly that it sounded like it was being yanked off.

I stood up, feeling a need to draw myself to my full height as the door opened and the driver got out. It was a man in his early twenties, his face burned lobster red from the sun, his mousy hair short and bristly. He had no neck, big powerful shoulders, large stubby hands, and a beer gut. He was wearing a yellow-and-black-hooped Rugby shirt, faded jeans, and Adidas sneakers. He regarded me with hostile indifference, then turned to lock the door of the Espace before lumbering up to me. He looked down at my chest before turning his eyes to my face.

"Nice car," I said.

"It's me mum's," he replied as though I were being dim. "Are you the woman what rung me dad?"

"Yes," I replied, deciding to drop any attempt at civility. "I'm worried about my brother."

"I know. He told me." He put his hand in his pocket and pulled out a big bunch of keys. "Come on, then."

He pushed past me, reeking of sweat, and I followed him into the house. As he clumped upstairs I wondered whether I ought to warn him about the fiddleback, but again I kept my mouth shut to protect Alex. If my brother had brought the spider—and who knew what else?—into the house without Cressley's permission, then he would most likely get in trouble for it. I wasn't so worried about the police being involved—I'm sure Alex had all the right licenses and stuff—I was more concerned about what Cressley and his thuggish son might do. I could easily imagine them stomping Alex's collection to a pulp, and quite literally throwing him and his stuff out onto the street.

"Who gave you my dad's number?" Cressley's son suddenly asked.

We were on the landing outside doors 3 and 4, and I tried not to give anything away. "Why does it matter?"

He nodded at the door to flat 3, and without bothering

to lower his voice said, "I bet it was that silly cow, wasn't it? Always sticking her nose in where it's not wanted."

I flushed angrily. "Nobody stuck their nose in anywhere."

He smiled unpleasantly. "Good job, then, isn't it? 'Cos people who stick their noses in more often than not get 'em chopped off."

I wanted to tell him not to be so pathetic, to stop trying to sound like some crap TV gangster, but I couldn't bring myself to say anything. The thing was, I was wary of this man, as I'm sorry to say I'm wary of a lot of men now. Oh, I know he was ignorant and transparent, and I know he wielded his aggression openly (unlike Matt, who had kept his tucked away out of sight until the time came for him to give terrifying vent to it), but that didn't mean he still wasn't dangerous. Besides, it wasn't as if he was being obstructive—just disagreeable—and uncomfortable as I felt, I could live with that. If it meant getting peace of mind about Alex, then what did a few hostile stares and moronic intimidation tactics matter?

So I shrugged, let it ride, and we proceeded to the top floor, me continuing to scan the stairs for the fiddleback. He kept twirling the big bunch of keys around his finger, jangling them, until he stopped outside the door to my brother's flat, found the one he wanted, and thrust it in the lock. As he twisted the key I stepped forward to follow him in, but he turned before pushing the door open.

"What d'you think you're doing?"

I was taken aback. "Nothing. I mean . . . just waiting for you to unlock the door so we can go in."

He shook his head. "I'll go in. You wait here."

"But I want to see if my brother's okay."

"Are you deaf or just daft? I'll go and see, you stay here."

"Why? What are you hiding?"

"I'm hiding nowt, love. But this is private property. We can't let any Tom, Dick, or Harry look round us tenants' flats."

"But I'm Alex's sister."

"So you say."

"What's that supposed to mean?"

He rolled his eyes. "Why does everything have to mean something? All I'm saying, love, is that I don't know you from Adam. You *say* you're this bloke's sister, but how do I know you're not working with some gang, looking round places to see what folk have got before ripping 'em off?"

"That's ridiculous," I said.

"Maybe it is. But you can't be too careful, can you?"

"I can show you something with my name on it," I said. "My driver's license. It's in the car."

"I'm not interested in all that. I haven't got time to piss about. I'll just go in, have a quick look, and come out and tell you what's what. Then we'll both be happy."

"But I want to see for myself," I said.

"Why? Do you think we're keeping him prisoner here or something?"

"No, of course not."

"Well, then."

"It's just that . . . I know him better than you. I might see something you'd miss."

"If he's in here, love, I think I'll see him easy enough."

"No, I didn't mean that. I meant—"

"Oh, for fuck's sake, I'm not standing here arguing the toss with you all day. I've got stuff to do. Now, either I go in and have a look or we just leave it and I fuck off home, all right?"

I wasn't happy, but I didn't see that I had much alternative. I nodded. "All right."

"Right, then." He opened the door and went inside. Before he shut it behind him I caught a glimpse of a narrow hallway and the edge of a bookcase that was lining one wall of it, making it seem even narrower. That was all.

Less than a minute later he was back. "Well?" I said.

"There's no one in there."

"And how does everything look?" I asked him.

"Fine. Bed's made. Everything looks normal."

I thought of the fiddleback. "There's nothing . . . broken or overturned?"

"Not that I could see."

I was itching to ask about Alex's collection, but I kept my mouth shut. "And there wasn't a note?"

"Not that I could see," Cressley repeated.

"Maybe you missed it."

He sighed. I could see I was really beginning to get on his nerves. "Why would he leave a note in his own flat? There's only him what's got a key to it."

"And you," I said.

"He's not going to leave me a bloody note, is he? I don't give a toss where he's gone."

I clenched my teeth, then said, "I thought he might have left his rent or something."

"Yeah, well, he didn't. Rent's not due for another week. And before you say anything else, I'm not answering any more questions. I'm off home before I get old and die."

He pocketed the keys and stomped away. I waited a minute so I wouldn't have to speak to him again, then followed. I was frustrated that I hadn't got to see Alex's flat, but I thought Cressley Junior was probably telling me the truth when he said Alex wasn't there. Maybe my brother *was* at school, after all. Maybe he had just been busy and hadn't had a chance to return my calls. If that was the case I should be happy that he was finding so much to do here, that he was building a new life for himself. I *should* be, but I couldn't help feeling a bit resentful. What did that say about me? Was I selfish? Was I as clingy and possessive as Cressley had accused me of being? I didn't think so, but then I suppose people are blind to their own faults, aren't they? If they weren't, they'd rectify them. I'd always looked out for Alex, but then he'd always done the same for me as well. So it wasn't all one-way traffic on my part; he rang me as often as I rang him. Did that make both of us possessive? We just needed each other, I suppose; we each felt stronger when the other one was about. We were damaged goods. We bruised easily. Or at least I did after all the horrible stuff with Matt. It used to be that Alex was the vulnerable one, but he'd got over all that now; he was happy with his sexuality. I'd been there for him, he'd been there for me. He was the one constant in my life.

I walked outside and turned my face up to the sunshine. For a few seconds I basked in its warmth. It soothed me as I thought about what to do next. It looked like I'd be staying in Greenwell, at least overnight. I'd already told Alex in my note I was going to stay at the

Solomon Wedge. If he didn't get in touch with me there, I'd try to find out which school he was likely to be teaching at and make my way there tomorrow morning. And if I *still* had no luck, then what? Back to his flat, I suppose, with a crowbar if need be.

Galvanized by my plans, I drove back to the center of town. There was a stone archway beside the Solomon Wedge, with a sign above it which read: CAR PARK (FOR RESIDENTS ONLY). I drove my car through the arch and found a space, which wasn't difficult because there were only four other cars there. One was a spotless electric-blue Porsche, which looked as out of place in these surroundings as a brilliant ray of sunshine on a stormy day. I got out of my car with the Puma sports bag I'd packed the night before, locked it, walked round to the front of the pub, and went inside.

I expected the interior of the pub to match the drabness of the rest of the town, so was pleasantly surprised to find it was actually quite nice in a chintzy, Laura Ashley kind of way. I also half expected the place to be full of locals who would fall silent and turn hostile faces toward me the second I walked in, like in that film, *An American Werewolf in London*. However, there were only three or four men sitting or standing around, and no one paid me much attention beyond an appraising glance. I walked up to the bar and dropped my bag on the floor by my feet. A man who I presumed was the landlord was at the other end, sharing a joke with a skinny, scruffy man with a straggly beard. From the landlord's appearance I guessed that he was the owner of the Porsche. His whole look shouted money, but in a vulgar, ostentatious way. Chunky gold bracelets jangled on his wrists, and the gold rings he wore on each of his fingers were so big and thick they looked more like knuckle-dusters than jewelry. His burgundy silk shirt, shimmering like dolphin hide stretched tight over his beer belly, might have made him look camp if it weren't for his heavy build and pug-nosed face, which gave him the air of an ex-boxer.

I wondered where his money had come from. Business could hardly have been booming in a town like this. Maybe he *was* an ex-boxer who'd retired on the proceeds of a sparkling career to run a pub in his old hometown. Or maybe he was a local gangster and the pub was a front, the legal, modest face of a far more lucrative criminal organization. Then again, I thought, smiling to myself, maybe his lottery numbers had come up and he liked people to know about it.

The landlord and the scruffy man ended their conversation with a roar of laughter, and the landlord came over to me. He was wearing a pair of polychromatic glasses, which had gone quite dark in the sunny pub, reducing his eyes to nothing more than pools of shadow.

"Now then, miss, what can I do for you?" he asked, his voice softer than I'd expected it to be.

I returned the smile he gave me. "I'd like a room, please, if you've got one. I saw your sign outside."

"No problem," he said. "In fact, we've got nine rooms. Nine rooms, nine vacancies. Take your pick."

"Business a bit slow, is it?" I said.

"It's the off-season," he said, and laughed. "People don't come here for their holidays, but businessmen come here sometimes. Conferences and stuff. It's all or nothing with us."

"Okay, which room is the nicest?" I asked him.

He put his elbows on the bar and leaned toward me. I got a whiff of expensive aftershave. "Oh, they're *all* nice. It's all top-quality accommodation here, none of your rubbish. En-suite bathrooms, color TVs. We've even got cable, though not your adult channel," he said with a grin and a wink, "but then you can't have everything, can you?"

I smiled amiably along with him, though cautious not to let him think I was doing anything other than sharing his joke. "Which one is the quietest, then?" I asked.

"That'll be our attic room. Number nine. Furthest away from the bar."

"Sounds perfect," I said.

He got the accommodation register and we sorted out the details. I told him I wasn't sure how long I'd be staying, but paid for two nights, half of which he said would be refundable if I only stayed for one.

"If you give them two a chance to finish their game, I'll get one of them to cover while I carry your bag up," he said, indicating a couple of men playing pool in the corner. "The wife's out shopping and the bar staff don't come in till later. You could have a drink while you're waiting. On the house, of course."

"It's all right," I said, picking my bag up. "I can manage. It's not very heavy."

He grinned again. "You modern women, eh? You'll be the death of old-fashioned blokes like me. Hang on a sec then, love, and I'll get you the keys."

The door that led upstairs was to the right of the bar.

To make up for not carrying my bag, the landlord held the door open, puffing out his chest as if he expected me to swoon with desire at the sight of the little gray curls that poked out of the V of his shirt neck. "Name's Jim, by the way," he said.

"Ruth," I replied.

"No, Jim," he said, deadpan, then laughed. "Sorry, couldn't resist that. I already know your name, though, don't I?"

"Do you?" I said warily.

"Oh aye. I can read upside down."

"I beg your pardon?"

"When you signed the register. Comes through years of practice. Ruth Gemmill, isn't it?"

"Yes," I said. "Does that name mean anything to you?"

"I don't think so. Should it?"

"My brother lives in Greenwell. Alex Gemmill. He's a teacher at the local secondary school."

"Oh aye?"

"I don't suppose you've happened to come across him, have you? Maybe he's been in here for a drink?"

"Happen he has, love. Lots of people come in here. They don't all tell me their names, though."

"No, I don't suppose they do." I paused, then added, "It's just that I'm a bit worried. I haven't been able to get in touch with him for a few days. I've driven up from London to see if he's all right."

"Oh, I'm sure he will be, love. There's not a lot happens in Greenwell. Someone sneezes round here and everyone knows about it."

I nodded, trying to mask my concern with a smile, thinking that that wasn't the impression I'd got of the town at all. It seemed an apathetic place, not an inquisitive one. If the landlord was telling the truth, though, and there was no reason to suspect he wasn't, then it was obvious that I'd underestimated what I'd seen and heard so far. Just because there hadn't been any blatant curiosity shown toward my arrival didn't necessarily mean there wasn't any.

"I'm sure you're right," I said, "but I was due for a visit anyway. To be honest, I don't even know the name of the school where Alex teaches."

"Well, if he teaches in Greenwell he'll be at the high school, won't he?"

"Greenwell High School?"

"Solomon Wedge."

"Ah," I said. "Who is this Solomon Wedge anyway?"

"Town benefactor. He paid for the high school and the hospital and the civic buildings to be built. Mind you, he was a bit of a bugger, by all accounts. Ruled his family and his employees with a rod of iron. Hit his wife over the head once with a walking stick, nearly bloody killed her. Got things done, though. You can't fault him for that."

I thought of Matt. Matt and his big, bony fists. Matt and his terrifying rages.

Got things done, though. You can't fault him for that.

I smiled before the memory could grow strong enough to show on my face, and said, "Well, thanks for your help, Mr. . . . um . . . Jim."

"My pleasure, love," he said. "Now, if there's anything else you want, just give me a shout, all right?"

I went up to my room, two floors above the bar. The final staircase was narrow and led to a landing no bigger than the inside of a lift. Two doors faced each other across the short gap, one numbered 8, the other 9. I unlocked the door of my room and went inside.

It was a lovely light room with a sloping ceiling and a skylight. The walls were yellow and the duvet on the brass-framed double bed was white with yellow flowers. With the bed taking up so much floor space, together with a big pine wardrobe against one wall, a dressing table against another, and a color TV sitting on top of a little chest of drawers in the corner, there wasn't much room to move around, but that didn't matter. I just wanted somewhere to dump my stuff and lay my head.

After unpacking my bag, I made myself a cup of tea, courtesy of the Solomon Wedge, and sat on the bed, my back against the headrest, my legs stretched out. I tried to relax, but I couldn't. I wondered what Alex was doing now, where he was. After drinking the tea and eating the two pieces of shortbread that had also been provided, I took out my mobile and dialed Alex's number. I didn't expect him to reply, but I still felt disappointed when after five rings his answering machine cut in.

I gave a brief account of what I'd done that day, said I was at the Solomon Wedge waiting for his call, and hung up. I looked at my watch and was surprised to see it was already twenty past twelve. How had the morning slipped by so quickly? I ought to get some lunch, especially as I'd skipped breakfast that morning, anxious to be off, but I was so full of nervous energy that I wasn't hungry. My stomach had felt jumpy all day, as if I'd been preparing to take an exam. Promising myself that I'd eat a large meal that evening, hopefully with Alex for company, I adjusted the pillows behind me, lay down, and closed my eyes.

The mattress was incredibly comfortable, and even though I was only lying on top of the duvet I felt enclosed by warmth. Lying there, trying to unwind, I realized that I was clenching my fists over my belly as though anticipating a punch there, and that my feet were crossed at the ankles. I forced myself to unclench them, to place my hands by my sides, and to uncross my ankles, even though it felt unnatural to do so. A year or so ago, when I was staying with Alex after the whole Matt thing, my brother bought me a relaxation tape which consisted of a soothing female voice with sounds of nature in the background—running water, gentle birdsong, that kind of thing. The woman on the tape talked about uncrossing arms and legs, allowing negative energy to flow from the toes and the fingertips, and it wasn't until then that I realized how stressed out I was. It was a defensive instinct, I suppose. I was bracing myself against attack, drawing myself in to make as small a target as possible. I'd made a real effort to change—I might *be* a victim, but I didn't want to look like one—but even now, during times of aggravation, I still catch myself retreating like a snail into its shell. Sometimes I become aware that my fists are aching because I'm clenching them so tight.

I lay on my back and imagined the negative energy flowing out of me, and after a while, in the warmth and comfort and silence, I forgot where I was, what time it was, why I was there. My thoughts began to drift, my head filling up with nonsense that in my semiconscious state seemed to make a weird sort of sense. Somewhere along the line, drugged by fatigue and unable to resist, sleep kidnapped me.

"Shit." I came awake to the sound of my own voice. Immediately I felt anxious, as though there were something vital I had forgotten to do. I looked around, blinking. Where the hell was I? What time was it? I felt utterly confused. I've often wondered if this is what Alzheimer's is like, a permanent state of the kind of disorientation you feel when you wake up in a strange place at an odd time of day.

I held my watch in front of my face and stared at it, waiting for it to make sense. Eventually it did, and as I registered the time—twenty to five—I realized why I felt so agitated. I'd drifted off to sleep with the half-baked notion that maybe I could meet Alex when he came out of school. But now it was too late for that, and I felt bad. Despite everything I'd done, I couldn't help feeling that falling asleep meant I didn't care about my brother enough.

I reached for my mobile and punched in his number again. Getting no reply felt like the punishment that I thought I deserved. I broke the connection as his answering machine cut in. I had nothing to add to my last message beyond asking him where he was and why he hadn't rung me, which I couldn't have made sound anything other than whiny.

In spite of my nap I still felt exhausted, but I made myself sit up and swing my legs over the side of the bed. The room had become hot, stuffy. I opened the skylight and pushed my face up to it, trying to catch what little breeze there was. I felt grimy in my clothes, even though

I'd dressed for the Indian summer we'd been enjoying in London, in shorts and a sleeveless top. I crossed to the door in the corner of the room beside the dressing table and looked into the en-suite bathroom. It was small, modestly decorated, but nice and clean. There was an overhead shower in the bath, and the color of the bathroom suite was what would probably have been called "avocado" in the brochure. I decided to have a shower to try to wake myself up a bit. Once I'd got undressed it took a while to get the temperature right, as I stood in the bath, fiddling with the dial, trying to avoid the powerful jets of water that were spattering up off the plastic, veering between boiling hot and freezing cold. I wanted the water to be lukewarm so it would cool me down. I've never been very good with things that are too hot.

Eventually I got the temperature right, and I stood under the water for a long time, savoring the warm, gentle pummeling on my head and shoulders, feeling cozily enveloped in the spattering barrage of sound. As a little girl I used to pretend I was caught in a tropical downpour whenever I took a shower. I'd sit at the periphery of the jets of water and pretend I was sheltering under a tree while the rain hammered down in front of me.

After a while, I turned off the shower, toweled myself dry, and stepped out of the bath. I crossed to the mirror and squeakily wiped the condensation away with my fingers. I'm thirty-one, and work out, swim, and run when I can, so I guess I've got a pretty good figure. I'm small (five-one) and slim, and more often than not people use the adjective "cute" to describe me. This sometimes makes me feel like a chipmunk, but I guess on the whole it's okay. In the early days, before he revealed his psycho tendencies, Matt used to say I looked like a dark-haired Meg Ryan. I mean, I'm not *that* cute, but I'm lucky in that I come from a good-looking family. Alex is tall, with sandy blond hair, dark eyebrows, and cheekbones to die for, Dad is chiseled and straight-backed, like some ex–sergeant major who has never allowed himself to run to seed, and I've got a picture of Mum in her twenties sitting on a beach in a swimsuit, looking like a blond Elizabeth Taylor.

I dried my hair, which I'd had cut quite short recently, and scrunched some mousse in it to give it that Natalie Imbruglia tousled look. As I put on clean underwear and a pale lilac dress with thin shoulder straps, I started to think about food. It was now five-thirty, and despite the unfocused nervousness still festering in my stomach, I was feeling pretty hungry. Grabbing my shoulder bag, I went downstairs to the bar.

There were more people there than before, maybe thirty or so, mostly a cross section of men who'd come in for a drink after work. Apart from myself there were only four other women in the room: a girl in her late teens, who was flirting shamelessly with a group of lads over by the pool table; a woman whose partner and herself were dressed up enough to make me guess that they were just calling in for a quick one before going on somewhere a bit more salubrious; a thickset, red-faced woman who was sitting with her equally thickset, red-faced husband, both of them staring silently into space as if they'd run out of things to say to each other decades ago. . . .

And the landlady.

To say that she took an instant dislike to me would be an understatement. As soon as I entered the room, she shot me a look of such open hostility that I faltered in my stride. Then I thought that I must have been mistaken, that her filthy look couldn't possibly have been intended for me. I walked up to the bar and smiled at her. She didn't smile back.

"Hi," I said, "I'm—"

"I know who you are. You're the one my husband gave a room to upstairs."

She was a well-built woman with dyed blond hair and a face like a baleful bullfrog. Her aggressive stance made her bright red dress seem like a declaration of war.

"That's right," I said, the smile stiffening on my lips. "Is it a problem?"

"Oh no!" she exclaimed, clearly meaning the opposite. "It's no problem at all!"

"Because if it is," I said, "I'll find somewhere else. I don't mind."

"I said it's no problem!" she snapped, her eyes flashing. "How *is* your room?"

"It's very nice," I said. "Lovely, in fact."

"I'm *so* glad."

"Er . . . I wondered whether you did evening meals?"

She looked at me as if in some way I was adding insult to injury. "No. We don't," she said curtly.

Refusing to be intimidated, I said, "I don't suppose you'd know somewhere nearby, then, would you?"

She stared fiercely at me. Then she said, "Ask Tony. He'll know."

"Tony?" I queried, but she was already moving to

the other end of the bar without even asking if I wanted a drink.

"Someone call?" asked a voice behind me, and I turned to see a small, wiry man in his early thirties with a ferrety face and a receding hairline. He was carrying five empty beer glasses in each hand, a finger in each one, and despite his diminutive stature he looked as though he could handle himself. As he put the glasses on the bar, I noticed a tattoo on his wrist of a fanged cobra rearing up, its mouth gaping wide.

"Are you Tony?" I asked.

"I was when I looked earlier."

"The landlady said you might be able to tell me where I can get something to eat."

"Depends what you fancy. Fish and chips, Chinese, Indian . . ."

"Chinese might be nice, if it's a good one."

"It's not bad. The Red Dragon on Livermore Street."

He gave me directions. I thanked him, then just as he was about to move away I said, "Tony, do you mind if I ask you something?"

"Depends what it is."

I glanced along the bar at the landlady. "Is she all right?"

"How do you mean?"

"Well, it's just that I'm staying here for a night or two and she didn't seem to like it. She was really rude to me."

As I spoke, she turned and looked at me, giving me the impression that she could hear every word we were saying. Maybe Tony thought so, too, because he leaned forward and murmured, "Mirror, mirror."

"What do you—" I said, then cottoned on. "Oh yeah, I see what you mean."

I decided to walk to the restaurant. It wasn't far and it was still warm even though the evenings were drawing in. Despite the warmth, the air was muggy, something that seemed peculiar to the town itself. It was as though the dark brickwork of the narrow streets absorbed the light. I kept blinking, sure there was something in my eye, but there wasn't.

It was not hard to imagine the landlady as the evil queen in a fairy story. It was insulting to think that she might suspect me of being her husband's bit on the side, though maybe her hostility was due to bitter experience. I'd have to watch Jovial Jim for the duration of my stay at the Solomon Wedge, make sure I didn't say anything that he might construe as encouragement. As an added precaution, I'd keep my room door locked when I was in there, and my key in the keyhole. Not that I was overly worried. After my experiences with Matt I reckoned that, if the situation called for it, I could handle Jovial Jim without too much trouble.

The Red Dragon looked like most other Chinese restaurants. There was a black sign with red Oriental-style writing, the name of the place bookended by two dragons curled into an S shape, claws outstretched, breathing fire. Inside there were Chinese lanterns hanging from the ceiling and long strips of what looked like parchment in bamboo frames decorated with Chinese characters. There were about twenty tables, all empty except for one by the bar where four Chinese waiters were sitting, talking and drinking pale, milkless tea. The waiters all looked at me when I walked in. The one nearest the door pushed his chair back, stood up, and smiled.

"Table for one?"

My first instinct was to leave. I'd never been in a restaurant where the waiters outnumber the customers four to one. But now that I was here I was too embarrassed to walk out, and besides I was hungry and it seemed a nice enough place. So I said yes and was led to a table by the window. The waiter gave me a menu and asked if I'd like a drink. I ordered a glass of red wine, and after he left took my mobile out of my bag and tried Alex again. Answering machine as usual. I waited for the beep, then said, "Hi, Alex, it's me. Just to let you know it's about six o'clock and I'm in the Red Dragon on Livermore Street if you get back in time and you'd like to join me. I'm dying to see you. I hope you haven't gone away or anything."

I felt I ought to say more, try to express how nervous and anxious I was, but I couldn't think of a way to phrase it without sounding pathetic. In the end I just said lamely, "Anyway, bye," and broke the connection.

The waiter brought my drink and I ordered crispy fried seaweed, chicken with Szechuan sauce, and special fried rice. As I waited for my food, I sat and stared out the window at the dreary street, which seemed determined to shy away from the early evening sunshine. I rarely feel lonely—I like my own company, and I can always find a million things to do, even when I'm puttering around my flat on my own—but all at once, sitting here in this empty restaurant in this strange and miserable town, I felt a wave of loneliness so profound it almost left me breathless. Suddenly I wanted to walk out of there, get into my car, and drive home. I even started calculating in my head what time I'd get back if I left now. Alex wasn't here. He'd gone away for a few days. He'd call me when he got home. But Alex didn't do that sort of thing. Or maybe he did. Maybe in London I hadn't noticed it because I'd felt as though he were close by even when he wasn't. Maybe Cressley had been right. Maybe I *was* clingy and possessive. I closed my eyes and rubbed my forehead. I couldn't think straight. When I tried to remember recent events they seemed elusive. I couldn't get a handle on them.

The food arrived, and just as I started eating, thankful for the distraction, two people walked into the restaurant. It was the well-dressed couple I'd seen in the pub. They were in high spirits, giggling and laughing. Whenever I see a couple who are happy in each other's company I always immediately think, I wonder if he'll ever hit her. I wonder if he'll ever punch her to the ground, then drop a microwave oven on her head; wonder if he'll ever try to choke her by ramming a TV remote control down her throat; wonder if he'll ever kick her so hard in the stomach that it'll cause her to miscarry. Because that's what Matt did to me, among other things. We started off laughing and giggling and sharing secrets, and we ended up—*I* ended up—terrified for my life.

When Matt was in a rage anything could double as a weapon, as long as it was close at hand. Books, potted plants, crockery, the kettle, the toaster. He once hit me thirty or forty times across the head and shoulders and back with the Dustbuster until it fell apart. Once he even smashed me in the face with a bunch of bananas, which might sound comical, but believe me it wasn't. The bananas were as hard as a fist in my face. I had a black eye for weeks afterward and had to be treated in Casualty for a detached retina. Thanks to Matt I've got scars all over my body and a few around my eyes. They're not big ones, and they're not particularly disfiguring, but they're there all the same. Each one a reminder of over two years' worth of fear and agony.

The food was good, but even though I was hungry I still felt too jittery to enjoy it. I ate dutifully, simply because I needed to fill up the fuel tank. I was halfway through my main course when a group of four people came into the restaurant—two young couples. I turned to look at them and then back to my meal, and as I did so I glimpsed someone strolling by on the pavement outside, past the restaurant's main window. I looked up, and as I did the person walking past half turned towards me and for an instant our eyes met.

It was Matt.

I cried out and jumped up, knocking my chair over. Already Matt had walked on without acknowledging me, and was now out of sight. I was only peripherally aware of everyone staring at me as I dashed across the room and yanked the restaurant door open. I ran out into the street, but there was no one to be seen. I was about to make for the nearest corner, thinking Matt must have disappeared round it, when someone grabbed me from behind.

Certain it was Matt, that he had somehow doubled back and sneaked up behind me, I began to struggle frantically, kicking back with my foot, trying to get his shin. "Hey, you pay your bill!" a voice with an unmistakably Chinese accent said angrily. "You pay or I call the police!"

All the fight went out of me. I stopped struggling, stopped kicking. The waiter behind me still had a tight grip on my arms. "It's all right," I said, "I'm not going to run away."

He held my arms for a few seconds more, then let me go. I turned to face him. "What's your problem?" he demanded.

"I'm sorry," I said. "I wasn't doing a runner. I saw someone outside the restaurant who I knew and it gave me a fright. It was someone who shouldn't be here, someone I hoped I'd never see again."

He was still glaring at me suspiciously. I indicated my table, which I could see through the window, and my half-eaten meal. "Look, if I was going to leave without paying I wasn't very smart about it, was I? I left my bag in there. It's got my money in it, my credit cards, my mobile phone . . ."

He glanced through the window and saw that I was telling the truth. The scowl slowly faded from his face. "Are you all right?" he asked.

I nodded, but internally I was quaking. "I will be."

"You want to come back in and finish your meal?"

"I'm not very hungry," I said. "I mean, the food was very nice, but all this has shaken me up a bit."

"Who did you see?" the waiter asked, looking up and down the street.

"Just . . . someone from my past. It's a long story."

"Okay. Well, if you don't want to finish your meal, how about a drink? You look as though you need one."

I thought of going back inside, of everyone staring at me, but then I was going to have to do that anyway, to get my bag and pay for my meal. I took one last look up the street, then shrugged. "Okay." Already I was beginning to wonder if I'd even seen Matt at all.

Fair

THE FIRST TIME I saw Matt he was being killed by a space monster. He had to hold the thing's tentacles to his throat to make it look as though it were strangling him. I remember thinking how convincingly he gurgled and choked and writhed on the ground. I also remember thinking what a nice smile he had when I saw him joking with the crew between shots.

The film was a low-budget science fiction thriller called *Satan's Star*. Matt was playing a security man who had about three lines before meeting his grisly demise. I was the production designer, and although I've worked on better things since, I was really excited at the time because it was my first film. My work on the movie was effectively over, but I'd asked to stay on set to take some photos and make some notes. I never thought the film would amount to much, but I've actually got more work through *Satan's Star* than anything else I've ever done. It turned out to be a tautly directed, well-played, and well-reviewed little movie, and although its theatrical release was minimal to say the least, it's done—and continues to do—good business on video.

Matt was only around for a couple of days of the six-week shoot, but he came to the wrap party, which was where I saw him again. The director, Jack Proby, who has since gone on to direct that thing with Ralph Fiennes and Gwyneth Paltrow, the one set in China that won all the awards, had a friend who owned a nightclub in East London, which we basically took over for the evening. All the cast and crew were encouraged to bring as many friends as possible to fill the place out. I wanted to take Alex, but for some reason—I can't remember why now—he couldn't come.

So I went with Keri, my flatmate, who kept asking me if there were any hunky men in the cast (she only ever watched films starring hunky men, and I think she was genuinely disappointed when I told her that no, I didn't think either Brad Pitt *or* George Clooney would be there). I thought about mentioning Matt, but I didn't. I'd had no particular designs on him as I'd set out that evening, but, in truth, I felt an odd desire to keep him a secret. Instead I told her that the lead was nice-looking, if a bit dim, which cheered her up. In the end, though, she went off with Steve, the soundman, who was married with two teenage daughters. This led to all sorts of complications later on, but that's another story.

The party was in full swing when we got there, even though Keri and I hadn't exactly arrived late ourselves. That's the thing with film and TV people—they don't waste time when there's a sniff of a party around. Keri and I didn't waste time either. We were really in the mood for it, and got stuck into the cocktails straightaway.

Back at the flat, Keri had produced a bottle of Malibu, which we'd been drinking as we got ready, becoming increasingly giggly with each liberal top-up. It's a wonder my makeup wasn't smeared all over my face. Or maybe it was. To be honest, I just didn't care. Having said that, I felt instinctively that I looked good. I felt *hot,* as Keri would say—as she had *already* said, in fact. Back at the flat she had run her hands over her luxurious curves, barely contained by the little black number she'd poured them into, and had exclaimed, "Ooh, I feel *hot* tonight. Some bloke is going to get *very* lucky later on."

The thing about Keri is that she always felt *hot.* Her supreme self-confidence was one of the things I liked about her. She was a big girl—not fat but voluptuous— with a lustrous tumble of naturally corkscrew-curly black hair and her grandfather's Italian temperament. We'd met at college (she had a degree in economic history, but she always played down her academic side as if she were embarrassed by it). We had shared various flats together for almost ten years.

Although neither of us realized it until later, this night was to be the start of the downward slope as far as our friendship was concerned. Not that we fell out or anything, not seriously anyway; it's just that a certain set of circumstances were set in motion that forced us both to reevaluate our lives. For Keri there was Steve the soundman, the messy situation with Steve's wife and kids— which led on one occasion to Steve's wife, Sue, standing outside our building at two o'clock in the morning, screaming at the top of her lungs for Keri to come out and face her (Keri didn't)—and Keri's eventual decision to take a job in Holland to get away from the whole sorry mess.

And for me, of course, there was Matt.

"Matt, Matt, super rat," Keri was to call him later when he started hitting me. "Why don't you give him the fucking elbow, Ruthie?"

I've asked myself this question many times, and looking back I'm astonished that I put up with so much, - astonished that I didn't walk away from him the first time he laid a finger on me. But back then, embroiled in it all . . . oh, I don't know. I honestly thought it was my fault that he acted the way he did, that it was me who'd brought out the violent side of his nature, and that therefore it was up to me to exorcise it from his system. I knew he was capable of tenderness, and had seen how remorseful he became each time he hurt me (at first anyway). I could probably write a book on the complexities of our relationship, on my constantly shifting emotions, my ever-changing mind, but let's just say that nothing is ever as black and white as it seems, that love is not only blind but pathetic too. It can turn us into victims and fools, reduce us to the kind of people who infuriate us on soap operas, the kind you want to scream at for allowing the creep or the bitch to walk all over them.

Does that sound cynical and bitter? Sad even? If so, then tough tits. It's not that I don't believe in love; in *real* love. All I'm saying is, it's a jungle out there. It can be wondrous and beautiful, but it's also full of dangerous predators, and if you don't tread carefully then chances are you'll get eaten alive.

I can't remember the name of the club, but I remember the song that was playing as we walked in. It was an updated extended remix of Donna Summer's "I Feel Love." The beat that underlay Donna's breathy vocals was like a pumping heart, like the pulse of the club itself. The people, caught in splashes of colored light like a rapid series of photographic stills, were like components of the body's inner workings, plucked into frantic animation by the stimulus of the music. It was sexy and organic and abandoned, and as I've never been much of a clubber, it was special to me, rare and exhilarating. I turned to Keri with (I'm sure) a look of wide-eyed glee and exclaimed, "This is great!"

I was ready to head straight for the dance floor, but Keri pointed over to the bar. "Let's get a drink!" she shouted.

I followed her to the bar, thinking how glad I was that I hadn't come here on my own. Everyone who wasn't dancing seemed to be standing in groups, laughing and drinking and holding shouted conversations above the music. I recognized networking when I saw it. These people were cementing relationships, extracting or offering vague promises of future employment. I felt a pang. I should be doing this. If I wanted to get on in this cutthroat industry, I should be getting in with the movers and shakers, chatting with producers, directors, even actors, who weren't big names now, but who might be in the future.

To be honest, it was only a brief pang. It's not that I'm not ambitious, it's just that I'm not superficial enough to chat with people for the express purpose of furthering my career. I may be cynical about love, but not about work. Besides, I've done okay. I haven't won an Oscar, haven't even done a big movie—not yet anyway—but

I've done lots of TV work and little films. My job's interesting, I'm happy, and I make a good living out of it. When it comes down to it, surely that's all that matters.

The next hour or two alternated between drinking and dancing. Keri and I must have tried every cocktail in the place. Some of them had disgusting names—Keri took great delight in asking the barman, a young, shaven-headed black guy with the most amazing body I've ever seen, for an Oozing Purple Helmet—and I have no idea what was in most of them, but we drank them regardless.

"We're going to be very ill," I said to Keri as we sipped electric-green liquid through the straws in our long glasses. I had no idea what time it was at this point, or how many drinks we'd had.

Keri regarded her drink—I think it was called Goblin on a Toadstool—and shook her head. "Nah, they're nearly all fruit juice, these things. Anyway, we're sweating out the alcohol down on the dance floor. It'll be squirting out of our pores in little jets."

"Lovely," I said, deciding not to tell her that I was already feeling queasy.

Keri finished her drink by eating the piece of kiwi fruit that came with it, then removing the straw and the cocktail stick and chugging it all back, ice and all. She banged the glass down on the unoccupied table we'd found near the bar, looking a little dazed and wearing a green moustache. She burped just as one dance track segued into another, then looked up, eyes glittering, over-bright. "Oh, I *love* this one!" she exclaimed. "Come on, Ruthie."

"I think I'll sit this one out," I said, crossing my arms on the table and resting my forehead on them.

I sensed her crouching down beside me. "Are you all right?"

"Just a bit tired," I said. "You go. I'll wait here."

She said something else, but I didn't catch it, and then she was gone. I sat for a while, my upper body slumped over the table, finding comfort in the darkness behind my closed eyelids. The music seemed far away, tuneless; only the rapid thump-thump of its beat seemed to penetrate my senses. I could have slept there quite happily, knowing that Keri would eventually come back and look after me, if the darkness I was suspended in hadn't suddenly started spinning.

There is a philosophy that everything we do is preordained, that there is some Great Plan in which we all play our part. My personal philosophy is that that's easy enough to believe when things are going well. It's easy to look around when you're happy and healthy and think that there's a meaning, a purpose, a *symmetry,* in everything you experience around you. But when your life is shit, when you're stuck in a nightmare you can't see your way out of, then there's no symmetry whatsoever—there's just clinging, howling chaos. Look at the concentration camps, look at Rwanda, Vietnam, Kosovo. Look at bereaved parents, raped women, the victims of torture. Are they part of the Great Plan? Is there a symmetry and a purpose to what has happened to them? They say that God moves in mysterious ways. But why? Why should He? What's the fucking point in that? Does He test us by murdering our children? By inflicting pain and terror and misery on kind, hardworking, law-abiding people? I sometimes wonder, if there is a God, why He had it in for me? What had *I* done to piss Him off? What possible purpose was there in moving Matt and me into conjunction on that fateful night?

If I'd had less of an alcohol tolerance I'd have been puking my guts out in the ladies' room sooner, or would maybe even have been dozing in a cab on my way home; if I'd had more I'd have been down on the dance floor with Keri, boogeying to M People or Livin' Joy or whoever was playing at the time.

But no. Fate decreed otherwise. It produced Matt just as I'd pretty much forgotten about him. Earlier in the evening I'd been covertly looking around for him, but in the end had decided, with only a hint of disappointment, that he wasn't going to show. For the past hour or more (like I say, time was no longer a concept I had any grasp of), I hadn't given him a second thought.

The need to be sick didn't so much sweep over me as surge up through my body like an irresistible tidal swell. I stood up quickly, with the vague impression that I'd knocked something over—my chair or a glass maybe. The room was swaying and spinning around me. I was disorientated, but I instinctively knew where the ladies' room was. I saw the lilac neon glow of the lettering blurring and doubling, maybe fifty yards away to the right of the bar.

I edged around the table and began to head in that direction, feeling as though I were trying to make my way across the lurching floor of a funhouse. I managed to stagger about halfway with no great mishaps, and then the floor abruptly tilted (or so it seemed to me) and I went flying.

Maybe it would have been better if the floor had broken my fall. Maybe if I'd bruised my dignity it would have saved a whole load of physical bruises later on. Or maybe my fate was already sealed. I never asked him, but it could have been that Matt had been watching me for some time.

It wasn't Matt I staggered into, though. It was a guy in a trendy suit whom I'd never seen before. He was tall and thickset, dark-haired, and with the kind of heavy stubble that made it look as though he shaved about four times a day. Even in my drunken state, I remember thinking that he looked a bit like Oliver Tobias in his younger days. I sprawled into him and knocked his glass of whiskey all down the front of his trousers. Ice cubes bounced off his crotch. His glass smashed on the floor, the sound of it drowned out by the pounding of the music.

He spun round aggressively, his glare only slightly diminishing when he saw me. Oddly, despite the music, I heard every word he said. "Oh, thanks a lot. Now I look as though I've pissed myself. What the hell were you trying to do?"

The person he'd been talking to at the bar, a chubby guy in a green shirt who was clutching a bottle of lager, grinned and shouted, "It was a hell of a way to get your attention."

I held up a hand in apology (I felt so ill I didn't trust myself to talk) and tried to move away. However, "Oliver" curled his hand around my upper arm, not roughly but strongly enough so that I would have to make a point of yanking it from his grasp.

"Hey, hey," he said, starting to smile, "you can't just walk off after making me spill perfectly good Scotch over my bollocks. Aren't you at least going to say you're sorry?"

"Watch him, love. He'll be asking you to lick it off in a minute," his fat friend said.

I felt another surge inside me, and this time what seemed like several pints of pukey bittersweet alcohol rushed up my throat and into my mouth. I clamped my teeth together, my cheeks bulging, and tried to wrench free of his grasp in a panic to get to the toilet. "Oi!" he shouted, and instinctively gripped my arm tighter, enough to bruise.

I threw up all over him.

There was really nothing I could have done to stop it. All the multicolored cocktails I'd quaffed jetted out of me like water from a high-pressure hose. My first gush of vomit went down the guy's front, staining his shirt, soaking his tie, ruining his jacket. A look of utter horror crossed his face and he jumped back, pointlessly late, though at least he avoided the secondary gush, which hit the floor and spattered up the bar. Even after that my stomach kept spasming; I felt horribly weak, boneless, as if everything inside me were being crushed to liquid and ejected from my system. As well as the puke that was coming out of my mouth, there was sweat trickling from every pore, snot running out of my nose, and tears being squeezed from my eyes. I wanted to get out of there—even in that state I was mortified by my conduct—but I couldn't. My body was intent on ridding itself of the poisonous stuff I'd been subjecting it to all evening.

Tears were running down my face now, forced out

through the pressure rising up from deep within my guts. It was while I was raising my head and drawing in a breath that I felt a hand on my chest just above my left tit. My initial instinct was that the guy in the puke-covered suit was taking advantage of my situation to cop a feel. But then the hand shoved me with a force that caused pain to flare hotly in my breastbone and I was propelled backward, far too quickly for my legs to cope, my arms pinwheeling vainly.

I landed on my bum with such a jarring thump that it sent a white zigzag of pain up my back and into my head. I lay there, the pain so bad that I couldn't move; I felt sure that I'd broken my spine. There was a roaring inside my skull and what seemed like a black buzzing swarm of flies across my vision. I brought trembling hands up to my face and rubbed my eyes. My hands came away wet with tears and a few moments later my senses started to return.

The roaring, I realized, wasn't in my head but outside. The guy I'd puked on was leaning over me, ranting and raving, going on about his suit and calling me a stupid bitch. If I'd been in any fit state, I'd have calmed him down, apologized, and told him I'd pay for the damage. But I was incapable of doing anything. My surroundings seemed dreamlike; only the sickness in my stomach and pain in my head and back seemed real.

The next thing I remember is the T-shirt, so blindingly white that I had to screw up my eyes. The man wearing it came up behind the guy I'd puked on, seemed to tower over him for a moment because the guy I'd puked on was still bending over me, shouting and breathing whiskey fumes in my face. What I remember happening next (and this may not be such an accurate account because I was pretty much out of it by this time) was the man in the T-shirt reaching down, his hand seeming huge, like the clawed scoop on an excavator, and grabbing the guy by the shoulder. Then he seemed to yank the guy backward with ease. I have a (no doubt false) memory of the guy's feet actually leaving the ground like a character in a cartoon, of the almost comically startled expression on his face. I'm not sure what happened next—presumably words were exchanged, maybe even blows. All I know is that suddenly the Oliver Tobias guy was no longer there and Matt—his T-shirt like the breastplate of shining white armor—was kneeling beside me, cradling my head, asking me if I was all right.

Five

THE HOUSE IS TALL and narrow. There is a black wrought-iron gate which creaks when I push it, and a mosaic floor in the vestibule. I don't know why I'm here, but I know it's important that I am. I twist the doorknob and the door opens. I walk into a high-ceilinged hallway with a tiled floor. There are pictures on the walls, and a mirror which has candleholders built into the wooden frame. Two red candles flank the mirror, and when I look into the glass I half expect to see an image from some Gothic fairy tale staring back at me. Overhead is a stained-glass lampshade, the dark bulb coated in a fine layer of dust. The place is quiet, like an early morning house preparing to come alive. There is a door to my left, and at the end of the corridor, beyond the wide staircase hogging two-thirds of the hallway's space to my right, is a kitchen, its door standing open. I see dust motes twisting in the glowing air. I see pine wall cabinets, and at the back of the room I see a sink with old-fashioned brass taps beneath a window.

I go upstairs. Greeting me on the first landing is a bookcase crammed so full that books are lying horizontally across those that are vertically stacked, using up all of the available space. There is a bathroom decorated in blue-and-orange-striped wallpaper and a bath on clawed feet, and a toilet seat and lid that are of clear melamine with dozens of plastic creepy crawlies—spiders and beetles and cockroaches—embedded in them. Above the toilet is a large framed black-and-white photograph depicting beautiful buildings on a misty morning. The word VIENNA is printed in white across the bottom of the picture.

The second room on this floor is small and plays host to a blue-and-white-striped sofa bed and two large bookcases. The sofa bed has a dust sheet partly covering it. Another sheet completely covers a wicker armchair by the window, conveying the look of a crouching figure. How do I know that there is a wicker armchair beneath the sheet? Similarly, how do I know that there is an Apple Mac computer and laser printer beneath the sheet draped over the desk between the two bookcases?

I cannot answer these questions. I try to peer into my own head, to retrieve the information that I know is stored in there, but my memory is as shrouded as the items in the room.

The final room on this floor takes me back to the front of the house. It is a large room, a bedroom with a rust-colored carpet, an old brass bed, and bulky pieces of furniture draped with more dust sheets. Above the bed is a large gouache painting, in browns and greens and mustard yellows—autumnal colors—depicting two grotesque figures seated at a table, eating a roast dinner.

The figures have big square teeth and leering expressions and they are holding serrated steak knives upright in their hands as if about to do battle with them. It is a disturbing painting, and the most disturbing aspect is that the figures have black crosses instead of eyes and that both are wearing red crowns which look like the paper party hats you get in Christmas crackers.

The only piece of furniture in this room not concealed by a sheet is the bedside table on which there are three items. A foil-backed bubble-pack of Nurofen, two tablets of which have been removed; a lava lamp, switched off, the red wax lying at the bottom of the tube of yellow oil like a lump of congealed blood; a dog-eared paperback—*Birdsong* by Sebastian Faulks—with a Borders bookmark inside it.

All three items, and the surface of the bedside table, are coated with a fine layer of dust.

Dead skin, I think, as I go downstairs. Ninety percent of dust is dead skin, flaking off our bodies in minute fragments whenever we move, swirling into the air and then settling around us. Perhaps that's why this place is not dustier than it ought to be. There has been no skin here, dead or otherwise, for a long time.

Small bubbles of memory rise from the depths and pop before they reach the surface. I reach the bottom of the stairs, which creak comfortably beneath my weight. I enter the room closest to the front door.

This room makes me dry-mouthed, impels me to shy away, to turn my head and screw my eyes tightly shut. I don't know why. It is a long room, stretching from the front to the back of the house, divided into two by an arch. The wall to my left is dominated by large bay windows which overlook the street outside. Set a little in front of the windows, facing the room, is a small sofa. Set at right angles to that, to my immediate left, is a larger sofa. A long low coffee table stands in the middle of the floor, reachable from the two sofas, and although this table—like the sofas, like every other item of furniture in this room—is covered with a dust sheet, I think of it cluttered with magazines and newspapers and paperback books, with mugs of coffee and tea, with glasses of wine, with bottles of beer.

Beyond the expanse of the coffee table is a television and video (an Aiwa, I think, though I cannot see it beneath the sheet). Behind the TV and video, on the opposite wall from where I'm standing, are shelves full of videos. I can see *It's a Wonderful Life, Citizen Kane, Withnail and I, The Italian Job, Bullitt.* Between these shelves and more containing a sound system and hundreds of CDs is a large open fireplace with a tiled surround (a red Art Deco design) and a black marble mantelpiece covered with unusual pots, objets d'art, raku vases. Through the arch is a large dining table beneath a black iron chandelier holding a profusion of cream-colored candles. There are more fitted shelves, these full of books like the ones upstairs, and a grandfather clock, silent beneath its sheet. At the back of this room are French doors which lead out to an enclosed patio. The walls of this long room are painted a dark, rich red and the carpet is green. It would be a beautiful room without the dust sheets, dramatic, yet cozy, full of a life heartily lived. But it frightens me. It frightens me to my very core.

I step into the room. It is silent, but I expect to hear

some sound, some commotion—I have to resist the urge to cover my ears. My attention is drawn to the telephone and answering machine on one of the deep shelves that house the collection of videos. Dread is crawling in my stomach, but I walk to the telephone and lift the receiver. The line is dead. I try the answering machine. Also nothing. I put down the receiver, take a deep breath, and turn to face the room, as if about to make an important announcement. I register movement from the corner of my eye, and turn my head a fraction to focus my full attention on it.

Something is moving beneath the dust sheet covering the larger of the two sofas. At least this is what I think I see, because the instant I bring my gaze fully to bear on the spot where I noticed the movement, it ceases. It was not a significant movement. I walk across to the sofa. Because of the coffee table pressing against the backs of my knees, my bare legs are closer to the sofa than I would wish them to be. Nevertheless I reach down, take an edge of the sheet in my hand, and peel it back from the object beneath.

The mound beneath the sheet is not caused by an insect. Instead what I see lying on the sofa cushion is a book. It is a book I have seen many times before. Indeed, I have three copies of this book in my flat in London. I pick it up to feel the weight of it in my hand, and examine the cover. Beneath the photograph of the slender brown spider sitting on what appears to be a dried-out leaf is my brother's name. Above the photograph is the title of the book: FIDDLEBACK.

Six

THE BED IN THE Solomon Wedge was so comfortable, and my sleep so deep, that the vividness of my dreams made them seem more real than the world I woke up to. Certainly my first thought, the memory of seeing Matt pass by the window of the Red Dragon, seemed more dreamlike than my actual dreams had been. The recollection unfolded in my mind in slow motion: Matt swiveling his head like an owl, his eyes snaring mine; me rising to my feet, my chair falling over like a progressive succession of freeze-frame images, taking an eternity to hit the floor.

It wasn't him. Couldn't have been. The fact that I had woken up thinking about the incident made me angry. *Fuck off, Matt,* I thought, *I don't want you in my head. You're no longer important. You're insignificant to me. Only Alex matters.*

Alex. I tried calling him again, with the usual result. My stomach was still growling with anxiety, but I made myself eat a fried breakfast (something I never do at home), and was actually enjoying it until Jim the land-lord's wife stuck her head round the kitchen door and looked at me, an indeterminate expression on her face. That started me wondering whether she'd done some-thing to my meal. Spat in my food, or laced it with rat poison, or pissed in the teapot. I left the meal half eaten and went out, got into my car, and drove to the school, which was situated on the other side of town, beyond the outskirts, a mile or so into open country.

As I drove through the main gates, a sea of arriving pupils parted slowly, resentfully, before me. I saw fields and hills rolling away behind and to the side of the chain-link boundary that caged the football and rugby fields, like a tantalizing display of unattainable freedom.

It was the Chinese waiter at the Red Dragon who had told me where the school was. We got to talking over a drink when I went back in to get my stuff and pay my bill. Turned out he had a nine-year-old daugh-ter at the school, but he'd never heard of Alex. Mind you, the only staff member he did seem to know was Mr. Rudding, the headmaster. I got the impression he left that sort of thing to his wife.

Kids stared at me as I parked my car and got out. I hate walking into schools as a stranger, as a rogue ele-ment with no inkling of what motivates the unique in-ternal culture of such a place. I tried to appear blasé as I moved with the flow of human traffic, intimidated by the fact that half the older kids were taller than I was. Whenever I saw a tall, blond-haired male my heart momentarily leaped before sinking in disappointment. Eventually I saw a stocky man with a beard, whose main task seemed to be to tell kids not to run in the corridors. "Excuse me," I said to him, "I'm looking for Alex Gemmill."

He squinted at me from beneath wiry graying eyebrows. "Girlfriend, are you?"

He had a Welsh accent and pale blue eyes. I laughed. "No, I'm his sister, Ruth."

"Sister, eh? Well now, I don't think I've seen Alex for a few days. Mind you, we don't cross swords that often. Different departments, different timetables, you understand. That's the modern education system for you."

He grinned suddenly, small white teeth springing forward through the slit in his bristly beard.

"Have you any idea who might know where he is?" I asked.

He turned his pale eyes on a boy who was hailing a friend down the length of the corridor. Seeing him, the boy clamped up immediately. "Sorry, sir," he muttered.

"Mr. Rudding would be your best bet," the teacher said, turning his attention back to me. "Have you met our esteemed head?"

It was hard to tell whether he was being ironic or not. "No, I haven't."

He gave me directions, and then, as though welcoming a permanent fixture, extended a hand and said, "I'm Mr. Thomas, by the way."

Two minutes later I was tapping on the door of the headmaster's office. When a voice called, "Come in," I opened the door and stuck my head in. I saw a thin, almost scrawny man seated behind a desk that looked too large for him, opening letters.

"Could you spare a moment?" I asked.

"Several if it's important," he replied, making rather a show of placing a half-opened letter carefully down. "Which of our little clan is yours?"

"What? Oh no, I'm not a parent. I'm a teacher's sister. That is, my brother's a teacher here. Alex Gemmill. I'm Ruth."

He smirked at my rushed explanation. I'm not sure whether it was that or his cold, appraising eyes that made me take an instant dislike to him. "Oh yes," he said, emphasizing the second word. "I can see the family resemblance now. My, you are a pretty family, aren't you? Of course, you're far more appealing to me than your brother is. I wouldn't want to give you the wrong impression."

I offered a tight-lipped smile, then was immediately annoyed at myself for giving him even this, for allowing him to think that he had amused me even slightly. Ignoring his comments, I asked, "Mr. Rudding, has Alex been in to school this week?"

Instantly he looked playfully reproachful, an expression that made my skin crawl. "No, he hasn't," he said, his tone of voice mimicking his expression. "He's rather a naughty boy, taking time off without offering any explanation."

"I'm a bit worried about him," I admitted. "It's not like Alex to be so unreliable."

"I'll have to take your word for that," Rudding said.

I looked at him, but his eyes, though appropriately attentive, were unreadable. "What do you mean?"

"Simply that I've only known Alex for a few weeks. It takes time and effort to develop a level of trust between two people. I'm afraid Alex has rather jeopardized that already."

I felt anger welling up inside me, though what Rudding was saying was reasonable enough. "Did my brother seem happy here, Mr. Rudding?" I asked. "Or rather, what I mean to say is, had he settled in okay to his new job?"

Rudding steepled his fingers as though about to pray. "My staff and I have made every effort to ensure that he was comfortable."

Comfortable. It was an odd choice of words. It made Alex sound like a hospital patient. I had the feeling that I was losing the thread of this conversation, that there was a hidden meaning behind Rudding's words. Could it have something to do with Alex's sexuality? Had he been ostracized because of it? In a place like Greenwell it was easy to imagine that he had.

Treading carefully, I asked, "Is Alex popular with the other staff? And with the pupils, too, come to think of that?"

Those oily, watchful eyes. That slight smirk. "Is there a reason why he shouldn't be?"

I was getting more annoyed, but I didn't think it would do me any good to show it. "Of course not," I said. "Alex is a lovely person. But that doesn't answer my question, Mr. Rudding."

Rudding's steepled fingers meshed together. It was like watching some probing sea-creature suddenly retreat into itself for protection. "I certainly find him a very pleasant young man," he said almost primly.

"And the rest of the staff? No problems there?"

"None that I'm aware of, though you'd have to speak to them about it."

"And what about Alex's pupils? Have any of them caused him any trouble?"

"Enough to make him flee, you mean?"

I scowled at his obvious amusement. "Of course not. I'm just trying to get to the bottom of things. There must be *some* reason why Alex has disappeared. As I said, it's not like him to do something like this. He's a very conscientious person."

Rudding cocked his head to one side and appraised me condescendingly. "Miss Gemmill," he said, "or is it Ms.? You young women are so touchy about such things these days."

I waved a dismissive hand. "Whatever."

"*Miss* Gemmill," he resumed, "as far as I am aware, your brother is a good and popular staff member. In my limited dealings with him, I have, until these past few days, found him to be both reliable and efficient. Now, why he has suddenly decided to leave us in the lurch like this, I have no idea, but rest assured, when he does deign to turn up I shall listen to any explanation he might care to offer with a sympathetic ear."

"Right," I said, "good. And if he does get in touch with you, you'll let me know?"

"If he wishes us to do so, certainly."

I wrote down where I was staying and the number of my mobile and gave it to him. He glanced at the slip of paper, then put it in the top right-hand drawer of his desk. Then he stood up, leaning forward slightly as though to kiss me. "And now, Miss Gemmill, I really must excuse myself. I have assembly in five minutes."

"No problem," I said, and stood up too. "Thanks for your time."

"My pleasure," he said obsequiously. He jabbed a hand toward me and I responded automatically. He caressed my fingers for a moment until I pulled my hand away. "Try not to worry, Miss Gemmill. I'm sure Alex will turn up."

"I'm sure he will too," I said.

I walked hurriedly away from his office, as if afraid he might come after me. My meeting with Rudding had left me with a sense of distaste, disquiet. There were few people in the corridors now. A couple of children making their way to their classrooms or assembly, that was all. My sandals clopped like hooves on the floor. I passed posters carrying warnings about drug and alcohol abuse, about AIDS. I walked out into bright sunshine and headed for the car park. As I turned the corner at the side of the building and my car came into sight, I saw three children standing by the driver's door.

At first I thought they were up to no good, and was about to call out, but then I realized that they were just standing there as if waiting for someone. There were two girls and a boy. They couldn't have been more than eleven or twelve. One of the girls had ginger hair and freckles, the other had blond hair kept neatly in place with an Alice band, and the boy was stocky with an unruly mop of dark hair.

They reacted when they saw me, looked at each other, and nodded, and I realized with a little jolt of alarm that they must have been waiting for me. The girl with the Alice band strode forward. "Excuse me, miss," she said.

"Yes," I replied warily.

"Sorry, miss, but are you Mr. Gemmill's wife?"

I smiled, relaxing a little. "No, but you're the second person who's made that mistake today. I'm his sister."

"Oh," the girl said, "but are you looking for him?"

Taken aback, I said, "Yes, I am. Do you know where he is?"

The children looked at each other, the boy raising his eyebrows at the girl with the Alice band, as if to say, *You tell.* "What is it?" I asked, alarmed for a different reason now. "Please tell me."

The girl with the Alice band looked solemnly at me. "He's been taken by the gray man," she said.

"What—" I began, but could get no further. A bellowing voice behind me made me jerk my shoulders so violently that a bolt of pain shot through my neck.

"You three! What are you doing out of school? Didn't you hear the bell?"

The children looked suddenly terrified. Still recovering from the shock, I turned and saw the previously watchful, self-assured Mr. Rudding, now crimson-faced, apoplectic with rage. Before any of them could respond, he screeched, "Get to assembly this instant!"

The children turned and fled, footsteps like a receding hailstorm. I glanced at them, then turned back to Rudding, my heart pounding. "I hardly think that was necessary," I said.

His momentary fit of rage was abating as abruptly as it had appeared. His face was paling, the terrifying bolt of emotion he had unleashed retreating back beneath his composed façade.

"The children should have been in school," he said. "I was concerned that they were intimidating you."

"Well, they weren't," I snapped. "They were just trying to be helpful."

"Oh? In what way?"

I briefly considered telling him what they had said, then decided against it. He seemed too eager, and at the same time too calculating. He seemed, in fact, like a man who was keeping secrets, which was why I decided that I would keep mine. "It's not important," I said. "Good-bye, Mr. Rudding."

I got into my car and drove away.

Seven

I WAS HALF A mile from the school before I realized that Alex was truly missing. Until now I had expected to catch up with him somewhere, had imagined myself walking into a homely staff room to see him slouched in a tatty old armchair, sipping a mug of tea, engrossed in his *Guardian*. I had even envisaged what he would be wearing: his blue Ted Sherman shirt, his mustard-yellow moleskins, his black suede Timberland boots. He would look up and a grin, half astonishment and half delight, would appear on his face.

"Ruthie!" he'd cry. "What are you doing here?"

I had expected to come away from the school with everything settled again, with all of yesterday's dislocating strangeness diminished to nothing more than an un-usual sequence of events to relate over an uproarious supper. But instead I had come away in turmoil, scared and disturbed not only by the confirmation that Alex had gone AWOL but by my encounter with Rudding and the children.

He's been taken by the gray man.

What had the little girl meant by that? Was it some childish epithet for an actual person? Some village bogeyman?

I had the disturbing impression that all of the odd occurrences since I had arrived here yesterday slotted together into a kind of pattern that nevertheless made no sense.

Omens. Omens and signs. But of what?

Something wicked, I thought. By the pricking of my thumbs, something wicked this way comes.

I shuddered, then laughed, a brittle sound. I was getting ridiculous. Fatigue, anxiety, the disorientation of being in a strange place; that's all it was. I needed to do something positive, something real. I decided it was time to report Alex's disappearance to the police.

The station, which I found after a bit of driving around, having vaguely remembered seeing one on my way into town yesterday, was parochial, unimpressive. It was a low, squat building with pebble-dashed walls blotched with patches of damp. It crouched behind a car park with space enough for two dozen cars, but which at this moment contained less than half of that capacity. I parked my own car and got out. The unseasonably warm air was undisturbed, giving me the impression that the place was poised, as I walked up to the only door I could see and entered the building.

The entrance vestibule was tiny, facilitating no more than three steps in any direction before leading into a wall. Opposite the door was what looked like a ticket window in a local railway station, a Perspex screen behind it and a canvas blind pulled down behind that.

There were a few dog-eared posters on the walls about drunk driving and the like. One poster showed a chubby, dark-haired girl grinning out from beneath the word MISSING, printed in red block capitals. I skim-read the text and noticed that she had disappeared from home while on an errand over five years ago.

I tapped on the Perspex screen and the canvas blind shot up, scaring me half to death. The police officer who'd been standing behind it had short, prematurely graying hair and a stern expression. "What is it?" he demanded, as if I were trespassing.

"Um . . . I've come to report a missing person."

He stared at me, unblinking and thin-lipped, as though he thought I was giving him a hard time, as though weary of the same punch line. And then, so flatly that I didn't know whether it was a prompt to continue or an acknowledgment of something he'd been expecting, he said, "Oh yes."

"Yes. It's my brother. Alex Gemmill. I haven't been able to get in touch with him for about four days now. He's not in his flat, he's not been to work, he's just disappeared. He's a teacher at Solomon Wedge School, he hasn't lived here long. It's not like him to disappear like this. I'm really worried about him."

The officer stared blankly at me for a moment longer, then bent down behind his desk. As he did, he muttered what sounded like "Fucking queer."

I leaned forward so I wouldn't lose sight of him. "Excuse me, what did you say?"

The policeman straightened up with a white form in his hand. "Pardon?"

"I just wondered what you'd said just then, when you bent down."

"I didn't say anything."

"Yes you did. I heard you."

Though his expression was fixed, contempt shone in the policeman's eyes. I could almost see the sneer curling behind his professional mask. His lips barely moved as he said, "What did you think you heard me say, madam?"

I hesitated, was on the verge of saying that it didn't matter, that it wasn't important, and then I said, "I thought I heard you say 'fucking queer.'"

Still the policeman's expression didn't change. "Really? And why would I have said that?"

I licked my lips. "It doesn't matter. I was probably mistaken. It's not really relevant, is it?"

"You obviously think it is, madam," the policeman said.

I was silent for a moment, trying to decide whether an explanation would help or hinder my cause. Then I thought of Alex and of how he was never ashamed of his sexuality, was always open about it.

"All right," I said. "Maybe it is relevant. It's just that my brother's homosexual. I thought you were making a prejudicial comment about him."

"I've never met your brother, madam," the policeman said.

"Yes. Look, I realize that. I'm sorry. I'm just a bit wound up."

I wanted the officer to laugh it off, to tell me that it was all right, but he didn't. He pushed the form through the two-inch gap at the bottom of the Perspex screen and said, "If you could just fill out this form, madam. Let me know when you're finished."

He yanked the canvas blind down before I could reply.

I was furious enough to want to do something childish, like stick my middle finger up at the blind, but I didn't in case there were security cameras recording me. Instead I took the form and filled it in, giving them four pages' worth of information about Alex. When I'd finished I rapped hard on the Perspex screen, hoping the policeman would be the one to jump this time. The blind went up and there was a younger man there, a bit horsey-looking, thick wet lips, freckles populating his hairline.

"Yes?"

Taken aback, I held up the form as if I were handing in homework or lines to a teacher. "I've filled the form in," I said.

The young man barely glanced at the sheets of white paper. "What form?"

"The one your colleague gave to me. Information about my missing brother."

"Oh, right," said the young man indifferently. "Pass it here, then."

I slid the form beneath the gap in the Perspex screen. The young policeman took it (I noticed a rash of pimples where his collar rubbed against his throat as if he had not long ago started shaving) and shoved it somewhere under the desk without really looking. This did neither my confidence nor my temper much good.

"So what happens now?"

The young officer shrugged. "You can leave it to us. We'll sort it out."

"You'll start looking for my brother straightaway, will you?"

"If we think it warrants it."

"What do you mean, if you think it warrants it?" I asked, struggling to keep my temper in check. "My brother's missing. Something bad could have happened to him. It's your job to deal with things like this. It's what you get paid for."

The young policeman sighed as if I were some minor irritant. "You don't need to tell me what my job is, madam. We're extremely busy here. We have to look at each individual report on the strength of its merits. We have to prioritize."

"Extremely busy doing what? Finding lost cats? Ticking kids off for scrumping apples? Handing out parking tickets?"

For the first time the young policeman looked me square in the eye, his indifference changing instantly to cold hostility. "What do you know? You don't live here. You're just a stuck-up bitch with no idea what goes on in this town. So why don't you stop interfering in our business and fuck off back to where you came from."

He pulled the blind down hard. For a moment I stood there, stunned, as though he'd just reached out and slapped me. I felt the sting of his words in my head, the sour jolt of unexpected vitriolic confrontation in my gut. I shouldn't have taken it, I know. I should have bashed on the Perspex screen, demanded an apology, an explanation, the right to see a senior officer and make a complaint. But instead I got a sudden and no doubt irrational gut feeling that the young officer was coming to get me, that the reason he'd pulled the blind down was so that he could engage me not only verbally but physically. Shaking, on the verge of panic, I turned to the door that led outside and threw it open. I staggered out into a pearly daylight that hurt my eyes and half ran to my car, expecting him to appear from around the side of the building, fists clenched, maybe wielding a truncheon. It seemed to take forever to fumble my keys from my bag, fit them into the lock of the door, get in, and start the engine. I drove away and as I picked up speed, still looking in my rearview mirror, I thought of the smiling dark-haired girl who'd disappeared over five years ago, gone missing while on an errand.

Eight

FOR THE MOMENT ALL I could think about was retreating to the relative comfort of my room at the Solomon Wedge to lick my wounds. I couldn't believe what the policeman had said to me. The words he had used kept running through my head, and each time they did they seemed to become more sinister, more laden with meaning.

You're just a stuck-up bitch with no idea what goes on in this town. What the hell did that mean? What *did* go on? And was the town really small enough for him to be so certain I wasn't local? Evidently so, which suggested word had got around that I was here looking for Alex. But why? What did the people of Greenwell have to hide? Although I tried to stop myself, to tell myself I was going way over the top, my feverish thoughts were nevertheless making me wonder whether Alex had been scared off, got rid of in some way. The possibility that the whole town may be in cahoots, involved in some plot or vendetta, was surely too far-fetched an idea even to contemplate.

I had to brace myself before entering the pub. It was barely midmorning, but I couldn't help thinking that the place would be full and that my antics at the school and then the police station would somehow have preceded me. I sat in my car in the car park for a good ten minutes, trying to regain my composure. Eventually, the trembling in my stomach seeping into my legs and hands, I got out of my car and forced myself to walk across the car park and in through the main door of the pub.

Conversations stopped; the sound of chinking glasses ceased; heads turned to look at me—but only in my imagination. It took me maybe two uncomfortable seconds to realize that, apart from two old ladies sitting drinking tea at a table in the corner, the pub was empty.

Neither of the ladies looked up as I stepped inside. Nor did Jovial Jim, who was idly feeding money into one of his own fruit machines. I slipped behind him, walking almost on tiptoe so as not to make any sound on the carpet, but he turned and saw me.

"Gotcha!"

I offered him a smile which I felt nervousness trying to pluck at. "Pardon?"

"Thought you'd try and sneak past without me noticing, did you?"

He grinned, but I could feel my cheeks burning. I grinned ferociously back at him and said lamely, "You looked so engrossed that I didn't want to disturb you."

He ambled over to me. He was wearing a navy blue

silk shirt today, as tight and shimmery as yesterday's. He looked like an old crooner who'd gone to seed. "Settling in all right, are you?" he asked. "Bed nice and comfortable?"

It would be a lot more comfortable if you were in it with me. Is that what he wanted me to say? Instead I replied, "Perfect, thanks," and then, before I even fully realized I was going to say it, I added, "Actually there was something I wanted to ask you about."

He spread his hands expansively. "Fire away."

"I wondered whether you knew anything about the gray man."

His face didn't exactly fall, but it became expressionless. "The gray man?" he repeated.

"Yes. It's a local legend apparently."

"I know that. Who told you about it?"

"Oh, a couple of kids mentioned it. I just thought it sounded intriguing."

He snorted. "Load of old rubbish, more like. Just a daft story from a time when folk didn't know any better."

"So who's the gray man supposed to be? Some sort of local phantom?"

"Aye, something like that. It's said he stalks the lonely places at night and inflicts a terrible death on whoever comes across him."

It sounded as though he were quoting this last sentence from a pamphlet or guidebook. "What kind of terrible death?" I asked.

He shrugged. "It's all a bit gruesome. Not worth repeating."

I laughed. "It's all right, you won't upset my female sensibilities. I like a nice gruesome story, especially one that isn't true."

"Aye, well." He poked a stubby, bejeweled finger beneath the thin golden frame of his spectacles and rubbed at the pouchy flesh in the corner of his right eye. "The story goes that down through the ages, people have been found mutilated, their eyeballs gouged out." He gave another shrug as if adjusting a weight on his back. "Like I say, load of old rubbish."

Jim's story didn't exactly unsettle me, but I spent the rest of that morning in a state of anxiety, and even a little fear, all the same. Most of the fear came from my notion, fanciful or not, that after my encounter in the police station I was under hostile surveillance. Every time I heard a noise in the pub I tensed, thinking that it was the police downstairs, coming through the door that led up to my room. I knew it was ridiculous, but it didn't stop me from expecting to hear the thunder of booted feet as they ascended toward me.

I tried phoning Alex again, mainly because I wanted the comfort of hearing his voice, even if it was only a recorded message. I didn't mean to say anything, but after the beep I found myself wailing, "Oh, Alex, *where are you?*" Then an image came to mind of dark figures sitting like vultures around Alex's answering machine in his flat—heavy, shadowy shapes, listening to my despair and sniggering. I killed the connection with a shudder, and as I slumped back onto my bed it occurred to me for the first time what I was actually doing.

I was hiding. I was doing the adult equivalent of

sticking my head under the covers and hoping the bogeyman wouldn't get me. As I realized I was doing this, I also realized how pointless it was. A child's blind, naïve faith was no good to me now. I was in my room because I didn't want to feel exposed out on the streets, but the truth of the matter was, I was far more vulnerable here. If people *were* keeping tabs on me, then they would certainly know where to find me. The fact that no one had come meant one of two things: either I was being paranoid and no one *was* interested in me, or they felt confident enough to keep uncoiling the rope in the sure knowledge that eventually I would hang myself.

So what were my alternatives? Stay here and keep a low profile (what would be the point in that?); go back to London and forget about the whole thing (and abandon Alex? Unthinkable); or stick around and continue my—for want of a better phrase—investigations, and run the risk of suffering the consequences of sticking my nose where the people of Greenwell would no doubt claim it didn't belong.

I wasn't really hungry, but I decided to sit in the pub and have some lunch, brazen it out. I heard voices coming from behind the door that led into the bar even before I'd got to the bottom of the stairs, but despite feeling as though I were the uninvited guest, I marched forward and pushed the door open.

As before, however, no one paid me much attention. When I entered the room, the nearest people to the door—a white-bearded man smoking a pipe, and a heavyset man with a helmet of thick, dark hair who was wearing a dusty checked shirt and clutching a pint—

glanced at me with no more than the normal amount of interest a man will show when a reasonably attractive woman enters his line of vision.

"Excuse me," I said, and they moved aside to let me through, the dark-haired man even offering a smile. I moved to the center of the bar, looking around as casually as I could.

A good two-thirds of the clientele were in their fifties or older. Elderly couples sitting eating lunch; old-timers in flat caps who'd popped in for a pint and a ham roll; workmen with beer bellies and black-rimmed fingernails; a harassed young couple trying to keep their two preschool children quiet with lemonades as they scanned the menu board by the bar.

Normal. Nonthreatening. Parochial. My wild thoughts began to seem almost shamefully silly in this context.

I ordered a prawn salad and a lime-and-lemonade from a chubby girl I hadn't seen before, who was serving at the bar. I ate it amid gentle chatter, the occasional curl of cigarette or cigar smoke, the musical burble of the fruit machine.

No hostile glances, or even any curious ones. Even Jim's wife ignored me, and I didn't get the impression she was doing so studiously either. It was as if she hadn't even noticed I was there.

Buoyed by this, I decided to go for a walk after lunch. I wandered around aimlessly for a while, the quiet streets as drab on foot as they had seemed from the car. It was turning cold. The sky was hazy, the dark-stoned buildings again giving the peculiar impression that they were sucking the light out of it.

I walked a circuitous route, coming back past the

Red Dragon, which was closed (OPEN AT 6 said a sign in the window) and looked deserted. I had almost reached the Solomon Wedge when a police car cruised past me. I tensed, but the car didn't stop or even slow down. I tried to make out the features of the two people inside, but they were little more than silhouettes. I swallowed, licked my lips, and the police car turned the corner. As soon as it was out of sight my mobile phone started the inane little jingle that I'd meant to change ever since I'd bought it.

My heart leaped, even as my tight stomach cramped. *Alex, where have you been?* I imagined myself exclaiming as I scrabbled to pop the press-stud on my little shoulder bag. I managed it on the third ring and scooped the phone free, scattering plastic—Visa, Sainsbury's, Blockbuster Video—and loose change at my feet. I pressed the Call button and gasped "Hello" as I stooped to pick up what I'd dropped.

"I know where your brother is," said a male voice that I didn't recognize.

My bent legs began to shake so much that I had to steady myself on the pavement with my free hand to stop myself from sprawling like a drunk in the street. "What?" I asked. "Who is this?"

"Meet me tonight at the railway station. Ten P.M." the voice said.

"Who is this?" I asked again. "Where's Alex?"

But the caller had rung off.

Nine

I TOLD MYSELF THAT I wasn't seeing what I thought I was seeing, that my mind was playing tricks. Time flies, people say, and I thought that maybe it lies too. It carries us along through life, and is cruel and duplicitous throughout the entire sorry journey.

I told myself that what I was seeing was nothing but an old branch line. Long-disused, fallen into disrepair, like so many in this part of the country. They were probably standardized, same design to save money, same materials, maybe even built by the same firm, a lot of them. It couldn't be the same place, and yet it was (or at least in what I was beginning to think of as my fractured mess of a memory it was). The railway station at Greenwell—right down to the overgrown dirt track that led to it, the weed-strangled, rubble-strewn car park, the smoke-blackened stonework, and the denuded roof—was a replica of the one Matt had taken me to three years ago, the one just outside Preston, where the smooth, blank sheet of his future had been screwed up, stamped on, damaged beyond repair.

Sitting in my car, staring at the place, I suddenly felt as though I *was* Matt, or rather that I had changed places with him. Three years ago it had been *his* tense hands on the steering wheel, *his* eyes that had held the fear.

This couldn't be, I told myself again. It was impossible. It was the darkness that was doing it; darkness was the most effective disguise of all. In the daylight this place would look so different that I would wonder how I could ever have seen the resemblance.

I got out of the car and stood beside it for a moment, unwilling to leave its side. The moon was a white, curved blade above the exposed rib cage of the station roof. It seemed to be the light it cast that was chilling the air, turning to a rime of frost where it touched the up-turned surfaces of the earth. As I walked slowly away from the safety of the car, toward the station entrance, the light shifted on the building's rough stonework as if it were trying desperately to form a face, or at least a mouth, with which to speak to me—welcome me in or warn me off.

He stalks the lonely places, Jovial Jim had said of the gray man, *and inflicts a terrible death on whoever comes across him.* The tangle of undergrowth bordering the car park behind me was growing fidgety in the rising wind, whispering as if in response to the soft, low moan of the wind itself.

I looked back once. Moonlight slid across the ice-smooth bodywork of my car as if attempting to gain entry. Either I was here first or the man who had arranged to meet me had used some other mode of transport. Perhaps he had walked; I thought of boot heels tapping steadily along the lightless road, gravel crunching softly underfoot. Something about the image—the walker's relentless, remorseless patience, his act of placing one foot steadily, unhurriedly, in front of the other with the world dark and silent around him—made me shiver.

I had tried to call him back, of course, but without success. I hadn't even been able to get hold of the number he had called from. I had spent all day wondering who he was, speculating, counterspeculating, my hopes and fears rising in equal measure. I had exhausted every possibility, every theory, had played through a hundred different encounters in my head. I had come prepared, or so I had thought, a knife I had bought that afternoon in one pocket of my jacket (not that I could ever imagine using it), a can of fly killer and a rape alarm in the other.

It was only when I arrived here, however, that I realized I wasn't prepared for this at all. I should have staked out my territory beforehand, made myself fully aware of what I was getting into. It hadn't occurred to me that the railway station would be remote and abandoned. It was Jovial Jim who had directed me here, but he had neglected to mention that the place was no longer in use, and I had never thought to ask. Before coming, I'd blithely reassured myself that nothing bad could happen, that a railway station was a public place, and that as long as I stayed in the busiest areas I'd be fine.

I stood now in the station entrance, hyperalert to the slightest sound or movement. I was uncomfortably aware of the building around me, of its dark corners, of how far away my car was. I thrust my hands into my jacket pockets and almost sliced open my finger on the knife that was already jabbing a hole in the pocket lining. The knife was a Kitchen Devil, small but incredibly sharp. Tentatively I found its handle and curled my fingers around it. It didn't make me feel any safer.

I took a deep breath to slow the ones that were coming too rapidly, and stepped forward into the station building. I moved as quietly as I could, but couldn't prevent the snap, crackle, and pop of broken glass beneath my feet.

Despite the moonlight that sidled into the room and alighted on the glass shards, making them wink and flash, there were still dark places here. My eyes jerked to them, one after another, imagining movement in every clot of shadow.

What would I do if I heard something? Slow footsteps tapping along the platform beyond the turnstile; the scraping of a match; the clearing of a throat; a voice speaking my name? I wondered about going back to the car, waiting there. Whoever was coming to meet me couldn't fail to see the car parked there, would know I'd arrived.

Unless, of course, they themselves weren't supposed to be here. It could be that the caller had risked a great deal to see me, and was now hiding somewhere in scared silence, waiting for me to approach. If I chickened out, a golden opportunity to find Alex might be lost. The caller might not be prepared or able to try again.

I moved slowly across the ticket office to the turnstile. I pushed at it, knowing it would be jammed. I climbed over carefully, thinking that this would not be good if I had to make a quick getaway. I emerged onto the platform, looked behind me to the far end, and felt my stomach lurch. There was the crossing point, the traffic light bent at an angle, a streak of moonlight climbing its metal pole. I walked forward to the WAIT-ING ROOM, the words written in faded gold script on faded blue paint, the IT amended with a black marker pen. I swallowed. It felt as though there were something sharp stuck in my throat. I reached out, grasped the handle, twisted the door open.

Moonlight flooded into the room so greedily that if it had had any substance it would have barged me out of the way. It was early October, and turning cold, but I could hear the drone of flies. My gaze was sucked to the room's center, where a figure hung like a life-sized puppet, its arms limp, like double pendulums at rest, its toes pointing downward as though straining to touch solid ground. The noose around its neck had caused the fig-ure's head to tilt almost coquettishly to one side. The flies I had heard, buzzing with idiot greed, circled and alighted on the body in an ever-shifting black cloud, like a soul attempting to shed itself of its mortal re-mains.

I couldn't see the corpse's face, and initially thought its features were obscured by shadow, or a mask of flies, before realizing that in fact the head had been covered by a hood. After an instant of wide-eyed disbelief, an in-stant where I wondered almost coolly whether what I was witnessing here was the result of a suicide or an exe-cution, the full horror of what I was seeing suddenly came screaming and flailing out of the darkness at me, and I staggered back as though under the onslaught of some invisible force, my internal organs contracting painfully, strength draining from my legs and blood from my head, making me terrified I was going to pass out. My surroundings receded; I felt as though I were being lifted out of my body. The only thing that kept me rooted to consciousness was the thought that whoever had done this awful thing might still be here, lurking in the shadows, watching.

I must have staggered the length of the platform and climbed over the rusted turnstile, but I don't remember it. All I recall is the sound and feel of breaking glass beneath my feet as I ran through the ticket office and out of the building. I halted for a moment, swaying, disorientated by the wide, cold spaces of the night. I looked up at the gleaming scimitar of the moon, and then I lurched over to my car, where I spent several horrible, exposed minutes fumbling for keys and trying to fit the correct one into the tiny lock with trembling hands before finally yanking the door open with such frantic force that I broke a nail, and sliding, falling, into my seat.

I pressed down the nub, locking the door, and for a minute or more just sat there, panting, half sobbing, trying to fight down the lurching nausea in my belly. I was in no fit state to drive. I took out my phone, jabbed 999, blurted "Police" even before the receptionist could finish asking me which emergency service I required. I was put through and began to tell them where I was and what I had seen, my words a garbled rush. My message must have been even more incoherent than I thought, because the person I was talking to kept telling me to calm down, take deep breaths, speak more slowly, assuring me that help was on its way.

When the phone call was finished, I abruptly burst into tears, great surging heaves of delayed reaction which almost choked me. I only snapped out of it—or rather, spasmed into life—when I heard something growling in the darkness behind the car. I twisted my head round, and saw white light cresting and shattering in the undergrowth. My senses were so heightened, my imagination so rampant, that it took me a moment to realize that what I was hearing and seeing were the engine and headlights of an approaching police car.

I looked at the dashboard clock—10:21 P.M. For the first time I wondered whether the killer (if there was one) was the man who had called me that afternoon, or whether he had arrived before me and been scared off by the terrible sight in the waiting room. The police car lurched to a stop and two peak-capped policemen in bulky jackets with luminous flashes got out. They were poker-faced, their eyes shrouded in shadow. I didn't unlock my door, merely wound down my window a couple of inches. The policeman who had been driving, the one who was closest to me, leaned forward and asked, "Are you the lady who reported the body in the station?"

"Yes," I said, thinking that if he asked me to get out of the car to show them where the body was, I'd refuse.

He didn't, though. He squatted on his haunches, the peak of his cap still making dark pools of his eyes, his colleague hovering at his shoulder. "Would you mind telling us exactly what it was you saw?"

I told him, starting with the phone call that afternoon, the reason for my being here. He listened without reacting, and when I had finished he straightened up. "All right, we'll check it out. Would you mind waiting here, madam?"

They seemed to be gone a long time, during which my mind continued to race without purpose. At last a dark figure appeared at the station entrance. I tensed briefly, then saw a second figure, a pair of peaked caps pecking at the air as the policemen strode toward me. I wound my window down a little further, but didn't say anything. The policeman I'd spoken to earlier came up to the car, put a hand on the roof, and leaned down. "You say the body you saw was in the waiting room, madam?"

This wasn't what I'd been expecting him to say. "Well . . . yes," I stammered. "Why?"

"We've made a thorough search of the building and we've found nothing. No body, nor any indication that there was ever one there."

"But . . . but that's impossible!" I said. "There *was* a body. I saw it quite clearly."

The policeman beside my car turned briefly to his colleague, who made some remark, his voice too low for me to hear. When he turned back to me, there was a grin on his face, which vanished before he said, "With all due respect, madam, it's a dark, creepy place, this. The imagination can play some strange tricks when you're spooked."

It sounded like a line from a bad horror movie. The fact that he was trying to patronize me with it made me furious. "I know what I saw!" I snapped. "It was a man. He had a noose around his neck. There were flies buzzing around him. I didn't imagine it."

The policeman who was doing the talking exhaled deeply through his nose as if he found this all very tiresome. "Well, there's nothing there now, madam. Perhaps someone was having you on."

Was that possible? I didn't see how. I thought of the last time I had had contact with the police in Greenwell, the young, horsey-looking officer snarling at me, "You're just a stuck-up bitch with no idea what goes on in this town." Could the entire police force be in on whatever was happening here? It seemed incredible, and yet suddenly I needed to be sure.

"Show me," I said.

The two policemen exchanged a glance. The talkative one said, "I beg your pardon, madam."

"Show me," I repeated, pushing open my car door, aware of how reckless, how foolish, this action might be, but unable to stop myself. "I want to see."

The policeman stepped back as the car door swung toward him. "There's nothing *to* see, madam. That's the whole point," he muttered.

"Just indulge me. I want to set my mind at rest. It'll only take a minute."

I could sense their exasperation, or maybe it was something else. But the talkative policeman abruptly nodded. "All right, then. If it'll make you happy."

I walked between the two of them, the talkative one shining a powerful torch ahead of us, piercing the shadows with ashen light. At the turnstile the lead policeman handed the torch to his colleague, then vaulted the barrier with ease and held out a hand to assist me. I hesitated a moment, then took his hand and climbed over. His strong, dry grip, the way he supported my weight, suggested a tensile strength which I knew I would have no answer to if he decided to use it against me.

We walked along the platform to the waiting room, our irregularly spaced footsteps like the tapping of some secret code on the concrete. My stomach hurt; my head throbbed dully; there was a prickling sensation behind my eyes. We stopped at the waiting-room door, which the policemen must have closed behind them.

Without preamble, the talkative one reached out and shoved the door open. He motioned at the room's dark interior. "You see?"

I stepped forward, though it was already evident that the room was empty. In the pitiless light from the policeman's torch I could see that the place was a hovel, strewn with beer cans and litter, smelling of piss. Plastic bags billowed and gaped in the breeze that blew in off the track; graffiti etched the moldering walls; shadows fled like timid night creatures at the periphery of the torchlight.

The policeman pointed his torch up at the ceiling, and though he didn't say anything I could see what he was getting at. The plaster was pocked with holes, stained and scabrous with water damage. There was nothing to which a rope could have been attached—no roof beams, no ceiling hooks, no protuberances of any kind.

"I know what I saw," I said stubbornly. "I didn't imagine it."

The talkative policeman shrugged. "That's as may

be, madam, but without any evidence there's not a lot we can do. I suggest you go back home, make yourself a nice cup of tea, and forget all about it."

I was frustrated and mystified, and I wanted to snap at him for being so condescending, but I held my tongue. Because, to be honest, he was right. What else *could* I do? And what could I expect the police to do if there was nothing here to corroborate my story?

I sighed, admitting defeat. "All right, I'll go home like a good little girl. But I *did* see a body. Maybe if you got a forensics team down here, they'd be able to find something."

His face remained deadpan, but I could tell that he was thinking: *Yeah, right, we're always calling teams of experts out in the middle of the night to investigate the claims of hysterical women.*

"I'll tell you what, madam. I'll pop back here in the daylight, have a poke around, see if I can find anything that warrants it," he said.

I shrugged. "Whatever." Then, hating the attitude of forced tolerance I was being shown, I turned abruptly away from the waiting room. "Come on, then."

We walked back to the cars in silence. Once there, the talkative policeman said, "Do you feel able to drive, madam?"

I still felt shaky, but gave a brisk nod. "Yes, of course."

The wind was picking up now, the trees and bushes around the station thrashing from side to side as if trying to tear themselves from the earth. They took my name and the details of where I was staying, then the talkative one said, "Thank you, Miss Gemmill. If we need to get in touch with you in due course, we will."

The two of them stood and watched as I drove the car out of the overgrown car park and turned onto the dirt track that led up to the road back to Greenwell. Their scrutiny made me uneasy. They were probably only watching to ensure that I was capable of driving after my traumatic experience, but it still made me feel self-conscious.

Perhaps surprisingly, I drove steadily, calmly, back to the pub. However, as soon as I cut the engine in the car park, a shudder blossomed out from my belly and into my limbs, so prolonged and violent that I thought even from a distance it must look as though I were having some kind of fit.

For the second time that day I found myself trying to compose myself in order to enter the pub. I didn't want to break down in front of all the people in there, especially as some of them might have been involved with what had happened tonight. I took a series of deep breaths, then braced myself and went inside. I was grateful to see that it was a lot quieter than it had been when I'd left over an hour earlier. I'd fully intended to go straight to bed, but now I realized that I could murder a drink. Brandy was supposed to be the thing for shock, but I didn't fancy that, so I ordered a G and T from the chubby girl who seemed unaware that I was the pub's only paying guest. I took an exploratory sip, unsure of how my system would take it, and immediately felt a comforting warmth spreading through me, quieting my nerves. I gulped down the rest of my drink and ordered another, and by the time last orders were called I'd sunk four of the things in rapid succession. My head was buzzing like the flies around the corpse in the waiting room, but I ordered a final double. "Nightcap," I explained to the chubby girl, who'd been watching me gulp one drink after another with wary fascination.

I wondered if I was slurring my words. I didn't care. I tried to take my time with my last drink, but it was gone in three minutes. As I made my way carefully across to the door that led upstairs, all but oblivious now of my surroundings, I heard somebody say my name.

I halted, paused a moment as I worked out how not to get my feet entangled in each other, then turned round. Jovial Jim was leaning over the end of the bar, glancing round, presumably in fear of his wife, who for the moment was nowhere in sight.

"Hi," I said, raising a hand and realizing immediately how drunken the gesture must appear. He seemed not to notice, however. In a low, confidential voice, he asked, "How did you get on at the station?"

I wasn't so drunk that I didn't immediately become suspicious. Deciding to give nothing away, I said, "Oh, fine. The bloke I was supposed to meet didn't turn up, but then that's the story of my life."

"Who were you supposed to meet?" he asked.

I smiled and tapped the side of my nose. Then I waggled my fingers at him. "Nighty night, Jim. See you in the morning."

I felt quite pleased with myself as I walked up the stairs, the alcohol in my system suppressing all the bad emotions of the day, making what I'd seen that evening seem dreamlike, distant. I let myself into my room and set about the task of making myself a cup of tea, but halfway through, with the tea bag in the cup and the kettle halfway to boiling, I suddenly felt incredibly tired, and stumbled over to my bed.

I fell onto it face-first and fully clothed, intending to have a few minutes' rest until the kettle clicked itself off. The next thing I remember was waking up with a jolt, convinced that I was not alone in the room. I was lying on my back and I was naked. I could feel the chill air on my skin. My head felt heavy as a rock. It took a real effort to raise it from the pillow. When I did I saw a naked man standing at the end of my bed, holding his erect penis in his fist and looking down at me.

My eyes jerked up to his face and I saw that it was Matt.

I screamed and hurled myself to my left, intending to throw myself off the side of the bed, onto the floor. Matt, however, was too quick for me. He leaped onto the bed, landing heavily on top of me, his long, strong fingers grabbing my upper arms with painful force, pinning me down. I bucked and thrashed beneath him in an attempt to throw him off, tried to knee him in his groin, but it was no use. He had always been lithe and incredibly strong. His hands slid along my arms until they were clamped around my wrists, whereupon he forced them up above my head, stretching the skin tight on my stomach, making my breasts ride up. He brought my wrists together and transferred both of them into his left hand, his long fingers clenched around them in an iron grip, my bones grinding together painfully. I felt a familiar sense of bitter humiliation at the fact that he could subjugate me completely by exerting only a fraction of his full strength.

His right arm was free now. As he raised it, I
flinched, turning my head aside, expecting him to start
punching me in the face. Instead his hand hovered for a
moment between us, then his fingers probed at the hollow beneath his breastbone, as if trying to pinpoint a
flare of pain, a touch of indigestion.

His fingers disappeared into his chest, sank in to the
knuckle, as though his skin were putty. He moved his
hand down, fingers rigid as a blade, opening himself up,
slitting himself from breastbone to navel. A black wound
gaped. There was no blood. I saw busy movement inside him. Then something slipped out from between the
lips of the wound and scuttled diagonally across his rib
cage.

A spider. A fiddleback.

The bloodless wound bulged, widened, and all at
once they surged up and out of him like ants from a disturbed nest. There were dozens of them. Hundreds. A
boiling mass of delicate, pale brown bodies, thin scuttling legs. They flooded out of him in every direction.
They fell on me, ran across my stomach and chest and
throat. Ran into my hair. Ran in a tickling frenzy across
my face.

I was frantic, hysterical, desperate to jump up, to get
them off me. But I couldn't move and I dared not
scream for fear they would be attracted to the soft,
warm cavity of my mouth. Terror and revulsion was es-
calating inside me, a pressure that seemed colossal, un-
containable. I felt sure something would rupture, that
my brain would burst in my skull like a balloon pumped
with too much air.

I felt the sting of myriad bites. I knew that if this didn't stop soon I would die. Through the blur of brown spider bodies scurrying across my face, I saw Matt ball his free hand into a fist. *Now he's going to hit me,* I thought, but instead of bringing his fist down hard he lowered it toward my face, pressing his bony knuckles against my lips. I tried to keep my mouth closed, but the pain of my lips being crushed against my teeth was too much. When I parted my lips a fraction, he forced his fist between them. I tried to bite him, but felt my jaws being slowly prised apart like the jaws of a mantrap. He bore down on me, spiders still swarming over and around us, using all his weight and strength, ramming his fist into my mouth. I started to panic as my lips and jaw stretched wider than they were supposed to. I made squealing, terrified animal sounds in my throat that resounded in my head. My jaws stretched still wider, impossibly wide. I couldn't breathe. I started to feel incredible pain.

Then something cracked. It felt as if my whole skull had given way. The pain engulfed me, vast and unendurable. Something exploded behind my eyes—blazing light, then screaming dark, my thoughts shattering. I felt myself being sucked down and then I don't remember any more. It was not sleep I fell into, but oblivion. Dead. Black. Nothing.

I don't think I came to gradually. I remember simply clicking back to life like an electric lightbulb and instantly remembering all that had happened to me. I was lying on a bed, on my front, my eyes closed, my fingers digging into the mattress as though clinging to a vertical rock face. I knew I should have been in terrible pain—but I wasn't. I opened my eyes.

I was in my room at the Solomon Wedge. I had half expected to wake up in a hospital, my jaw wired shut, my pain deadened by drugs. I could see my hand and arm, a good portion of the mattress, the wall beyond. I wriggled my fingers experimentally.

For a few moments, remembering the immense cracking sound that had reverberated through my skull, I was frightened of moving my head. But my jaw felt okay. I ran my tongue cautiously along both rows of my teeth, then clenched them together. Using my arms for leverage, I pushed myself up and slowly heaved myself onto my side. I sat up and looked around. There were no spiders in my room, no bites on my skin, no bruises on my wrists where Matt had gripped me so tightly, no pain in my jaw. Unbelievable as it seemed, what had happened last night must have been nothing more than a particularly vivid dream. I didn't know whether to feel relieved or alarmed, couldn't fathom what this said about my state of mind, or whether it would happen again. I felt momentarily shell-shocked, and then the emotional horror of last night's experiences came flooding back to me. I started to weep and shake. I felt degraded, scared, and totally, totally alone. I curled up into a ball and wrapped my arms around myself and I cried and cried and cried, soaking the bedsheets with bitter tears.

Ten

"MATT, TALK TO ME," I whispered.

We were heading back to his place in a cab after a night at Graham and Kate's. Chris and Paula had been there too. Matt had met Graham and Kate before—got on well with Graham, had even started playing for his five-a-side team on Wednesday evenings—but he hadn't met Chris and Paula, even though we'd been promising to get together for ages. I'd wanted Matt to meet them, not only because I'd wanted to show him off, but because Chris was a TV producer, and the more people in the business I could introduce Matt to the better as far as I was concerned.

Matt, though, hadn't been keen, which had started the evening off badly even before we'd got there. It wasn't that he lacked ambition, it was just that he hated—as he put it—"these contrived meetings."

"It's not contrived," I told him as we sat with our drinks in the Blue Posts on Broadwick Street, which was where we'd arranged to meet after work (well, *my* work; Matt was currently resting). "Chris and Paula are my friends. I've wanted you to meet them for ages."

"Yeah, but there's this whole TV-producer thing going on," he said, swirling what was left of his Grolsch round in the bottle. "You just want me to impress him so he'll give me a job. You want me to *perform*."

I laughed. "Of course I don't want you to perform. I just want you to be yourself. If something comes of it, great. If not, no big deal. I mean, I want my friends to be your friends, Matt, and vice versa. And a lot of my friends work in film and TV because that's where I meet them. I met Chris about eight years ago when we were both working on a costume drama for the BBC, and since then he's thrown bits of work my way every now and again—it's just the way things happen. So, you know, if something eventually comes of you not only meeting Chris tonight but getting to know him, as I hope you will, then what's wrong with that?"

Matt was silent for several seconds, staring moodily down at his bottle. Eventually he said with more than a trace of bitterness, "It's true, though, isn't it? It's not how good you are in this business, it's who you know."

I shrugged. "That's life, I'm afraid."

"Yeah, well, it stinks."

"Why does it stink? It's what happens everywhere. Surely you're not naïve enough to think that it doesn't?"

We'd been going out for five months at this point and were still finding out new things about each other. Matt's revelation at the railway station was now two months behind us. On the few recent occasions when I'd brought up the subject, he had refused to talk about it. "Look," he'd say, "I wanted to tell you, but now I just want to draw a line under it and forget it. It's something that happened in the past. It's not important anymore, okay?"

Except that it *was* important, and not simply to me, but to him too. What had happened to him as a child had created something between us, a presence which I sensed hovering in the shadows from time to time. I didn't want to hassle him about the experience, but I felt strongly that he still needed to talk about it. It seemed clear to me that he still had some of the old poison left in his system, and that he would not be fully free of its effects until he allowed someone to draw it out of him.

Later, of course, I would blame myself for his violence, would put it down to my own mishandling of the situation. I'd ask myself why I couldn't have left well enough alone, would convince myself, despite evidence to the contrary, that if I had, then things would have been fine between us. It's only now that I know his lack of self-control, his propensity for violence, was his problem, not mine. It was in him, and of him, before we had even met.

But all that was to come. In the Blue Posts, when I suggested that he was naïve, he gave me a cold look, then muttered, "Don't treat me like a child, Ruth. I'm just disappointed that you have this attitude, that's all. Doesn't skill and talent and hard work and . . . and commitment count for anything these days?"

Not much, I was going to quip, but he patently wasn't in the mood. I reached across the table and took his hand. His palm was ice cold from clutching the bottle.

"Of course it does," I said. "What I'm saying is, it's good to have contacts, even friends, in the business, but of course you've still got to prove yourself to them, you've still got to show that you can do the job. I'm not saying Chris is going to employ you because he likes your jokes or thinks you're an okay bloke or whatever. But he might get you an audition for something. There's nothing wrong with that, is there?"

Matt pouted, but I could see that he was wavering. "Suppose not," he mumbled.

"Good. Drink up, then, and let's get going."

As far as I was concerned, the evening went pretty well. Matt was a bit quiet, which I put down to his shyness at meeting new people, but Chris and Paula seemed to like him well enough. In the cab on the way home, however, he turned stone cold on me.

"Are you okay?" I asked him. He didn't answer, just stared out the window, elbow on the thin sill, hand cupping his chin. I glanced at the driver. I could tell Matt was pissed off, but I didn't want an argument here, in front of this complete stranger.

"Matt, what's wrong?" I murmured, trying to keep my voice light. I put a hand lightly on his arm, but his skin seemed almost to squirm away beneath my touch, muscles tautening.

I left it for thirty seconds or so, hoping he'd come round, then I leaned toward him. "Matt, talk to me."

He mumbled something.

"Pardon?" I asked. When he didn't respond, I tried again. "What did you say, Matt? I didn't hear you."

He half turned toward me, shadows massing on his face like storm clouds gathering in an autumn sky. "I said I've got nothing to say."

"Why?" I asked. "What have I done?"

He gave me a contemptuous look. "You honestly don't know?"

"No," I said, "I don't."

He stared at me with such blank intent that I started to feel uncomfortable. Finally he said, "Think about it," and turned back to the window.

I was shocked and confused. What the hell had happened to make him like this? I wasn't that drunk, so I knew I hadn't done anything that I would regret later. I hadn't flirted with either of the boys, or made a big thing of the fact that Matt was an actor in front of Chris, or ignored Matt, or excluded him by indulging in in-jokes, or made a fool of myself. As far as I was concerned, it had been an evening of good food, good wine, and good company. So what was his problem?

He refused to talk to me all the rest of the way home. When we got back to his flat I asked, "Do you want me to come in with you?"

"Please yourself," he muttered, and got out of the cab, dropping a fiver on the seat.

My confusion was turning to anger now. If it hadn't been for the cabdriver, I would have shouted after him not to be so pathetic.

I considered going home, but I couldn't leave it like this, particularly as I had no idea what I'd done wrong. I paid the driver and got out, and was just in time to catch Matt letting himself into his building. "Matt, wait!" I shouted when it looked as though he was going to shut the door behind him. He didn't wait, but at least he left the door ajar. I ran up the steps and went in after him.

I didn't like Matt's place much. I always preferred it when we went back to mine. The building was dingy and always had a faint odor of cat pee. There was a man who lived on the ground floor who was always drunk, and kept slipping into diabetic comas because he didn't look after himself properly. Matt had called an ambulance out to him three times, having heard him moaning for help in a dreamy, distracted way as if he were stuck in the middle of a nightmare he couldn't wake up from.

Matt had left the door to his flat ajar, too, which I saw as a good sign, as a sign that he was willing to talk. I went in, prepared to be conciliatory, and found him in his poky sitting room, hunched forward on the edge of his armchair, clutching the TV remote control and staring intently at an old film in which all the men were wearing trilbies and extruding sharp, snappy, machine-gun bursts of dialogue.

His flat was clean and tidy enough, but no amount of embellishment could disguise the squishy, mismatching furniture studded with cigarette burns, the threadbare carpet, the sooty stain on the wall above the convector heater.

"Matt," I said, but his only response was to turn the volume up on the TV. That really irritated me, but I tried to keep calm. "Matt, this is silly. I don't even know what I've done."

He turned to me then, and there was a look on his face that was going to become all too familiar as our relationship started to spiral downward into ever darker and narrower alleyways over the ensuing months. It was an expression that managed to be both frighteningly impassive and yet brimming with contempt.

"How can you not know? Are you stupid or something?"

I felt my throat constrict with fury again. "No, I don't think so." I paused, took a few deep breaths to calm myself. Eventually I said, "But something's obviously happened tonight that's passed me by, and for that I'm sorry. I thought we'd had a good time."

"We were having a good time."

"So what happened to change that? Please tell me, Matt. I need to know."

Abruptly he jabbed his thumb down on the remote control and the TV picture was sucked into darkness. "I don't like being made a fool of," he said.

I gawped at him. "I'm sorry. I think I've missed something here."

"You made me look stupid in front of your friends." His words were clipped, hushed, almost emotionless.

"How?" I asked.

"You all had a good laugh at my expense, didn't you?"

"Did we? Why, what did I say?"

He tilted his head to one side, twisted his face into an expression of schoolground mockery, and said in a jabbering falsetto, " 'Ooh, of course Matt's a poor, destitute actor. He only goes out with me for my money. I'm your meal ticket, aren't I, Matt?' "

Realization dawned. It had been a tiny part of a much wider conversation, and I hadn't used anything like the tone that Matt had just spouted back at me. What I'd actually said was that Matt, like many young actors, was finding work hard to come by, but that I was making enough money for both of us to enjoy the little luxuries of life—meals out, visits to the theater or the cinema, the occasional weekend away. At the end of this, I'd nudged Matt and smiled and said, "Regular meal ticket, aren't I, Matt?"

I laughed, relieved that what lay at the root of his discontent was nothing more drastic than this.

"Oh, Matt, it was only meant as a joke. No one took it seriously. Everyone who was there tonight knows how tough it is being an actor."

He said nothing, simply sat staring at the blank TV screen. I went over and crouched down by the side of the chair, put a hand on his arm.

"I'm really sorry, Matt. It was insensitive of me. But I honestly didn't mean anything by it."

Still he didn't say anything. Still he didn't look at me. I rubbed his arm, leaned forward, and kissed him on the side of his head. "Can we be friends?" I asked.

I expected him to turn and sigh and nod, maybe even to murmur an apology for being so touchy, but still he continued to stare straight ahead as though I weren't there. I knew how serious and determined he was about his career, and how touchy he became if anyone said anything even slightly disparaging about it.

"I'll make us some coffee," I said. "I really am sorry, Matt." I walked into the kitchen.

I felt bad about having upset Matt, but at the same time I knew I hadn't said anything too awful. In Matt's narrow, mildewy kitchen I filled the kettle with water and set it to boil, got two mugs down out of the cupboard, and reached for the jar of coffee.

It was at this point that I sensed a presence beside

me, and half turned, sure it would be Matt coming to make up. I glimpsed his impassive face and then the impression of something dark and blurred flying toward me. I had barely begun to flinch when the thing connected and crunching pain exploded in the side of my head. My vision flashed with a starburst of light, and then I was falling.

I put out my hands to break my fall, but misjudged the distance and fell heavily, bending my wrist back and bashing my hip. I remember thinking I must have had an accident, that something had fallen from above and hit me on the head. When I looked up, dazed, and saw Matt looming over me, I thought he was there to help, to reach down and lift me up, and I raised a hand toward him. Then he hit me in the face.

His fist connected with my lips this time, the bottom one of which burst like a tomato. I felt pain rushing up from my jaw into my skull. I think I screamed and rolled away from him. My mouth was awash with blood. Its coppery slickness made me gag. I knew Matt had left when the overhead fluorescent light, which his body had been blotting out, suddenly zinged back into view, its harsh brightness piercing my vision.

I lay there for a while, unable to believe what had just happened. It seemed like a sickening betrayal of all Matt and I had shared in the past few months. It was the end, it had to be the end. I had always vowed that if a man ever showed any violence toward me, I would leave him—no questions asked, no chance for an apology, no looking back. But when I'd said that, I hadn't really thought it would ever happen. I hadn't reckoned on the fact that I could ever build a relationship with a man who was capable of doing this. I'd told myself that if I ever met such a man I would know immediately, would smell it coming off him like a musk, and so walk away.

But I hadn't, had I? I hadn't had a clue. There had been no gradual buildup (though later, when it was all over, I would see little signals along the way), no warning, no nothing. It had simply come at me from out of nowhere—bang, bang—with devastating suddenness. The fear of walking the streets alone at night, the fear of being mugged or attacked, had suddenly invaded what I'd thought was a safe place in my life, and the result was disorientating, shocking. I didn't know what to do, how to react. What was I *supposed* to do? What were the rules?

I lay on Matt's kitchen floor for a while, and then I pushed myself up groggily into a sitting position. The pains in my face felt like weights that shifted uncomfortably each time I moved my head. My dress was covered in blood from my busted lip. I felt sick and dizzy. I sat against the wall for a bit, taking deep breaths, feeling the throb of pain each time I inhaled through my nose. I listened, but could hear nothing. Had Matt gone out? I didn't feel scared of him at this point, just shocked at what he had done. It was as if he had peeled his face off like a rubber mask to reveal an entirely different countenance underneath.

Eventually I got to my feet and went through to the bathroom, cupping my hand to catch the blood that was still dripping from my chin. I washed my face in cold water and then I looked in the mirror. I was relieved to see that I didn't look as bad as I'd thought I was going to. My bottom lip was split and swollen, but you wouldn't have known I'd been hit on the side of my face, even though it felt stiff and sore. I sat on the side of the bath, holding damp toilet paper to my lip until the bleeding stopped. My head was telling me to walk out of that place, get a cab home, and never see or speak to Matt again.

I opened the bathroom door, and straightaway I heard sobbing. It was the full-blooded, heart-wrenching sobbing of the utterly bereft. Perhaps I should have derived strength from it, reveled in it, but I couldn't. I didn't exactly feel pity, or a need to comfort, but all the same I knew I couldn't simply walk away from someone who was that unhappy.

I followed the sobbing to Matt's bedroom. He was lying on his front, arms stretched out in a crucifix shape, face buried in his pillow. I watched him for a moment and then in a thick voice I said, "Matt."

He stopped his crying abruptly, sort of swallowed it down with a gulp. For a few moments he remained in the same position and then he slowly turned his head and looked at me. His face looked as if he'd had raw onion rubbed in it. He looked stricken and ashamed.

"Ruth," he whispered. "I'm sorry, I'm so sorry."

"You hit me," I said. "You *attacked* me, Matt."

"I know." His face crumpled as if he were about to start crying again. "I know I did, and I can't . . . it was unforgivable. I can't tell you how sorry I am. You'll leave me, won't you?"

The bluntness of the question threw me. *Yes,* I should have said, *yes, I fucking will leave you,* but the thought of it just ending like this—despite what he had done— horrified me. We'd had five months of happiness. How could it all finish so abruptly and brutally? I hesitated for a moment, and then I said, "I should."

"I know," he blubbered. "I know you should."

"Why did you hit me?" I asked him.

My voice was plaintive, like a little girl's. Matt rolled over onto his back, then heaved himself upright and sat on the edge of the bed. Head bowed, shoulders slumped, he looked exhausted, shell-shocked.

"It was . . . it was all closing in on me. I felt as though I was being laughed at, that nobody was taking me seriously. That's not a good enough reason, I know, but I just . . . I just lashed out. And now I feel so awful and so sick and so sorry."

"You hurt me," I said.

"I know. I know I did." He started to cry.

I went to him. I know, I know, bloody mug, bloody sucker, but I went to him and put my arms round him and made shushing noises, just like a mother whose small child has banged his head or cut his knee. He cried in my arms, and I felt so terrible for him, even though I know I should have been feeling terrible for no one but myself.

At last his tears stopped and he whispered, "You'd better leave me."

"Why?" I asked softly.

"Because I'm not good enough for you. I hurt you. I'm just so fucked up, and you . . . you don't deserve what I did to you. You're such a sweet, lovely person, and I'm just . . . just such a shit. Just fucking, fucking shit for doing what I did."

Part of me wanted to agree with him, but seeing him so distraught far surpassed my physical pain. And seeing him so full of remorse didn't exactly nullify but certainly softened the mental shock of what had happened.

So I continued to hold him and whisper to him and comfort him. I didn't tell him everything was all right, because it wasn't, but—fool that I was—I was already beginning to think I could see how we might move forward from this.

After a while, he raised his head and whispered again, "I'm so sorry, Ruth. I'm so sorry."

Eleven

AFTER MY DREAM ABOUT Matt and the spiders, my primary instinct was to pack up and go home. I couldn't, though, because if I didn't look for Alex, who would? I wondered how long I might have to stay here, what would happen if I didn't find him, how far I could go before admitting defeat.

"Stop it," I said out loud. "You *are* going to find him."

For the time being I still had options, lines of inquiry to pursue—I tried not to see beyond that. There were people I could talk to—the Chinese waiter, children and staff at the school—but my priority was to get into Alex's flat and see what I could find. After last night's experiences I was scared, but if what had happened at the station had been intended to scare me away, then in a curious way it had had the opposite effect, had bound me to the town even tighter than before. Something was happening here, something bad, something that Alex had been sucked into. Maybe he had found out too much, or maybe it had to do with the fact that he was gay, or an outsider—or maybe it was none of these things. The why wasn't important. The fact was I believed he was in danger, and I couldn't leave here until I'd got to the bottom of what was going on. The gray man, Matt, the fiddleback on the stairs, the body at the station—they were all glimpses of a bigger picture whose composition I had yet to clearly perceive.

Unlike yesterday, when the hostile reception I'd encountered at the police station had incapacitated me, sent me fleeing to the dubious sanctuary of my room, last night's far more disturbing events had perversely encouraged me to be proactive, to approach the day with a very definite plan. Even though I was more frightened than ever, I had come to realize that you couldn't give in to it. If you hid you would be found. If you cowered you would be nothing but prey.

I ate a solitary breakfast in the lounge bar of the Solomon Wedge, then sought out Jim and paid for two more nights' accommodation. I watched him closely as I told him I wanted to stay longer. If he was surprised by my decision he didn't show it. I couldn't decide whether or not he was involved in whatever was going on in Greenwell. He had a far more expensive car than he ought to have been able to afford, and he had neglected to tell me that the railway station was long disused when I'd asked him for directions to it yesterday, but what did either of these things prove?

In my car I fished out the grubby strip of paper the girl in Alex's building had given me and dialed Cressley's number. He picked up on the fifth ring and barked out his name.

"Mr. Cressley," I said, "this is Ruth Gemmill. I called you the other day about my brother, Alex. He's a tenant of yours at 5 Moxon Street."

"Oh aye," Cressley said. "You're the one what dragged our Lance out on a wild-goose chase."

I ignored the jibe. "Mr. Cressley, Alex still hasn't turned up and his family and friends are getting very worried about him. I was wondering, therefore, whether it would be possible for me to drop by and pick up the keys to his flat. It's possible that there may be some clue to his whereabouts in there: a diary, an address book, something that might tell us where he's gone."

Cressley sighed. "I thought our Lance had already had a look round."

"A cursory one, that's all. He was only in the flat for thirty seconds."

"Aye, well, I'm not in the habit of giving out keys to my properties willy-nilly."

"But this is an exceptional case, surely?"

He snorted. "*Every* bloody case is exceptional, love. You'd be surprised some of the stories I've been told."

"All right, then," I said, "if you won't lend me the keys, I'll have to call the police, see what they have to say."

I was hoping that the magic P word would encourage Cressley to reconsider, but he merely said, "Yeah, you do that, love."

"You don't mind the police getting involved?" I said, a little deflated.

"Why should I? I've got nothing to hide."

"Right. Well, the police it is, then," I said. "Good-bye, Mr. Cressley."

I waited for him to say something, to sigh and concede that maybe we could get this matter sorted out between us, after all, but instead he put the phone down without saying another word.

"Pig," I muttered, frustrated. I had no intention of going to the police. They and Cressley were probably in cahoots, involved up to their fat red necks in whatever was going on. No, if I was going to get anywhere I had to resort to more drastic measures. What I was planning made my stomach squirm with trepidation, but I was determined not to be deflected from my course of action. I drove out of the car park and around Greenwell for a bit until I spotted a hardware shop, then I bought what I needed and headed up to Moxon Street. I kept my eye out for Cressley's Espace, but all was quiet. Parking my car a little way up the street in the hope that he wouldn't spot it if he or his son turned up, I put on my jacket and slid the crowbar I'd bought up my sleeve.

As I walked back down the road to number 5, I had to make a real effort to stop myself from glancing shiftily from side to side. I even had to concentrate on walking normally, my legs felt so stiff and uncooperative.

My heart was pounding when I reached the door and pressed the buzzer for flat 3. What would I do if Cressley turned up now? Run for it? Try to bluff it out? "Come on, come on," I muttered, and pressed the buzzer again, even though I'd only given the flat's occupant maybe five seconds to answer my first summons.

She must have been nearly there when I'd buzzed the second time, because almost immediately there was a crackle and a voice said, "Who is it?"

"Hi," I said, "it's me again. Ruth Gemmill. Could you buzz me in, please?"

There was a pause, then the girl said, "I don't think I'm supposed to. You got me into trouble last time."

"What sort of trouble?" I asked. When the girl didn't answer, I said, "They didn't hurt you, did they?"

"No," said the girl. "They threatened me. They said they'd throw me out if I let anyone else in who didn't live here."

"Oh," I said, "I'm sorry about that." And I genuinely *was* sorry, but my need to get into Alex's flat overrode my guilt at the further trouble I might be about to land her in. I'd never considered myself very good at lying, but now in an easy, lighthearted tone I said, "But it's okay this time. My brother's still not turned up, so Mr. Cressley's given me a key to look round his flat. The only thing is, he didn't have a spare key for the house. He said there'd be somebody here to let me in." I paused, and then took what I knew was a big gamble. "You can ring and ask him if you don't believe me."

I fully expected her to say, *All right, I will,* but after a wait of maybe ten seconds the door buzzed. I pushed it open triumphantly. I was in! Excited and scared, I ran up the stairs, bypassing the girl's closed door and all the other closed doors in the building, all the way up to Alex's flat.

Breaking in felt like crossing an invisible line. Despite my good intentions, I knew it was an act that could drop me in the biggest pile of kak imaginable. The only remotely unlawful thing I'd done in the past was to steal a sugared jelly snake from our local corner shop when I was eight years old. As I rammed the curved end of the crowbar into the gap between the door and the frame and heaved, I felt that exact same terror rush of adrenaline that I'd experienced all those years ago. I winced and gritted my teeth as though that alone could cushion the sound of wood splintering. The noise of the door giving way seemed abysmally loud in the silent building. I expected doors to open all the way up from the ground floor, residents to come rushing out to see what was going on. But nothing happened, and with a final groaning crunch the door to Alex's flat swung open.

The damage to the lock didn't look too bad. I thought that if I cleared up the bits of wood that had fallen on the floor, pushed some of the splayed splinters back into position, and closed the door when I left, then there was a chance that no one would even notice the flat had been broken into for a while, maybe not even until Alex returned to it. I glanced behind me, then squatted down and cleared up the debris, which I carried together with my crowbar into the flat. Just inside the door was the note I'd pushed under the first time I'd come here. I picked it up and scrunched it in my fist, then closed the door behind me.

Alex's flat was dim, the curtains closed, and it smelled of dusty unoccupation. But beneath that smell was another—a warm, homey smell, a smell that you couldn't really define except by saying that it was Alex's smell. I breathed it in, and was surprised to find that it brought a tear to my eye, a lump to my throat. It was like being a hairbreadth away from him and yet unable to hear or see or touch him. At that moment I longed to look up and see him standing there smiling at me, longed to hear him say, *Hiya, Gemmo. How's it going?*

"Alex," I whispered, but the word sank into nothingness, deadened by dust.

His flat was as cluttered as all his other rooms and flats and houses had ever been. Despite his sexuality my brother was a typical man. He collected things, and like all men who collect things, if he had one of something then he had to have them all. If he found an author he liked, he wouldn't be happy until he'd bought and read every word that author had ever written. If there was a band he enthused about, he had to own every song they'd ever released. He had to buy every episode of a favorite TV series on video, or every film of a particular actor or director. And the trouble was, Alex had a mass of wild and eclectic passions: Alfred Hitchcock, Wim Wenders, and Stanley Kubrick; Australian movies; Carry On films; Kenneth Williams and Joe Orton; *The Avengers, Blakes' 7,* and *Friends;* Hammer Horror; Sherlock Holmes; *Star Wars.*

As a result, wherever he lived was always crammed to the rafters with stuff, much of it tat to you and me, but a treasure trove to Alex and his like-minded friends.

And then there was his work too. However passionate Alex was about all these other things, he was doubly passionate about his work.

As I glanced down his narrow entrance corridor to the open door at the far end, I saw what I always saw wherever he lived—shelves crammed with books and videos and CDs. I walked down there, bypassing a door on my left (bathroom) and one on my right (bedroom).

The open door at the end led to the main room, the living room, which was large and rectangular. It contained a sofa bed and a matching armchair in pale blue material, which I knew came from IKEA because I had gone with Alex to choose it God knows how many years ago. The armchair faced a big TV and VCR, videos and magazines stacked beside it haphazardly. The TV stood in front of a heavy old sideboard on which stood a lava lamp, a large glass ashtray containing a pile of bits and pieces (paper clips, elastic bands, a book of matches from a restaurant, a broken skeleton key ring, a plastic cockroach, a black marker pen) and tons of action figures—Darth Vader and Godzilla; a Dalek which I knew talked when you pressed a button on the top of its head; an alien from *Independence Day;* Dracula sitting up in a coffin; a large and fearsome-looking scorpion; Pinhead from *Hellraiser;* some kind of robot which looked vaguely familiar; a few others that I couldn't identify.

Alex's life was so enriched by his many, many interests, that I find the only trouble when describing him—as now—is that sometimes I'm reduced to lists. Whenever I think of my brother, it amazes me that one person could be interested in so much. Because as well as all these sedentary, insular pursuits, Alex loved being outdoors too. He loved mountain-climbing; he'd been on expeditions; his work had taken him to some of the remotest places in the world. He had friends from all walks of life—mountaineers and explorers and archaeologists were forever staying with him in London. He regularly received E-mails from places like Tibet and New Zealand, China and Tanzania.

Standing here in his flat, surrounded by everything

that *was* Alex, everything but the man himself, brought it home to me how incredible and unlikely his decision to relocate to Greenwell had been. What was going on? There had to be some hidden agenda that I couldn't (or was refusing) to see. I felt like a murder detective, surrounded by every clue you could possibly need, and still unable to grasp the solution. I stood there looking around, as if wondering what to tackle first, and eventually walked over to his desk.

It was at the far end of the room, next to a glass-fronted bookcase containing multiple copies of Alex's books. I turned on his computer and waited for it to boot up. When it had I clicked on Outlook Express to check his E-mails, but there was nothing in either his inbox or sent items file. Strange. I rooted around in the papers on his desk, but it was all academic stuff, journals and photocopied articles and copious reams of notes; nothing personal whatsoever. Also, oddly, there was nothing that related to Alex's teaching post at the school—no piles of homework to mark, no dog-eared curriculum, no missives bearing the school crest.

I straightened up, licking my dry lips, disturbed not by what *was* here but by what was missing. It was as though someone had come in and carefully excised every part of Alex's recent life. But why? There was only one reason I could think of: in order to remove any incriminating evidence. I searched the flat, but even though it was all achingly redolent of Alex (the *Millennium Falcon* hanging above his bed; the climbing equipment heaped in the hallway; the clutter of Body Shop toiletries in the bathroom beneath a poster of Hitchcock's

The Birds), there was no clue as to where he might have gone.

There was, however, one thing in his flat which gave me hope, which led me to believe that he may have left here willingly. In his bedroom was a large shelving unit stacked with around two dozen empty glass tanks. The tanks were where Alex normally kept his menagerie—his spiders and scorpions and snakes and exotic beetles. If he had been abducted then surely these tanks would now be full of dead or dying creatures. Of course, there were other possibilities—maybe Cressley had insisted Alex get rid of his pets, or maybe someone had taken them, perhaps transferring them from their large tanks into more portable containers. It did cross my mind, thinking of the fiddleback I had seen on the stairs, that someone may simply have come in here and let them all go. However, if that had been the case, there would surely have been some evidence of their occupation. The flat had been closed and locked up, and most of Alex's collection would have been too large to squeeze under the door. Some would have been eaten by others, some would have sought refuge in the nooks and crannies, but there would still have been enough of the little darlings around for me to feel as though I'd blundered into some phobic's nightmare.

Wouldn't there?

I shuddered and looked around, up at the ceilings and walls. I took a step back from the bed that I was standing too close to in case something large and black and many-legged scuttled out from beneath it.

Moving more warily now, I made my way back to

the main room. As I stepped through the door, my eyes darting everywhere, a memory suddenly jumped to the forefront of my mind. I had a recollection of something moving at the periphery of my vision, of turning my head and glimpsing a lumpy shape beneath the dust cover on a settee. It's hard to explain how, but all at once the memory seemed to spark a connection in my head, and I rushed over to Alex's old IKEA sofa and, regardless of what might be lurking under there, pulled off the cushions and threw them on the floor behind me.

There, as I had somehow known it would be, was what I had been looking for. With a trembling hand I reached down and picked up the two books bound together with an elastic band. One was an address book, the other a chunky blue clothbound diary. I removed the elastic band and opened the diary. It felt unreal somehow, even magical. I half expected to hear the tinkle of tiny bells, see a glittery puff of fairy dust, as if by opening the book I had broken the seal on some enchantment.

I knew the books had been left for me. I don't know how I knew, I just knew. I realize that sounds trite, but I felt there were already enough forces working against me in this town, and that this little bit of good fortune was simply no more than I deserved.

Alex had moved to Greenwell around seven weeks ago. I turned to the twelfth of August, the date he had arrived. In his diary, in his looping, sloping script, which always seemed to convey a sense of excitement and enthusiasm, was written "Arrived in Greenwell! Moved into 5 Moxon Street!"

I smiled. Alex always wrote significant personal

events down in his diary because he was a great one for anniversaries. He'd often say things like: "Do you realize it's seven years to the day since I broke my leg falling down that mountain?" Or: "You wouldn't believe it was exactly ten years since I left home, would you?" Or even: "It's Joe Orton's birthday today. If he was still alive, he'd be sixty-five. Officially an old-age pensioner."

It would drive me mad sometimes. "So?" I'd ask him. "What's your point?"

"Well," he'd reply, "it makes you think, doesn't it?"

"No," I'd say, "not really," to which he'd cry in exasperation, "What's the matter, girl? Have you no sense of history?"

It's funny how little things that irritate us about the people we love often make us feel affectionate toward them when they're no longer there. I knew that next August 12th Alex would be saying, "Do you realize it's exactly a year since I moved to Greenwell?" I grinned at the thought, but beneath the grin was an overwhelming sense of sadness. If I could only find Alex he could spout all the anniversaries he wanted at me—well . . . for a little while at least.

I flicked forward through the diary, and on August 21st found the proclamation: "MET KEITH AT THE LAME DUCK!!!" There were several other references to the mysterious Keith before, on Monday September 4th, I came across an entry which read: "Started at SW! Met Liz!" SW was presumably Alex's abbreviation for the Solomon Wedge High School, but who was Liz? It was odd, but even though Alex and I had talked at length over the phone for the first six weeks he'd been here, I couldn't now recall anything concrete about our conversations. Had he told me about Keith and Liz? About his new job? About the town? More importantly, had he ever even *hinted* that anything was wrong here? Because if he had had even an inkling that things were not as they should be, then he would have told me, I'm certain of it.

Hard as I tried, all I had in my head was a vague recollection of sitting in my flat with a phone in my hand, talking to him. But as to what was said between us, I couldn't remember a thing. What was wrong with me? Had Matt hit me over the head one too many times? Were my sleeping pills messing up my memories? Certainly parts of my recent life seemed hazy, certain events insubstantial. Disturbed, I tried to focus on the matter at hand.

There were various references in the diary to Keith and to Liz, sometimes separately, sometimes together. September 11th: "Keith and Liz. Bellini's. 7:30"; September 13th: "Liz. Badminton. 6:30"; September 15th: "Keith's Farewell Meal. La Dolce Vita, 8:00"; September 27th (a week ago—was that the last time I'd spoken to Alex?): "Dinner at Liz's."

Keith and Liz. Were they a couple? Was Liz perhaps Keith's wife or girlfriend? No, because Alex had met Liz on September 4th, the day he'd started teaching at the Solomon Wedge High School, which would seem to suggest that she was also a teacher there. Besides, his meeting with Keith had been written in huge, joyous capitals. "It's definitely wedding bells, darling," Alex's willfully camp friend Charlie would have said.

I put the diary aside and picked up the address book. As I pored carefully through it, I wondered why Keith had had a "farewell meal." Was he changing jobs, moving away from the area, or was this perhaps Alex's blackly humorous way of marking the end of a brief relationship? Scanning the pages of the address book, I couldn't help but feel jealous that I had no input into this part of Alex's life, which brought to mind Cressley's snide comment about my possessiveness. I scowled and flipped the page over. I was already on S. And then I saw it, the last entry on the page. "Liz Sykes."

There was no address, just a phone number. I took out my mobile and dialed. After four rings came an answering machine message. "Hi, this is Liz. Sorry I'm not here to take your call, but if you leave your name and number I'll get back to you as soon as I can."

I switched off my phone, cutting off the beep. I'm not funny about answering machines, but on this occasion I really didn't want to leave a message. I'm not sure why, it just made me feel too exposed somehow. It wasn't that Liz didn't sound nice, because she did. Chirpy, friendly, full of life. It's funny how much we can glean just by hearing someone speak a few words. She sounded like someone you could trust, someone you could talk to. I hesitated for a moment and then dialed the number of the school, which was one of the few things I had managed to commit to memory.

Almost immediately a clipped female voice (the antithesis of Liz's) said, "Solomon Wedge High School."

"Good morning," I said. "Is Liz Sykes available, please?"

"She's probably teaching. Who shall I say is calling?"

"It's her sister," I said without hesitation, and immediately thought, *What! What did you say* that *for?*

There was a pause, during which I expected the woman (I pictured her as waspish, uptight, navy blue cardigan buttoned up to her neck) to say coldly, "Miss Sykes hasn't got a sister. Who the hell *is* this?"

But instead she said, "Is it important?"

"Quite important," I said. I felt intimidated enough to almost add something like, *It's about our mother.* However, I managed to restrain myself, thinking it wise not to get in any deeper than I already was.

There was another pause and then the waspish woman said, "Just a moment. I'll try to locate her for you."

My heart thumped and my hand holding the receiver was slick with sweat as I listened to the silence at the other end. A couple of times my courage almost deserted me, my thumb touching the button that would break the connection, but not pressing it. I imagined the woman telling Liz that her sister was on the phone, Liz looking puzzled and saying, "But I haven't got a sister." When I heard the *clunk* of the receiver being picked up after what seemed like ages, all the moisture drained from my mouth. Then the voice from Liz's answering machine said, "Hi, Moira. What's up?"

For a moment I was thrown. I swallowed and licked my lips, aware of the silence stretching between us. Finally I said quickly, "Hi, Liz. I'm afraid it isn't Moira. I just said that so I could get to talk to you."

"Oh?" said Liz. She didn't sound annoyed, just intrigued.

"My name's Ruth Gemmill," I said. "I'm Alex Gemmill's sister."

"Oh!" she said again, but this time it was a happy exclamation. "Where is he? I've been really worried about him."

"I was hoping you might be able to tell me that," I said. "I've come to Greenwell to look for him. Actually, I was wondering whether we could meet up, pool our resources."

"Sure," she said without hesitation. "Where and when?"

"Well, are you free tonight?"

"I think I can squeeze you into my busy social calendar," she said, her tone making it obvious she was joking. "Where do you want to meet?"

"You suggest somewhere," I said. "I don't know Greenwell very well."

"Whereabouts are you staying?"

"The Solomon Wedge. It's a big pub off Wedge Square."

"I know it," said Liz. "Well, why don't we meet there?"

"I'd rather not," I said. "Too many prying eyes."

I half expected her to ask me what I meant, but instead she said, "Okay then, how about . . ." She thought for a few seconds, then said, "There's a decent pub called The Rooster about five minutes' walk from the Solomon Wedge. It's on Roslyn Street. How does that sound?"

I walked over to Alex's desk, found a spare bit of paper and a pen, and wrote it down. "Great," I said. "About half past seven?"

"See you there," Liz said. "Bye, Ruth."

It was only as I was putting my phone back in my bag that I realized I had forgotten to ask her about Keith. Oh well, no problem. I could ask her tonight. Taking Alex's diary and address book, I had a last look round the flat, lingering in each room as though desperate to commit every detail to memory. Then I left, hurrying down the stairs, expecting at any moment to hear the sound of the front door opening below, the heavy tread of feet in the hallway.

As I drove back into the center of town I felt almost euphoric. I glanced at the car clock and was shocked to see it was almost midday. My watch told the same story. Where had the time gone? Had I really been in Alex's flat for two hours? I decided to see whether the Red Dragon was open for lunch. It was, and I celebrated by ordering the businessman's lunch, three courses for seven pounds. There was a party of—surprise, surprise— businessmen in there, six of them in all. One or two kept casting lascivious glances in my direction, but I ignored them. When the waiter who had chased me out of the restaurant a couple of days ago (I had started to think of him as *my* waiter) arrived with my first course of crispy duck pancakes and black bean sauce, I asked him if he had time for a quick chat.

He glanced at the businessmen, said, "Two minutes," and sat down. Between mouthfuls of pancake I asked him about life in Greenwell.

It was not a particularly productive conversation, to tell the truth. Either he was giving very little away or he was simply unable to perceive the shadows that I sensed everywhere in the town. He had been here for eleven years, business was good, the people were very nice, his wife was happy, his daughter liked her school. When I asked him if anything odd ever happened in Greenwell, he replied with such seriousness that I wasn't sure whether he was joking, "People sometimes run out of my restaurant without paying. But they are usually outsiders and I usually catch them."

As he got up to leave, I asked him whether he had heard of the gray man. I watched him closely, but there was not even the faintest flicker of recognition in his eyes. He shook his head slowly. "No, I haven't. I'm sorry." I finished my meal, found a bookshop, where I bought a map of the area (so that I wouldn't have to keep asking for directions and thus tipping off the locals about my intended whereabouts) and a copy of *The Orton Diaries* edited by John Lahr (which I felt would bring me closer to Alex somehow), and then, unable to think of anything else to do before my meeting with Liz, made my way back to the Solomon Wedge.

I went up to my room, found Roslyn Street on the map, then lay back on my bed and started to read my book. All the food I'd eaten had made me sleepy, however, and after twenty minutes of trying to fight my drooping eyelids I gave up and allowed them to close. Instantly, despite fearing a repeat of the terrible dream I had had last night, I felt myself drifting away. As I did so I thought how odd it was that since I had been here I hadn't had to take a single pill to help me sleep. I resolved that once I got back to London, I would ceremoniously flush all my pills down the toilet. It would be another symbolic step toward a new and happier life— or perhaps a step back to the life I'd known before Matt, if such a thing was possible.

That was my last thought before I woke up several hours later. I came to slowly, enjoying the stillness around me. I looked at my watch and saw that it was ten past five. I got up, had a long bath, changed my clothes, then made myself a cup of tea and sat on my bed, reading my book. I couldn't concentrate, however. I felt edgy, eager for the time when I could leave the Solomon Wedge and go to meet Liz. I put the book aside and turned on the TV. The news was on, but it seemed distant, unrelated to me, as though it were being beamed in from another world. Greenwell seemed beyond time and space. It existed purely within its own boundaries. It was like a plague town of old, spurned and isolated, rotting away from within.

I set off earlier than was necessary, having committed my route to memory. It was more a ten-minute walk than a five-minute one, but I didn't mind; it killed some time. The Rooster looked out of place in Greenwell. It was spick and span, having evidently been recently modernized and refurbished. There was a new, brightly colored sign hanging outside the front door (a grinning, strutting, cartoonlike rooster, its chest puffed out) and the interior smelled of fresh carpets and polished woodwork. A chalk blackboard boasted dishes more exotic than your normal pub fare, and there were panels of gaudily colored stained glass partitioning the separate areas. There was even a family section where mums and dads could enjoy a quiet drink whilst their kids hurled themselves around the soft sculpture play area. In London I avoided such places like the plague, but here, in this dreary town, I applauded The Rooster's determined cheerfulness, its contemporary values.

Perhaps not surprisingly the pub was almost deserted. The two staff members I could see—one polishing glasses, the other wiping tables in the dining area—were both young and smartly dressed in crisp white shirts and black trousers. I went to the bar and ordered a gin and tonic and then, as an afterthought, a plate of corn-fed-chicken sandwiches. Then I found a table within sight of the entrance doors and sat down to wait.

At one minute to half past the left-hand door was pushed open and a woman entered. I'd been there half an hour by then, during which time I'd eaten my chicken sandwiches and was on my second G and T. As the woman turned her head to look at me, I gasped.

I realized that Liz Sykes was exactly as I'd envisaged her. Small and neat and healthy-looking, her strawberry-blond hair was drawn up in a loose but stylish twist, held in place by a tortoiseshell clip. She was wearing a sleeveless black ribbed crop-top and black stretch pants. Her arms were brown, her muscles well toned, and her stomach, which I saw in glimpses when she moved, was also tanned and enviably flat. Perhaps the only surprising thing about her was the silver ring that she wore in her belly button, though I'm not sure exactly *why* I was surprised by this. I guess maybe it was because I still subconsciously viewed teachers from the perspective of my schooldays, still thought of them as staid establishment figures, not subject to the whims of fashion and youth culture.

She grinned when she saw me and strode across the room, hand outstretched. "Hi, you must be Ruth. Alex has told me a lot about you. Oh God, I promised myself I wouldn't say that."

I laughed and took her hand. Though it was small and slender, her grip was surprisingly strong.

"Hi," I said. "Thanks for agreeing to meet me."

She cheerily waved away my gratitude. "Hey, it's a pleasure. If we can put our heads together and work out where Alex has got to, then you'll be doing me a favor too. Alex is a lovely guy. I've missed him like mad this last week or so."

"I miss him too," I said. "Would you like a drink?"

"My shout," said Liz, and gestured at my glass. "What are you having?"

As Liz ordered drinks at the bar, I wondered how much she knew about my brother. Had he told her he was gay? Presumably so if she had been out with Keith and Alex together. Besides, if she was as good a friend to Alex as it appeared, then he would almost certainly have told her. Alex didn't wear his sexuality like a badge, but I know he liked to be open and honest with friends and colleagues, claiming that it avoided awkward misunderstandings later on.

Liz came back with the drinks. "Thanks," I said as she put a glass before me. "What's that you're drinking?"

"Rum and Coke," Liz said, holding up her glass. "But I can't have too many. I'm driving."

"Do you live far away?"

"Not too far. In a little village called Shelton, about five miles north of here. It's a lovely place. Not like Greenwell."

"What makes you say that?"

Her eyes widened slightly. "Oh, sorry, I didn't mean to offend you."

I leaned forward conspiratorially. "No, what I mean is I agree with you. Greenwell's a hole."

Liz looked relieved. "It is. So dreary and depressing. I keep trying to persuade Alex to move out to Shelton."

"How well do you know Alex?" I asked.

"Pretty well, I think, considering we only met about four weeks ago."

"And has he told you . . . much about himself?"

Liz smiled. "Oh yeah, we hit it off from the word go. It's been real info-dump time between us." She paused. "He's told me he's gay, if that's what you're getting at."

For a moment I considered denying that I had meant anything of the sort, then I shrugged sheepishly. "Actually, that *was* what I was getting at. I did wonder whether you had a romantic interest in my brother."

She gave an unladylike snort. "Hardly."

"That's all right, then," I said. "I'm glad we've got that one out of the way." I leaned forward, elbows on knees, all too aware that our voices were practically the only sound in that cavernous place. "I gather he was seeing someone called Keith?"

"That's right. Keith Thornley. Another nice guy. They were well suited actually."

"And Keith had to go away, did he?"

She looked at me quizzically.

"I'm sorry. The only information I've got about you and Keith is from my brother's diary. One entry reads 'Keith's farewell meal.' "

"Oh, *right,*" she said, tilting her head coquettishly as realization dawned. I'd noticed that little tilt of the head a couple of times since we'd started talking. The cuteness of the gesture in such a poised, self-assured woman was totally endearing, and I surmised that there were almost certainly dozens of adolescent boys whose initial sweaty sexual fantasies involved the delectable Miss Sykes in a starring role.

"No, Keith's gone to Australia to visit his parents," Liz said. "They emigrated there after his dad retired a few years ago. The meal was just a bit of a joke because Alex and Keith were being so pathetic about not seeing each other for a couple of weeks."

"I see. So when was the last time you saw Alex?"

"It would be . . . let me see . . . this time last week. Wednesday. Alex came over to my place for dinner. He seemed okay, we had a good time, but then he didn't show up at school on Thursday. I called him, but there was no answer. I haven't seen him since."

"What did you think when you couldn't get hold of him?"

"At first nothing. I was a bit disappointed because we'd planned to go for a walk on the weekend and I'd been looking forward to it. I love Alex's company, especially when we're out in the countryside. He's just so knowledgeable about everything, points out things that you wouldn't ordinarily notice. Not in an arrogant way, though. In a way that makes you feel good."

I smiled, feeling suddenly close to Liz. I knew exactly what she meant. Alex didn't make you feel as though he was preaching or showing off when he told you stuff, but as though he was enriching you, confiding in you. It was a very appealing trait, one that had caused men and women alike to fall head over heels for him.

"So where did you think he'd gone?" I asked.

"I assumed Alex was ill or that something had come up. I asked Geoff Rudding, our headmaster, whether he knew where Alex was, but he was his usual snide, unhelpful self."

I filed that one away. Liz wasn't keen on Rudding either. I was beginning to like this woman more and more.

"If Alex had been ill," I said, "he would have let someone know he wasn't coming to work. He wouldn't have just not turned up."

Liz nodded. "That's what I thought too. I mean, I know I only met him a few weeks ago, but he'd always seemed to be someone you could trust, someone who was one hundred percent reliable."

"He *is* reliable," I said. "He's always been there when I've needed him. Always."

We lapsed into a brief silence, both of us, I suspect, thinking the same thing. Alex had always been there for me (not in person sometimes, admittedly, but he'd always been at the end of a phone line or computer terminal), and the fact that he wasn't now could only mean that he was somehow being prevented from contacting me.

I took a gulp of my drink—my head was beginning to spin a little—and said, "I had a strange conversation with three of the children at your school yesterday."

"Did you?" asked Liz. "Why was that?"

I told her how they had been waiting by my car after my meeting with the headmaster. "I don't know how they knew I was looking for Alex, but they said they knew where he was. When I asked where, they said he'd been taken by the gray man."

Liz looked at me for a moment, then gave an exaggerated shudder, like someone shaking the cold out of themselves when walking from a winter street into a warm house. It was a reaction that surprised me. I had expected her to laugh or roll her eyes.

"What does it mean?" I asked.

She recovered her composure quickly and smiled. "It doesn't mean anything. It was just the way you said it, the tone of your voice. It gave me the shivers."

"But there must be some reason why the children said it."

Liz shrugged. "You know what kids are like. I remember when I was nine or ten, my friends and I spent a whole summer convinced we were being stalked by a golden monster. The reason for this was that we'd found a spatter of gold paint on the pavement outside my friend Melanie's house. After that, we found all sorts of 'clues' that proved the existence of this beast. Broken sticks that we told each other he'd been chewing to sharpen his teeth; divots in the field behind my house that we claimed had been gouged out by his claws. We convinced ourselves on the flimsiest of evidence that this thing was after us. We *terrified* one another." She shrugged again. "It's what kids do. The ones you saw had probably become obsessed with the local legend, and as soon as Alex failed to turn up for school on Thursday, they put two and two together and made five."

"You've heard of the gray man, then?"

"Vaguely. Isn't he supposed to be some portent of

doom or something? I don't know the origins of the story."

"He haunts the lonely places," I said.

Liz smiled and looked around. "I wouldn't be surprised if he put in an appearance here tonight, then."

"He kills whoever he meets," I said. I was trying to steer the conversation round to telling Liz about all the odd things that had happened to me since I'd arrived here without making myself sound like a lunatic. The trouble was, even as I was speaking I knew that this wasn't the way to go about it. If I told her now about the figure I had seen in the field and about my experience last night, wouldn't she assume that I was insinuating the gray man was responsible for the body in the station? I was desperate to tell someone everything, in order to get an objective perspective on the events of the past few days, but I felt instinctively that this wasn't the right moment. Liz was just about the only person I'd really connected with since I'd been here, and the last thing I wanted was to alienate her during our first meeting.

"He sounds like most of my year ten class," Liz quipped, but I sensed behind her smile she was a little perturbed by my intensity. I forced myself to smile, too, and then Liz surprised me by saying, "Actually, I *do* remember something about the gray man."

"Oh yes," I said. "What's that?"

"You're not supposed to see his face. If you look him in the face, you'll die."

I finished my drink and went to the bar for more. Liz had a Coke without the rum this time. I had another

G and T, telling myself that if I wanted to avoid another night of terrible dreams I'd better make it my last. As I sat down, I said, "You don't think Alex might have followed Keith to Australia, do you?"

Liz did that little tilt of the head again. "It did cross my mind, but . . . no. It wouldn't make any sense, would it?"

"I suppose not," I said. All the same, it was a faint hope to cling to. "When is Keith due back?"

"I'm not sure. He was going over for about two and a half weeks, so it could be any day now."

"Do you have his number?"

"Yes, I do." Liz rummaged through the small shoulder bag which she had placed on the seat beside her and took out a tiny black address book. She copied Keith's number down on a beer mat and handed it to me.

After that our discussion about Alex's possible whereabouts became a more general conversation about my brother. I told Liz things about him that Alex would have been too modest or embarrassed or forgetful to tell her himself. She in turn told me what a good teacher he was, and how popular he'd become with his pupils despite the short time he'd been there.

"How about the staff?" I asked. "Is he popular with them too?"

She hesitated a moment, then said, "He's certainly not *un*popular. The younger staff members like him. It's just that the school has its share of . . . dinosaurs. Traditionalists."

"People who don't like the fact that he's gay?"

"Oh, I don't know if it's that so much. I'm not sure they even *know* about that. No, it's more that they don't like any change to the status quo. They view new people and new ideas with suspicion. It's symptomatic of the whole town."

"Was Alex surprised by that attitude when he came here?"

"He rose above it. He didn't let it affect him. We talked about it now and then, but I don't think he even regarded it as an issue. I guessed he'd coped with far greater prejudices."

I asked Liz about herself. She'd been at the school for five years. Before then she'd lived in the village where she had been born, had taught at the school that she herself had attended as a little girl.

She was easy to talk to and we got on well. I always liked the people that Alex chose as his friends. It worked the same the other way around, too, apart from Matt. It wasn't that Alex and Matt were antagonistic toward each other in those first few months, it was just that there had never been a spark between them. Despite the fact that I found both of them interesting to talk to, they just couldn't seem to find any common ground. Their conversations would peter out into awkward silences, and when I asked Alex about this, he would say—to my annoyance—that Matt made him uncomfortable, that he wasn't really interested in what you had to say, and that he had no sense of humor.

I should have listened to my brother. He was a better judge of character than I was. But with Matt I had a blind spot. I took issue with Alex's assessment of him, accused him of not giving Matt a chance. *I* got on well with him, I told Alex, *I* was able to talk to him, and most of my friends seemed to like him well enough. Alex would just shrug and apologize and say that he didn't want to have an argument about it. "Maybe it's just me," he'd say. "Sometimes you meet people, people who you feel you ought to get along with, but you just can't, you're like repelling magnets. Each time you come close you just veer away from one another. Your minds never touch."

Liz and I stayed in The Rooster until closing time. During that period only eight or ten people entered the building. The staff stood around looking bored and pissed off, probably wondering where their next wage packet would be coming from when this place closed down. At times I found myself casting surreptitious glances in their direction to ensure we weren't being watched or overheard, and then silently admonished myself for doing it. Had I really become so paranoid that I believed the staff here—most of whom looked like college kids out to earn some extra money—were in on the underhanded goings-on in this town? Several times I almost told Liz everything, but on each occasion the time didn't seem quite right, and I couldn't get the words out. All the same, by the time we left the pub I felt I had a new friend and ally. We exchanged phone numbers and promised to keep each other informed of developments.

"Don't feel as though you need Alex as an excuse to keep in touch," Liz said. "If you just want a friend to talk to or you fancy a night out, then give me a call. I'm usually in."

She offered me a lift back to the Solomon Wedge, but I decided to walk in an attempt to clear my head. We said our good-byes by Liz's car, which I was astonished to see was a red Spitfire. "It's not as impressive as it looks," she said. "A friend of mine's brother does them up. I've got it on a sort of extended loan."

We shook hands a bit awkwardly like business colleagues at the end of a meeting, and then Liz reached out and enclosed me in a brief but fierce embrace.

"He'll turn up sooner or later," she said. "Try not to worry." I nodded, her hair tickling my face, absurdly grateful for the physical contact.

We broke apart, Liz clasped my hand briefly once more, then she got into her car and drove away. She stuck her hand out the window in a wave as she turned the corner. I waved back, and then she was gone.

The engine noise faded, leaving me alone in the dark. There were streetlamps lining the pavement at staggered intervals, but typically for Greenwell, they were all but ineffectual. The glow from their soft orange heads seemed flat, stifled by a darkness that was thicker here than anywhere else I had ever known. I imagined shadows seeping from the dark stone of the buildings around me at night, clotting the streets with a near-physical presence.

I started to walk. Despite the treacle-thick darkness, my footsteps—heels clopping the pavement, insteps crackling on the gritty surface—seemed exaggerated, like a cinematic sound effect. The sky was starless, so inscrutable that I could just as easily have been looking at a black lid that had closed over the town at night. There was not a sound to be heard, and thinking about it I realized how oddly quiet Greenwell was at all times. Stand outdoors in any other populated area and you would hear birdsong, distant voices, the rumble of engines. But here

I honestly couldn't remember hearing or seeing a single bird. It made me think of Auschwitz, where, it is rumored, birds will not fly.

I had been walking for two, perhaps three minutes when I heard a sound behind me. It was a soft sound, hard to describe. A kind of swish, like a large curtain being pulled suddenly back. I turned round, but saw nothing untoward. The noise was so intriguing, so hard to decipher that I considered walking back to see if I could get to the bottom of it. Then I thought of my room at the Solomon Wedge and decided that at this moment all I really wanted was to be there. I turned and walked on.

For the next minute or two the sound occupied my mind. I thought of a swooping bird, a cape being flung over a shoulder, a knife or sword slashing the air. This last image made me uneasy and I walked quicker, my breath starting to tug in my chest. After last week's brief Indian summer, the days, and especially the nights, were beginning to turn chillier, though not cold enough yet to fog my breath.

I passed a churchyard that was raised above road level, the stone wall on my right almost as tall as I was. The wall was sagging outward, and I thought of it giving way beneath the weight of the earth behind it, smothering me in a landslide of dirt and human remains.

Hurrying on, I passed a row of shops which were succumbing to neglect and the ravages of decay. Weeds sprouted from the stonework of Sublime—Hair and Beauty Specialists; pale brown tape and rain-damaged rectangles of white cardboard held the cracked front window of Great Clobber in place. Across the road an expanse of scrubby grassland ended in a chain-link enclosure where swings and a roundabout and a slide linked to a climbing wall by a rope bridge stood spindly or squat, like safari park animals waiting for daylight. Close to the roundabout was a wooden bench, beside which a bush, paler than the surrounding objects, stirred.

Slight though it was, the movement caught my eye, my head twisting so sharply that I felt a spasm of pain in my neck. The bush wasn't a bush at all, but a man. A man dressed all in gray.

He was far enough away for his face to be nothing but a blurred oval. His arms appeared molded to his body, hands stuck in the pockets of a clay-colored gown or overcoat. When he began to move in my direction, seeming to glide over the spiky clumps of grass, I ran.

It was a wild, panicked run. I didn't dare look behind me, not until I was three streets clear of the park, not until my heart was burning so hotly in my chest that I *had* to stop. Even so, I carried on until I reached the relative sanctuary of a bus shelter, twisting round even as I collapsed against the glass wall, panting, leaving a greasy, long-fingered smear from the hand I used to steady myself.

The road behind me, made tunnel-like by an arch of high, stooping trees, was empty. I listened, but I could hear nothing except the sound of blood pounding through my head and veins.

I shoved myself up from the bus shelter and began to lurch along the pavement, my head trying to turn in all directions at once. I was passing blocks of flats on my left, residential houses on my right. As I glanced at each building I realized something else about Greenwell.

Though it was gloomy and claustrophobic, there was no dropped litter, no graffiti, no vandalism. Something to rejoice about, you might think, but I felt a heavy, somehow oily sensation in my stomach, and a mental jolt of what I can only describe as dread. Greenwell was a bad place, a *wrong* place. I'd heard of houses having a bad atmosphere, an evil aura, but I'd never experienced that feeling until now, had never thought that such a notion could apply to a whole town. Maybe this will sound crazy, but I couldn't help thinking that the Greenwell that surrounded me was nothing but a disguise, a masquerade of stone and glass and concrete and metal concealing something far worse.

I was approaching the center of town now, only a few minutes' walk away from the Solomon Wedge. The closer I got to the heart, the denser the streets and the taller the buildings became. I felt as though I were sinking, as though I were heading not only inward but downward too. There was not a soul about. Not a single soul. Even as I thought this, I glanced to my left, up a street that bisected the one I was on, and—so quickly that it was nothing more than an impression—glimpsed a gray figure sliding out of sight around a corner at the street's opposite end.

The thought leaped instantly into my head: the gray figure in the park was not trailing me directly, but had taken a shortcut and was now trying to cut off my route to the Solomon Wedge. Panic rushed through me once more, and though the ebbing of the initial adrenaline surge had enervated me, I again started to run. I felt as though I was running clumsily, as though thick, soupy darkness were clinging to my legs like mud, dragging me down. The sooty buildings on either side seemed to lurch forward with each erratic footstep. I had to turn right, run up another street, and then I would be in Wedge Square, within sight of the pub.

If I could get to my room I would be okay, I told myself. A child's faith again: the bogeyman can't get you if you reach "home" before he does. I should have known better, of course. Experience had taught me that the bogeyman can get you anywhere at any time. He is not afraid of the light, he is not afraid of running water or garlic or silver or salt or ancient symbols chalked within a protective circle. He is no respecter of boundaries, he does not have to be invited in in order to reach you. All the same I needed something to cling to, something to believe in. I staggered to the end of the street. I glanced behind me, then slowed momentarily to peer around the corner, and saw nothing in either direction.

Relieved, I picked up my pace again, knowing that at the end of this street was the Square, and that at the other side of the Square was the Solomon Wedge. In twenty or thirty seconds I would see the lights shining from its windows. In a minute or two I would be able to run up to it, open the door, let myself in. I began to allow myself to believe I had beaten the darkness.

And then, just as I least expected it, just as hope was rising in me, the dark shape of a man stepped from a shop doorway to my right.

I cried out, slid to a halt, tried to turn, but the figure flowed swiftly, purposefully, toward me. It reached out and enclosed my arm in a tight and painful grip.

I struggled to escape, my head turned away from the figure, fearful of looking into its face.

"It would be better for you if you didn't struggle," a voice suddenly hissed in my ear.

Shocked, I swung round and saw a square, pudgy face beneath the dark dome of a policeman's helmet.

"What are you doing?" I cried with a mixture of relief and indignation. "Let me go!"

He cleared his throat, and then in an officious monotone he said, "Ruth Gemmill, I'm arresting you for criminal damage and burglary. Would you please come with me."

"Criminal . . . ? You've got to be joking!" I exclaimed. But his face held not even the vaguest hint of a smile.

twelve

AT THE CORNER OF the Square a police car was waiting, its engine silent, its lights extinguished. The policeman led me to it, his grip so tight on my arm that I was sure his fingertips would leave bruises.

Was this it, then? Had they allowed me so much leeway before finally now deciding to put a stop to it? What were they going to do? Make me disappear like Alex?

I was scared and nervous, but at least that was better than a minute or two ago when I'd been terrified.

As we approached the car, it revved into life, the engine clearing its throat before settling into a purr, the headlamps casting cones of light before them. In the backseat a shadow leaned across and opened the door.

"Get in," the policeman said, placing a hand on my head and forcing me to bow into the car.

I obeyed without protest, deciding to remain silent for now, to argue my case at a more opportune time. I wondered how they'd found out that I'd broken into

Alex's flat, unless they'd been keeping me under constant surveillance. I suppose the fact that they felt they needed an excuse to arrest me ought to have given me hope, but I was worried by the accusation of burglary. Did that mean they knew I'd taken the diary and the address book, or were they referring to something else?

The inside of the car smelled cloyingly of meat. Burgers. My already nervous stomach turned slowly over again. I wanted to ask for some fresh air, but I didn't want to give them the satisfaction of refusing. So I sat silently, staring between the two front seats at the world beyond the windshield, and tried to concentrate on not feeling ill.

The policeman who'd arrested me removed his helmet and also got in the back, forcing me to shuffle into the middle, squashed now between his considerable bulk and the slighter frame of the man who'd opened the door. I didn't look at either of the men, but I was aware of the pudgy policeman draping his arm across the back of the seat so that his hand was touching my hair, and of his warm, meaty breath on the left side of my face. I had the impression he was gazing at me, waiting for me to acknowledge him.

"So we meet again," the man on my right, the one who had opened the door, said.

I jerked my head in his direction and realized it was the young, horsey-looking policeman I'd given the missing persons form to.

I went cold. I didn't know what to say, so I said nothing.

"Been a naughty girl, haven't we?"

I faced front again, hoping in vain that if I ignored

him he would get bored and leave me alone. He shuffled closer to me and sniggered. It was the snigger of the little man who had always craved the power and authority of the big and had now finally been given the chance to wield it.

"Playing hard to get, are we?" he jeered and—as the car pulled out into the road—reached toward me.

I flinched, thinking he was going to either slap me or molest me. "My, my," he said, "aren't we nervous."

I flushed with rage and embarrassment when I realized that all he was doing was pulling out the seat belt from the slot beside my hip. He leaned across my body, dragging the seat belt behind him. I tensed as I felt the weight of his body press against me, felt his hand brush across my breast, slide across my stomach, fumble beside my hip. Then the catch slid into its socket with a metallic *chunk* sound and he leaned back.

"There," he said, "isn't that better?"

Nothing more was said on the short journey to the station. When we arrived, I released my seat belt quickly before Horse-Face could lean across me again. For the last few minutes I'd been breathing in the hot, beefy, onion-breath of the chubby policeman who had arrested me, and as soon as the door opened I scrambled out of the car after him to gulp in the fresh air.

The shape of the building, its long, low flat roof, made it look as though it were being crushed beneath the considerable weight of the starless sky. By night it looked not merely drab but ominous, like a military holding block in some far-flung dictatorship. The globe of light above the door I had entered the last time I'd been here should have added a sense of welcome, of refuge, but its harsh glow seemed contained and thus only darkened the shadows around it. I took a step toward the door, but Horse-Face grabbed me by the wrist.

"Where do you think you're going?"

I hated the feel of his skin on mine, but I endured it, determined not to do anything to provoke him or the others. "Inside," I said, then couldn't stop myself from adding, "or are we staying out here in the car park?"

He grinned and tugged on my wrist, pulling me closer to him. Still grinning, he hissed, "Don't get clever, bitch." His face was only two inches from mine, and I could smell his breath, which had a meaty odor every bit as pungent as his colleague's. "This way," he said, and led me by the wrist to the far side of the building. I was furious at being dragged along like a dog, but this time I managed to keep my mouth shut. The four of us—Horse-Face yanking me along, Onion-Breath lumbering behind me, the silent, unseen driver bringing up the rear—moved around to the side of the building and stopped at a set of locked double doors.

"Tradesmen's entrance," Horse-Face said, and tugged on a loop of chain at his hip, one end of which was clipped to his belt, the other attached to a ring of keys that arose from his trouser pocket. He selected a key and the lock scraped open. A moment later we were in the building.

The walls of the corridor we entered were taupe, the vinyl floor tiles a thin, watery blue. The bulbs overhead, contained in square mesh cages, offered such feeble illumination it seemed there was some sort of energy drain, that the place was operating on half power. What light there was made everyone look slightly jaundiced.

"You can let go of my wrist now," I said when the outside door had been locked behind us. Horse-Face grinned again, his teeth slick, as if newly varnished.

"And here's me thinking we were on the verge of a beautiful relationship."

He stared at me deliberately for a moment, his grin never reaching eyes whose pupils seemed almost entirely black, then he very deliberately sprang his fingers apart.

"Thank you," I said, resisting the urge to rub my wrist, even though it felt hot and sore.

Onion-Breath placed a hand on the small of my back and gave a little push. "Keep walking."

We came to the end of the corridor, then turned right into another one, almost identical to the first. Halfway along we stopped at a door marked INTERVIEW ROOM 12. Onion-Breath leaned forward and opened it wide. "In here," he said.

I went in and thought that he was following me. However, he merely stepped inside to grab the handle of the door, then pulled it shut with a bang, leaving me alone. I didn't mind that so much, but when I heard the scrape of a key in the lock I crossed back to the door. "Hey, what's going on?"

I heard Horse-Face snigger. "Don't worry, sweetheart. You'll be dealt with soon enough."

Dealt with. With a rush the night's events seemed to suddenly catch up with me, and all at once I felt so scared it was like sickness. The strength-sapping sensation that slithered up from my legs into my midriff was like the beginnings of the limb-aching fever ("Ruth's lurgy," Alex calls it) that always grips me when I come down with flu. I wanted at that moment to protest, to reason with them, even to plead, but I managed to resist the instinct, to maintain my silence. It would do no good to beg. In fact, they would probably have liked nothing better than to have me groveling at their feet.

The interview room contained only a chipped Formica table bolted to the floor and a big, old double-headed tape recorder built into the wall. I desperately needed to sit down, but there weren't any chairs, so I sat on the floor in the corner farthest from the door, my back against the wall.

How long I stayed in that room alone I'm not sure. I didn't have a watch, and it probably seemed a lot longer than it actually was, but I'd estimate I was there for about an hour and a half. The debilitating terror stayed with me for a while; a couple of times I almost threw up at the thought of what might happen to me here. As time dragged on, however, I began to grow restless, to wish that something *would* happen. I wondered why they didn't get on with it, what they could possibly hope to gain by keeping me hanging around. I thought about the body in the station. If that had been intended to scare me off, then it had been not merely a poorly judged attempt but an act of crass stupidity. Did my persecutors honestly believe I'd flee Greenwell and say nothing? My brother was missing and a man was dead. Did whoever was responsible for all this truly think I'd put all that behind me, go back to London, and get on with my life? Perhaps they had intended me to conclude that the hooded body in the station was Alex, though at no point had I ever entertained that possibility. Although it had been dark in the station and I'd got no more than a glimpse of the hanging man, I had known instinctively that it wasn't Alex dangling there. Perhaps it was something about the build or the corpse's hands . . . I don't know. I simply felt that if it *had* been Alex, I would have recognized him immediately.

Throughout my incarceration I heard not a single sound in the rest of the building. I began to wonder whether they'd all gone home and left me, whether I was going to have to stay in here all night without food or drink or toilet facilities. At one point I even wondered whether they were planning to leave me here indefinitely. After all, Greenwell was a small town and it was unlikely that anything would ever happen that would necessitate the use of twelve interview rooms simultaneously. This room could remain locked for weeks, months even, and no one would even raise so much as an eyebrow. Perhaps the same fate had befallen Alex. Perhaps he was less than an arm's length away, separated from me by nothing more than a foot-thick wall.

Such notions, ridiculous though they may seem in the cold light of day, gained a terrifying energy and significance in that barren, locked room. For a few minutes, stir-crazy, I lost control, abandoning my previous determination to hold on to my composure. I banged on the door, screamed to be let out, but no one came. Eventually, my fists aching, several of my knuckles bloody and bruised, I retreated to my corner and sank for a while into a kind of torpor.

Exhausted, though nervily awake, I was wondering whether I ought to bed down for the night when I heard footsteps in the corridor outside. I scrambled to my feet as a key turned in the lock. The door opened and two men came in. They were both big and broad-shouldered. One was wearing a pale gray suit, the other dark gray. The one in the pale gray was pudgy, with a scrunched-up face, thinning hair, a moustache, and sideburns. His colleague was younger and fitter. He had neat, sandy-colored hair and a square-jawed face with a pronounced dimple in the center of his chin.

The younger man closed the door. Both men were carrying chairs, which they placed at opposite ends of the Formica table. The older man sat down in his chair, the younger man simply put his into position, then went to stand by the door, hands crossed loosely in front of his crotch like a footballer in a defensive wall.

I looked at the two men and licked my lips. My stomach cramped nervously. I needed to go to the toilet, but I didn't want to ask because it would give them power over me, the power of adults over a child.

"Sit down," the older man said coldly.

I lingered for a moment, eyes flitting between the older and the younger man. "Do you mind my asking who I'm speaking to?"

The older man regarded me steadily. "Yes."

I was confused. "I'm sorry . . . yes what?"

"Yes, I do mind. Now sit down!"

The venom with which he spat out these words shocked me. The saliva in my mouth turned to porridgy glue instantaneously. I had to sweep my tongue across the front of both rows of teeth before I could unstick them from my lips enough to talk. Trying not to sound nervous, I said, "I think I'm entitled to see some ID."

The older man leaned forward in his seat, his large stomach pressing against the edge of the table. "You are entitled to fuck-all," he said. "You have no rights here. Now, either you sit down or we'll break your legs so you've got no choice."

I could feel my chin trembling, but I was determined not to cry. I sat down and shielded my face with my hand, aware of the policemen's eyes on me. I swallowed and blinked in an effort to regain my composure. Finally I felt able to talk, though the question I asked still came out as a squeak. "Why are you doing this to me?"

The younger man laughed. "You honestly don't know?" His voice was hard and clipped, a local accent. I don't think I'd met anybody in Greenwell who didn't sound as if they'd been born and bred there.

I wasn't sure what to say, how deep to dip my toe. I didn't know how much they thought I already knew, or had guessed. Finally I said, "I only broke into my brother's flat because I'm worried about him. I'm not a criminal."

The older man pushed himself back with a snort as if he couldn't believe what he was hearing. "You commit a crime, you're a criminal."

I shook my head. "This is a farce. It's not as though I killed anyone. I don't deserve to be treated like this."

"If you can't take the consequences, you shouldn't have committed the crime."

"I had no choice. No one was willing to help me."

"There's always a choice. Why didn't you bring the matter to us?"

Because you're all bloody in it together, and you know it! I wanted to shout at him. But instead I said, "I did, but one of your officers told me to fuck off back to where I came from."

"I can't believe that," the older man said as if weary of dealing with liars.

"I don't care whether you believe it or not. It's true," I said.

The older man gave me a contemptuous look. "So make an official complaint," he said.

"I'm making one now," I said, then glanced at the double-headed cassette recorder. "Shouldn't you be taping all this?"

The older man leaned back in his chair and looked at his colleague. "Hear that? She's trying to tell us how to do our job now?"

Except that that wasn't exactly what the older man said, because after saying "Hear that?" he spoke what I can only assume was the younger man's name. The thing was, it didn't sound like a proper word at all. It didn't even sound like a foreign word. It sounded *strange*. Dragging and crackly, like a poor recording that bleeds through onto the back of a cassette tape and comes out backward and muffled on side B.

"What did you call him?" I asked.

The older man turned back to me, all weary aggression once more. "What?"

"Just then. You said something. Made some sort of weird noise. What was it?"

The older man stared at me for so long that I felt the nervousness inside me careering toward panic. I glanced at the younger man. He was staring at me, too, his face so immobile that he looked to be in a trance.

"We don't stand for people like you in this town," the older man said suddenly.

I blinked. "What?"

"Cunts like you. Coming here. Causing trouble. Disrupting our lives."

A terrible cold fear sluiced through me. "I just want to find my brother," I whispered.

"Cunts like you have got to be punished. Made an example of," the older man continued flatly. "We don't want vermin overrunning our town, infecting us with their filthy ideas."

Was he talking about Alex? Was I finally about to discover what had happened to my brother? I felt something tickling the fine hairs on my bare forearm and glanced down. A fiddleback spider was walking up my arm.

I reacted instinctively, jumping up from my seat and brushing at the spider with my other hand. I saw the spider fly off, but I didn't see it land. My chair fell over with a clatter.

The older man jumped up, too, consumed with rage. Eyes bulging, cheeks almost purple, he screamed, *"Sit down! Sit down, you fucking bitch!"*

I cringed, certain he was going to follow his verbal onslaught with a physical one. I tried to explain about the spider, but he drowned out my words with his screaming.

"I'm sick of your shit! Sick of it!" he shouted. *"Take your clothes off!"*

I halted, midexplanation, and gaped at him. I wasn't sure I had heard him properly. "What?"

"Take your clothes off! Take them off now! Get your fucking clothes off!"

I could see he meant it. I wanted to throw up. My need to pee was almost unbearable. At that moment I wished desperately that he would collapse with a heart attack. If he had clutched his chest, if his face had gone the color of new denim, if he had crashed to the ground, I would have done nothing to help him. I had done a first-aid course once, a million years ago back in London, but I would have stood by and watched him die, would have willed it with a fierce glee.

Shaking my head, I backed into the corner. I had all but forgotten about the spider now.

"No," I said, "I won't. You can't make me."

The younger man grinned and allowed his hands to drop to his sides. "Yes we can," he said. "If you don't take them off yourself, we'll rip them off you. It's your choice."

My head seemed to be shaking of its own volition. My hands moved protectively to cover my crotch and breasts as if I were already naked. "Leave me alone," I said. "You can't do this. It's sexual harassment. It's rape."

"So tell a fucking policeman," said the older man, and laughed. The younger man's grin widened and he moved toward me.

I felt myself becoming hysterical at what was about to happen to me. *"Leave me alone!"* I screeched. *"Leave me alone! Don't touch me!"* I began to scream for help, but the two policemen just laughed.

"You hold her down, I'll get her kit off," the older man said.

I sank into a crouch, arms hugging myself desperately, head hunched into my shoulders. They were standing over me. I had my eyes closed, but could sense them, smell them, could feel their cold shadows falling across me.

"Last chance to do it yourself," the younger man said, "before we tear your clothes off your fucking back."

I sensed them waiting, heard the older man's quick, animal-like panting. I sensed his fat, hot hands reaching down for me. *"No!"* I screeched suddenly, my head snapping up, eyes opening. His sweaty face was looming over me, bloated with lust.

"No," I said again. "I'll do it. You keep your fucking filthy hands off me."

The two men backed off, the older one reluctantly. Slowly, in the hope that something would intervene to save me from having to do this, I began to unlace my boots. The two men watched, the younger one with a deadpan expression, the older one feasting his eyes on me. I tried to blot them out as I took off my boots and socks. I lifted my little shoulder bag over my head and put it on the table, then unzipped the jacket I was wearing and placed it on top of my boots on the floor. Now I was wearing nothing but a knee-length dress and my underwear. I hesitated.

"And the rest," the older man said.

"Stand up," said the younger man. "Stand up straight so we can see you."

I looked up at the younger man. "Please," I whimpered, "please don't make me do this."

"Stand up so we can see you," he repeated, his voice lifeless.

I felt tears swelling at the back of my eyes. I had been determined not to cry, but I felt a few stray ones squeezing themselves from the corners of my eyes, fleeing in glittering tracks down my cheeks. I stood up clumsily, my legs shaking, my hands trembling as I gripped the hem of my dress, dragged it up over my hips, over my ribs, over my head. I dropped it on top of my jacket. Without it I felt cold and small and horribly vulnerable.

"Now the bra," the older man said throatily.

I was unable to prevent myself from weeping now, my hands shaking so much that I couldn't unhook my bra. When the hook popped free it did so almost unexpectedly. I dipped forward as my breasts became exposed, scooping them to me with my left hand and arm, squashing them against my chest. I dropped my bra on the pile of clothes at my feet.

"Now the knickers," the older man rasped.

I removed my knickers with my right hand, again stooping forward to conceal myself as much as possible. I placed my right hand over my crotch and flicked the pants onto the pile of clothes with my foot.

"Excellent," the younger man said. "Now stand up straight, legs slightly apart, arms held out by your sides."

I was still weeping. "Please," I begged. "Please don't make me do this."

"Do what we tell you," the older man said. It was evident he was enjoying this. When I didn't immediately comply, he said, "If you don't do what you've been told I'll stick my finger so far up your fucking arse that you'll be on fucking tiptoes."

Slowly I straightened up, but it took a huge effort of will to place my arms by my sides, to expose myself fully to these two men. As I raised my arms I was shaking not only with fear but with cold; I felt literally frozen with shock.

"Legs a little wider apart, please," the younger man said.

When I was standing in what the two men considered a satisfactory position, they began to examine me. They didn't touch me—if they had I would have curled up into a ball on the floor and screamed the place down—but simply walked around me as if I were an exhibit in a museum, peering at different parts of my body. At one point the younger one got down on all fours and gazed candidly between my legs.

It was a horrible, horrible ordeal. They made me feel like an object, made me feel worthless and used and without dignity. I couldn't stop weeping, but they were oblivious to my feelings. When I tearfully asked them why they were doing this, what they were looking for, the younger one just smiled and told me not to pretend I didn't know.

At last the older man bent down and gathered up my clothes. To my disgust he buried his face in them for a moment, and I heard him draw in a deep breath. Then he turned and lumbered across to the door, the younger man following, grabbing my bag from the table as he went. Without another word the two men left the room.

Naked, shaking with the trauma of my ordeal and unable to stop crying, I sank to the floor. I had tried to contain the sobs as much as possible when the men were in the room, but now I gave them free rein. They tore themselves out of me in great rasping whoops, leaving my stomach feeling raw, my chest aching. They went on for a long time and when they finally began to peter out they left me feeling so drained that I couldn't move.

I think I dozed off at some point from sheer exhaustion, or at least slipped into a kind of traumatized torpor. It was the sound of the door opening once again that jolted me back from my semi-trance. I didn't know how long I had been sitting there; all I knew was that I was shivering with cold and that my bladder was an aching anvil inside me. I think I'd been dreaming about Alex, about one of the big dinners we used to have—a few of his friends, a few of mine—where we'd hardly been able to eat we were laughing so much. The sound of the door ripped that memory away like a layer of skin, and suddenly I was back in a place that was too harsh, too hard, too real.

My body clenched, tensing itself against more humiliation. I hadn't been physically abused, but I felt battered and ground down all the same. I raised my eyes, expecting to see the two men reenter the room, but instead a dumpy uniformed policewoman came in, carrying my clothes, boots, and bag. She put them on the table and said, "You can get dressed now."

I stood up gingerly, feeling exhausted and stiff with cold, my bladder crippling me. I tried to blot out the thought of the older man burying his red, sweaty face in my clothes as I got dressed. I zipped my jacket up to the throat and picked up my bag. "I need the toilet," I said, surprised by the hoarseness of my voice.

The policewoman hesitated, and I said, "Don't let me go, then. I'll just piss on this floor. I'm not bothered."

The policewoman pursed her lips, but then said, "Come with me."

She led me out of the room and down the corridor to an unmarked door. She pushed the door open. "In here," she said.

The toilet was smelly and only perfunctorily clean.

Despite my swollen bladder I cleaned the seat with several sheets of the tracing paper that passed for toilet roll, then laid little squares of it all around the seat before sitting down. I gasped when I finally let my bladder go, closing my eyes in near ecstasy. My innards still ached when it was over, but I felt a thousand times better. I remained seated for longer than I needed to, just to give myself time to properly compose myself. I decided to look in my bag to make sure they hadn't taken anything. The first thing I saw when I opened it, however, was something that shouldn't have been there at all.

It was a small rabbit brooch that appeared to be made of gold. The rabbit was running, but curling back on itself, as if chasing its own tail. Where its eye should have been was an empty socket that looked as if it were intended to hold a gemstone of some kind. I turned the brooch over in my hands. It was not my sort of thing, but it was a beautiful piece of work.

I wondered how it had got into my bag. Had it been put there by accident or planted deliberately? If the latter, then why? Was the brooch some kind of a clue? Was someone trying to help me? Or was it the Greenwell equivalent of the evil eye?

I checked the rest of my bag's contents and found that nothing else had been taken or added. When I came out of the toilet, I held up the brooch and said, "I found this in my bag."

The policewoman glanced at the brooch and shrugged. "So?"

"So it isn't mine. Someone must have put it there by mistake."

"What do you want me to do about it?" the policewoman said.

"Put it back where it came from. Someone might come in to claim it."

I held the brooch out toward her. The policewoman took a step back as if she didn't want the thing to touch her skin. "Keep it," she said. "It's nothing to do with me."

I regarded her for a moment, then slipped the brooch into my jacket pocket. It might be a useful thing to keep hold of, if only to find out its significance.

"So what happens now?" I asked. Fully clothed and with an empty bladder, I felt stronger, more able to cope.

"Now you can go," the policewoman said.

"Just like that? You're not going to charge me with anything?"

"Not at the moment."

"So what was the point of all this?" I asked. "Apart from humiliating me, of course?"

"We're currently pursuing several lines of inquiry," the policewoman said. "If we need to speak to you again, we'll get in touch."

"But I've admitted I broke into my brother's flat. What else is there to say?"

"I'm not prepared to discuss the nature of our inquiries with a potential suspect."

I glared at her. "This whole thing is a joke. Okay, well, at least tell me this: why was I made to take my clothes off? What were those two creeps looking for?"

She gave a contemptuous snort. "What do you think?"

"I really have no idea."

"They were looking for witch marks," she said, and suddenly burst out laughing as if she had just cracked a joke so hilarious that it had taken even her by surprise.

I looked at her, bewildered and disturbed. What were these people on, for God's sake? Reality seemed constantly to be shifting out of alignment in Greenwell, like a radio station that keeps wavering and blurring into static on a long car journey. Suddenly I felt weary. I just wanted to be out of there. "I'd like to go now, please," I said.

The policewoman stopped laughing. "This way." She led me to the end of the corridor, then turned right. I assumed she was leading me to the front entrance. I started to follow, then heard an explosion of laughter behind me. I turned and caught a glimpse of three men entering a door farther down the corridor. Two of them were the men who had ordered me to strip. The third was Matt.

"Hey!" I shouted, and raced after them. Enraged, I reached the door I had seen them go through and wrenched it open. The room beyond was larger than I'd expected. It was a busy open-plan office, full of noise and people. How had the door in the corridor managed to contain so much chatter, the constant ringing of telephones, the tapping of fingers on computer keyboards? I stood on the threshold of the room, taking everything in, but there was no sign of Matt and the two men. I took a step into the room and abruptly everything stopped—all noise, all movement.

I remembered the feeling I'd had the first time I'd stepped into the Solomon Wedge, how I'd half expected everyone to break from what they were doing and stare silently at the stranger in their midst. When it hadn't happened, I'd laughed it off, poured scorn over my hyperactive imagination. But now it was happening here.

It was like a dream. I felt reality slipping out of alignment, disintegrating into static again. As I stood there, one hesitant step into the room, every head turned in eerie unison toward me, every eye regarded me with a blank and depthless gaze.

WHY DO WOMEN STAY with violent men? Why do they cover for them, stick up for them, feel a sense of duty toward them? I regard myself as an intelligent, clear-thinking, independent woman, and yet I stayed with Matt for over a year after he started hitting me.

Why?

There's more than one answer. There's a whole complex array of answers. Some of them sound so pathetic that if I'd heard them from anybody else I'd have shaken my head in sorry disbelief. One of the answers is this: I felt *responsible* for Matt's violence. I felt as though I were the one who'd inadvertently opened the cage and released the wild animal, and that it was my duty to catch the beast and lock it up again.

Another reason I stuck with him—and I guess this is intertwined with what I've just said—is because I felt I could help Matt, change him. For a long time I didn't see him as a calculating person, or a cruel one. I saw him as a tragic figure, as a victim of his past, saw his violence as something separate from him, like a buildup of toxins that he had to expel every now and again to prevent his entire system from becoming poisoned.

For the first few months, in between the bouts of violence, Matt could be attentive, humorous, tender. But each passing day was like a barbed wire fence, snagging a little more of his goodness. He became increasingly sullen and irritable. At the time I thought it was my fault that he was behaving like this, but with hindsight I now believe that his behavior probably followed the same pattern throughout the course of each of his relationships. I think that for Matt the initial buzz of a new relationship was enough to keep the demons at bay. And maybe he would be genuinely happy for a while, thinking that his past was finally behind him. But as time wore on, and routine and familiarity set in, there wasn't enough to distract him, and the demons would come whispering again.

It was three days before Christmas. This would have been our second Christmas together. Except I had come to the conclusion that I didn't *want* to have a second Christmas with Matt. After eighteen months, I had finally decided that enough was enough, that the relationship was destroying me. Six weeks previously Matt had wrestled me to the ground and kicked me three times in the stomach, causing me to lose the baby I'd been carrying. Matt hadn't known about the baby. I'd got pregnant by mistake, and had still been of two minds about what to do. In fact, it was getting pregnant that had actually made me realize that I didn't want to be with Matt anymore. When I thought of the child inside me, I thought only of a manacle that would chain the two of us together for the rest of our lives. It might sound strange, but I had been surprised—shocked, even—to discover how much that prospect horrified me. I knew then that I was going to finish it sooner or later. Looking back, I don't know why I didn't end it immediately after the miscarriage. Maybe I was too scared of what his reaction would be.

I never told him about the baby, and I never told him about losing it either. He would only have said its death was my fault for not telling him I was pregnant in the first place. I had avoided a beating there, but I hadn't been able to avoid the last one he had administered, three weeks earlier. We had been sitting in his flat late at night, watching a movie together, *The Piano*. Halfway through it Matt had announced he was bored and wanted to go to bed, and had got up off the settee and walked across to the TV, arm outstretched.

"Hey, what are you doing?" I asked.

"I'm turning this off, it's shit."

"No it's not," I protested. "How can you say that? It's a great film. I'm really enjoying it."

"Well, I think it's shit, and I want you to come to bed."

You can see it coming, can't you? And yes, I could see it coming too. But what do you do? Demurely go along with everything he says just because he can hit harder than you, or stand up for yourself, make him aware that you have your own needs and opinions, and that they deserve just as much respect as his?

I won't dwell on the argument. It was familiar,

depressing, and inevitable. Suffice it to say that it ended with Matt sitting on my chest, trying to ram a TV remote control down my throat. I struggled frantically, panic-stricken by the thought that this time he would go too far, that he wouldn't stop until he'd killed me. Eventually, starved of oxygen, I blacked out, and came to sometime later, still lying on the carpet, the remote lying next to my head. There was blood in my mouth and on my face and in my hair and on the carpet. The remote had broken one of my teeth and badly cut the roof of my mouth. My throat was so bruised and swollen that for almost a week afterward I couldn't swallow solids.

I struggled to my feet and cleaned myself up in the bathroom. Afterward I went to look for Matt and found him in bed, sleeping peacefully, taking deep, long breaths. The first few times he'd hurt me he'd been so contrite afterward that I'd ended up comforting him. Now, though, he was indifferent to what he had done to me. Whenever I tried to get him to talk about it later, he always refused, accused me of dwelling on things unnecessarily, dragging up stuff he'd rather forget.

I watched him for maybe a minute. In sleep his long, bony face looked so peaceful, almost childlike. I'd known our relationship was doomed even before tonight, but now, for the first time, I realized that I loathed him so much I didn't care what happened to him anymore. This was the end, I was going to stop seeing him, and if that led to him throwing himself off London Bridge or under a tube train, then good riddance. As I stood there I actually found myself looking idly around the dark room for something to bash his skull in with as he slept.

I clenched my fists as if it were the only way of preventing myself from picking up a weapon. "It's over," I whispered to his sleeping form, and quietly closed the door.

I called a cab and waited outside in the freezing cold for it to arrive. As I watched my breath spiral away into the night, I wondered why it had taken me so long to reach this moment. Watersheds should be significant and dramatic, but this was quiet, contemplative, compounded by a sense of loss, of mourning, permeated with relief. I knew I would never again set foot inside Matt's flat, and suddenly felt a virulent, soaring joy that managed to surprise me. My broken tooth throbbed, my mouth felt like an open wound, but my physical pain was vindication for my newfound resolve to leave Matt to face his twisted demons alone.

Over the next couple of weeks Matt called me incessantly. At first he sounded irritated that I hadn't been in touch, accused me of being petty.

"Matt, you were trying to choke me with a TV remote control," I said, as if trying to explain to an aberrant child why his behavior was wrong. "I lost consciousness. You could have caused me permanent brain damage, or even killed me."

"Don't be ridiculous," he said. "It was just an argument that got a bit out of hand, that's all."

For the last I don't know how long I had been pussyfooting around Matt, subconsciously weighing up what I was about to say before saying it, for fear he would take it the wrong way. Now, though, I didn't care anymore. Emboldened by my conviction that I would never again be alone with Matt, I said, "An argument? You have *got* to be joking. You don't argue, Matt, you attack. You need some serious help, otherwise one day you're going to kill somebody."

There was a silence, which meant that either Matt was thinking about what I'd said, was too outraged to talk, or was trying to intimidate me. I waited patiently, feeling icy cool, completely in control. What did I care? It was his phone bill.

At last he said curtly, "I didn't ring up to talk about this."

I sighed. "Matt, there's nothing else *to* talk about. It's become the biggest thing in what's left of our relationship."

"I don't want to talk about it," he repeated.

"Fine. Then let's not talk about anything ever again." Before he could respond, I put the phone down.

Despite this, his calls kept coming. After a couple of days of vainly trying to explain to him why he should take responsibility for his actions, I gave up and simply stopped picking up the phone, allowing the answering machine to act as a protective shield between us.

Matt left lots of messages. Listening to them chronologically was like listening to a case study of someone who was progressing ever deeper into madness. At first, as I've said, he started off sounding irritable, as if *I* were the unreasonable one. Then, when he realized that this time I wasn't going to come crawling back to him on the strength of a curt apology and a halfhearted promise that he would never hurt me again, he turned needy, saying that he couldn't cope without me. When that didn't work he started to become abusive—on one day he left twenty-nine messages, the last dozen of which managed to sound vicious despite being totally incoherent; on another memorable occasion he filled up a whole tape by repeating the word "bitch" over and over again.

I toyed with the idea of calling the police, but in the end decided that before I involved them I would make an effort to formally end the relationship myself. Closure, the Americans call it. Matt and I had never had closure. I'd simply walked away from the job, leaving live wires exposed all over the place.

And so I called him, arranged to meet him at Marco's, an Italian restaurant just off Tottenham Court Road that we'd been to a couple of times. "We need to talk," I told him. "We need to sort a few things out."

He was sullen, monosyllabic. He'd been trying to get me to agree to see him for over two weeks, but now that I had he didn't seem bothered. "So you *will* be there?" I asked. "Wednesday the 23rd. You won't forget?"

He grunted. Exasperated by his behavior, I put the phone down without saying good-bye. *You'd better bloody be there, you looney,* I thought. I wanted it all over for Christmas, wanted him out of my life for good.

I rehearsed the evening in my head many times before it arrived, planned exactly what I was going to say to him, as if learning lines. I tried to anticipate his counter-arguments and to come up with responses for them. Tried, too, to imagine what sort of mood he would be in, and found it virtually impossible. I pictured him being sullen, being angry, being upset. The fact that I couldn't predict exactly what his reaction might be saddened me; had it really taken me eighteen months to realize that I didn't know him at all? I talked things over with Alex, a couple of times into the early hours of the morning as we killed several bottles of Australian red. We even role-played to see how I would cope with unexpected responses. I decided I was going to play it calm and friendly, but cool. I wasn't going to get emotional, because that would only provide fuel for his fire. Alex and I spent a lot of time deciding what I was going to wear, how I was going to do my hair, how much makeup I was going to put on. I wanted to look nice, but I didn't want Matt to feel I was mocking him by dressing as attractively as I could, or give him the false impression that I was trying to win him back.

I arrived at the restaurant twenty minutes early, because I wanted time to collect my thoughts. I didn't want to come in out of the rain and the cold, flushed and disheveled, to find him waiting for me. I wanted to be sitting at the bar, sipping a G and T, looking calm and assured. *That* part of the evening went as planned, at least, even though I didn't *feel* all that calm and assured. I don't quite know what I expected, but I certainly didn't expect Matt to turn up in an Armani suit and silk tie, looking healthy and happy. Yet suddenly there he was, a bouquet of red roses in his hand, an ecstatic grin illuminating his face.

"Ruth," he said, "it's brilliant to see you. You look fantastic." He leaned down with the obvious intention of kissing me on the lips. I turned my head quickly aside and felt his mouth graze my earring.

"You look very nice yourself," I said, wanting to ask him how, when he'd had no work for the past few months, he'd been able to afford a five-hundred-pound suit.

"One has to make an effort for a special occasion," he said good-humoredly. "These are for you, by the way."

He handed me the flowers. Their scent was incredible, but I was uncomfortably aware of everyone at the bar regarding me with an expression somewhere between humor and pity. Marco's was the kind of place that attracted young and trendy city types, and I knew exactly what they were thinking: Red roses. How *obvious,* how *gauche,* how *embarrassing.*

I wondered whether Matt had bought me the flowers as a genuine token of . . . what? Love? Affection? Apology? Reconciliation? Or whether it had been an ironic gesture, calculated to place me at a disadvantage. I forced a smile and said, "They're beautiful, Matt, thank you." Then I turned and smiled at the barman. "Could you possibly put these in water for me?"

Matt ordered drinks and we were shown to our table. He seemed relaxed, completely at ease. I wondered how much of it was an act. It was certainly hard to reconcile this elegant, confident individual with the person who'd mumbled incoherent threats over my answering machine, who'd repeated the word "bitch" over and over for the best part of an hour. I felt tense, wary of being lulled into a false sense of security. We sat down and were handed menus, and when the waiter went away I said, "So, are you okay?"

Matt glanced up from his contemplation of the menu, a quizzical smile on his face. "I'm sorry?"

"I just asked you whether you were okay. I mean, you look great—"

"I feel great," said Matt. "I've been doing a lot of thinking, sorting things out in my head."

Since when? I wanted to ask him. It was only four days since I'd last been in contact with him and then he'd seemed like a prime case for institutionalization.

"Well, that's good," I said. "So what have you been thinking about specifically?"

"Us," he said, making it sound portentous, staring into my eyes.

I held his gaze. "Me too," I said. "For the last few weeks I've thought of nothing else." I found my fingers toying nervously with my fork, and forced myself to clench my fist. "And I think we both know that we can't go on like this, don't we?"

"Oh, absolutely," he said.

I tried not to show my surprise. "You really mean that?"

"Of course I do. We've just been letting things drift on, haven't we? We haven't been going anywhere. Things have been getting stale."

"Well, that's only part of it, Matt," I said. "Isn't it?"

Before he could reply, a waiter appeared at our table with a basket of warm ciabatta rolls. Matt broke open his roll and raised it to his face as he breathed in deeply, eyes closing in a languid blink.

"Best smell in the world," he said. He opened his eyes and looked at me. "This is all I want from life, you know, Ruth. You, me, the smell of fresh bread . . ."

"If only it could have been that simple," I said curtly.

"I think it still can."

I started to shake my head, but he held up both hands as if to shield himself from any negative gestures or comments I might direct at him. "Look, let's order our food first, okay? Then we can talk properly. I know you're not happy with the way things are—neither am I—but I think I know what the answer is, if you'll just hear me out. Red okay?"

He was waving the wine list. I shrugged and nodded. Matt called the waiter over and we ordered our food.

When the waiter had gone I said, "I'm glad that you're okay. After some of those messages you left on my answering machine, I didn't know what to expect tonight."

Matt grimaced as though I'd drawn attention to some mildly embarrassing misdemeanor. "I suppose I did go a bit over the top, didn't I? To be honest, the last couple of weeks have been something of an odyssey for me. I stayed in my flat and forced myself to think about things I've never really thought about before. It fucked my head up, made everything a bit of a blur, but it was worth it in the end. Thanks to you I'm a better person now. I know exactly what I want, who I am."

Matt talked quietly, reasonably, but there was something in his manner that set me on edge. Beneath his earnest humility I sensed the intense glitter of the fanatic. It seemed he'd chosen a path for himself and was walking assuredly along it in a straight line. But what if the path were to curve unexpectedly, or even disappear altogether? What would that do to him?

The wine arrived. Matt tasted it and proclaimed it excellent—a happy customer, full of Christmas cheer. The waiter filled each of our glasses two-thirds full and then departed. I leaned forward and asked, "What if you can't get what you want?"

Matt smiled at me, as if my lack of faith amused him.

"I don't entertain the possibility of failure anymore," he said. "I refuse to acknowledge negative thoughts. This is the new me, Ruth. The new improved version. I've shed my skin. I've left the past behind once and for all."

"And it's really as easy as that, is it?"

"No, it's not been easy. I didn't say it had been easy. In fact, it's been really hard. It's been like going cold turkey. But I'm through it now. From this day forward, things can only get better."

Our food arrived. Matt had a spicy pasta thing, with prawns and cream. I'd ordered a chicken and bacon salad.

"Well, if that's the case, then I'm really pleased for you, Matt—" I began.

"For us," he said. "This change will benefit both of us." He grinned suddenly, put down his knife, and dipped his hand into his jacket pocket. He produced a small velvet box, which he placed on the table between us. I felt my stomach contract.

"What's this?"

"Open it," he said, eyes glittering eagerly. "I was going to give it to you a bit later, but I can't wait any longer."

I stared at the box for a few moments, then reluctantly put down my cutlery. My heart punched at the base of my throat. With a sense of foreboding I took the box in my trembling left hand and opened it. Inside was what I had been dreading and expecting—a beautiful white gold ring studded with a cluster of pale topaz.

My head was pounding so much that Matt's voice throbbed in my ears. "I want you to marry me, Ruth. I want us to make a fresh start, a new life together."

I stared at the ring. For a minute or more I couldn't

move or speak. All other sounds in the restaurant seemed to recede. We were enclosed within an umbrella of silence.

"Well?" Matt asked at last. "Aren't you going to say anything?"

I closed the box and pushed it back across the table toward him. "I'm sorry, Matt, I can't," I said.

Again he offered me that quizzical smile, as if I had told a joke whose punch line he didn't quite get. Then he gave a snorting half laugh and said lightly, "What do you mean?"

My mouth was dry. I took a gulp of wine. "I can't marry you, Matt."

He blinked. "Yes you can."

"No, Matt. I *can't*."

"Why not?" he asked, looking genuinely bemused.

"Because I don't love you, Matt. Because you frighten me. Because you hurt me." Two weeks ago I had loathed this man. Now I couldn't help feeling sorry for him.

He frowned. "Haven't you been listening to a single word I've said? All of that is behind me now. If you'll just . . . just say yes, it'll never happen again."

I actually thought at this point that our relationship was going to end with a civilized conversation. I leaned forward so that I could speak gently, softly. "I'm sorry, Matt, but I'm not willing to take the risk. Too many times in the past you've said how sorry you were, how you'd never hurt me again—"

"But this time I mean it!" he said.

"And you never meant it before?"

"Well, yes, but it's different this time. I promise you it's different. Just give me a chance, Ruth."

I ran my tongue along the roof of my mouth, along the cut which was healing now, but which still tasted raw, metallic. I shook my head.

"Sorry, Matt. I haven't got any more chances left to give."

He clenched his teeth. "But this is so unfair, Ruth, don't you see? For months I've been fucked up and you've stood by me. But now, when I'm finally better, when I've finally come out of the other side of the tunnel, you drop me like a hot brick. It doesn't make any sense."

I sighed, picked up my fork, prodded halfheartedly at my salad. "I'm sorry, Matt, really I am. I really wish it could have worked out between us—"

"It *will*," he insisted. "I promise you, Ruth, it will."

"No," I said, "it's too late. I don't trust you anymore. You frighten me. You say you're better, but I'm just not prepared to put that to the test. This is the end, Matt. I'm sorry."

"It's *not* the end," he said. "I won't let it be the end."

"Matt, you've got no choice. I don't want to see you again. Nothing you say will persuade me otherwise."

There was desperation on his face. He picked up his glass and gulped down the wine, poured himself another, and drank that like water too. His face contorted as though he were in pain.

"Why did you have to spoil it?" he said. "Why did you have to fuck everything up? Do you get some sort of sick pleasure from seeing me suffer, is that it?"

"Calm down, Matt," I said. "Of course I don't like seeing you suffer. I've been trying to help you for God knows how long. And what have I got for my efforts? Punches, kicks, pain. I'm not prepared to take it anymore."

"Why don't you ever fucking listen to me?" Matt said, suddenly vicious. Then, before I could respond, he snatched up the third-full bottle of red wine, stood, and clubbed me on the side of the head with it.

I closed my eyes a split second before the bottle impacted with my skull. Thankfully the glass didn't shatter, but it was a hard enough blow to knock me off my chair, to make lights explode inside my head. I didn't feel any pain at first. As I hit the floor I felt only a sinking inevitability, and oddly, a sense of embarrassment at the spectacle Matt was forcing me to make of myself. I raised my head, blinking the sparks out of my eyes, and was just in time to see the table and all its contents sliding and toppling toward me.

I ducked and rolled away, felt something hard smash into my shoulder, causing instant pain before I was surrounded by the crashing of crockery and glass, the jangling clank of cutlery. I was spattered by something wet and warm, heard angry shouts. I pushed myself upright and looked around, caught a glimpse of Matt running out of the restaurant and into the bar, pursued by one of the waiters. Everyone was staring at me. Some looked shocked, some curious, some had obviously enjoyed the spectacle. The overturned table was next to me, its smashed contents strewn over an extensive area. Most of Matt's dinner had splashed up my left arm and the left side of my dress. I was sitting in a puddle of sauce and salad dressing. A waiter with a plump face and very dark, bushy eyebrows appeared by my side and crouched down.

"Are you all right?"

My shoulder was full of hot pain and my ankle throbbed as if I'd twisted it, but I said, "Yes, I'll live."

"You've got blood in your hair," he said.

"Have I?" I raised my hand to the side of my head and my fingertips came away red. "Oh yes."

"Can you stand?"

"I think so. My ankle hurts."

"Take my hand. I'll help you up."

He supported my weight as I got to my feet, wincing, bits of food sliding off me. The waiter who had chased Matt came back into the restaurant, red and panting, shaking his head.

"Come with me. I'll take you to the staff rest room. You can clean yourself up there."

I thanked him. He escorted me through the door into the kitchen and out of another door into a short corridor made narrow by the crates of wine stacked up in it. At the end on the right was a clean and sizeable toilet and sink.

"Take your time," he said. "When you've done, go back into the kitchen and get one of the guys to give me a shout. I'll get you a cup of coffee or something."

"Thanks," I said. "This is really good of you. I'm so sorry about what happened in there."

"Looks like it was the other bloke who had the problem, not you."

"You could say that. He's my boyfriend. Or rather, my ex-boyfriend. He's a bit unstable. He'd come here to ask me to marry him, but I'd come to tell him it was over. He didn't take the news very well."

"Looks like you had a lucky escape," the waiter said.

I held out my hands, palms up, and looked down at my ruined dress. "If you can call this lucky."

The waiter left me to it and I cleaned myself up as best I could. As I sponged the mess from my dress, I thought, *Well, if that wasn't closure I don't know what is.* It had been a typical and rather fitting way for Matt to acknowledge the end of our relationship. I wondered whether I'd ever see him again. I thought about him saying how much he'd changed, how he'd never hurt me again, how he just wanted another chance, and then I thought of him hitting me on the head with the bottle, and I laughed until I cried.

I didn't stop for a coffee. I just wanted to get away. I apologized to the waiter who'd helped me and offered to pay for all the mess, but he refused.

"I'll bill your friend," he said. "Just give me his name and address. If he doesn't pay up we'll sue."

I told him I didn't want that, that it would only be an excuse for Matt to contact me again, if only to stir up trouble. In the end the waiter grudgingly allowed me to pay for the meal we'd barely touched, but he dismissed the breakages as unimportant.

"Occupational hazard," he said. "The amount of crockery we buy, those plates only cost us a few pence each."

He told me that getting rid of Matt was the best Christmas present I could have given myself, then he called me a cab. I found myself giving Alex's address, because instead of going home to lick my wounds I realized that what I really wanted was company, the kind I could be myself with.

Alex was watching *The Birds* for about the four hundredth time when I turned up on his doorstep. The only illumination in his front room came from the flickering TV, a lamp on the mantelpiece which was shaped like a clenched fist holding a red bulb, and a small artificial Christmas tree we'd had since we were kids, which was standing proudly in the center of his dining table, festooned with strings of fairy lights.

He opened the front door, took one look at my dress, and asked, "What did the bastard do this time?"

I shrugged, but I felt my voice cracking with emotion. "He hit me over the head with a bottle and then threw a table at me."

Diagonal shadows sliced across Alex's face as his jaw clenched in anger. "Right, I'm going to kill the fucker," he said, and looked as though he would have rushed out of the house there and then if I hadn't placed a hand on his arm.

"Alex, please," I said. "It's two days before Christmas and I'm so . . . so *sick* of violence." All at once emotion engulfed me and I reached out for him. "Just look after me," I sobbed into his chest.

Alex apologized, settled me in the front room, made me a cup of tea, fetched me a change of clothes.

"You watch the end of this while I have a bath," I said when I'd drunk my tea and put my dress to soak in the kitchen sink. "Then we'll talk."

An hour later I reappeared, hot and damp and languid, the bath having enervated me almost to the point of inertia. My shoulder was throbbing where the edge of the table had caught it, but my head and ankle felt much better.

"It'd better be over," Alex said.

I plopped down. *The Birds* was finished and there was a Bond film showing now, Pierce Brosnan, without sound.

"It is," I said. "I'm going to start going out with *him*." I nodded at the screen.

"Not if I get there first," said Alex.

I grunted a laugh and Alex turned the TV off with the remote. "Shall I open a bottle of wine?"

I shook my head. "It'll just send me to sleep."

"Okay." He settled back on the settee. "Do you promise me it's really, *really* over?"

"Yes," I said. "If I never see that bastard again it'll be too soon. He's a nutter, Alex."

"I've been trying to tell you that for the last year."

"No, I mean he's . . . he's not just violent, he's seriously unhinged. He belongs in a straitjacket."

"He belongs at the bottom of the Thames with a sack of rocks round his neck," Alex said.

"You know, I really don't give a shit what happens to him now. He could throw himself under a bus for all I care."

"You really mean that?"

"Yes," I said. "My Matt period is definitely over. It's onward and upward from now on."

Alex swung himself into a sitting position. "I will open that bottle of wine, after all," he said. "That's definitely something worth drinking to."

As he stood up, someone knocked on the door—or rather thumped it. Five hard thuds.

Immediately I felt everything tighten inside me. I looked at Alex, and saw his eyes narrow, his mouth set in a thin line as his jaw clenched.

"If that's that fucking animal—" he muttered.

"Please, Alex, don't make a scene," I said. "I don't think I can stand any more tonight. If it's him, just pretend I'm not here, pretend you haven't seen me."

"I'm not hiding inside my own house," he said. "I'll just tell him to fuck off."

"Please, Alex . . ."

"Don't worry. If it's him I won't even open the door."

He stomped through to the hallway and turned on the light. The upper half of the front door was a stained-glass panel through which Alex would immediately be able to see who was standing outside. I folded my arms and braced myself as if for impact.

Sure enough, after a few seconds I heard Alex shout, "Fuck off!"

From here the actual words of Matt's response were indistinct, but I could hear the anger in his voice.

"Well, she doesn't want to talk to you," Alex shouted back. "In fact, she never wants to see you again. So why don't you just get out of her life for good, Matt. Go and see a fucking psychiatrist or something."

More shouting from Matt. When he had finished, Alex retorted, "I've already told you, she doesn't want to see you. Now piss off or I'll call the police."

But Matt didn't piss off. Instead he started kicking the front door, the savage echoes of which reverberated round the house. He raised his voice several decibels, too, until he was almost screeching. "Let me in, you fucking queer! Let me in!"

Alex shouted at Matt to stop kicking the door, then he came storming into the room, eyes blazing, searching for something. "Where's my fucking baseball bat?" he said. "I'm going to brain that bastard."

"Please, Alex, don't sink to his level," I said, uncurling myself from the chair. I ran across the room to the telephone and snatched up the receiver. "I'm calling the police. Tell him I'm calling the police."

Alex looked at me a moment, then he gave a sharp nod and ran out of the room. I punched 999, pressing the receiver hard to my ear. I was still aware of shouting and crashing in the background, but I tried to keep calm, tried to concentrate on being as concise and coherent as possible. When the call was over, the first thing I heard was the sound of footsteps thudding up the stairs. This was followed by another crash as Matt kicked the front door again, and then a sudden high-pitched howl of pain which seemed to make every one of my nerve endings leap to attention.

I ran out into the hallway. I sensed movement to my left and whirled to see Alex coming down the stairs, savage satisfaction on his face.

"What's going on?" I asked.

Alex raised his right arm and I saw that he was holding a kettle. "I poured boiling water on the fucker out of my bedroom window."

"Alex, you didn't!"

"I warned him. I warned him that if he didn't stop I'd do it, but he just carried on."

I can't deny that there was a part of me that wanted to rejoice, to revel in my brother's actions. After all those things Matt had done to me, the bastard deserved some pain. Nevertheless I said, "Alex, this is really serious. You could have scarred him for life."

"I hope I have," Alex said.

"But you might go to prison for . . . for . . ." I didn't really know what for. Assault, grievous bodily harm, one of those sorts of things.

"No, I won't," Alex said, "because if he goes to the police, all the suffering he's put you through this last year or so will come out, and we'll soon see who the real psycho is."

It was only now that I realized Matt's assault on the door had stopped. I pointed this out to Alex.

"Let's hope he's got the message and buggered off," Alex said.

"What if he's passed out on your path because he's so badly scalded? That's not going to look very good when the police arrive, is it?"

Alex looked at me, then put the kettle down and walked up to the front door. It was a good stout wooden door which had stood since the house had been built in the mid-1800s. All the same, Matt's assault had taken its toll. There were bulges on the inside where the paint had cracked and the wood had splintered slightly. It was clear there was no one on the other side of the door now. Though the view through the stained glass was distorted and murky, you could make out an impression of the pale path leading to the front gate, the dark patch to the right which was the flower bed encircling the minuscule front lawn. Alex crouched down, lifted the flap of the letter box, and peered through it.

"I can't see him," he said. "I think he must have— *shit!*"

I glimpsed a blur of movement through the stained glass and then heard an almighty shattering of glass from the front room. I didn't know until Alex told me later, but what had happened was that Matt, spattered by hot water but not seriously hurt, had gone across the road and picked up one of a pile of breeze blocks that was stacked inside a neighbor's front gate. He had then run back across the road and hurled the breeze block through Alex's big front window.

Alex went bananas. He scrabbled at the front door, wrenched it open, and catapulted out into the night. Barefoot, I went after him, shouting at him to come back. Matt was standing on the pavement outside the house, hands spread wide as if offering himself. Alex crashed into him just as a police car turned the corner, headlamps illuminating the row of parked cars on the other side of the street. I jumped up and down, waving my arms, and the police car came to a halt in the middle of the road. By the time two uniformed officers had got out and were running toward me, Alex had Matt by the lapels of his Armani suit and was banging his head on the pavement.

Fourteen

THE RABBIT BROOCH IS on my bedside table. I don't remember putting it there. I remember very little between leaving the police station and crawling exhausted into my bed at the Solomon Wedge. My eyes are closed, but I know that the brooch is there, because it is calling to me. I feel it behind my eyelids, pulsing like a little heart. I sit up, reach for it. It is warm in my hand, and it does not feel hard like metal, but soft like skin. It translates a sense of urgency to me, a need to perform a vital, but unknown, task. I get up, walk down the stairs, through the dark and deserted pub. I am barely aware of myself or my surroundings; details are irrelevant. All that matters is where I am going, what I am about to do. I do not remember leaving the pub, but suddenly I am in my car, driving, the brooch on the seat beside me.

I drive for a while, and gradually become aware that there are no more buildings, only trees and hedges and fields. I stop at the roadside beside a large field, pick up the brooch, and get out of the car. There is no moon, no lights. It is dark and silent. I walk across the field. Am I wearing shoes? Am I clothed? Is it cold? I don't know. I walk across the field until I know it is time to stop. Then I drop down onto my knees, and using a sharp stone and my fingernails I begin to dig.

It seemed as though I was wondering what had really happened even before I woke up, because the instant I became conscious the thought was there. I was back in my bed in the Solomon Wedge, daylight struggling feebly through the curtains. Had I really left my bed in the middle of the night? Had I really walked into the middle of a field and begun to dig a hole with my bare hands? The memory of doing these things was vivid, but the details were less than vague. And in the cold light of day, the impetus for my actions seemed not merely vague but ludicrous. In my befuddled state last night I hadn't thought to question the fact that the brooch was influencing me, directing me, that to all intents and purposes I was in its possession. I turned my head and looked at the bedside table, and felt a little jolt of surprise when I saw that the brooch was still there.

I hesitated a moment and then reached for it. It was made of cold, hard metal. I held it in front of my face, looking at it now as if for the first time. The design had a fluidity, a sinuousness, but without the gem that fit into the setting of the eye socket, the rabbit looked dead.

It was difficult to tell what it was made of. Brass? Copper? Gold? Or perhaps some kind of alloy? As I turned the trinket over in my hand, I suddenly realized I had all the proof I needed that last night's episode had been nothing more than a dream.

My fingernails were clean. If I had really been digging in the dirt only a few hours before, there would still have been some residual muck either beneath them or embedded in the pores of my fingertips, no matter how hard I might have scrubbed them when I got in. I threw my duvet back and saw that the rest of me was clean too. Furthermore, a quick look around assured me that none of my clothes or shoes had any mud on them.

I felt an odd mixture of relief and disappointment. I put the rabbit brooch in my shoulder bag and thought about the dream all through breakfast, which this morning was served up by Jovial Jim's wife. She all but threw my fried breakfast down in front of me, causing tomatoes and beans to slop over the side of the plate.

Okay, so it had been a dream, I wasn't refuting that, but was it possible that it had actually been more than a dream? Could it have been . . . I don't know . . . *guidance* of some sort? A wild assumption, I know, but in the context of everything else that had happened to me it didn't actually seem that far-fetched. But guidance from whom or what? It was probably best not to dwell on such questions. Better instead to merely follow your feelings, go with your gut instincts, let everything else take care of itself.

After breakfast I went out and bought a spade. Then I rang the school and asked to be put through to Liz.

"Hi, Ruth," Liz said. "Did you get back okay last night?"

"Eventually," I said. I told her everything that had happened at the police station.

Liz was so outraged about the way the police had treated me that I felt guilty I wasn't at least just as angry myself. Perhaps I would have been if my ordeal hadn't been superseded by the dream, which seemed to be all I could think about.

When I told Liz what I intended to do, she laughed and said, "You're not serious?"

"I am actually," I said. I paused, then asked, "Do you think I'm losing it?"

"Well . . . no," she said. "If you feel this strongly about it, then I think you should go for it."

"Thanks," I said. "The only thing was, I was wondering whether you'd come with me."

"Me? Why?"

"Because you're the only friend I've made since I came here. And because . . . I suppose I just need someone to tell me I'm not crazy."

"I can't promise I'll do that," said Liz with a laugh. Then her voice became semiserious. "But hey, what if we *do* find something?"

"We'll deal with that if and when," I said. "So you'll come?"

"Yeah, why not? Lunch is at half twelve. Why don't you meet me by the main entrance?"

I spent the rest of the morning vainly scouring Alex's address book and diary, looking for anything that might offer a clue as to his whereabouts. Just after midday I set off to pick Liz up from the school.

As I parked round the back, children started to spill out through the doors as if the school were becoming too small to accommodate them. I locked my car and took a shortcut up some steps and along a walkway between buildings. The walkway led to the top right-hand corner of the playground, which I had to cross to reach the main entrance. I was aware of groups of teenagers scrutinizing me as I passed. I didn't look at them, not because I was afraid of their hostility, but because I was afraid of the recognition I might see in their eyes.

I was three-quarters of the way across when I became aware of three children—a boy and two girls—huddled against a wall to my left, whispering together and casting glances in my direction. When I looked at them I realized that they were the children who had been waiting by my car two days ago, the ones who had told me about the gray man.

"Hello, miss," the boy said as I caught his eye. "You're not still looking for Mr. Gemmill, are you?"

"I am actually," I replied.

"You won't find him," the girl with the Alice band, the one who had done all the talking last time, told me bluntly.

I looked at her, feeling a flash of anger at her offhandedness, which I was unable to disguise from my voice. "Because he's been taken by the gray man?"

She nodded.

"And how do you know that?" I asked.

The children all turned their heads slowly to look at one another. It was eerie. It reminded me of the police station last night, of how everyone in the office I'd burst into had stopped what they were doing and had turned in unison to regard me, their faces expressionless.

"We saw it happen," the boy said.

My eyes widened. "You *saw* it? What do you mean? *Where* did you see it?"

"In one of the viaduct arches near the far woods," the girl with the Alice band said.

I squeezed my fists together. It was the only way I could stop myself from reaching out and grabbing her by the arm to shake the information out of her. "When was this? What did you see exactly?"

The girl shrugged, her gaze wandering momentarily, as if she were bored by this conversation, as if it were unimportant.

"It was last week. We were down by the arches, playing. When we heard someone coming, we hid. We saw Mr. Gemmill and the gray man. They were talking, but we couldn't hear what they said. As soon as we saw the gray man we ran away. We were ever so quiet. I don't think him or Mr. Gemmill heard us."

I thought of the figure in the field, the colorless wraith that had seemed to pursue me through the town last night. "But . . . but what did he look like? The gray man, I mean. How did you know it was him?"

The girl gave me a withering look. "He was gray."

"But his face?" I asked. "What did he *look* like?"

The girl's expression became even more scornful. "We didn't see his face, of course."

"If you see his face you die," the boy explained.

"But Alex . . . I mean, Mr. Gemmill . . . you said he was talking to the gray man?"

The children all nodded as if their heads were being jerked by the same string.

"Then *he* must have seen the gray man's face."

"That's how we knew we'd never see him again," the girl with the Alice band said.

I took a step backward as if I didn't want to be poisoned by her words. "No, the gray man is just a story, a silly superstition."

She shrugged, unwilling to offer an argument. The other two children stared at me.

"What did the man who was talking to Mr. Gemmill look like from the back?" I asked. "What kind of clothes was he wearing?"

"Gray clothes," the girl said.

"Yes, but what *kind* of gray clothes? A suit, do you mean? A gray suit?"

The girl seemed not to understand the question, then shrugged again. "I can't remember."

Frustrated, I turned to the others, my voice perhaps sharper than it should have been. "What about you two? Do *you* remember?"

They shook their heads.

"Right," I said. "Do you know what I think? I think you're making all of this up."

I expected the children to react, to protest, but the girl with the Alice band simply shrugged her shoulders yet again. "We're not making it up," she said calmly. "We're just telling you what happened."

"We're trying to help you, miss," said the boy.

I was more dismayed than perhaps I should have been. What I wanted to be offered, from any quarter, was hope, not a resigned acceptance that Alex was gone for good. "Okay," I said. "Maybe you aren't making it up, but I think you're mistaken. Whoever Alex was talking to, it wasn't the gray man. It was just a man. Flesh and blood, like me and you. Maybe the arches would be a good place to start to look for him. Or maybe . . ." As soon as I realized what I was going to say, the words evaporated. Subconsciously I had been thinking of my dream last night, of the shiny new spade in the back of my car. The implications of such thoughts terrified me. I felt ashamed that I had allowed them ingress. Again speaking more harshly than I had intended, I asked, "Have you told anyone else what you've just told me?"

The children shook their heads. If this had been anywhere other than Greenwell I would have been furious at their inability to recognize the significance of what they had seen. Resignedly I said, "Okay, then. Thank you." And unable to think of anything else to add, I walked away.

Liz was waiting for me by the main entrance. As soon as she saw me, she asked, "Are you okay?"

"Sort of," I said. "I'll tell you on the way."

We walked the same route back to my car, but the three children were now nowhere to be seen. When we reached the car park I opened the passenger door so that Liz could get in first, then walked round to the driver's side. As I pushed the key into the lock, I felt a sudden compulsion to look behind me. When I did, my gaze was immediately drawn to an upper window of the main school building. I saw a figure standing there which, although virtually in silhouette, I knew immediately was the headmaster, Mr. Rudding. His arms were raised and his bunched fists were resting on the glass as though he had been pounding on it. Although his face was nothing more than a dark blob, I got the strong impression that he was furious—maniacally, ragingly so. I imagined his eyes glaring into mine and looked away with a shudder. I got into the car, started the engine, and drove away. I didn't say anything to Liz, but I felt the power of Rudding's baleful gaze following us all the way up the drive and out of the school gates.

"So what is it you have to tell me?" Liz asked. She looked radiant, as if the autumn chill agreed whole-heartedly with her complexion. By comparison I felt dowdy and jaded. I related the conversation I'd had with the children.

"I'm sure you're right," she said. "I know the place the kids mean. We could go there now if you like."

I briefly considered it then shook my head. "No, I feel as though I have to do this first. While it's still fresh in my mind. I feel a sense of . . . urgency. I can't explain it."

Liz nodded, happy to go along with whatever I wanted. "What do these kids look like?" she asked.

I described them, but she was none the wiser. "They may only have started this term. There's a lot of the litt-leys I'm not that *au fait* with yet."

I didn't feel much like talking, so we drove in silence for a minute or so. I was conscious of Liz's scrutiny, guessed that she was assessing my state of mind, perhaps wondering whether to bring up last night's ordeal.

"So," she said when she finally did speak, "where are we going exactly?"

Her question broke the spell. Until that moment I realized I had simply been driving, allowing the auto-matic pilot in my head to guide my movements. Sud-denly I felt like the subject of a hypnotist who has been instructed to wake up. I faltered, lifting my foot from the accelerator. The car slowed.

"I don't know," I said.

"What do you mean, you don't know?"

"I just don't. I'm driving to the field in my dream . . . only I don't know where it is."

"But you seemed pretty sure until I asked the question."

"Yes, I did, didn't I? But it was like . . . do you ever drive home from school, and because you've done the journey so many times you just switch off? You arrive home, and all at once it's like coming out of a trance?"

Liz gave that little tilt of the head again, and sighed. "Every day."

"Well, that's how I felt just then," I told her. "It was as though the dream had taken over."

"And now?" Liz asked.

"Now I haven't a clue where I'm going."

"Oh." She was silent for a moment, then she said contritely, "I'm sorry. That was my fault. I shouldn't have said anything."

I focused on the road ahead, tried to relax, to clear my mind. I felt that I needed a distraction, something else to talk about, in order to allow my instincts to take over once more. "As well as being arrested last night, I think I was followed," I said.

"Followed?" exclaimed Liz. "By the police, you mean?"

"No."

"Then by whom?"

I hesitated for a moment before blurting out my answer. "The gray man."

Liz looked at me as if unsure whether she should laugh or look alarmed. "What do you mean?"

I told her about the figure I had seen standing in

the children's playground, moving across the grass toward me.

"Creepy," agreed Liz. "But you don't honestly think it was the gray man, do you?"

From her tone of voice and the expression on her face I guessed that my next answer would prove vital. We were getting on well, but we still barely knew each other. I forced a smile.

" 'Course not. But it might have been the same man who met Alex under the arches."

"Come to shut you up, you mean?"

I shivered. "It's not a nice thought, is it?"

"No," agreed Liz. "But are you sure this guy was following you? Maybe he was just taking his dog for a walk or something."

"He didn't have a dog."

"Well, maybe it had run away and he was looking for it then."

I glanced at her. "You think I'm paranoid, don't you?"

She didn't answer immediately and I laughed. "You do, don't you?"

"No, it's not that," she said. "I think you have reason to be paranoid. If it was me, I'd probably be the same. And I certainly wouldn't want to walk round Greenwell at night. The whole town gives me the creeps."

"I just have this feeling that everyone I meet is hiding something from me, present company excepted, of course. On the other hand, maybe I'm just being hypersensitive because of Alex. Maybe I think everyone is actively working against me when all it is really is that no one except me seems to care what's happened to him."

"Hey, *I* care," said Liz, putting her hand briefly over mine on the steering wheel. "I care a lot."

"Oh, I know you do," I said. "I was talking about the people in Greenwell."

"Inbred imbeciles, the lot of them," Liz said.

"Including all the kids at the school? Including the teachers?"

"Ha! Don't get me started on that one."

"What do you mean?"

"Just that I could tell you some stories."

"Go on, then."

Liz smiled. "Some other time, maybe."

"I'll hold you to that." I faltered, then said, "Some really odd things have happened to me since I've been here."

"Odder than what you've told me already?"

"Some of them, yes."

"Like what?"

"I'll give the same answer you did, and not just because I'm playing tit for tat."

"Looks like we've got a lot to talk about," said Liz. "How about dinner at my place tonight? It'll get you out of Greenwell. You could even stay over so you can have a few drinks."

I didn't need to think about it. "That would be great, but are you sure?"

"Sure I'm sure. I'm not asking out of charity. It'll be fun for me too."

"Okay," I said. "It's a date. Shit!"

"What is it?" exclaimed Liz, alarmed by my sudden change of mood.

I was looking out of the driver's-side window, my

foot easing gently down on the brake. "We're here," I said, and turned to look at her. My whole body was tingling. "That's the field from my dream last night."

"You're certain?" asked Liz as I pulled in at the side of the road and stopped the car.

"Absolutely positive."

The words were barely out of my mouth when a feeling of claustrophobia swept over me. I opened the door and scrambled out, then stood up straight, breathing in deep lungfuls of chilly air. I didn't know *how* I knew this was the right field, I just did. I had never been to this place before, and there were no particular landmarks I recognized; it was simply as though my head were a spirit level, and after wavering from side to side, the bubble had now come to a stop dead center. I felt a sense of equilibrium, of balance. It's hard to explain or justify the sheer sense of *rightness* in my head. This was the place. I simply knew it as surely as I'd ever known anything. I opened the trunk and lifted out the spade I'd bought that morning.

I glanced at Liz. She was standing beside the car, hands on the roof, looking at the field as if she had expected something more. It was a big field, a large uneven area of muddy pastureland, surrounded by a rickety wooden fence that in places had almost been overrun by weeds and undergrowth. In the far corner stood a huge, gnarled oak tree, undressing for winter, leaves scattered around its base like old scabs. I put my hand into my pocket and grasped the rabbit brooch. It wasn't warm, it wasn't pulsing, but I liked the shape of it in my hand.

I walked across the grass verge, still wet with dew,

tossed the spade into the field, and climbed in after it. The fence swayed alarmingly beneath my weight; it appeared that the vegetation that made it look more like a hedge was holding it upright.

"I haven't got the shoes for this," said Liz, looking ruefully down at her smart black zip-up boots.

"Do you want to wait there?" I asked.

"No way. I've come this far. I'm not going to miss the great climax."

The ground was a bit squelchy, but firm enough, beneath my feet. I took a couple of steps back to the fence and held out my hand. Liz grasped it and climbed up, the fence creaking ominously when she reached the top. She jumped down from a crouching position, still holding on to my hand. She landed awkwardly, stumbling into me. I put my arm around her waist to steady her. Her cheeks were red, either from the cold or the exertion. "Thanks," she said. We trudged across the field, to the place where I had dropped to my knees and begun digging in the dream. I now had no doubt where that place was. I think I could have found it with my eyes shut. When I came to a halt, Liz looked surprised, as though she'd expected there to be a big white cross painted on the ground.

"Are you sure this is right?" she asked.

There was nothing to indicate that the ground had been disturbed, but I nodded. "Positive."

I started to dig. The ground was soft and my spade cut into it easily. Within a minute I had created a mound of earth inversely proportionate to the hole beside it. Liz stood beside me, peering into the cavity of almost-black soil, wrinkling her nose at the sight of a halved worm flipping and writhing. Occasionally she glanced around. "If a farmer appears with a dog, or a big shotgun, I'm off," she said.

The hole was maybe a foot deep when I met resistance. My spade cut through an inch or so of soil, then clunked against something that jarred my hand.

"I've found something," I said.

"What is it?"

"I don't know. Something solid."

"Maybe it's just a stone," Liz said.

"I don't think so. It feels like something hard but hollow."

Liz said nothing, but she seemed suddenly anxious. I knew what she was thinking because I was thinking it too. Was there a skull down there beneath the soil, or perhaps even more than a skull?

With my spade I scraped the layer of mud away from whatever was lying beneath it. Both Liz and I were bracing ourselves for the sight of bone, and so were surprised when the object was revealed to be not white but terra-cotta-colored.

"It's a pot," Liz said, leaning forward. "Careful, don't break it."

I scraped the mud gently away from the pot. It was circular, like a gourd, with a stubby spout on one side that had been sealed with wax. It was hand-fashioned, not machine-made; it looked like an old drinking vessel.

When I had cleared as much of the mud away from it as I could, I reached down into the hole and lifted the vessel out. I laid it carefully on the grass, then squatted on my haunches and looked at it, absently rubbing my muddy hands together.

"I wonder what's in it," said Liz. "We could take it back to the school, heat a knife up with a Bunsen burner, and use it to cut through the wax seal."

"Or we could just do this," I said, and picking up the spade that was lying on the ground beside me, I struck the pot with the point of the blade.

It broke into several large pieces, like a chocolate egg. I thought I saw a flurry of spindly legged movement from within, and jumped back. Then I recovered my composure, embarrassed and annoyed with myself. How could there possibly have been anything alive in there? For God's sake, pull yourself together, girl!

Liz must have thought I'd been wary of flying shards, because she didn't say anything. I bent over the pot, my heart thumping, suddenly frightened of what might be inside it. I could see a twist of blond hair, some teeth (which still had tiny shreds of skin and dried blood on the roots as though they had been ripped out forcibly), and a small red gemstone.

My heart began to beat even faster. I picked up the gemstone, then reached into my pocket and brought out the rabbit brooch. With a vertiginous sense of inevitability, I slotted the red gemstone into the metal rabbit's empty eye socket. It was a perfect fit.

"This is very, very weird," Liz said quietly.

I felt dizzy and sick and scared. As though the rabbit brooch had suddenly turned red hot, I unclenched the fingers that were gripping it. The brooch with its new red gem of an eye fell into the remnants of the pot. I grabbed the spade again and used its broad blade to push the broken pot and its contents back into the hole.

"What are you doing?" Liz asked as I scooped up a spadeful of the soil I'd dug out.

I dropped the soil into the hole. It spattered dark on the brooch, partly covering it. "I'm burying it," I muttered, and scooped up another spadeful of soil. All at once I felt feverish, eager to complete the job. "I'm burying the lot."

Fifteen

DRIVING AWAY FROM GREENWELL that evening was not as liberating as I had hoped it would be. All it did was make me realize that I wouldn't be free of the place until I had found Alex. It was as though the town were encased within a vast dark bubble, and that rather than bursting free of it, it was simply stretching around me, clinging to my skin, the more I tried to distance myself.

Shelton appeared to have taken Greenwell's share of charm as well as its own. The place was all quaint cottages and country pubs. There was a bridge over a stretch of gurgling river. Hanging baskets, some still clinging tenaciously to summer's glory, were a seeming prerequisite beside every front door.

Liz had told me to look out for the ancient church and then to turn left at the drinking fountain whose spout was the carved stone head of a wild boar. Down Primrose Lane, past the little primary school on the right, then second left, which was Thornham Grove.

Liz's stone cottage, number 8, was set back from the road, a wooden gate opening onto a winding path that sloped down to a tiny red front door peeping shyly from beneath a wooden porch smothered with a sinewy briar of roses. A quartet of fruit trees, denuded by autumn's ravages but still proffering the odd brown-mottled apple or shriveled pear, diminished the light from the cottage's leaded windows to a shifting glitter of yellow shards.

I was surprised and slightly embarrassed to see that Liz had dressed up for the occasion. She was wearing a little black number, stockings, and heels, and whereas I wasn't exactly in sweatshirt and jeans, I couldn't help feeling that my pink cashmere sweater and black velvet trousers didn't quite hack it. I wondered whether to apologize for my lack of effort, but decided almost in the same beat that that would merely have made us both feel awkward. In the end I merely grinned at her ebullient "Hi!", stepped forward into the vestibule, and kissed her on the cheek.

"You look fantastic," I said, and then quickly, to save her feeling obligated to respond in kind, "And what a brilliant house! It's like something out of a fairy tale."

"It was my grandmother's," Liz said. Her eyes were sparkling and her cheeks were flushed. Either it was hot in her kitchen or she was already a couple of glasses ahead of me.

"How long have you lived here?" I asked.

"Seven years."

"You inherited it?"

"No, I bought it. The stairs got too much for Gran so she put the place on the market. I was renting at the time and kind of thinking of buying somewhere, and Dad just said, 'Well, why don't you buy your gran's place?' I was really lucky. I'd always loved the house, and Dad gave me some money toward it. I don't think he wanted to see some stranger taking it over. He was born and brought up here."

The idea of generations of Liz's family making their home in this wonderful place gave me a cozy rush of nostalgia. "It's a lovely idea," I said, "passing a house down through the generations. Maybe you'll do it too eventually."

"There's not much chance of that," Liz said, evidently amused by the idea.

"Why not? You're young yet. You've got plenty of time."

"Hmm," said Liz, then took my arm. "Anyway, come in properly, let me show you around. Didn't you bring an overnight bag?"

"It's in the car," I said. "I thought I'd bring it in later." She turned and led the way into the house, patting the yellow walls on either side of her. "This is the hallway," she said, "and this is the lounge." She indicated the only door on the right beside a steep, narrow staircase.

I poked my head in dutifully and saw a roaring open fire, terra-cotta–colored walls, bookcases in the two alcoves flanking the chimney breast. There was a beautiful old wooden sideboard, thick rugs on the floor, a sumptuous three-piece suite upholstered in fine air force–blue needlecord.

"Wow!" I said. "This is fantastic."

Liz grinned and pointed up the stairs. "Thanks. Those

are the stairs, believe it or not. I could show you round now or we could have a drink first and do the guided tour thing later."

"Let's have a drink," I said. "I could do with one after today."

"What'll you have?"

"Anything. What are you drinking?"

"I took the liberty of opening a bottle of sauvignon."

"Great," I said. I handed her the bottle I'd brought. "You might want to put this in the fridge."

She led me into a kind of back lounge or dining room dominated by a large inglenook fireplace with a cast-iron hood. The room smelled deliciously of wood smoke and cooking. The lighting consisted of the dancing, twisting flames of the fire, the glow of a rose-colored Tiffany lamp and various strategically placed candles. Liz went through an arch into the kitchen whilst I sat at the table, which had been set for two, nibbling tortillas and listening to Macy Gray as I stared mesmerized into the fire.

"Have you done much to the house since you moved in?" I asked, raising my voice above the popping and crackling of logs.

Liz reappeared, bearing a glass of wine which trapped the reflection of flames within it. "Not structurally. I had the place rewired and a new bathroom suite put in, but most of the changes have been aesthetic ones—carpets, curtains, paint."

"I hope you don't mind me asking, but is your gran still around?"

"She is. Still going strong at ninety-three. She lives with my mum and dad now on the other side of Shelton."

"And how does she feel about the changes you've made? I know if it was me I'd be worried that my gran would take offense every time I undid something she'd done."

"Oh, she's great about it all," said Liz. "In fact, she seems to take a huge delight whenever I do something new to the place. And the brighter the colors I use the better, as far as she's concerned."

We wandered through into the narrow, cluttered kitchen, and as Liz busied herself with the food, I leaned against the doorjamb, sipping wine. I told her about my parents, about Alex turning up at my cousin's wedding with his then-boyfriend, Joe, which was the first time Mum and Dad had discovered he was gay. "It was a bit fraught at the time, but it's funny in retrospect," I said. "Joe was a sweetie. I was sad when he and Alex split up, but he couldn't cope with Alex zipping off around the world all the time. He turned up with Alex at Lucy's wedding in a brown leather suit with shoulder-length, bleached blond hair. You should have seen my dad's face. In the bar before the reception, he sidled up to Alex and me when Joe was in the loo and said, 'I don't want to get personal, son, but are you sure that mate of yours is all right?'

" 'Course, I knew what he meant straightaway and I'm sure Alex did too, but Alex said, 'Yeah, he's fine, Dad, he's just a bit nervous. Why, what's he doing? Throwing up in the toilets?'

"So Dad gave Alex this look as if he was being facetious and said, 'No, son, I mean is he *all right*? Is he *normal*?'

"And Alex said, 'As normal as you are, Dad,' and at

that moment I knew he was going to tell him, that it was going to come out, and part of me wanted to run away and part of me wanted to be there for Alex, to support him.

"Anyway, Dad snorted and stood up very straight and thrust his chin out like an army colonel or something, which is a stance he always adopts when he's getting on his high horse about something. And he said, 'I doubt that,' and Alex went very still, and then in this quiet voice, which sent a shiver through me, he said, 'What's that supposed to mean?'

"And Dad said, 'Well, let's just say that if he was a friend of mine—not that he would be, mind, but if he was—I certainly wouldn't bend down to tie my shoelaces if he was behind me.'

"For a moment I thought Alex was actually going to hit Dad, but then he smiled and said, 'Don't worry, Dad, you're not his type.'

"Dad looked surprised for a moment, then he said, 'So what are you telling me, son? That your friend really is a woofter?'

"And calm as anything, Alex said, 'Well, either that or he's been faking it every night in bed with me these last three months.'"

Liz whooped with horrified delight. "You're kidding! So what did your dad do?"

"Well, at first he didn't realize what Alex had said. He sort of half laughed, and then suddenly realization dawned and his face went beetroot red, and he took a sudden step back as if he thought Alex was going to pounce on him and he said, 'What the bloody hell are you talking about?'

"And Alex said, 'What do you think I'm talking about, Dad? I'm gay. I've always been gay. It's no big deal.'"

"Good for Alex!" Liz said. "So what was your dad's reaction to that?"

"Oh, he blew his top as you'd expect. Said Alex was disgusting, that he'd brought shame on the family, all the usual crap. He tried to get me on his side, but when he found out I'd known for years he had a go at me too, said I'd encouraged Alex. It was all very depressing, all very predictable, but that's Dad, he's like a walking cliché. All he does is repeat what he's read in the papers or heard on the telly."

"So did he create a scene in front of all the guests?" Liz asked.

"Not really. He just told Alex to keep out of his sight and then he stormed off. Alex turned to me and said, 'Well, I think that went rather well,' but I could see he was upset and angry and trying to conceal it. Joe came back from the toilet and freaked out when he heard what had happened and thought Dad had gone off to get a lynch mob or something. He wanted to leave, but Alex told him that they were staying, that they had nothing to be ashamed of.

"And so it went on, Dad furious but trying not to show it in front of our relatives because he was terrified that they would find out and think it was somehow his fault, Mum getting all upset and sniveling a lot, Alex defiant, Joe getting more and more nervous, and me stuck in the middle, getting flak from my dad, calming down Mum and Joe, and trying to be supportive to Alex. I was knackered by the end of the day, I can tell you."

"I bet you were," said Liz. "So what are your parents like now?"

"Oh, Mum's fine. She came round pretty quickly. Dad's okay so long as it's never mentioned. He and Alex can be civil to one another just as long as Dad can ignore the fact that Alex is gay. If the subject ever comes up, then they usually have a blazing row. Especially if there's some family do coming up—Christmas or a wedding or whatever. Dad wants Alex to be there, but only on his terms, which means he doesn't want Alex to bring what he calls 'any of them poofs' with him. Oh, he's a model of open-minded, forward-thinking liberalism, my dad. Bless his little cotton socks."

"Parents, eh?" said Liz. "Who'd have 'em?"

"Well, yours seem all right," I said.

"No, they're great. They've always supported me and Moira, whatever we've done. My gran too. I've been lucky, I suppose."

"I'm lucky to have Alex," I said. "He's much more than a brother. He's the best friend anyone could wish for."

At once I felt a lump in my throat and a moment later—to my own surprise—I was sobbing. I covered my face with my hands and felt Liz stroking my hair.

"Hey, come on," she said. "Don't cry."

After a minute or so I pulled myself together. "Sorry," I said. "That kind of snuck up on me. I didn't mean to go off like that."

"We'll find Alex," Liz said. "You'll see."

"Do you really think so?"

She smiled, but her answer scared me because it was

an avoidance of the question. "You've got to have faith, haven't you? You can't give up."

"I won't give up," I said, "not until I've found out where he is."

She stared into my eyes and a strange moment passed between us, a brief hiatus where neither of us seemed certain what to say or do next. Then Liz reached for the wine bottle and said, "I think you need a refill."

"I think you're right," I said, holding out my glass toward her.

As she poured the wine she asked, "Are you ready to eat?"

"Definitely," I said. "I've been starving myself for this."

"I've made vegetarian," said Liz. "I hope that's okay."

I ate as if I hadn't eaten for days, and as if I wouldn't be eating properly again for quite some time. Liz had made eggplant and sesame pâté for starters, peppers stuffed with pine nuts and apricots for the main course, and a raspberry meringue gâteau for dessert.

The two of us drank as if it were going out of fashion too. I'm not sure how much wine we had, but I remember Liz opening at least two bottles during the meal.

It was only afterward, with our empty dessert bowls in front of us, that I finally brought up the subject I'd been putting off since I got here.

"So what did you think of what happened this afternoon, of what we found?"

Liz sighed, reached for her glass, and took a gulp of wine as if she needed it to fortify herself. "I've been trying not to," she said. She tapped her fingernails against the side of the glass, then looked at me. "Remind me again how you knew that we'd find something buried there."

I told her about the brooch, about my dream (I referred to it exclusively as a dream now, even in my own mind; anything else would have been too strange).

"So the brooch led you there?" Liz asked.

"My *dream* about the brooch led me there."

"But if you hadn't had the brooch, you wouldn't have had the dream?"

I shrugged. "Who can say?"

"But it was the police who planted the brooch on you, wasn't it? They put it among your personal effects, insisted that you take it."

"So what are you saying?"

She gazed into the fire, a thoughtful look on her face, and for a moment I thought she was going to come up with some blinding insight, produce some vital puzzle piece I'd overlooked. Then she shook her head. "I don't know what I'm saying. It's all too weird."

"It's not the only weird thing that's happened to me since I've been here," I said.

"No, you mentioned that before. So what else has been going on?"

I hesitated, then said, "I'll tell you, but only on the understanding that I'm not reading anything into these incidents—I'm just relating them as I experienced them. And I'm not prone to wild fancies. I've got an open mind, but I'm not gullible. I've never had any psychological problems, never taken any hallucinatory drugs—well, I once tried some magic mushrooms at college, but they had no effect whatsoever—and I was perfectly sober, on the whole, when these things happened."

Liz held up a hand. "And do you promise to tell the truth, the whole truth, and nothing but the truth, so help you God?"

"Now you're making fun of me."

She laughed, though not vindictively. "Sorry, Ruth, but you seem so serious."

"I just don't want you to think of me as a crank," I said.

She looked upset that I could even think she would, the alcohol making her face more mobile, her expressions more exaggerated. "I'd never think that, Ruth, whatever you told me."

The wine was making my own head swim, but even I could tell that Liz was heading rapidly toward rat-arsed. Maybe she wasn't as used to it as I was, or maybe she'd been more than a couple of glasses ahead of me when I'd arrived. Regardless, her drunkenness gave me the confidence to relate all that had happened since I'd arrived in Greenwell, if only because I half hoped she might have forgotten it by the morning. Liz watched me with wide, slightly glazed eyes, swaying slightly on her seat and taking occasional sips from her glass. When I got to the end of my story I marked it with a simple shrug. Liz still didn't respond, and just continued to stare at me. I left it for fifteen seconds or so, then smiled nervously. "Well, aren't you going to say something? Get out of my house, you mad-eyed loon? Something like that?"

Liz blinked slowly. "It's a lot to take in," she said. "I'll have to think about it for a while."

"Right," I said, and stood up. "While you do that, I'll make some coffee."

I went into the kitchen, and as I did so the intruder light came on in the back garden, making me jump. I looked out the window, which had framed only blackness before. More apple trees, ashen and eerie in the half-light, raised their myriad spiny limbs to the moon as though in proclamation of some arcane god. I thought of Rudding earlier that day, his arms upraised as he pressed himself against the window, face twisted with rage.

I told myself that an animal must have activated the light—there was certainly no sign of an intruder—but I shuddered nonetheless. I felt vulnerable standing there in the brightly lit kitchen, and wished there was a blind I could pull down to shield myself.

Because the kitchen was unfamiliar it took me a good ten minutes to make the coffee. I half expected to emerge from the kitchen to find Liz facedown on the table, snoring quietly, but she looked up almost alertly when I came back in with a tray. "There's some after-dinner mints in the cupboard above the fridge if you've got room for one," she said.

"I saw them," I said, "but I didn't want to presume, so I left them where they were."

"I'll get them." Liz clutched the edge of the table for balance as she stood up. "Do you want to carry the coffee through to the lounge? We might as well sit on the comfy seats."

I did as requested, placing the tray on the floor by the hearth and throwing a couple more logs on the dying fire. I lifted the poker from the companion set and jabbed at the glowing embers until they responded with a lick of angry flame.

"Good move," Liz said, offering me an after-dinner mint from the box in her hand. We sat at opposite ends of the vast, comfy settee, our legs tucked beneath us, sipping coffee and nibbling chocolate mints.

"So?" I said. "Any thoughts on what I said?"

"It's scary," Liz said. "It gives me the creeps. I can't explain any of it."

"But do you believe that I'm telling the truth?" I asked.

"I believe that you think you are."

"What's that supposed to mean? You think I've been imagining things, hallucinating?"

"Please don't get mad with me, Ruth," Liz said plaintively.

"I'm not getting mad. I just know what I've seen. But I've got no explanation for any of it either."

Liz paused a moment, blinking sleepily into the fire, then said, "The thing is, it's all so strange that the most *normal* explanation is precisely that you have been hallucinating it all, or at least misinterpreting what you've seen."

"Or it could be that I'm being manipulated," I said. "Everything I've seen and heard and experienced may be an attempt by the people of Greenwell to scare me off."

"Except it hasn't, has it?" said Liz.

I smiled. "I'm made of strong stuff, me."

Liz wiped a hand across her face as if attempting to clear away cobwebs. "I'm a bit pissed," she admitted, "but it seems to me that if they *are* trying to scare you away then they could be more direct about it. I mean, all this stuff with the spiders and the pot and all that—it's creepy, but it doesn't exactly send you screaming all the way back to London, does it? There was the body in the station, I know, but then that doesn't really make sense either. I mean, if they're prepared to commit murder, then why haven't they just done away with you and got rid of your body? If the police are in on it, then they're virtually untouchable, aren't they?"

"I don't know. Maybe they're playing some kind of ritualistic game. I keep getting the feeling that there's something I'm not seeing, that I'm too close to everything, and that what I really need to do is step back to see the bigger picture. But I can't. I can't tear myself away."

Liz took another sip of her coffee. "Well, if it's any consolation to you, I can't either, and I'm not as close as you are."

I sighed. "But then again, maybe that's because there's nothing *to* see. Maybe I am just . . . seeing things that aren't really there."

"It's all to do with seeing and not seeing," Liz said a little blearily.

"What do you mean?"

Her mouth opened, then closed, then opened again. Finally she said, "I'm not sure really. I'm rather drunk. I don't quite know what I'm talking about."

We looked at each other and giggled. It seemed the only thing to do under the circumstances. "What about these stories you were going to tell me?" I said. "About the school?"

She dismissively wafted the hand in which she was

holding her cup, slopping coffee on her black dress. "It's not very interesting really. Just gossip. Sordid little stories about sordid little lives."

"Like whose?"

"Well, Rudding's mainly. It all stems from him."

"Don't tell me—he's the leader of a satanic cult. He and his followers dance naked around the goalposts at midnight."

"It wouldn't surprise me, the stuff I've heard about him."

"Like what?"

Liz leaned forward as though afraid of being overheard. "It's said he got a fifteen-year-old girl from the school pregnant, but that the pregnancy was blamed on a boy in her class. Apparently the boy's father was a school governor and had had a bit of a run-in with Rudding earlier in the year. Because it was an underage issue, the police got involved, and the boy ended up committing suicide. He was found hanging from a tree in the woods behind the school."

"That's horrible," I said. "Is it definitely true?"

"Who knows? It's all hearsay, whispers. But the bit about the boy killing himself is true. I remember it being in the local papers."

"So when was this?"

"It would be about . . . yes, about six years ago. It was about a year before I started working at the school."

"So has anything happened since you've been there?"

"One or two things. A fourteen-year-old girl who'd stayed behind in the school one night for some reason claimed that a masked man had chased her through the school, out into the playground, and across the playing fields before she'd managed to lose him. I spoke to the girl at her home the next day and she was genuinely terrified, shaking and crying as she was telling me the story. Rudding, though, more or less called the girl a liar and refused to do anything about it. Then, about nine months after that, Rudding tried to rape my friend, Beverley."

"He tried to *rape* someone? You're kidding," I said.

"I'm not. Beverley was really sweet. She was from Newcastle. We got on really well. She taught drama, and she'd only been at the school about two months when it happened. She said she'd gone to Rudding's office one lunchtime and when she got there he just attacked her. She said he didn't say a word, he just went for her, like an animal. She got away by hitting him with the phone."

"The phone?" I said, surprised. I had no idea why that detail should jump out at me, but I got a sudden, almost overwhelming sense of déjà vu.

Liz nodded. "Again the consensus of opinion was that she was lying, but she wasn't, Ruth. I spent time with her afterwards and I know she was telling the truth. Rudding, though, said it was her who'd come on to him and that she'd gone ape shit after he'd politely resisted her advances. He made her out to be some deranged nymphomaniac, he got everybody on his side. The newspaper headlines were sickening—Beleaguered Headmaster blah blah blah. And the things he said! He kept calling Bev a poor child and said that he bore her no ill will and that she obviously needed help. The really weird thing, though, is that Bev disappeared one day."

"Disappeared? Left, you mean?"

"Well, that's what everybody thought, but the thing was she'd always said to me that even if she was driven out by this thing, even if she was forced to leave, we'd always stay friends and keep in touch. But then one day she was just . . . gone. I never heard from her again."

"Maybe she'd had enough, just wanted to break all ties to the place."

Liz made a face. "Maybe. Doesn't quite ring true, though."

We both lapsed into a meditative silence. I almost didn't want to voice what was going through my mind, but at last I said, "What happened to your friend sounds exactly like what's happened to Alex. Disappeared without trace."

Liz might have been pissed, but that didn't mean she didn't know when to be reassuring. She shook her head and said, "No, no, Ruth, this is totally different. Alex hadn't had a rud-in with Running . . . I mean, a . . . a run-in with Rudding. There was no reason for anyone to *make* him disappear."

"None that you know about, you mean."

Again she shook her head. "No, if there had been anything he'd have told me, I know it."

"Rudding sounds like a monster," I said.

"He *is* a monster. He's a despicable human being."

"Has he ever given you any hassle?"

"Not yet. Not directly. I try to keep out of his way."

The wine had made me feel melancholy. Once again my own tears took me by surprise. I had no idea I was shedding them until I felt them wetting my cheeks.

"Hey," Liz said, her slow, liquid-eyed drunkenness

exacerbating the tenderness of her voice. "What's the matter?"

"I don't know," I said between sniffs, the tears still coming. "I'm just crying because . . . because I am."

"It's all getting too much for you, isn't it?"

"I s'pose so."

"Well, that's okay. Just let it all out, girl. Get it gone. Clear out that toxic waste."

As if her words were the permission I needed, I cried harder. I was only half aware of Liz moving the box of after-dinner mints out of the way, shuffling toward me across the empty middle ground of the settee, and holding out her arms. I sank into her embrace, snuggled my wet cheek against her breast, heard her utter a wordless sound, a breathy moan that I assumed was intended to be soothing. She stroked my hair, then adjusted her position slightly so that she could wipe away my tears. Next I felt her hands on my cheeks, tilting my head up, and then her warm, soft lips on mine.

At first, unsure what was going on, I didn't react. Then her tongue, tasting of wine, darted between my lips and teeth, flickered inside my mouth. I pulled away, startled and confused. I broke free of her embrace and stared at her, my eyes searching her face. Her cheeks were crimson, her lips wet, her eyes already downcast to avoid mine.

"I'm sorry," she mumbled. "I'm sorry. I was drunk, I read the signs wrong. I'm sorry."

She pushed herself up from the settee and hurried out of the room, one hand pressed to her cheek. I sat there, at first stunned by the turn of events, and then, as it began to dawn on me what had happened, ashamed at the way I had reacted. I wasn't gay, but the reason I had recoiled so violently hadn't been because of Liz's pass at me, but because it had taken me by surprise. Now, though, I felt terrible that the vehemence of my rejection had caused Liz to flee, hurt and embarrassed. Liz had been nothing but kind to me, and I'd treated her as if she had some disease. What was more, I felt that by responding to Liz as I had, I had somehow let Alex down. I was well aware of all the shit he had had to take over the years, and I felt sick that I had now contributed to somebody else's similar burden.

I sat for a while longer, working out what I would say, then went after Liz. I entered the little dining room and saw that she'd left a note for me on the table. I picked it up and read:

Dear Ruth,

I'm so sorry about what happened. Heat of the moment, too much booze, whatever. I've gone to bed to sober up. I've made up the spare bedroom for you in the attic, but I'll understand if you don't want to stay. I should have told you before, but I stupidly thought, being Alex's sister, you'd just pick it up. What a moron I am. Again, I'm so sorry.

See you in the morning?

Love,
Liz

The lump which had never quite gone away rose in my throat again. I let myself out of Liz's cottage as quietly as I could and went to my car. It was raining thinly and steadily. The fruit trees, guardians of the house, whispered between themselves. I opened my trunk, took out my overnight bag, and went back to the cottage. I closed and locked the door, put guards over the two fires, and then went upstairs, wincing each time a step or floorboard creaked.

Sixteen

DRY-MOUTHED, I WALK along the tiled hallway, particles of grit too tiny to be registered by the human eye bursting beneath the soles of my shoes. I pass the mirror with the wooden frame and catch a glimpse of myself flashing past. When I reach the door to my left I stop. My mouth is shriveling up from the inside and my stomach is digesting itself. I raise my hand, the palm and fingertips of which are slippery with sweat, and place it on the doorknob. I watch with mounting dread as I take a grip on the knob and turn it. My sweaty hand slips on the polished wood, but there is enough friction for the knob to turn. The door opens, not as if I am pushing it, but as though it is being pulled from within. Not wishing to, but feeling as though I *have* to, as though all that I do is inevitable, preordained, I step into the room.

Something terrible has happened here. I know that as soon as I enter. I have a peculiar impression that past and present have collided, that one is overlaid on the other. Dustcovers still shroud the furniture, and many things are still in place—the furniture itself, the TV, the shelves of CDs and books and videos, the dining table beneath its black chandelier, the objects on the mantel-piece above the fireplace. But some things are not in place, some things are different, and these things carry a charge, an energy, that resonates within me, that touches me on some primal level. There is a dropped plate of dried-up pasta on the floor, and the telephone that sat on the shelf behind the TV is now on the floor, too, its receiver detached and smeared with blood. Most terrible of all, however, is the blood on the settee and the carpet, pools and trails and spatters of it, dried to a reddish-brown crust.

The blood itself is shocking, but it is not that which terrifies me. The awful thing is what lies behind the blood, what it signifies, what it means. I shake with terror because I am afraid of what my own mind may reveal to me. I know instinctively that it will be the worst thing in the world. I know it will be unendurable.

And so, terrified of discovering or rediscovering what happened here, I turn and flee. And as I run, I scream, not merely to give voice to my panic, but also to drown out the memories that threaten to unwrap themselves like poisonous sweets in my head.

Seventeen

IT WAS THE SUN slanting through a gap in the curtains and stretching itself like a sword of light across my face that woke me the next day. My eyes opened a crack, then closed again as light that felt like white heat rushed to fill the crevice between my lids. I groaned and rolled over. A wine hangover, like sour, fermenting grapes in my stomach and head, gleefully announced its arrival. I might have tried to sleep it off if I hadn't suddenly remembered how last night had ended.

I sat up, groaning, feeling like shit for several different reasons. My priorities were twofold: I needed some water and I needed to know if Liz was okay. I dragged myself to the orange-walled bathroom, splashed water on my face, then rinsed out what looked like an already clean mug and filled it from the cold tap.

My legs were feeling wobbly, so I sat down on the toilet while I drank. The house was silent and I felt almost peaceful sitting there. I wondered what time it was. It was light, so it couldn't have been too early. After five minutes or so I felt well enough to go and see if Liz was okay.

As I crossed the landing it occurred to me that perhaps I ought to get dressed first. I was wearing a skimpy T-shirt, and didn't want to appear provocative. As soon as the thought crossed my mind, however, I felt angry with myself. What did I think Liz was going to do? Leap on me because she'd be overcome with lust at the sight of my bare legs? As a result of my annoyance I knocked harder on her door than perhaps I should have done. All the same there was no reply.

"Liz," I called softly. "Liz, are you in there? It's me, Ruth."

As if it could be anyone else. Was I going to be this dumb, this clumsy, throughout the coming encounter? I needed to be able to say the right things, to express myself properly. I took a deep breath, then opened the door and leaned forward to peek inside.

Liz's bedroom made me think of royalty, everywhere purple and gold. Or perhaps a harem, with its four-poster bed swathed in purple fabric, matching the drapes at the windows. But the drapes were tied back with gold cord, allowing chill autumn light to spill across the neatly made bed. I pulled the door closed and stood at the top of the stairs. "Liz," I called. "Liz."

I think I knew even before calling that the house was empty. I padded downstairs and into the back room. There was still a faint glint of orange in the gray embers of the fire, but the room was cold enough to raise goose bumps on my legs.

Liz had set the table for breakfast and left me another note.

Dear Ruth,

I've gone to work. I was hoping we might talk this morning, but I couldn't bring myself to disturb you. Once again I'm so sorry about last night. I hope it won't stop us being friends. Please help yourself to whatever you want for breakfast.

Speak to you later?

Love,
Liz

Liz obviously felt as guilty about last night as I did. I ached to apologize, and half wished I'd written her a note before going to bed, though I always preferred dealing with important stuff face-to-face. I wasn't very hungry, but I made myself some toast and sat nibbling it while I reread her note. After the toast I made myself a cup of tea, which warmed and settled my stomach, but only at the expense of exacerbating the icy chill that was seeping into my bare feet. I stood up and began to walk around, cringing because my toes ached like bruises from the cold, my hands clasped around the warm mug.

Idly I studied the books on the bookcase behind the little sofa that was angled toward the fire. Wainwright's walking books; books on gardening and interior design; a bunch of novels by Alice Walker and Toni Morrison; some Penguin classics; the *Time Out* film guide. As I browsed I realized that I didn't even know what subject Liz taught. I'd have said something in the arts—English or drama or art itself. But if Liz had taught any of these subjects, I would have expected to see more evidence of it around her house. Shouldn't an English teacher's house be crammed with novels? An art teacher's with . . . well, art, and books on art, and art materials? Perhaps she taught math then, or geography, or history, or a foreign language. But again, whatever her subject, I would have expected to see more evidence of it.

I suppose I was thinking about Alex, thinking of how passionate he was about the things he was interested in, and how evident those interests were just from looking around the place where he lived. I guess I had always had this rather naïve, schoolgirlish notion that a teacher's subject was merely an extension of his or her hobby, that they were constantly and happily immersed in whatever they taught.

I moved from Liz's books to the framed photographs displayed on various surfaces around the room. Here was a middle-aged couple, wrapped up warm on a winter's day and grinning like teenagers despite their red noses, who must be her parents; here was a copper-haired, heavier variation of Liz, who must be her sister, Moira, sitting astride a bicycle; here was Liz herself with her arm around an old lady who was undoubtedly her grandmother; here was Liz again, her hair bleached blond and her skin tanned by the sun she was squinting into. And here beside Liz, her arm draped across Liz's shoulders, was another blond-haired girl with a wide, laughing mouth and brown sparkling eyes.

Instantly I felt something—a frisson of recognition. I *knew* this girl. I picked up the photograph and stared at it, filled with a fierce but infuriating sense of familiarity.

Her face, her name . . . The memory was so tantalizingly close, like a taste that filled me with nostalgia, but which I couldn't quite identify. I stood there for several minutes, waiting for the thin veil to tear, for the memory to break through, but it failed to do so. In the end I put the photograph back on the bookcase, unsettled to the point of anger. I washed up my breakfast things, then stomped upstairs to shower and dress, my mind working so furiously that by the time I left Liz's cottage it felt as though a steel plate were being screwed tighter and tighter into my forehead.

Driving back to Greenwell, I remembered what I had said to Liz last night, about not being able to stand back and see the bigger picture. Being unable to recognize the girl in the photograph felt like part of that, part of something I was missing. And it was not just the fact that I couldn't recognize her, but that she was with Liz. If I knew her as well as I thought I did, how could she be friends with Liz too? It was not beyond the bounds of possibility, of course, but it felt like something far more significant than a coincidence.

Abruptly it started to rain, big fat drops spattering like colorless bugs on the windshield. The dark clouds, lowering themselves oppressively toward the earth, reflected my mood, though more pertinently seemed to mark Greenwell's boundary, to define the outer edge of the pall that hung permanently over the town. Never mind that I had arrived in Greenwell a few days ago in sunshine. That seemed now like nothing more than a mocking reminder of the life I had left behind. Greenwell's boundary on that occasion had been defined differently, that was all. Defined not by gathering rain clouds but by the death of the hare beneath the wheels of my car, and—as though the sacrifice had awoken it—by the gray figure striding across the field toward me.

I turned my windshield wipers on and put my lights on half-beam. I slowed down, too; my annoyance at not being able to identify the girl in the photograph was making me speed. The roads between Shelton and Greenwell were narrow and twisty, country lanes bordered by high, unruly hedges and trees that craned over the road, leafless branches extended and splayed as though in frozen startlement. As abruptly as it had started, the power of the rain increased, battering angrily on the roof as if frustrated it couldn't extract me from my metal box. My windshield became a shimmering wall of water, beyond which trees and hedges and the dark thread of the road were a blur of constantly moving shapes. I shifted down into second and put my wipers on full. They squealed as they whipped from side to side, struggling to fend off the deluge. I leaned over the steering wheel, peering grimly through the instantly deliquescing arcs that the wipers created and constantly renewed. The landscape was deadened by the rain, starved of light and color. On a straight stretch of road, a narrow corridor between tall trees, I saw a gray bush about fifty meters ahead, so close to the roadside that I was forced to make a slight adjustment to my wheel to prevent myself from plowing into it. The bush was only twenty meters away when I realized it wasn't a bush at all but a gray-clad figure. The instant I realized this the figure began to turn slowly toward me.

Time seemed to freeze, and my shoulders clamped with dread. I felt cold pinpricks tingle across my skin as I recalled the boy in the playground telling me, *If you see his face, you die*. I tore my eyes away from the figure, which was half turned now, and stamped on the accelerator despite the driving rain. An almighty shudder rushed through me as the car swept past, the figure a fleeting block of gray in the passenger window.

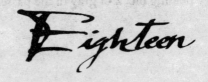

Eighteen

THE MAN WAITING FOR me at the Solomon Wedge was gorgeous. Maybe not Brad Pitt gorgeous, but he drew my eye like a sparkling object the minute I walked into the room. He was sitting at a table by the window, drinking tea—a little Earl Grey label was attached to the piece of white thread that dangled from the metal teapot in front of him. I knew he was waiting for me as soon as he glanced up and smiled.

He had dyed blond hair (not usually my thing at all) and very chiseled features. His broad shoulders and big hands, and the way he sat upright, straight-backed, on his seat should have made him appear powerful, yet the insipid light washing in through the window gave him a sense of ethereality. He reminded me of a vampire, anemic, in need of blood. I didn't know who he was, but I wasn't instantly pleased to see him. I was still shaky after my encounter on the road, and had been planning to do nothing more than chill out in my room for a while.

The man stood up. At that time in the morning he was the pub's only customer. Indeed, he and I were the only people in the room. "You have *got* to be Ruth," he said. He was tall, dressed in a gray linen suit and a black polo neck.

"Have I?" I replied cagily, which seemed to surprise him.

"You *are* Ruth, aren't you?" he said. "You must be. You look so much like Alex."

Hearing this stranger speak my brother's name was like a hammer blow to my gut. "How do you know Alex?" I demanded.

"I'm Keith," said the man. "Has Alex not mentioned me?"

"Keith!" I exclaimed. "Of course! Liz told me you were in Australia."

"I was. I got back late last night and called in at the school this morning to see Alex. Liz told me that Alex had gone missing and that you were staying here." He shook his head. "I don't understand, Ruth. What's going on? Where's Alex?"

"No one knows," I said. "He disappeared without a word just over a week ago. I came to find him, but I'm not having much luck."

"And he didn't leave a note or anything?" Keith asked, then admonished himself. "No, of course he didn't. Sorry. It's just that this all seems so unreal. I was so looking forward to seeing him. This is the last thing I expected to find when I got back."

"I know," I said, and shrugged, momentarily at a loss for words.

"Look," said Keith, gesturing at the seat opposite

him, "come and have a cup of tea and a chat. I hope you don't mind me saying, but you look a bit done in."

"I am. Thanks." I walked over and slumped gratefully into the seat opposite his. It had stopped raining. Something approximating gauzy sunlight was leaking through the clouds overhead.

"I'll order some more tea," said Keith. "I think everyone's clearing up after breakfast. Hang on."

I watched him as he moved away from the table, out of the milky light, and saw that I had been wrong about him. He didn't look anemic at all, he looked tanned and healthy and fit. Yet for all that he still retained an air of fragility. Or perhaps not fragility, but vulnerability. It was ridiculous—I had only known him for two minutes, but already I was feeling a primeval urge to protect him from some of the possibilities I was being forced to contemplate.

He returned with a tray of tea things which he set before me. "Thanks," I said and poured myself a cup.

"Has Alex done this sort of thing before?" Keith asked. "Gone off without a word?"

"No."

"But he has traveled a lot?"

"Yes, but he always keeps in touch. Phone calls, letters, E-mails. This time, though, there's been nothing."

"Perhaps he's trying to contact you at your London address," Keith suggested.

"No, my friend Sarah's monitoring that. She'll let me know if anything arrives." I looked at him. "I was actually hoping you might be able to shed some light on his whereabouts. Liz and I did wonder whether he'd followed you to Australia on a whim."

"No such luck." Keith looked thoughtful for a moment, then shook his head. "And I can't think of a reason why he would just go off without a word. He was happy here. Everything was going well."

We sipped our tea for a moment, listening to faint sounds of activity from the kitchen. Then Keith said, "Did you check the *Fargo* box?"

"I'm sorry?"

"The *Fargo* box. Alex once said to me that if he ever had to leave me a secret message he would leave it in the box that contains his video of *Fargo*—you know, the Coen brothers' movie? Did he ever mention that to *you* as well?"

"No," I said, trying not to sound jealous, "he didn't."

"I asked him why he'd ever want to leave me a secret message and he just shrugged and said, 'You never know.'"

I smiled. That sounded like Alex. He was like a kid sometimes, he loved secret places. As kids we'd had numerous hiding places in the house and garden which no one else knew about. I used to forget where half of them were, but Alex had them all logged in his head.

"I assume you've checked out his flat?" Keith inquired, interrupting my thoughts.

"Yes." I leaned forward. "I didn't have a key, so I broke in."

Keith looked both appalled and admiring. "You didn't!"

"I did. The police found out about it too and arrested me."

"What happened?"

I thought of my ordeal in the police station, but decided

against sharing it. "Nothing much. They let me go eventually." Suddenly I no longer wanted my tea, nor to chill out. I stood up. "Come on, let's go and check out the *Fargo* box."

We went in Keith's car, a banana yellow Punto. I was quite prepared to break into the house, but Keith produced two keys on a Wallace and Gromit key ring, one for the outer door, one for the flat itself. The house was silent as usual. I wondered whether Alex and the reclusive woman in flat 3 were the only tenants. It wouldn't surprise me. The longer I spent in Greenwell the more difficult I found it to believe that someone would actually choose to live here. As we went up the stairs, treading softly and saying nothing, I allowed myself a brief, optimistic fantasy: maybe living in Greenwell, simply being here in this dreary, soul-numbing town, had done Alex's head in to such an extent that he'd had to go away to think for a while with no distractions. To find himself and not tell anyone.

Even as the notion formed, warming me briefly with its optimism, I sensed hairline cracks of illogicality tracing their way across its brittle surface. We reached Alex's floor. I half expected to see some evidence that the police had been here, and was worried that we'd find the door to his flat secured by some kind of impenetrable barrier, but everything was just as I'd left it. Keith produced his key, but I gestured guiltily at the splintered wood around the lock that I'd attempted to tease back into place. I pushed the door and it swung open. Keith and I stepped into Alex's flat together.

Everything was just as I had left it. Perhaps the place

smelled a little mustier than it had previously, perhaps a greater number of dust motes swirled and spun as the air billowed around us, perhaps time had done a tiny bit more of its painstaking, infinitesimal work, but to all intents and purposes, nothing had changed.

I walked into the main room, my eyes scanning the shelves so rapidly that I saw nothing. Keith stepped past me and went straight over to a shelf on the opposite wall. I only saw the video of *Fargo*—white spine, red writing—when Keith placed his forefinger on it and teased it from its slot. I stepped forward, holding out my hand.

"Can I have it?"

He glanced at me, eyebrows raised, and I thought I must sound like a petulant little girl. I forced myself to smile and he shrugged and said, "Of course." But he handed the plastic box over with what I felt was a degree of reluctance. I took it from him, trying not to snatch, and opened it. I saw immediately that there was something tucked beneath the video. I lifted the video out, was so impatient I would have tossed it across the room in the vague hope it would land on the settee if Keith had not been there to take it from me. I lifted out the white unmarked envelope that had been nestled beneath, then shoved the plastic box into Keith's hands too. I tore open the envelope and extracted what was inside. Two photographs, nothing written on the backs. One of the photos was of me and Alex in London, him with his arm around me, both of us grinning like lunatics. The other was of me and Alex as little kids, sitting in our sandpit in the garden. I was holding a bright yellow plastic spade, engrossed in my digging. Alex had a blue spade and was squinting happily into the camera, a white sunhat on his head.

I held the photographs, one in each hand, and stared at them. As I did so I felt an all-engulfing wave of longing, regret, and awful, unbearable sadness break over me. My eyes flooded with hot tears, the photographs blurring like fragile memories. I sagged as the energy drained out of me. I felt Keith's hands on my arms, holding me up.

He spoke to me, and even though his words were a mush of meaningless sounds, blurring and blending one into another, his voice was soothing, coaxing, comforting. I clung to him, desperate for his strength, his support. I felt as though I were standing on the edge of a cliff, and that if I let go I would stumble over it into darkness. The awful grief that was surging up and out of me was like a drug, a heavy sedative, veiling my perceptions. I was only vaguely aware of what I was doing and of my surroundings. Keith and I were no longer standing up but sitting down; I had my face buried in his chest, could smell his clean skin; his hands were moving on my body, stroking, caressing; I lifted my face and felt the soft, warm wetness of his mouth on mine.

All of this seemed like a dream, a fantasy, and yet at the same time it was intense, life-affirming. It filled me up and I drank it in, craving it. Keith's skin against mine, his mouth on me, was the salve on my wound, the shot of morphine to deaden the pain. I don't recall undressing, but all at once I was naked and he was naked, and he was moving on me, sliding on me, and his mouth was on my breasts and on my stomach and between my legs.

I stretched out my arms, my hands forming fists, fingers hooking into claws, scrunching up the photographs I still held. Except that they weren't photographs, they were softer than photographs, more pliable. I had the sense of becoming aware, rising up as though from a deep sleep. All at once it occurred to me that what I was clutching were handfuls of bedsheet. I opened my eyes.

I was lying on my back, staring up not at the ceiling of Alex's flat but of my room in the Solomon Wedge. I was approaching orgasm, exquisite threads of sensation curling up through me as the tongue between my outspread legs lapped and probed. I raised my head groggily, looked down the length of my body, and saw not Keith's short bleached hair, but hair that was lustrous, long, strawberry blond.

My pleasure turned immediately to freezing, cramping panic. I dug my heels into the bed, let out a sound like a grunt of pain, and propelled myself upward into a semisitting position. I scrambled backward, my back thumping the headboard, as Liz, naked, raised her head and looked at me, eyes dewy, hair tousled, mouth wet. "What's the matter?" she said somnolently, raising herself on all fours and moving toward me. Barely realizing what I was doing, I kicked out at her, my foot impacting with her shoulder.

"Get away from me!" I screeched at her. "What's going on?"

She sat up, rubbing at her injured shoulder, her face full of pain and bewilderment. Then abruptly her eyes narrowed, her face hardened. Suddenly she was furious. She scrambled from the bed, snatching up clothes that were strewn on the floor. "What's your fucking problem?" she demanded.

I shook my head, dragging the sheets up to cover my body. "Don't be angry, Liz. Just tell me what's happening."

Liz was dressing quickly, jerking on her clothes. "You're crazy," she snapped. "You're a fucking schizo. You ought to see someone, get your head sorted out."

"I don't know what's happening!" I wailed.

"You've lost the plot, that's what's happening," said Liz, and stormed out of the room.

Nineteen

WHEN ALEX HAD CAUGHT up with him in the street, Matt had not fought back. He had simply gone limp, had not even tried to push Alex away when Alex had started banging his head on the pavement. It was creepy and scary. Who knows what might have happened if the police had not arrived and dragged Alex away from Matt's prone body? Later Alex said to me that Matt was a coward, that he only attacked those who were weaker than himself, but I wasn't so sure. I couldn't help thinking that Matt was more cunning than that, that he was playing mind games with us. By capitulating, by soaking up the pain of a nasty beating without retaliation, I believe that Matt was trying to make a kind of warped point, was trying to let us know that nothing we could possibly do to him would deflect him from his chosen course of action.

As a result of that night's events, both Matt and Alex were bound over to keep the peace, and Matt had a court injunction imposed on him, forbidding him to come near me. I spent a quiet Christmas with Alex that year, and an edgy, uncertain winter, wondering whether it really was all over. It was only as the hard frosts gave way to softer ground and new buds, and as the days began to stretch out their arms, that I finally began to relax. I'd spent a lot of time at Alex's house, feeling vulnerable on my own, but now I began to live a more independent life again. I got a good job on a movie, a crime caper starring Pierce Brosnan and Rachel Weisz, with Michael Caine doing a cameo as a shadowy underworld boss. The first part of the shoot was in London, but in April we were all due to fly out to Venice to do some location work there.

I was happy and excited about that, and although there were the omnipresent mental shadows lurking beneath the surface, I felt as though I was finally getting my life back on track. I wasn't in a relationship, but that's because I didn't want to be. I didn't think about Matt constantly anymore—if I had enough other things to think about, then I found I could push him right to the back of the queue. I could never rid myself of him completely, however, which was why I could never settle to anything—I needed to be perpetually busy to keep him at bay.

One March morning, toward the end of the London shoot, I came out of my house and started walking down the street toward the tube station. The film company was happy to pay for cabs, but if there weren't any holdups on the line the tube was much quicker. It was three months since I'd last seen Matt and I'd stopped jumping at sudden noises, stopped automatically looking over my shoulder whenever I left the house. More fool, me.

I don't know how long he'd been watching me. Maybe only a day or two, maybe since Christmas. I also don't know why he'd left it until now to act—maybe he hadn't had the opportunity before, or maybe it was simply that crazy people don't do things in a logical manner. On this occasion I didn't even see his face. All I was aware of was the brief—very brief—sound of running feet behind me and a flash of movement in my peripheral vision. Then I heard a sharp crack and felt a searing pain that shot down from the top of my head, blacking out my thoughts as effectively as a bolt of lightning fusing a string of lights looped along a seafront promenade.

I woke up in hospital, feeling as though my head had been split in two, weeping with the pain of it. For several minutes I was unaware of any other sensation in my body. I didn't even know Alex was beside me, clutching my hand, until he leaned forward to gently kiss my cheek.

"Hey," he said, "come on, you're safe now. I'm here. I won't let anyone hurt you."

"My . . . head . . . hurts . . ." I managed to tell him, and even though I was whispering, each word felt as though it were jabbing at the agonized nerve endings in my skull.

He gave me some pills to swallow, some water to sip, which again was excruciating, and then I drifted back into sleep. When I woke up later he was still there, watching over me. It was dark in the ward now; people coughed and rustled, there was the occasional quiet groan.

I felt marginally better. The pain in my head was just about bearable. Alex smiled.

"How are you doing?"

"Great," I murmured and his smile widened, then diminished.

"You do know who I am, don't you?" he asked.

What a ridiculous question. It took me a moment to realize that they must have been worried the blow to my head would result in brain damage. " 'Course I do," I whispered, and curled my lips into a little smile to show I was joking. "You're Dale Winton."

The smile reappeared on his face. "Do you remember what happened?" he asked.

"Someone hit me."

"Matt," replied Alex. "He was seen. Positive ID the police said." He hesitated a moment, and then, choking up, he said, "He hit you with an ax, Ruth. Fractured your skull. You could have died . . ."

He struggled to conceal his tears and anger and disbelief. I squeezed his hand.

"I'm okay," I whispered. "I'll be okay."

Alex rubbed his other hand across his face, recovering his composure. Quietly he said, "The police haven't caught him yet, but if they don't find him, I will. And if I find him I promise you, Ruth, I'll kill him. I'll kill him for everything he's ever done to you."

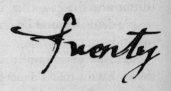

twenty

SUDDENLY I WAS LOOKING up at the ceiling, with no memory of having traveled through the interim state between sleep and conscious thought. I felt drained and fragile, my limbs weak, as if I were trying to fend off a debilitating bout of flu. As my memory returned it was accompanied by a slew of emotions—confusion, shame, self-loathing, fear. Fear because I didn't know what was happening to me. Was it simply that I was starting to seriously lose it? Was this what going mad felt like?

I sat up with an effort, my body feeling as though it belonged to someone else, and was unwilling to haul itself out of bed. I tried to piece together my last few memories, but after finding the photos in the *Fargo* box there seemed to be nothing but fragments. Had I made love to Keith or to Liz—or to either? What had happened between being in Alex's flat with Keith and waking up here? If I wasn't losing it, what other explanation could there be? Perhaps I had been drugged, but how? I hadn't eaten or drunk anything since . . .

Since Keith had fetched me a pot of tea when I'd met him downstairs earlier.

Was that the explanation? Had Keith, my brother's boyfriend, drugged me? He'd had the opportunity, but if that was the case then it must have been a hell of a strong drug, because I'd only taken a couple of sips from my cup.

Yet now that I came to think about it, how did I even know that the man I'd met had been Keith? I'd never seen a picture of him, so he could just as easily have been an imposter. The fact that he had keys to Alex's flat and knew about the *Fargo* box didn't mean a great deal. But if he wasn't Keith, why had he drugged me and lured me to the flat? Just to fuck me? Was it really as banal as that?

I had the impression I was forcing the pieces into place, that none slotted in neatly of their own accord. Where, for instance, did Liz fit into all this? The way I remember her reacting to me it was as if I'd seduced her and then gone schizoid, flipped into another persona altogether. Or maybe she and "Keith" had preplanned the whole scenario together, simply to disorientate me. It was a hateful idea. The last thing I wanted was to regard Liz as an enemy, but in the circumstances could I afford to trust anyone entirely?

Still feeling as though I'd been through the mill (could it be the drug wearing off?), I reached for my alarm clock. From the dim, pearly quality of the light in my room I guessed it was early evening, that I'd slept most of the day away, but it was only when I realized that the clock was edging toward 7 A.M. and not 7 P.M. that it struck me I'd lost about sixteen hours! My God, what had happened to me in that time? Hopefully most of it had been spent here sleeping, and there had been nothing worse than I remembered. I crawled out of bed, staggered into the bathroom, and sat down in the shower, hugging my knees to my chin.

I dozed for maybe twenty minutes beneath the comforting barrage of water. When I emerged I felt better, more capable. Grabbing my mobile, I dialed the number that Liz had given me. After four rings the phone at the other end was picked up and a voice blearily said "Hello."

"What happened yesterday, Keith?" I said.

"Pardon? Um . . . who is this? Ruth?"

"Don't piss me about, Keith. I want to know what's going on."

There was a pause, then Keith said, "Um . . . I don't know what you're getting at. Have I done something to annoy you, Ruth?"

"What happened yesterday?" I repeated. "Tell me what happened after I found the photos in the *Fargo* box."

"The *Fargo* box?" Keith asked, still sounding bemused. "Oh, you mean when we went to Alex's place on Friday?"

"Yes, that's what I said. Stop pissing me about, Keith."

"I'm not, I'm sorry. It's just . . . it threw me when you said yesterday."

"What are you talking about?" I snapped, feeling as though the conversation was slipping away from me.

"Well, yesterday wasn't Friday, was it? Yesterday was Sunday."

For a moment time seemed to halt in its tracks. "What?"

"What do you mean, 'what'?"

"What . . . what day is it today?"

"It's Monday, of course. Are you okay, Ruth?"

Monday! So I hadn't lost sixteen hours, after all. I'd lost three whole days! What the hell was happening to me? My head spun, and I felt as though I was going to faint.

"Monday?" I managed to say, my voice sounding as though it came from a long way away.

"Yes, of course. Ruth, are you okay? You sound really strange."

I tried to pull myself together, reminded myself that Keith may well be in on this with the rest of them, that he may be reveling in my confusion. I summoned up all the conviction I could muster and said, "I'm fine. I'm just tired, that's all. Now are you going to answer my question or not?"

"Um . . . s-sorry, Ruth," stammered Keith. "I've forgotten—"

"What happened after we found the photos in the *Fargo* box the other day?" I demanded.

I've got to give it to him—Keith sounded genuinely mystified. "Right, well . . . um . . . well, you got upset, *really* upset, and you started crying, and you were swaying about as if you were going to faint. I steadied you and led you over to the settee, and we sat down and I gave you a hug. You were crying for a long time. I put it down to all the stress you'd been under recently. I kept telling you to let it all out. Afterwards you were so exhausted, you could barely speak. You said you wanted to go back to the Solomon Wedge, so I drove you. I saw you in and asked if you'd be all right, and you said yes, you just wanted to sleep. I told you to call me when you felt better, and you said you would."

"And that's all, is it?" I asked, my voice curt but my resolve evaporating a little.

"Yes, that's all. Why do you ask?"

"It's not how I remember it," I said.

Sounding baffled, Keith said, "I see. So how *do* you remember it?"

"I remember you . . . taking advantage of me."

"*What?*"

"I remember us taking our clothes off, having sex."

There was a brief pause, and then Keith said quietly, "What is this, Ruth? What are you trying to do to me?"

"I'm not trying to do anything to you," I said. "I'm just trying to find out the truth."

"The truth is that you got upset, I comforted you, and then I drove you back to the pub. We didn't have sex, Ruth. I'm gay, for Christ's sake!"

"You say you are," I said.

"What's that supposed to mean?"

"You say you're gay. You say your name is Keith. You say you're Alex's boyfriend. But I don't have proof of any of this, do I?"

There was a longer pause this time. If Keith really was who he said he was, then I could guess what he was thinking. Who was this crazy woman he'd got lumbered with? What the hell was she up to? At last he said, "All right, Ruth, if you want proof then I've got proof. I've got my driver's license, my passport. I've got photographs of me and Alex together. I'll come round to the pub to show them to you now if you like. All I want to do is help, Ruth. I love Alex too, you know."

I felt the new fragile membrane that had formed around my emotions threatening to crumble again. Trying to sound brisk, but succeeding only in sounding harassed, I said, "Not now. Maybe later. I've got something to do first."

"All right, Ruth," Keith said, "whenever you're ready. Give me a call, okay?"

"Yes," I said. I was going to switch the phone off, but before I could Keith asked, "Are you going to be okay?"

He sounded genuinely concerned. Confusion was grinding inside me. I wanted to shout, *Don't do this to me. I don't know whether I can trust you!* Instead I said, "I'll be fine. See you later." Then I snatched the mobile from my ear and punched the disconnect button, as if the phone were a trap I had lured him into and now sprung.

Despite having apparently not eaten for three days, my appetite was still nonexistent, though I thought it wise to try to get something down before I flaked out completely. I went downstairs and nibbled my way through several rounds of toast and butter. Tony, who was serving today, brought me a pot of tea and looked at me strangely when I requested bottled orange juice instead and stipulated that I personally wanted to open the bottle. After breakfast I felt stronger, more centered, as though my wildly fluctuating thoughts were settling, wavering back into alignment.

I needed to talk to Liz to find out what had happened between us. I wasn't relishing the prospect, but I couldn't ignore it, not if I wanted to try and salvage the only real friendship I'd made in Greenwell. I sat in my car and started dialing the number of the school, then killed the connection. No, it would be better to give her no forewarning of my arrival.

It was only when I got to the school that I realized I'd got the timing all wrong. The school day—a new school week after the weekend I'd lost—had only just begun. Liz would be teaching. I couldn't just barge in and demand to speak to her. I thought about driving round for a bit, seeing a bit of the countryside, but then I remembered the gray figure who'd been standing by the side of the road the other morning. I decided I didn't want to tempt fate, didn't want to turn a corner to find the figure there waiting for me again—or worse, in the middle of the road this time, its arms perhaps outstretched to halt the car.

I was giving myself the willies. I pulled into a lay-by just beyond the school and turned on the radio in the hope of banishing my demons with pop music. Finally, over the D.J.'s increasingly irritating patter, I heard the trilling of the school bell. Break-time at last. Suddenly, aware that I had no more than fifteen or twenty minutes before Liz would be teaching again, I started the car and drove round to the car park at the back.

I fought my way through hordes of children in the corridors, whose sole purpose in life seemed to be to hamper my progress. At last I reached the staff room and knocked on the door. I felt disheveled, breathless with urgency—but maybe that was the best way to face her; she might take pity on me when she saw what sort of state I was in. When the door opened, my heart skipped as I thought at first my knock had been answered by Liz herself. I almost instantly realized that this woman was taller and thinner and older than Liz.

"Can I help you?"

"Is Liz . . . um, Liz there?" I asked, unable for the life of me to remember her surname, compounding my feeling of stupidity.

The woman scrutinized me for a moment, and I wondered whether Liz had confided in her about me—I squirmed with embarrassment at the thought. I half expected her to tell me brusquely that Liz didn't want to see me, but instead she said, "I'll see," and retreated into the room, making a point of closing the door enough so that I couldn't see inside.

As I waited, I was aware of the seconds until the end of break ticking by. I considered walking away, thought that maybe it would be better if I came back later, caught Liz just as she was about to go home, and suggest we go for a drink. Yes, that might be the best idea. But even as the thought occurred to me the door swung open. The expression on Liz's face was not encouraging.

"Why have you come here?" she demanded. "What's wrong with you?"

I felt like a wayward child, totally inadequate. I was the same height as Liz, possibly even taller, but I felt I was looking up at her.

"I need to talk to you," I said, then immediately wished I'd rephrased it, had said instead, "*We* need to talk."

"Well, I don't think I need to talk to you," Liz snapped. "There's nothing to say."

"Yes there is, there's plenty to say!" I protested.

She folded her arms. "Like what?"

I looked around. Passing pupils were casting curious glances in our direction. "I just want a chance to explain myself," I said. "Look, isn't there somewhere more private we can go?"

She was silent for a moment, arms still folded tightly as if to provide a buffer against me. Then she said, "Come on, then," and stomped past me down the corridor, not bothering to check whether I was following.

She ran up a flight of stairs and I ran after her, past lingering pupils whose furtive glances made me uneasy. We went down another corridor, Liz moving so swiftly that I thought she was trying to lose me. She came abruptly to a halt outside a closed classroom door and shoved it open. I arrived at the threshold just in time to see a startled teenage couple hastily disentangle themselves from the snog they'd been having, the boy whipping his hand out from beneath the girl's skirt, their faces flushed.

"Out!" Liz snapped, and the couple scrambled to obey, the girl wiping her mouth guiltily on her sleeve, the boy mumbling, "Sorry, miss," as he passed with his head down.

I closed the door and then Liz and I were alone. She perched on a desk and folded her arms again. "Well?"

For a moment I was too flustered to think. Everything I'd rehearsed silently in my head, the different approaches I'd considered to deal with whatever mood Liz might be in, had either fled from my brain or were jammed in there so deep I was unable to extricate them. I raised my hands in a vague gesture of conciliation.

"I'm sorry."

"Is that it?" Liz placed her hands on the desk as if to push herself upright prior to leaving.

"No!" I said. "Of course not. It's just . . . I'm so confused, Liz. I don't know what's happening to me. Please don't be angry. You're the only friend I've got here."

"I'm not surprised if this is the way you treat them."

"I know, I know, it's just that . . . oh, this is going to sound so feeble."

"Try me," Liz said tersely.

I took a deep breath. "When I opened my eyes and saw that you were in bed with me, I freaked out because . . . well, because I didn't expect to see you. I thought I was in bed with someone else."

Liz looked at me with contemptuous disbelief. "Come again?"

She hadn't moved, but I raised my hands as if to bar her exit, or perhaps to protect myself against physical attack. "Look, I know how mad this sounds, Liz, believe me. I don't know what's going on myself. I was hoping *you* might be able to tell *me*. But the truth is, the reason I reacted like I did is because I honestly thought I was in a different place with a different person."

"I see," she said cynically. "So who did you think you were with?"

"Keith."

"Keith! Alex's Keith?"

I nodded.

She looked angry and confused. "I don't know what the hell you're on about."

I was desperate for answers, but I thought it best to tell her my side of the story first. I took her through my encounter with the gray figure at the side of the road, my meeting with Keith, my lost weekend. "The thing is," I said when I had finished, "I've got no proof that the man I met even *was* Keith. I've never seen him before, so I don't know what he looks like. All I know is that the man waiting for me said he'd been to the school and you'd sent him to find me at the pub."

"That's right. Keith did come to the school. I told him you'd stayed over with me the night before, but that you had a room at the Solomon Wedge, and that if he went there he'd catch up with you sooner or later." She fell silent.

"So," I said nervously, "*you* tell *me* what happened."

"You seduced me," Liz said bluntly. "You called me on Saturday morning and said you needed to see me straightaway. You said it was important. When I arrived you hardly said anything to me, just that you'd been thinking about what had happened between us, and you wanted it to go further. Then you started kissing me . . ." Her voice trailed off.

I pressed my hands to my cheeks. They were trembling, the fingertips cold. My heart was thumping frantically with fear. "I have no memory of that," I whispered. "No memory at all. Oh God, what's happening to me?"

"I don't know," Liz said frostily.

"So where does this leave us?" I asked. "Are we still friends?"

Liz gave a small, bitter smile. "I hated you after the way you treated me. I haven't been able to sleep since Saturday, I've been so twisted up with anger and humiliation."

I hung my head. "I'm so sorry," I mumbled. "I didn't mean to make you feel like that. I would have done anything not to hurt you. You're the only friend I've got here."

Neither of us spoke for a moment, then Liz sighed as if saddened by her own lack of empathy. "Maybe it's not your fault."

"What do you mean?" I asked.

"I don't know. Maybe you were drugged or something."

"By Keith?"

She screwed up her face. "I can't believe that."

"Who, then?"

"I don't know. By someone at the Solomon Wedge maybe."

I thought about it. It was possible, I suppose, but for what purpose I couldn't fathom.

"What if I was right before?" I suggested. "What if the man I met at the Solomon Wedge wasn't Keith? What if someone intercepted him en route and took his place?"

"It's all a bit far-fetched."

"It's possible, though, isn't it?"

"Well . . . just about, I suppose. Hang on a minute." Liz was wearing a pair of silk charcoal-gray combat trousers. She unbuttoned one of the pockets and took out a small, square, black leather wallet. She opened the wallet and teased out a photograph. As she did so, another one came free and fluttered to the floor. "Oh bugger."

I moved forward to pick it up. The photo was lying facedown. When I turned it over I realized I was looking at the same girl who had been in the photo with Liz on her mantelpiece, the one who looked so familiar to me.

"Who's this?" I asked, handing the photo back to Liz.

Liz looked at it, a wistful smile on her face. "Jenny. My ex-partner."

All at once the door to my memory swung open, the name Liz had provided like the last elusive digit of a combination lock. "Jenny Sayer?"

"Yes, as a matter of fact. How did you know?" said Liz, taken aback.

I laughed. "Jenny Sayer was my best friend at school when I was fourteen. Then her family moved away and we lost touch. I thought I recognized her when I saw her picture in your house, but I couldn't place her. She's changed quite a bit. She looks thinner and her hair's a different color. How is she?"

Liz paused, and though it was only for a split second I suddenly knew that the news would not be good. Liz's voice was flat, emotionless. "She died of stomach cancer fifteen months ago."

I hadn't seen Jenny for almost two decades, but my body jolted with shock. "Oh, Liz, I'm so sorry. Oh no. Oh, poor Jenny."

"These things happen," Liz muttered, and handed the other photograph to me. "Here's a picture of Keith."

It was the same man I had met in the Solomon Wedge, the same man I had gone to Alex's flat with. He was wearing a basketball vest with a number 20 on it. He was grinning into the camera and he had his arm draped around Liz's shoulder, dwarfing her. Liz had a black vest top on, and was laughing so hard you could see her fillings. It was a sunny day, light haloing their hair.

"It was taken on one of our picnics," she said.

"Alex took this?"

"Yes."

I handed the photograph back to her. It was strange, but seeing them so obviously happy made me feel unbearably sad. "It's the same man," I said, at which point the bell rang.

Liz pushed herself off the desk. "I've got to go."

I looked at her with something like panic. "So what happens now? We are still friends, aren't we?"

She didn't answer me straightaway, and when she did she simply said, "Give me a ring. We'll talk later."

"But we are friends, aren't we?" I asked, aware of how pathetic I sounded but unable to help myself.

Liz looked troubled. "I hope so. I need some time to think, though, Ruth."

"I'll ring you at home," I told her as she moved to the door. "Perhaps we can go out for a drink or a meal."

She gave me a noncommittal smile, then opened the door, and almost immediately stepped back. "Of all the cheeky . . ."

Someone had been standing on the other side of the door, eavesdropping on our conversation—this much I understood. I stepped forward, past Liz, and caught the merest glimpse of Rudding, the headmaster, scuttling around the corner like some great black spider.

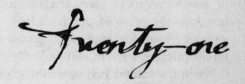

SEVENTEEN SUMMERS AGO MY main objective in life was to get Richard Prince to go out with me. He was in the year above me at school, and he looked like Simon Le Bon without the peroxided hair. My campaign manager in this venture was my best friend, Jenny Sayer. I looked up to Jenny. She was everything I wanted to be. She was blond and bubbly, she had big boobs, and she was popular with the boys. I, by contrast, was mousy and shy and underdeveloped.

I did used to wonder sometimes why she went around with me, though it was nice to bask in the warm glow of her reflected popularity. In my more anxious moments I thought that she'd chosen me as her friend simply in order to make herself look good, though there was certainly never any evidence to back up my apprehensions. Indeed, Jenny and I spent most of our time together, and a great proportion of that when no one else was around— in the evenings after school and during the holidays. We always got on great, and I think it's largely thanks to

Jenny that I started to come out of my shell at around this time. Jenny was forever trying to convince me how attractive I was, was always telling me that this or that boy fancied me.

Jenny had six or seven boyfriends during the eighteen months or so of our friendship. The reason we weren't friends for longer was because we'd gone to different primary schools, and had only got to know each other in the second year of senior school when she got moved up to my class following a reshuffle after the first-year exams. When her dad was offered a job in Holland a month or two into the first term of our fourth year, we wept in each other's arms and vowed we'd stay in touch forever. We wrote regularly for three months or so, and then, as our different lives and our new friends began to lay claim to our attention, sadly lost touch.

That summer term, though, at the end of our third year, was the height of our friendship. We were both fourteen going on fifteen, and we thought we were the coolest creatures on the planet. Once New Romanticism (if that was the right term for it; I never was sure) started to hit the charts in a big way, we "discovered" it and made it ours. We were into Tears for Fears and Spandau Ballet and the Human League. My own personal fave, though, was Simon Le Bon out of Duran Duran. To my fourteen-year-old eyes he was almost angelic in his perfection. The crush I had on him made me feel dizzy and weak and sick with longing. So enamored of him was I that I didn't even notice Richard Prince looked a bit like him until Jenny pointed it out to me.

"No he doesn't" was my instant, indignant reaction. I regarded it almost as a personal insult that she could think anyone could have even so much as a fleeting resemblance to the magnificence that was Simon.

"Yes he does," she insisted. "He's got the same cheekbones and the same eyebrows. If he grew his hair a bit and dyed it blond he'd be the spit."

I continued to refute Jenny's suggestion, yet over the next couple of days I must admit I saw more and more what she was getting at. Richard Prince didn't look exactly like Simon, but he did look a bit like him, and in my book even a second-rate Simon had to be pretty yummy.

"I could ask around, find out what he does on weekends," Jenny suggested.

"Why would you want to do that?" I asked, feigning indifference.

"So that you can talk to him."

"I don't want to talk to him."

"Yes you do."

And it was true. I *did* want to talk to him. Almost solely through the strength of her personality and her powers of persuasion, Jenny had managed to convince me that I had a major crush on this guy.

For a while we shadowed Richard's movements with no luck. We went to places we wouldn't normally have been seen dead in, but received not so much as a nod or a smile. Whole evenings would drift by with me on the verge of going over to speak to him, but not managing it because the circumstances were never quite right. I felt terribly inadequate. I knew if Richard had been Jenny's target and not mine she would have had him in her clutches by now. All the same, she was incredibly pa-tient with me. She coaxed and cajoled, but she never bullied me or blamed me for another wasted evening or poured scorn on the pathetic feebleness of my efforts. Time and again I urged her to forget it, tried to con-vince her that we were wasting our time, that he wasn't interested, but she was having none of it.

Spring slipped into summer, and as the holidays ap-proached I began to feel a sense of relief. I was in tur-moil, and saw the impending break from school as a chance to get my head together, to put distance between myself and the ongoing, agonizing Richard Prince situa-tion. My feelings toward Richard at this time were oddly ambivalent. As he became (in my eyes) less attainable, my crush on him seemed to increase exponentially, until it had reached a stage where he was all I could think about, where I would spend whole lessons dreaming of what our perfect date would be like, whilst idly doo-dling his initials, intertwined with mine, in the back of my exercise book. And yet another part of me wanted him to disappear, never to be seen again. He had derailed my life and I wanted to get back on track as soon as pos-sible. If this is what love is all about, I thought, then I want no part of it.

Jenny, though, had other ideas. As soon as we broke up for the school holidays, she persuaded her dad to make us both members of the tennis club that Richard belonged to. She presented this information to me as though it were a gift I'd be rapturously thankful for, but I was horrified.

"It's okay," Jenny said, misunderstanding my stricken

look. "Dad doesn't mind. He thinks it means I'm turning normal again. He doesn't mind paying for you, too, either, because he thinks if I've got someone to play with I'll stick at it longer."

"But I don't—" was as far as I could get before the last couple of months of hormone-induced tension overwhelmed me and I burst into tears. Jenny looked completely bewildered, but after a moment she wrapped her arms around me and held me close.

We were in my bedroom, playing Duran Duran's *Rio* album. We were alone in the house. Dad was at work, Mum was down at the shops, and Alex was out somewhere with his friend, Nige.

"Don't cry," Jenny kept saying. "What's the matter?" But it was a while before I could speak.

Finally I blubbered, "It's all right for you."

"What's all right for me?"

"Well, you've had loads of boyfriends. But I never know what to do or say. What if I say something really stupid and he laughs at me?"

Her expression softened. "Come here," she said. With her arm still around me, she pulled me down so that we were no longer sitting on the bed, but lying on it, side by side, our noses almost touching, her hair tickling my forehead.

"What you've got to learn, Ruth," she said softly, and her breath was sweet like bubble gum, "is not to take it all so seriously. It's a game, a bit of fun. So what if he laughs at you? You just laugh right back at him. Boys are immature. Use 'em and abuse 'em, that's what I say."

"It's easy for you," I said.

"It's easy to do. Just try it."

I was silent for a moment. "But you've had experience."

"So what are you saying? That I'm a slut?" But she was laughing as she said it.

" 'Course not. But what I mean is . . . all right, what if him and me started going out and he wanted to . . . you know . . . do it?"

"Do *you* want to do it?"

"No. I don't know. Not yet."

Jenny stroked my arm and shrugged. "Then don't do it. It's up to you. It's your body."

"But what if he chucked me because I didn't want to do it, or because I was no good at it?"

"Then he'd be a shit and not worth knowing anyway," said Jenny. She carried on stroking my arm for a minute, then she said, "We could practice if you like."

"What do you mean?"

"I could pretend to be Richard and you could be you."

I giggled, but felt a little squirm of anticipation in my belly. "Don't be daft."

"What's daft about it?"

"I don't know. It just is."

"Up to you," said Jenny airily. "I was only offering you the benefit of my experience."

We lay there for a bit longer, me thinking of what she had said, and unable to shake off that feeling of delicious anticipation, and then at last I said, "Go on, then."

"What?"

"Let's practice."

"You sure?"

"Yeah."

"Okay, then." She wriggled a bit on the bed as if trying to get more comfortable and I felt her boobs pressing and moving against me. "First off," she said, "tell me what you've done so far with a boy."

"Not a lot."

"What does 'not a lot' mean?"

I thought about it. "I've snogged."

"Is that it?"

"Yeah."

"How many boys have you snogged?"

"Two."

"Tongues?"

"No," I said, thinking of Reece Jarvis's (the last boy I'd snogged at Tracey Quentin's birthday party) tongue, and trying not to be repulsed.

"Okay," said Jenny. "Well, if you snog someone with tongues, it's called a French kiss because that's the way the French do it."

"I know *that*," I said.

"They're very passionate, the French," said Jenny. "A French kiss is like this." To my surprise she dipped her head and clamped her lips on mine. After a moment she broke contact and looked at me. "Well, open your mouth, then. I can't show you unless you open your mouth."

"I didn't know you were going to do that," I said.

"Well, we can't practice unless we do stuff, can we?"

"No," I said, "I suppose not."

"So open your mouth."

I opened my mouth. Jenny leaned forward and kissed me again. After a moment I felt her tongue clashing with mine. I was alarmed, but it was a nice feeling, too, thrilling and forbidden. I responded to her, my tongue wrestling with hers. We entwined our arms around one another and began to move together on the bed, our bodies gently wrestling as our tongues were. The music in the background seemed to recede as if someone were slowly turning down the volume control.

Then I felt her hand on the warm flesh of my stomach and I raised my head, our lips disengaging with a wet smack. "What are you doing?"

"Ssh," she said, her eyes dewy, half closed, her lips red and shiny plump. "Just relax, go with it."

"What are you going to do?"

"Something nice. Nothing that will hurt you. If you tell me to stop, I will."

I settled my head back on the pillow and closed my eyes when her face came close enough to blur. We were kissing again, our lips sliding, our tongues moving constantly, but my mind was now almost wholly focused on what Jenny was doing with her hand. It was palm-flat on my stomach and she was stroking me gently, her fingertips moving in a circular motion across my flesh, leaving pleasurable shivers of sensation in their wake. And as her hand languidly circled my flesh, so it rose higher with each revolution, until her fingertips were stroking the material of my bra, and then her hand was gently caressing my breast.

I was in a dilemma, part of me wanting to blurt out at her to stop, part of me wanting her to carry on. My head told me that what we were doing was wrong and dirty and sinful, but I liked it, I liked it a lot.

She slipped her fingers under my bra and cupped my naked breast, her fingers toying with my nipple. I tensed and shuddered, and whispered into her mouth, "Should we be doing this?"

"What harm are we doing?" she murmured. "I'll stop if you want me to."

"I don't want you to stop," I said.

"Will you do to me what I'm doing to you?" she asked me.

"Yes."

Later, when we were lying in each other's arms, momentarily sated, Jenny asked, "Do you ever touch yourself?"

I blushed and refused to meet her eye. "A bit. Sometimes. Do you?"

"All the time," she said, and she looked at me with wide lustful eyes, making me quiver with apprehension and excitement. I felt that I was moving into uncharted territory, into a place rife with both dangers and wonders. I didn't know how to respond.

"Are you shocked?" she asked me.

I shrugged, trying to be blasé. "Nah, 'course not."

"Have you heard of the G-spot?"

I wracked my brains, trying desperately to work out what she might mean. It was probably somewhere in town, a nightclub maybe, where you had to be eighteen to get in. Jenny probably went there on the nights when we weren't together. She could pass for eighteen easy, if she wanted to.

"I've heard of it," I lied, "but I've never been there."

To my surprise, she burst out laughing, and once she'd started she couldn't stop. After a couple of minutes I started to get irritated. I slapped her arm. "What? What, Jenny? Tell me." But she just laughed.

At last I got really angry, and I shoved her away from me and sat up. "Well, if you're going to be such a horrible bitch," I said, "I'm going downstairs." I was nearest the wall, so had to scramble over her to get out. As I was doing so she grabbed me and pulled me down on top of her.

"Sorry," she breathed through her giggles. "Sorry, Ruth. I wasn't laughing at you, honest."

"Yes you were," I said.

"No I wasn't. I was laughing at what you said, not at you."

"There's no difference."

"Yes there is. It's just that . . . well, the G-spot isn't a place you go to. It's here."

Before I realized what she was doing, she had grabbed my hand and pushed it up between her legs. Because it was a hot day she was wearing a short skirt and no tights. Her panties were damp and warm, and she groaned as she applied pressure to my fingers, pushing them deeper into the softness of her crotch. She clamped her lips to mine and kissed me hard, then panted, "Will you keep your hand there?" into my open mouth.

Too terrified and excited to do anything except what she told me, I nodded. She released her hand from mine, then dug me in the ribs with her elbow as she raised her arms slightly. I was so overwhelmed by what was happening that I didn't realize what she was doing until I felt the material of her pants ruckle beneath my palm, followed by the sensation of wiry pubic hair beneath my fingers. *She's pulling her pants down!* I thought, and again the thought was a yell of both thundering terror and heart-stopping excitement.

"Put your finger in me," she said.

"Which one?" I asked stupidly.

"It doesn't matter. Here." She put her hand over mine again and applied pressure, and my middle finger slid inside her. She was slippery and roomy and fleshy, wetter than I'd ever been when I'd tentatively explored myself. Her back arched and she let out a little shriek. If her hand hadn't been clamped on top of mine, holding me in place, I'd have pulled away from her, thinking I was causing her pain, even damage.

"Are you all right?" I asked, looking at her screwed-up eyes, her panting mouth, her blazing cheeks. She reminded me of the woman in the film about childbirth we'd had in biology.

"Ah, that's so good. Push your finger in deeper, move it around a bit," gasped Jenny.

I did it until my wrist ached, until she finally let out a scream and grabbed me and clung to me, her grip like iron, her fingers digging into my shoulders.

"What's wrong, Jenny?" I cried. "What's wrong? What's wrong?"

It was a terrifying thirty seconds before she answered.

"I'm fine," she gasped, and sank back onto the bed. Her eyes were half closed. She had a look of dreamy contentment on her face. "That was so good," she murmured.

"Was that your G-spot?" I asked.

She nodded slowly and raised her arms. "Hold me for a while," she said.

I'm not sure how long we lay there, but it seemed like forever. Jenny, her skirt still rucked up around her waist, her knickers round her ankles, snoozed happily, but I remained awake and tense, worried that Mum or Alex might come back at any moment. I was relieved when Jenny finally roused herself and reached down to pull her pants up.

"Your turn now," she said.

I shook my head quickly. "No, it's okay."

"But it's not fair if I get all the fun," said Jenny.

"It's all right, honest. Mum or Alex might be back any minute."

So we just talked, and Jenny told me about the G-spot, and about the clitoris, and about orgasms. She told me that G stood for Girl, because only girls knew about it, because it was our Big Secret.

"Boys are pretty useless really," Jenny said. "They don't know how to make us happy. Only we can do that."

It was a long, sexy summer, a summer of awakening, of—thanks to Jenny—a burgeoning confidence in my own sexuality. Who knows where it might have led if she hadn't moved away? All I know is that my time with Jenny was tender and wonderful and massively, overpoweringly exciting. Maybe it was the newness of it, the incredible sense of self-discovery, the feeling that we were doing something daring and forbidden, but whenever I think back to that time I still recall the thrill of it all, and perhaps oddly, I get a warm, almost cozy flush of happiness, of nostalgia.

I don't fancy women now. My experiences with Jenny have left no residual longings, no buried desires. The thought of sleeping with women doesn't disgust me, but it doesn't remotely appeal to me either.

However, the thought of sleeping with *Jenny* again,

with Jenny alone of all women, *does* appeal, or at least the thought of reliving those days, with sleeping with the Jenny that I knew. But of course the Jenny that I knew has gone forever, and now even the Jenny that she became has gone forever too.

Life, I discover as I grow older, is full of such disappointments. Happy times pass away, dreams gradually fade. Sometimes it makes me wonder why we carry on at all.

twenty-two

ON THE DRIVE BACK from the school to the Solomon Wedge, I was struck by an almost epiphanous sense of realization. Despite what I had said to Liz about ringing her to arrange a meeting, it suddenly occurred to me that I wanted no further part in whatever was going on here. It was as though the thought had been introduced from outside myself, injected like a drug into my system. It delivered me from the draining experiences of the past few days, filled me with a sense of nervous anticipation. My first instinct was to reject it out of hand, but the more I considered it the more reasonable it became. For the first time I realized that there was really no point in me staying in Greenwell any longer.

It wasn't as though I'd be abandoning Alex; his trail, such as it was, had turned stone cold, and I was certainly not going to get any help finding him from the local authorities. I'd probably serve him better by going home and trying to put my head in order. In fact, extricating myself from Greenwell's sticky web was surely the only way that I *could* help him. At least in London there would be people who would listen to my story, who would take me seriously. As soon as it was discovered how appallingly I had been treated here, the authorities there would surely feel compelled to act. I could even get the papers involved, whip up a public outcry. I allowed myself to relish the prospect that this time next week Greenwell wouldn't know what had hit it. The corrupt mechanisms operating at the heart of this rotten little town would be laid open like the innards of a laboratory rat, exposed for all to see.

Back at the pub I packed quickly, feeling purposefully efficient now that I had made my decision. It was almost midday, and the sun, which had all at once sprung through the haze which capped the town as though in approval of my decision to leave, was angling through the skylight above my head, draping a band of light across the duvet and the floor beyond. I zipped up my bag, then crossed to the small, lace-curtained window that overlooked Wedge Square. I had glanced perfunctorily out of this window only once before, and wasn't sure why I was doing it now, except perhaps to gain one final overview of the town before I put it behind me, hopefully for good. I lifted the net curtain and leaned forward, and immediately noticed a group of men standing in the center of the square below, as if waiting for something. It took me a moment to focus on them, to register who they were—and then I suddenly went cold.

There were four of them in all: Rudding, the two policemen who had ordered me to strip, and another with his back to me. It was this one, whose face I couldn't see, who frightened me the most.

As if sensing my fear, drawn to it, the fourth figure slowly turned, then tilted his head and looked straight up at me. I saw the glint of his teeth when he smiled, the sharply angled bone structure of his face. It was his eyes, though, that lured me in. They seemed to burn through the distance between us, as if their very gaze could slice through flesh, cause pain.

"Matt!" I gasped, lurching back as though pushed. I was still gripping the curtain, and before I let it drop I saw Matt turn to the others and gesture up at my window. All three of them swiveled their heads in my direction. Though their features were no more than vague blots at this distance, I sensed zealous rage emanating from Rudding and grim satisfaction from the two policemen. Matt himself was a void, merely a shape that disguised a terrible and enveloping darkness. Rudding let out a cry, almost a shriek of triumph, and then the four of them were swarming (if four people *can* swarm) toward the Solomon Wedge.

I let go of the curtain and looked wildly around the room. What could I do? They were coming to get me and I had nowhere to run. I'd hear their feet pounding on the stairs in a moment. The skylight? No, the Solomon Wedge stood alone—there was no Batman-like escape to be had over the rooftops. The window, too, offered nothing more than a sheer forty-foot drop to the concrete below.

I dithered for a moment, then rushed into the bathroom and pulled the shower curtain across. Then I ran back out of the bathroom, tugging the door closed behind me. As I climbed into the big pine wardrobe against the wall, I was shaking with fear, all too aware how obvious and desperate my plan was. What I was hoping was that all four of my pursuers, thinking I was in the bathroom, would pile in there, whereupon I would emerge from the wardrobe and leg it down the stairs. It was the sort of thing that would probably have worked in some kids' crime caper, but if it worked here it would be a miracle. My insides felt like water. I was shaking so much I wondered whether I'd be able to run even if I did get the chance.

I pulled the wardrobe door closed behind me, cloistering myself in darkness. If I'd had my mobile I could have rung Keith, but it was packed away in my bag and in my panic I'd forgotten it. As I heard them coming up the stairs, I pressed myself against the back of the wardrobe, wishing desperately that I could merge with the wood behind me and disappear. There was a crash and suddenly they were in the room; I heard their thumping feet, the savage bark of their voices.

"Check under the bed." Each syllable Rudding uttered was like the snap of a steel trap.

I braced myself for the inevitable, unsure how I'd react when the door was finally thrown open, whether I would fight like a maniac or crumple with terror.

There was a bit of moving about in the bedroom, a few bumps and thuds, and then someone said, "In here."

I sensed movement receding from me, and I thought incredulously, *They've gone into the bathroom.* Surely my silly little plan wasn't going to work?

I knew I had no choice but to go for it. I pushed open the wardrobe door, feeling as though I was going to pass out with fear. I fully expected someone—Matt—to be waiting by the bed, arms folded, a grin on his face, but astonishingly the room was empty. What was more, the door on the far side was standing invitingly ajar. Moving as softly as I could, holding my breath, I crossed toward it.

I almost made it out undetected. Less than a second later and I'd have done so. However, just as I was about to step onto the little landing, the bathroom door was pulled open and Rudding emerged. Our heads twisted, eyes locked onto one another; for an instant we both froze. Then his face contorted into an expression of pure rage, an incoherent screech leaped up from his throat, and he lunged across the room toward me.

I ran, my feet pounding the stairs, and almost immediately heard the wordless shouts of my pursuers bouncing off the walls. As I descended, the many centuries of human progress, of civilization, seemed to peel away from me in layers, so that by the time I reached the door at the bottom of the stairs that led into the pub, I was nothing but the same animal that has existed since life began on this planet, the one whose entire being is centered on simply running in terror, trying to keep ahead of whatever shape death may have taken behind it.

I ran into the pub, panic clouding my vision, barely aware of heads turning to look at me. Someone stepped into my path as I bolted for the exit door. I swerved to avoid them, and saw the red shimmer of Jovial Jim's silk shirt, his chubby, ringed hands reaching out to grab me. I lashed out, was aware of my hand connecting with something, heard a grunt of pain, and felt a brief lightning streak of glee across the dark, crushing sky of my fear.

There were bodies in front of me and behind me. I was struggling for air, for space, as if in a nightmare. I caught a fleeting glimpse of Jovial Jim's wife, her face uglied with hatred and gimlet-eyed fanaticism. Then something connected hard with my ankle, made me howl in pain, my feet became entangled with something else, and I was down.

A sizzling poker of pain shot inward from my right hip, which took the brunt of the impact with the floor. I heard a roar of triumph, or thought I did, through the thumping in my ears. I was surrounded by jostling bodies, which towered over me—I expected them to start kicking, stamping, and curled myself into a ball.

Then I sensed the crowd quiet and move away from me. I looked up and saw the bodies around me parting, people shuffling backward on either side to form a corridor. Down the corridor strode Rudding and the two policemen, Matt a dark presence at the rear. Without a word Rudding leaned over me—then his hands shot forward and grabbed my arms. I struggled, but his strength was deceptive for such a little man. I tried to twist my body to kick him in the side, but the older of the two policemen grasped my right ankle and held it in a grip that felt strong enough to bruise bone. The younger policeman took hold of my left ankle, and the three of them bore down on my limbs until I was lying on my back, spread-eagled.

I felt humiliated, vulnerable, and sick with panic. They had forced me into a position where they could do whatever they liked to me, where I wouldn't be able to do a thing about it.

Matt stepped forward and stood astride me. He was obviously enjoying himself, reveling in the power he held.

"Matt," I said, "please stop this. What do you hope to gain by it?"

He didn't answer. Instead he bent his knees, lowered his body down toward me, and then very deliberately knelt on my chest.

I gasped at the weight of him. His knees ground painfully against my breastbone. I thought I heard my ribs creak, was afraid they might snap, cave in.

"Matt, you're hurting me," I said, each syllable a wheezing effort.

For the first time Matt spoke. "I know," he said.

"Please," I begged him. "Please, Matt . . . I can't . . . breathe."

He responded by placing his hands around my throat. He squeezed, cutting off what little air I was managing to draw in.

The panic I had experienced up to now was nothing compared to this. It came roaring and flailing out of me like a mad thing, making me want to thrash and convulse and kick and scream. However, I could do none of these things; I was immobilized. All I could do was lie there and have the life throttled out of me.

The tightness in my head and chest expanded, became unbearable, then unendurable; I felt sure that the overwhelming need for air would drive me mad, that my heart and brain were swelling like overinflated balloons that would eventually explode.

My vision started to blur, my thoughts to fizzle out.

Oh God, I thought, *I'm going to die, oh God, I'm going to die, oh God, I'm going to—*

twenty-three

I WAS IN A dark place, a small place, a quiet place. Its confines comforted me. I wanted to stay there forever, alone and drifting, devoid of pain, memory, thought. But even as the notion lulled me, I felt my mind struggling for full consciousness, striving to restore my senses. It was as if there were two of me, one wanting to give up, let it all go, and the other determined to fight on until my last ounce of strength was exhausted.

Inevitably the fighter inside me won, made me open my eyes. Instantly my senses felt bombarded. Memory came flooding back, and with it, fear. I remembered Matt's hands around my throat, my terrible panic, my inability to move. I remembered thinking I was going to die, remembered the terror of that—and yet, despite that, I almost wished that I *had* died, because at least then there would be no more pain to come.

After the initial burst of stimuli, my senses were now beginning to settle down, enabling me to take in my surroundings. I was in what appeared to be a narrow, walk-in pantry. The light was dim, but I could make out rows of shelves on both sides of me, stacked with tins and jars, bottles and Tupperware boxes and food-stuffs wrapped in cellophane packaging. There were cardboard boxes of bottled French lager stacked on the floor beneath a thick stone shelf. The instant I saw them I thought, *He bought those on a day trip to Calais.*

I shuddered. Who? Who had bought them? My mind didn't seem to want me to know. Moments before it had flung itself open, allowing consciousness to stream in, but now I could almost hear metal shutters clanging down, vaults of information being sealed.

I clambered gingerly to my feet, my limbs stiff. Oddly, however, my throat and neck felt fine, despite Matt's attentions. Ahead of me was a door, and I moved across to it, tried the handle, expecting it to be locked. To my amazement it opened immediately.

My eyes were so unprepared for the light that accosted them after the dimness of the pantry that for a second it seemed as though the room in front of me was whiting out, like a photograph too rapidly exposed. I squeezed my eyes shut and stood for a moment, breathing in air that I suddenly realized smelled of tomatoes and garlic, onions and herbs, and watching the red branches of my own veins inside my eyelids. My senses seemed to reawaken one by one, so that what filtered through next was sound, a faint murmur of speech that I knew instinctively was not the natural discourse of two human beings responding instinctively to one another but the more measured, rehearsed cadences of scripted speech.

Accustomed to the red glare behind my eyelids now,

I opened my eyes once again. I was standing in the corner of a large, cluttered kitchen. There were pine wall cabinets; a large sink with old-fashioned brass taps beneath a window that looked out on a small, enclosed paved area bordered by flower beds; a big wooden table scattered with letters and leaflets and menus for take-away food places; a heavy old sideboard against the far wall beside a door that led into a tiled hallway.

The room was almost unbearably familiar. I had been in this house so many times, had so many happy memories of it. And yet the place distressed me, frightened me, and the reason it frightened me was . . .

Was because something bad had happened here.

No, not just bad. Cataclysmic. The worst thing that I could possibly ever imagine had happened in this place. I looked round, my eyes devouring details in the hope of enlightenment. I was terrified of the answers I might find, but I needed to know. It was *time* to know.

Details:

A large scorpion model on the sideboard.

A purple-and-pink-striped climbing rope hanging on one of a row of hooks by the back door.

Pictures on the walls—a framed poster of *The Goal-keeper's Fear of the Penalty,* directed by Wim Wenders; a portrait of Kenneth Williams in the style of Warhol's Marilyn Monroe; a photographic collage of exotic insects.

"No," I said and put my hand over my mouth. Then I was running, out of the kitchen, into the tiled hallway. I was aware of the staircase to my left, the wood-framed mirror inset with candleholders affixed to the wall on my right, the front door twelve feet in front of me.

Time seemed to slow as my senses suddenly sharpened. For a moment everything seemed crisp and perfectly aligned, details and textures almost quivering with their own unique vitality. The light pouring through the door's stained-glass panel made it look as though color were bleeding toward me, intending to entwine me in its cathedral-like radiance.

I went through the door to my right and entered two familiar rooms which merged together and became one. In truth it had been one room all along, but until now my mind had not allowed me to recognize the fact. I had walked this house in my dreams or my thoughts many times, and had always found it deserted and had always been fearful of it. But in person I had been here many times too. In my life *before*.

This was Alex's house. Alex's house in London before he moved to Greenwell. Before the gray man took him away.

And here *was* Alex, sitting on his sofa, feet perched on the edge of his low coffee table, watching TV and eating a plate of pasta.

As I walked in he glanced up at me and smiled. "Hiya, Gemmo, how's it going?" he said.

I gaped at him. He gave me an amused frown.

"What's the matter with you? You look like you've just—"

"Don't say it," I said quickly.

"Say what?"

"What you were going to say."

"Okay," he said slowly, but he was still smiling, still treating my behavior as a joke.

"What's happening, Alex?" I asked him.

He looked at me cautiously, as if this might be a trick question and he was wondering how best to answer. At last, like a doctor trying to placate a dangerous patient, he said, "Well, I'm eating linguine and watching *The O-Zone*. Then later—"

He got no further. The door crashed open and Matt lunged into the room.

He was holding a kitchen knife in his hand, and he looked utterly, utterly crazy. Both Alex and I were so shocked that at first neither of us moved or said anything.

Matt jumped forward, and holding the knife high above his head in his right hand, made a grab at my arm with his left. I reacted for the first time, snatching my arm away and stepping sharply back from him, banging the side of my knee against the low coffee table and losing my balance, sprawling half across the table, then ending up on the floor.

Matt lunged forward again, at which point Alex jumped up, the plate of pasta sliding from his lap, linguine and sauce spilling like guts onto the green carpet. Alex shouted something, I don't know what, then Matt rounded on him, sweeping his knife arm down with savage intent. The next thing I knew, Alex's arm had been slashed open and there was blood everywhere, on the carpets and furniture, across the coffee table and on me.

It didn't slow Alex down. I don't think he even felt it at first. He went for Matt again, reaching for his knife arm, but Matt was like a frenzied animal, twisting and fighting. I cried out—a combined warning and wail of horror—as Matt spun and slashed downward at Alex,

like a tennis player dealing with a tricky backhand. I
didn't see the knife go in, but I saw blood suddenly start
to pour out of Alex's side, just above his hip, like water
from a punctured bag. Alex staggered a little and Matt
moved forward again, and all of a sudden Alex was
turning to face me, and there was a knife, or at least the
handle of one, sticking out of his chest. Alex had a
strange expression on his face, the mild irritation of a
man who discovers a smudge of dirt on his fresh white
shirt. He reached for the knife handle with a hand that
appeared to be encased in a shiny red glove, but before
he could clasp it his hand started to shake.

Then he bent forward and was sick on the carpet.

Then he fell over.

At once he started to convulse. Shocked beyond reason, shocked almost to the point of primitivism, I
crawled across the carpet toward my brother. I didn't
notice Matt move toward me, was unaware of his presence until he grabbed my wrist and hauled me with
frightening strength to my feet. I looked into his face
and saw nothing there, his eyes twin voids of indifference. I struggled, and I think I screeched at him to let
me go, but I'm not sure; I felt so distanced from my
physical self. Matt's grip, however, was like a metal clamp,
and when he turned and dragged me behind him, I felt
as though I were struggling against a machine, as
though I were tied to the back of a slowly moving car,
trying to get it to stop by digging in my heels.

I looked desperately back at Alex, whose life was
flowing out of him with each pump of his weakening
heart, and then beyond him to the telephone on its shelf.

At once a wave of *wrongness* swept over me. I had a sudden mental picture of the telephone lying on the floor, its receiver detached and splotched with blood. This was how it should be, I thought.

Bizarrely, given the circumstances, the fact that the telephone was untouched made me feel more than anything else that something had gone badly awry here. Before I could reflect on this, however, I was hauled out of the room in which Alex lay dying, along the hallway, and out of the house. A police car idled at the curb. From the backseat, Rudding leered at me.

Twenty-four

I WAS MADE TO sit in the back between Matt and Rudding. The two policemen who had ordered me to strip were in the front. No one said anything during the drive, not even me. Rudding, his body overly warm and acrid-smelling, like a dog in heat, continually leered and tried to catch my eye, but I ignored him. For the most part I sat slumped, staring down at my clasped hands, trying to fathom what was happening. When, at one point, I did look up, I was not surprised to see I was back in Greenwell again.

I felt I was on one of a number of preordained paths, and that if I didn't choose carefully when my next opportunity came along, then this particular path might well lead to my own destruction. My thoughts were vague, largely unformed, almost instinctual, and yet I couldn't help feeling that they were accurate too. I was a pawn in a complex game, pivotal, and yet a pawn nonetheless. So far I had played the game bravely, albeit recklessly at times, but the odds were stacked against me and each time it had seemed as though I was making headway I had been outmaneuvered.

And now here we were at the endgame and I was losing badly and bereft of ideas. All I could hope for was guidance or else a flash of inspiration, but from where?

The car stopped. I looked up. I had not been aware of us bumping down the dirt track that led here, but I saw that we had come to a halt on the weed-blighted patch of rubble in front of the abandoned railway station. The last time I had been here I had found a dead man, a noose around his neck, a hood obscuring his features. Was I destined to be the next to be executed?

After the horror of Alex's stabbing, I had felt numb, almost weary, as if my own life were draining away in tandem with my brother's. Now, though, as Matt leaned forward to open the door, I felt an adrenaline surge kick-start my system into life once more.

"What are we doing here?" I demanded, feeling my body beginning to quiver with fear and suppressed energy.

When Matt didn't reply, I confronted Rudding. "Why are you doing this to me? What have I ever done to you?"

Even though he hadn't answered my earlier question, it was Matt who spoke now. I used to love his voice. It was deep and rich, a good actor's voice, one that carried even when he spoke softly. "They believe you've come to destroy their way of life," he said.

"Why?" I asked, bewildered.

"Because you have," said Rudding, his voice full of spite. "You come here causing trouble, asking questions."

"I only wanted to find my brother," I protested.

Rudding snorted, and the policeman in the front passenger seat shook his head as if he had never heard such a fanciful tale.

"Why else do you think I would come to this poxy little shit-hole?" I yelled at Rudding, suddenly furious.

Matt laughed and clapped his hands together. Incensed, I turned and aimed a punch at his head. Still laughing, he caught my hand in his own before it could reach its target, the interception such a blur of movement that it made me think of Superman stopping a bullet in its tracks.

For a moment he held my hand in his considerably larger one. Then he let it go with a dismissive gesture and opened the car door. On the other side of me Rudding opened his door too. As he was climbing out of the car, Matt reached back almost casually, grabbed my arm, and hauled me out into the sunshine.

I made a token attempt to shake myself free of his grip, but it was pointless. He began to walk toward the station entrance, and if I didn't want to be dragged along like an errant child, I had no option but to fall into step beside him. Rudding walked on the other side of me and the two policemen brought up the rear. I desperately wanted to ask what was going to happen to me, but I was too afraid of what the answer might be.

We crossed through the ticket office, the only sound the crackling of broken glass under our feet. Rudding slid up behind me and took my arms to allow Matt to climb over the rusty turnstile. I had to make a real effort not to recoil from Rudding's cold touch, from his reptilian breath on the nape of my neck. I felt almost relieved to be in Matt's clutches again once he was on the platform side of the turnstile and, in what seemed an oddly chivalrous gesture, had reached back to help me climb over.

There was an instant, jumping down from astride the turnstile to land on the platform, Matt lightly holding the fingers of my right hand to aid my balance, when I perhaps could have made a break for it. I saw myself racing across the platform and jumping down onto the disused railway track, fleeing like an Olympic athlete while my pursuers floundered behind me. I glanced at Matt and saw that he was grinning at me as if I'd been plucked from the audience at a seafront cabaret. It was an expression that made me falter (and therefore caused my tiny window of opportunity to slam irrevocably shut), not only because of its unexpectedness, but also because it couldn't help but make me wonder whether he could read my mind.

Even as I was thinking this, his grip fastened on my arm once again and he began to steer me along the platform. I knew where we were headed, but that didn't stop my stomach from writhing like a skewered snake. When we stopped outside the waiting room, I concentrated on trying desperately not to shake, so that Matt wouldn't have the satisfaction of feeling my fear vibrating through my skin. Rudding stepped forward and opened the waiting-room door. As light crept in, revealing what was inside, I gasped.

Lying on their stomachs on the floor, hands and feet bound, were Keith and Liz. At first I wasn't sure whether they were alive or dead, then Liz turned her head very slightly, perhaps not so much to look at us, but in reaction to the light. Keith had his eyes closed, and yet I had the impression he was not unconscious, but simply looking inward, perhaps attempting to distance himself from his current situation.

"What have you done to them?" I asked.

My question was ignored. Instead Rudding sneered at me. "Get down on your knees."

I twisted my head to look at him, felt anger flaring up inside me, and welcomed it. "Why should I?" I snapped. "Why should I do anything you tell me, you revolting little man?"

His eyes narrowed, his lips tightened. I thought for a moment he was going to lash out at me, but the knowledge that I'd got to him gave me a brief, fierce surge of almost pure joy. Rudding glanced at Matt as if seeking tacit permission to retaliate. Though I was not aware of any response from Matt, permission, it seemed, was not forthcoming. Rudding pulled himself together with an obvious effort, then marched stiffly across the room to the back-to-back rows of bolted-down metal chairs in the center. On one of the chairs was a petrol can. He picked it up. I heard its contents slosh.

"If you don't do exactly as we tell you," he said, "I'll pour this on your friends and strike a match." He bared his slick yellow teeth at me. "Now, will you please get down on your knees?"

"You fucker," I said, but I did as he asked. My arm throbbed where Matt had been gripping it so tightly. I wondered whether this was it, whether one of the policemen was going to step up behind me and put a gun to the back of my head or a noose around my neck.

I felt cold inside, cold with shock. Then I heard someone step up behind me.

My arms were pinioned behind my back and my wrists were tied together. I winced as the knots were tightened, clenched my teeth to prevent myself from crying out. A hand grabbed the back of my neck and shoved me face forward onto the floor. Without my arms to break my fall, I banged my chin hard enough to send pain searing up through my skull as my teeth clacked together. The floor was gritty and dry, but the urine stench which pervaded the room was stronger down here. I felt my feet being forced together so that my ankle bones grated one against the other, and twisted my upper body awkwardly to peer over my shoulder.

One of the two policemen—the younger, I think, though I could only see him in silhouette, framed by the light beyond the open door—was tying my feet together and being none too gentle about it. Panic flowed through me, cramping my stomach. I fought hard to remain calm, to keep my head as clear as I could. To be a captive of these men was bad enough, but to be incapacitated, too, was even worse, because it now meant I had no means to defend myself, I would simply have to submit to whatever they decided to do to me.

I closed my eyes, took long, deep breaths, and only looked again when I felt the bone-grinding tugging on my ankles stop, sensed the younger policeman rising to his feet, stepping away from me.

Whatever their plans, ideally I would have liked to have appeared defiant, contemptuous, but I was too terrified to carry it off. I knew if I tried to speak (which in itself was difficult as my saliva was so dry and congealed in my mouth it seemed more solid than liquid), my voice would emerge as a wavering falsetto. And so I remained silent and waited to see what their next move would be.

I didn't have to wait long. Rudding was still cradling the petrol can and now he began to unscrew the lid. He watched me as he was doing it, his eyes savage and gluttonous, his grinning mouth a rictus of warped glee.

I turned away from him to look at Liz and Keith. Keith still had his eyes closed, but Liz was looking at me steadily. She didn't look scared, she looked . . . I don't know . . . calm, maybe. Self-assured. As if she had accepted her fate, or as if she believed that no matter how bad things seemed, everything would ultimately turn out okay.

The sound of liquid splashing on the floor drew my attention away from her. I twisted my head again, saw Rudding emptying out the contents of the can onto the splintered, detritus-strewn tiles, sloshing it up the walls. Now the smell of urine was superseded by the pungent chemical smell of petrol. Despite the circumstances, I was momentarily transported back to my childhood, to long, sunny, holiday-bound car journeys punctuated by pub lunches, word games with Alex and my parents, raucous singsongs, and quieter periods engrossed in coloring books or Enid Blyton.

Matt stepped forward and I saw him take something out of his pocket. I didn't realize what it was until I heard a scrape-click and saw a tulip of flame rise from his fist.

"Cleansing by fire," he murmured, his face a cadaverous orange mask. "Burning the past away. Good-bye, Ruth."

"No, Matt!" I screamed, my voice tearing up from my dry throat. But it was too late. I saw him bend and touch the flame to the petrol. Suddenly and silently a wall of fire separated the three of us from the four of them. Without another word the dark shapes shimmering on the other side of the fire turned and walked away, leaving us to burn.

"No!" I screeched again. "No, Matt, come back!"

Already the fire was taking hold, crawling up the walls and licking its way across the ceiling. Its heat caused blisters of sweat to spring out on my skin; its smoke snagged in my throat, making me cough. I began to thrash and writhe, fighting futilely against my bonds.

"Turn your back," I heard someone say, and twisted my head to see Liz wriggling toward me like a wounded snake.

"Wha—" I said, the word foreshortened by a coughing fit.

"Turn your back," Liz repeated. Her voice was so calm and authoritative that I did as she asked.

I felt her doing something to the ropes that bound my wrists, something that made the rough hemp rub and chafe against my already raw and seeping skin. It was agony, like wearing hot, stinging bracelets; I screwed up my face and tried to detach myself from everything. In some ways I was aided in this by the smoke, which was making my head swim. I tried not to make any sound—I didn't want to discourage Liz if this was to be our only chance of escape—though I couldn't prevent the odd moan or whimper forcing its way out of my throat.

"There," she said at last, by which time her voice was booming oddly in my ears. I felt as though we were on an island in the center of a sea of flame, drenched in sweat. I couldn't breathe properly; every inhalation felt like sucking in soupy, smoke-poisoned heat.

"You can move your hands apart," she said, her voice echoing in my ear, as if from a great distance.

I tried it. My shoulders seemed to creak with pain. Exhausted, I rolled onto my back and held my hands up in front of my face. The ropes had been sawed and hacked through. There was blood on them where my chafed skin had given way. My hands looked bloodless, though they moved like dying crabs when I willed them to. The pins and needles surging through them was horrendous enough to almost make me pass out, but I welcomed it.

"Take this," Liz said, and I turned my head to see that she had her back to me and was holding something in her still-bound hands. I felt as though my brain wasn't working properly, as though my thoughts were connecting incredibly slowly. I seemed to look at the object in Liz's hand for an age before reaching down with my still-clumsy fingers and plucking it from her grasp. I stared at the object, unable to believe what I was seeing.

"But I buried this," I croaked.

It was the rabbit brooch, its jeweled eye intact.

"Nothing can stay buried forever," said Liz.

I stared at the brooch in wonder. Its eye, reflecting the fire that was devouring the walls around us, winked redly at me.

"Use it, Ruth," Keith said.

His voice broke the spell. I looked at him, and saw that his eyes were open now, staring intently at me.

For a moment I didn't know what he meant, and then I realized. The rabbit brooch's sharpest edge would not have been much use as a weapon, but it was all we had. I began to saw frantically at Liz's bonds, fighting hard to remain conscious. Several times the brooch slipped from my still-numbed fingers and clattered to the floor.

It seemed to take forever to cut through the ropes, though it could have been no more than a minute or two. As soon as Liz's hands sprang apart, she turned, took the brooch from me, and began to slash at the ropes around my ankles. I lay back, struggling for breath while she untied Keith. I wondered vaguely how she could appear so unaffected by the heat and the smoke. The next thing I knew, she was pulling me to my feet, shouting, "Come on, Ruth, we've got to get out."

My instinct was to protest, but I felt too drained to argue. I'm not sure whether I rose to my feet unaided or whether I was hauled upright. Neither am I certain exactly how the three of us got out. I remember seeing flames on all sides, then running on leaden legs and feeling incredible heat. The next thing I knew I was lying with my cheek pressed against cold stone and there was something roaring some distance away. And there was air, piercing and plentiful; its freshness as I gulped it in made me realize how bruised and scoured my fight for air had made my throat and lungs feel. I wondered abstractedly whether any permanent damage had been done, though I couldn't find the strength to care. I was simply grateful to be out, grateful to have avoided serious injury yet again.

"Isn't it time you put a stop to all this?" Keith asked.

I looked at him, or thought I did. My mind was slipping now; I was no longer certain what was real and what was thought, or dream.

"How?" I asked, though I may have merely formed the word in my mind.

"By going back," said Keith.

"Back? To where?"

"To where it all began."

It sounded like a fairy-tale answer, mystical and meaningless. Liz came forward and pressed something into my hand.

"Here," she said. "This belongs to you."

It was the rabbit brooch. The flames gouting from the open waiting-room door, veining the black smoke which boiled up from the building's roof, made its red eye glow and flicker, made it pulse like a beating heart.

"You have to set things back on the right path," said Keith. "It'll destroy you if you don't."

"What will?" I asked, or perhaps I merely wanted to, but lost the words somewhere in the pulsing of the tiny heart in my fist. The heart drew me in, or perhaps flowed out toward me, extending crimson tendrils, making the world around me seem flat and unreal, like a photograph obliterated by spilled ink. I blinked, and all I saw was red, all I heard was red, all I tasted and touched and smelled was red. I was a blood cell, racing through the deep caverns of the body I was keeping alive, rushing toward the heart.

I blinked again, and suddenly I was hurtling backward, or else I was still and the redness was rushing away from me. A solid world formed without warning around me, and I looked at the redness and saw that it was no longer a good thing, but a bad one. The redness was blood. Alex's blood. Alex's lifeblood, running out of him.

twenty-five

I WAS BACK IN Alex's house, sprawled on the carpet, having been shoved into the coffee table. Alex was lying in front of me, a knife sticking out of his chest, his feet making little pedaling, kicking motions. Looming over both of us was the fiend who had done this to my brother, his eyes like the eyes of something dead. I kicked back from him, and rage rushed up inside me.

"Look what you've done!" I screamed at him. "Look what you've fucking done!"

Matt didn't reach down and grab me this time. Instead, as though roused from a trance, his robotic composure fell away. He blinked at Alex and then at me, and his eyes were no longer blank but fearful. All at once he looked less like a monster and more like a stricken schoolboy who had overstepped the mark.

"It wasn't my fault!" he protested. "He came at me. He attacked me."

"You burst into his house! You had a knife!"

"But I wasn't going to use it," he said, indignant, defensive.

"But you *did* use it, didn't you? And now it's too late to take back what you've done."

I scrambled to my feet and made for the phone on the shelf behind the TV.

"What are you doing?" he demanded.

"I'm getting an ambulance for Alex."

"If you tell them what happened the police'll come." He looked scared, trapped.

"Probably," I said and picked up the receiver.

"No, you can't!" he shouted, and flailed across the room toward me.

I turned to meet him, the receiver still in my hand. I was terrified, traumatized even, but my sense of self-preservation and concern for Alex gave me an agile strength and a ruthlessness I had no idea I was capable of possessing. As Matt came within my range I swung the receiver at him with perfect timing and smashed it into the side of his head. His mouth opened and his eyes flickered and he staggered back. I couldn't see a wound, but blood suddenly blossomed at the side of his head. He put his long, bony hands, his hateful hands, up to it. I stepped forward, the telephone cord still allowing me plenty of leeway, and hit him again. The sharp clunk of the receiver impacting with his skull was immensely satisfying. He gave a little cry of protest. I hit him again, and again, and again, until he had been forced down onto his knees. Blood ran out of his hair and soaked his shirt, and there were smears of it, sticky as glue, on the telephone receiver. I stepped away from him, turned, and dialed 999, and slipped into a kind of funnel of calmness, where for the duration of the call my head was clear and I was as erudite and as concise as I had ever been.

It was only when I put the phone down that I realized how much my arm was aching. Not just aching, but really hurting; I'd put everything into those blows with the telephone receiver. The pain seemed to throb out of my arm into the rest of my body, to set up a chain reaction, and I sank to my knees, my shaking legs suddenly unable to support the weight of my body. After being so together on the phone, my mind now felt slow and syrupy, able only to absorb details as sharp little increments of information. I looked at the telephone receiver and saw strands of hair sticking to the blood that was smeared across it. This made me realize that for the last couple of minutes I hadn't even thought about what Matt might be doing. I turned my head, but seemed able only to do it slowly. Alex was lying on the carpet in a pool of blood, deathly still. Matt was nowhere to be seen.

I crawled across to my brother on spent limbs, my body still shaking. I crooned his name, stroked his hair, terrified of moving him in case it made things worse and snapped the delicate thread of life he might still be clinging to. His eyes were closed, which I told myself was a good sign, told myself that it meant you were sleeping, not dead. I was covered in his blood, but I didn't care. I lay down beside him, and that was how the ambulance men found us when they arrived.

I traveled with Alex in the ambulance, but I don't remember much about it. What I do remember is that one of the ambulance men put a big, warm orange blanket around me and gave me some tea out of a thermos flask.

I don't usually take sugar in my tea, but this had quite a lot of sugar in it and it tasted fantastic. The journey itself passed in a blur. I think I kept asking whether Alex would be okay, and received vague assurances from the medics that they would do all they could for him.

The wait in the hospital after Alex was wheeled through for emergency surgery was just as dreamlike as the trip in the ambulance had been. I sat in a corridor on a plastic chair, still clutching the orange blanket around me. Nurses appeared every now and again to ask how I was; on a couple of occasions I was even brought a hot drink. A policewoman spoke to me too. She touched my arm and her tone was gentle. I can't remember any of her questions or what I said in response to them.

There was a constant traffic of people shuffling up and down the corridor, but I registered them only as a lulling, ghostlike tide. I felt numb inside, anesthetized. I had slipped into a state where I couldn't quite believe that any of what was happening was real. I don't think I slept, but I drifted; perhaps one of the medics had given me something in the ambulance to countermand the effects of shock—I honestly can't remember.

I have no idea what time it was when I heard a deeper voice speak my name. I looked up and saw a portly man in his early fifties, whose iron gray suit, complete with waistcoat, matched the hair swept theatrically back from his wrinkled brow. Indeed, his whole face was deeply lined, and there were heavy bags under his pale eyes.

"Miss Gemmill?" he said again.

"Yes," I said, the word I spoke seeming to come from somewhere else.

"Miss Gemmill, I'm Dr. Lassiter. I'm the surgeon who operated on Alex."

All at once I was scared. I hadn't realized until now that I'd been dreading this moment. I wished I could slip back into my dreamlike state of waiting. "Yes," I said again.

"Miss Gemmill, Alex fought bravely, and we did all in our power to save him, but I'm afraid his injuries were too severe. He died a little while ago on the operating table. For him the end was very peaceful. I assure you he didn't feel a thing."

He spoke with genuine compassion, but his words to me seemed as cold and sharp and lethal as Matt's blade had been to Alex. I felt myself punctured, torn open. I felt as if a great howling pit were opening beneath my feet. I reached out and gripped the sleeves of the surgeon's gray jacket. "No," I pleaded with him, "no, no, no."

"I'm sorry, Miss Gemmill," he said, and he *looked* sorry, he looked heartbroken, in fact. I felt it all overwhelming me, felt something black spin inside my head, and the next thing I knew I was on the floor, and although I wanted to be left alone, people were pulling at me and talking to me, trying to drag me back into their terrible world, into a place I no longer wanted to be a part of.

I went to be with Alex for a while, and I sobbed over him and whispered his name and stroked his hair and wished with all my heart, with every fiber of my being, that tonight had never happened and that Alex could be alive and restored to me. We never realize how much we take for granted, or how achingly we love someone, until they are taken from us. Each day we carry on as though we're immortal and nothing is ever going to change. We go through our lives feeling bored or fed up, or at best blasé, little knowing what a wonderful and precious thing it is we've got until it is denied us.

"How am I going to manage without you?" I whispered and kissed him on his cool cheek. "Oh, Alex," I said, and then the tears came again and I could say no more.

The policewoman, younger than me by a good five years, drove me home. She came into my flat with me, switched on the lights, preceded me into every room. She was reluctant to leave, but I insisted that I wanted to be on my own, and eventually she went. She told me that they'd pick Matt up pretty soon, and that I wasn't to worry because a police car would be patrolling the area, passing in front of my house every five minutes, until they apprehended him.

When she had gone I sat in silence for a while, hands pressed between my knees. At that moment the thought of Matt coming after me didn't worry me in the slightest; he had already done the worst thing that he could possibly do. Eventually I got up and went to the window and looked out. After a couple of minutes I saw a police car cruise slowly past the house. I looked at my watch and saw that the time was 1:17 A.M. I waited for the police car to reappear, then consulted my watch again—1:24. The next time it came around it was 1:30. As soon as it had disappeared round the corner at the top of the road, I grabbed my car keys from their hook above the sink in the kitchen and went downstairs. I'd gone round to Alex's earlier that evening on the tube, so that I could have a drink, intending to get a cab back or stay over at his place. This meant that my car was still parked out in front. I got into it and drove away.

I drove on autopilot, my subconscious registering signs and signals and responding to them. I headed north, and by the time I got to Preston it was almost dawn. The dark skin of the sky was splitting open to reveal paler wounds. It was no longer the day that Alex died. Already his death had passed into history.

Without consulting a map, I drove unerringly to the old station where Matt had taken me on Day One. I jolted down the dirt road, and came to a halt, with an almost empty tank of petrol, on the cracked, weed-choked surface of the car park. The roofless, decaying building in front of me clung tenaciously to what re-mained of the darkness, like an old man attempting to conceal his sagging nakedness. I got out of the car and walked across to the main entrance.

The smell of human waste greeted me as I stepped into the ticket office. Coldness fell from above; with the breaking of dawn the building seemed stripped of two roofs, one of timber and slate, the other of darkness. I stepped across the broken glass and traversed pools of discolored water to reach the rusted turnstile. I gave it a little push, but it refused to move, so I climbed over.

The wind bowling along the platform was like a physical thing, flailing and howling at me. It was only when it whipped my hair about my face that I realized what sort of state I was in. My hair was dry and scratchy, like old twigs, which it took me a moment to realize was because it was covered in dried blood. I looked at my hands. They were covered in flakes of blood, too, and my fingernails were packed with it. Feeling as though I were waking up, or coming out of a trance, I looked down at my clothes, and saw that they, too, were stiff and dark with Alex's blood. This was his life here. This was the life that had seeped out of him. Suddenly I felt weak and sick and overwhelmed with the horror of what had happened. I stumbled to the edge of the platform, fell to my knees, and threw up on the overgrown tracks below.

Being sick was like pulling a plug out of me. For the next fifteen or twenty minutes I screamed and wailed and cried and yanked at my hair. I felt close to the brink, felt as though I would be driven mad with grief. Eventually, though, even this subsided, leaving me drained and wretched and lethargic.

After another ten minutes or so I hauled myself to my feet and trudged over to the faded blue door of the waiting room. The door was standing very slightly ajar. I took a deep breath, then pushed it open.

Pale, cold light angled slyly into the room from behind me. I heard a creak and a soft clunk at the same instant I saw Matt. He was in the center of the room, hovering three feet above the floor, glaring at me. For a moment I thought he'd become the demon I'd latterly thought him to be, but then I saw the hole he'd made in the ceiling, the exposed rafter he'd attached the rope to, the noose around his neck.

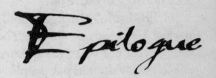

Epilogue

"RUTH, THERE'S SOMEONE HERE to see you."

The unexpected sound of Dr. Sykes's voice was mellifluous enough not to startle me. It was, after all, her job to soothe and reassure, which was why I had selected her as an ally, I suppose, during what I now thought of as my battle. I turned and squinted. The noonday sun crowned her strawberry blond hair with a dazzling white coronet of slow-burning flame. It threw her face into soft shadow, but I could see that she was smiling.

"Oh?" I said.

I was aware of a figure hovering at her shoulder, could sense the uncertainty, the anxiety, of the individual. Since reemerging, as it were, I'd felt . . . mellow. And I didn't think that was due wholly to the medication I was still obliged to take. My mind was sharp, clear, precise, uncluttered. I felt newly minted, unblemished by the stultifying emotional detritus of the past. All around me people seemed to be rushing hither and thither, their lives fueled by stress, by the fear of nonachievement. But I was content simply to sit and ponder and recuperate, to allow one day to slip into the next without worrying about the passage of time, about picking up the threads, about needing to move on.

"Hello, Ruth," the figure said, tentatively stepping forward, blocking out the sun. The voice, too, was hesitant, uncertain. I was the supposed mental patient, and yet I felt it my duty to put people at their ease.

"Hi, Kate," I said.

"Kate's been keeping tabs on your progress, Ruth," Dr. Sykes said.

"Or lack of it," I replied, and smiled to show I was joking. "I know. Keith told me you've been ringing up two or three times a week."

"I came to visit a few times too. But you weren't . . . I mean, I don't think you realized that I was here."

"I'll leave you two to it," Dr. Sykes said, and gave my shoulder a squeeze. "Don't go getting sunstroke out here."

"She seems really nice," Kate said once Dr. Sykes was out of earshot.

"She's the best," I said. "She was my greatest friend when I was . . ." I tapped the side of my forehead with my index finger. "She helped me get through it."

Kate was perched on the bench beside me, but she didn't seem particularly relaxed despite our idyllic surroundings. I gazed out on the rolling lawns and meticulously tended flower beds, taking delight in the ever-changing play of light on the leaves of the trees in the distance.

"And are you through it?" Kate asked. "Properly, I mean?"

I nodded. "I couldn't cope with Alex's death, wouldn't accept it. Severe post-traumatic stress. I just shut down so I wouldn't have to face up to it."

"But if you shut down, how can you be through it?" Kate asked. "I mean, you've been catatonic for six months, Ruth. The times I came to see you, you just stared into space. They had to feed you through a drip."

"I know," I said. "Poor old Keith has had a lot to put up with."

"And then one day you just wake up and say you're fine, you're over it. But how can you be when you still haven't faced up to anything?"

"But I have faced up to it," I said. "The reason nothing was apparent on the surface was because it was all happening internally. I don't know what you'd call it— a delusion, a dream, a mental landscape. All I know was that it was as real as this place. And even when it got strange and confusing, even when I didn't know what was going on, it still felt real."

"Do you want to talk about it?" Kate asked.

"Not really." I could see she was hurt by that. I reached out and took her hand. "No, what I mean is that I don't feel the need to. I thought maybe you thought I did, that you were seeing it as your duty. I mean, I'll talk to you about it if you really want to listen."

"I do," Kate said. "I'm interested."

"All right, then." I gave her a condensed version of what had happened in Greenwell as I had experienced it. Though I knew the place did not exist on any map, it was as real to me as the world I had reemerged into. If I had made the wrong choices in Greenwell, if I had allowed the darkness to engulf me, I felt sure I would still be trapped there now, that I might never have found my way home.

"So part of you must have been conscious, then," said Kate. "To incorporate so many elements from the real world, I mean."

I sighed. "I suppose so, although I wasn't even slightly aware of it. Having said that, when I woke up I wasn't surprised to see that Liz and Keith were real people. In a way, it was almost as if I'd been expecting it."

"So is Keith gay in real life?" Kate asked a little too innocently.

I thought of Keith in his white nurse's tunic and dark trousers, which was all I'd ever seen him wear in the hospital, and then I thought of him in Greenwell in his linen suit and black polo neck, and I thought of him naked and kissing me, kissing me between my legs, and in spite of myself I blushed.

"I don't know," I said. "It's not something we've talked about."

"He's a bit of a hunk, though, isn't he?" said Kate, her eyes twinkling mischievously.

I laughed. "I don't believe this. I've only been back in the land of the living for two minutes and already you're trying to matchmake."

"Am not!" said Kate, none too convincingly.

I squeezed her hand. "I'm so lucky to have a friend like you, Kate. A lot of people would have given up on me."

"No one's given up on you. We all knew you'd pull

through. Graham's been brilliant. On the few occasions that I did start to let myself think that you'd never come back to us, he pulled me out of it by saying that it was just a matter of time, that we just had to be patient."

"Good old Graham," I said. "How is he?"

"Oh, he's fine. Working too hard and drinking too much, as usual. He blamed himself for everything at first, you know, says he should have realized sooner that there was something not right about Matt. He said that sometimes, when they played football together, Matt used to really lose it." Then she checked herself. "Matt's probably the last person you want to talk about just now."

I shrugged. "He's dead. He can't cause me any more pain than he already has. It doesn't upset me to talk about him, it's just that he's not *worth* talking about."

"You're right," said Kate. She fell silent for a minute, and it saddened me to see that she was struggling to find something to say to fill what she evidently perceived as an awkward moment. Kate and I had always felt perfectly relaxed in one another's company, had never had to indulge in superficial chitchat to mask the fact that we really had nothing to say to each other.

"It's okay, Kate," I told her. "*I'm* okay. You don't have to make allowances for me. I'm not going to have a relapse every time someone mentions Matt—or Alex, either, come to that."

Kate gave me a rueful look. "I'm not handling this very well, am I?"

"You're doing okay," I said. "I'm sure I'd be the same if the roles were reversed."

This time, the brief silence that ensued was companionable. This was how I'd always measured the depth of my friendships. With true friends you can sit quietly and not feel uncomfortable. Hand in hand, Kate and I listened to the somnolent drone of the bees, the occasional murmur of distant traffic, the sharp clack of garden shears as one of the Greenwell Clinic's many gardeners shuffled along on all fours several hundred yards away, trimming the already immaculate borders.

"So what are your plans now?" Kate asked eventually. "When are you coming home?"

"When Dr. Sykes says I'm better, I suppose. I'm in no hurry."

"Have your mum and dad been to see you yet?"

"They came as soon as they could. Dad's been fantastic actually. The second time he came on his own and poured his heart out to me. He's devastated about Alex, but he was so, so happy—I mean, genuinely happy—to see me up and about. He cried his eyes out, and he hugged me like he didn't ever want to let me go. We talked more in a single afternoon than we have in the last fifteen years. Do you know he's even been paying the rent on my place in London?"

"Yes. I think it was his way of convincing himself that one day you'd be well enough to go back there."

"Well, I'm glad I can make at least that wish come true for him," I said.

Kate and I chatted for a little while longer before she had to leave. She hugged me and told me that she'd come again on the weekend, and that if I wanted to stay with her and Graham for a bit once I got out then I was more than welcome. I stayed sitting on the bench, turning to watch her as she crossed the sun-drenched lawn toward the elegant mansion that had once been

Greenwell Hall and was now the Greenwell Clinic. She paused on the steps to wave to me. I waved back.

Alone again, I stared out across the lawn toward the line of trees that marked the boundary of the woods a quarter of a mile away. Dr. Sykes had told me that bluebells and wild garlic grew there in profusion, and that once I was stronger, perhaps even as early as next week, I could walk in those woods. I remembered being in such places with Alex, recalled his enthusiasm as he pointed out details of flora and fauna that would otherwise have escaped my untrained eye. I closed my eyes and allowed my memories free rein, allowed Alex's life to play across the screen of my mind like a series of movie clips. His life may have been short, but it had been happy and fulfilled and packed full of the best experiences. When I pictured him now, I pictured his ebullience and his childlike wonder; in my mind he was never still and he was always grinning.

I opened my eyes again and sunlight flooded them. Blinking, I was surprised to see what appeared to be a figure, standing just within the boundary of the woods, almost concealed by leaves. I saw the sun flash on blond hair, and though the figure was too far away for its face to be anything more than a blur, I had the overwhelming impression that it was looking straight at me.

I stood up, placing a hand on the bench to steady myself. As I did so, the figure arced its right arm in a beckoning gesture.

"Alex," I whispered, and found myself moving toward the figure as though its summons were a hypnotic command that I couldn't resist. No one paid me any heed as I walked steadily across the immaculately shorn grass.

Everything around me seemed still, poised. Heat lay over the land like a sleep-inducing drug, allowing me to pass by, unnoticed.

As I drew nearer to the trees, the figure suddenly slipped into the shadows and strolled unhurriedly away. "Wait," I called, but the figure ignored me. If I wanted to catch up with it, speak to it, I had no option but to follow.

I stepped between two trees, to where the undergrowth immediately became thick and tangled, the ground uneven. The sunlight was unable to penetrate the tangle of branches above me; I gasped at the sudden gloom and chill, felt the hairs on my arms bristle as my skin rippled with goose bumps. I began to struggle forward through the thicket, pushing aside small, springy branches, forging through bushes and shrubs. The figure was some way ahead of me, a blur of dark moving among the shadows. Unused to exercise, I gasped and panted, feeling as though I were straining every sinew in my attempt to keep it in sight.

After five or ten minutes, sweat was running down my face and each breath felt like a length of hot barbed wire being dragged up from my lungs. My limbs were leaden, my back was aching, and my arms were covered in stinging scratches. I knew I couldn't go on much longer. If it wasn't for my desperate desire to catch up with the figure, I would not have been able to resist the impulse to sink to the brambly ground and give myself up to sleep.

I glanced up at intervals during my pursuit, and each time I did so I caught a dark glimpse of movement ahead of me, enough to give me the impetus to keep moving. But eventually, inevitably, the moment came when I looked up and the figure was no longer there. Desperately I scanned the confusing collage of bark and leaf, the nuances of shadow. As I realized that I had finally lost my quarry, the last of my energy drained from me. I staggered forward, my legs buckling, tripped on a mass of viney, exposed roots, and fell forward down a short incline, my arms going out in front of me like someone doing a belly flop into a swimming pool.

The ground was springy enough to prevent bruising, but I still hit it hard enough to cry out in shock. I didn't slide far, but when I finally lifted my head after coming to a halt I realized I was in a clearing that was roughly circular in shape, trees clustered around its edge like spectators at a cockfight.

Groggily I raised myself to my knees, wondering what Dr. Sykes would say when I returned to the hospital in such a disheveled state. I had leaves and twigs in my hair, and my hands and clothes were covered in mud and grass stains. My desire to find out who had been leading me through the woods had faded with my energy. All I wanted now was to go back to the clinic, have a hot bath, a cup of tea, and a long sleep in a comfortable bed.

I took a number of deep breaths to calm my pounding heart, then clambered unsteadily to my feet. My legs felt shaky, but I reckoned I could make it back if I took it slowly. One of my first priorities when I left the clinic would be to build up my fitness levels again. I hadn't put on much weight during the past six inert months, but my muscles, despite the physical therapy, felt atrophied; even a short walk left me breathless and aching.

I was about to turn and head back the way I'd come when a brief but violent flurry of movement on the far side of the clearing made me jump. It made me more than jump, in fact; it made me cry out and duck as though someone had fired a gun at me. My eyes darted to where the movement had come from, but I couldn't make out what I was seeing at first. A heap of brown fur. An arc of rusty metal. Blood.

Cautiously, my heart a dull thump at the base of my throat, I moved closer.

For maybe half a dozen paces I couldn't see what the bloodstained tangle of fur and metal was, and then all at once it slammed violently into focus. It was a hare caught in a mantrap, its back leg almost completely severed. It was lying on its side, the eye I could see open and glaring, mad with agony.

I could tell it was alive by the rapid rise and fall of its ribs as it silently panted its life away. I thought of the hare in Greenwell, crushed beneath the wheels of my car. But that hadn't really happened, had it, except in my own head? I had been sick then, I wasn't sick now. So what was this? The fulfillment of a premonition, or merely coincidence?

My head rang and spun. I wanted to get back to the clinic, I needed my medication. But first I had to help this poor creature. I had to free it if I could, or, failing that, put it out of its misery.

I moved closer to the hare, taking small, shuffling steps, obeying my heart even though my head was imploring me to turn back. As my shadow fell across it, it glared up at me and started to thrash in panic, ripping its wound even wider, exposing bone, releasing fresh gouts of blood.

"No," I murmured, feeling faint and nauseous, holding up my hands, "I'm here to help."

The hare began to scream. A piercing, unearthly cry, like the wail of a young child.

I knelt down beside it, my head swimming, and as I did so I sensed a presence behind me. As my shadow had fallen across the hare, so a larger shadow now fell over me. I started to turn but before I could I felt a sharp blow in the small of my back and then a weight which bore me to the ground. I struggled frantically, unable to prevent my arms from being pinioned behind my back or the large, bony hand from closing over my face, blocking the supply of air to my nose and mouth.

"Don't struggle," a deep, rich voice whispered in my ear. "Don't struggle and it will soon be over."

I did as I was told. I stopped struggling. As consciousness slipped away, I realized that the world was full of traps, and I wondered whether I would ever be free of mine.

J. M. MORRIS lives in North Yorkshire, England.